"*N*o woman should have to wash a man's underwear unless he's a real husband! Underwear and hankies are not things a woman should have to scrub unless she's utterly destitute, insane, or crazy in love!"

He watched her with wary eyes, the way a man would watch a burning fuse.

"Here I am taking care of some other woman's children!" Heat pulsed in her face, choked her. "Another woman that you loved and held and . . . and while you were doing all that I was embroidering hundreds of stupid pillow cases, remembering three kisses and wondering if I'd go to my grave without ever . . . without ever . . . You know what I mean. Of course you know. Being married to me didn't stop you from —"

His hands caught her waist and pulled her hard against his body.

A gasp broke from her lips. "What are you —"

Then his mouth came down hard on hers, hot, demanding, almost angry. This wasn't the kiss of an inexperienced youth. This was a man's kiss and a man's need that explored her mouth and pressed her hard against an iron body that set her mind and flesh on fire. . . .

THE BRIDE OF WILLOW CREEK

Maggie Osborne

IVY BOOKS • NEW YORK

Chapter 1

Of all the times to be late, this was the worst.

The instant Sam rushed out of the saloon, an acrid drift of soot and smoke wafting from the top of the street told him the train had already arrived. Damn. Being late was one more grievance to hold against his basically worthless attorney. If his attorney had kept a regular office instead of holding appointments at a table in the Gold Slipper, there might have been a clock that Sam could have kept an eye on. Of course, if he'd remembered to wear his pocket watch, he wouldn't be in this pickle to start with. Some days turned sour the minute a man left his house. He'd had a lot of those days lately.

Dodging pedestrians and street traffic, giving up on the narrow boardwalks, he ran toward the depot. Plenty of time tomorrow to think about legal problems and attorney's bills. Right now his most urgent problem came from the past.

And she was going to be furious that he hadn't been waiting on the new platform when the train steamed into Willow Creek. Their reunion—he guessed he could call it that—definitely was not beginning on a positive note.

Sam's steps slowed as he crossed Fifth Street and noticed only one person still on the platform. That answered his major question. He'd wondered if he would recognize her. Ten years changed people.

When he'd known Angelina Bertoli, she'd been as slender as a nail, and he could swear she'd been shorter. She had filled out considerably—and interestingly—but he would have recognized this older, more womanly version of the girl he remembered. In fact, and it annoyed him greatly, if he were meeting Angie today for the first time he would have been strongly attracted to her.

Striding forward, he noted details that awakened memory. The mass of reddish brown hair knotted on her neck beneath her hat. The wide sensual curve of her mouth. The smooth slope of her cheek. Her vitality. She had been so filled with curiosity and eagerness to experience the world. Now that vitality steamed and fizzed beneath the surface, giving an impression of movement although she stood still, clutching her handbag at her waist.

When she spotted him her gaze flared, then narrowed, and he remembered that her eyes were dark enough to seem almost black, but he'd forgotten how expressive those eyes could be. Once he had read tenderness in her gaze, and love. Had felt the wrench of watching tears form and spill. But until now, he hadn't seen the dark beams of fury. Temper wasn't a trait young women displayed to their suitors.

"Sam Holland?"

Her tone conveyed perhaps a 90 percent certainty that she recognized him, but the hint of doubt made him wonder what changes she noticed in him. He wore his hair long now, tied at the neck with a strip of leather. That probably surprised her. A life largely spent outside had weathered his features and etched lines that made him look older than twenty-eight. Maybe he'd filled out and grown taller, too. Hard to say. Possibly she'd expected him to wear a suit, as he had the last time they saw each other.

Actually, he'd considered wearing his suit, then decided on denims and a flannel shirt instead. Today's meeting wasn't about making a favorable impression. He could say his final good-byes in his everyday clothing.

Either he nodded to confirm or she decided on her own who he was. Later, when he reviewed the incident, he decided she wouldn't have hit him unless she felt certain of his identity.

The embarrassing thing was that he didn't see it coming. His attention was fixed on the bags, boxes, and trunks piled around her, and he was frowning, wondering why she needed such an excessive amount of luggage for an overnight stay.

Her fist caught him on the side of the head and knocked him backward. Astonishment widened his eyes as he worked his jaw and checked with his tongue to see if she'd knocked any teeth out.

He couldn't believe it. She'd hit him in public, and she'd hit him hard. She'd struck with enough force to send him reeling and damned if it didn't feel like one of his teeth might be loose.

Sliding a look toward Bennet Street, he swiftly scanned the traffic to see if anyone was watching. Gossip ran through mining towns faster than grass through a horse. By tomorrow everyone in Willow Creek would know that Sam Holland had offended a woman at the depot enough that she'd whacked him good.

"Years ago I promised if I ever saw you again, I'd give myself the satisfaction of breaking your jaw." She waved a gloved hand in front of her waist as if it hurt. He hoped it did. "I regret more than I can express that your jaw doesn't seem to be broken!"

"So that's how it's going to be," he said softly, staring at her snapping eyes and the fire blazing in her cheeks.

"Well, what did you expect?"

Since she was leaning forward and speaking through her teeth, furious enough to take another swing at him, Sam decided the prudent thing was to step out of range. "We'll have time to talk about the past," he said tightly. "But this isn't the place. Where are you staying? At the Continental or the Congress?"

"I didn't make any arrangements."

"Then we have a problem." His day was sinking from bad to disastrous. "The Morgan versus Fitzgerald fight is tonight and there isn't a vacant hotel room in town." Worse, he could see that his plans to attend the "fight of the decade" were fading by the minute.

She made a face of disgust. "Naturally I expected you to make the necessary arrangements after you received my telegram."

Her scathing tone implied that even a low character like him should have been gentlemanly enough to see to her accommodations.

The spring day had begun cool and comfortable, but now Sam felt the sun on his face and back, as hot as the anger rising in his throat. "The time for expectations passed a long time ago, Angie. Coming here was your idea, not mine. I didn't ask you to come, not this time." He felt a kernel of satisfaction in seeing her jerk upright and blink hard. "Your father should have made your arrangements."

"My father died six weeks ago," she said sharply, scowling as if her father's death was his fault.

Learning that Bertoli had died provided an additional

petty sense of satisfaction. He'd outlived the bastard. His instinct was to spit and say good riddance, but he managed to restrain the impulse. However, he didn't offer the obligatory and in his case hypocritical "I'm sorry." Instead, aware they couldn't stand here on the platform much longer without attracting attention, if they hadn't already, he turned his mind to the problem of where she could stay. Unfortunately, he could think of only one place.

"I guess you'll have to stay at my house," he said finally, his reluctance plain.

"If that's too objectionable, you could abandon me right here! Certainly you've done it before."

She thought that *he* had abandoned *her?* Biting down on his back teeth, he stared in disbelief. One thing was already clear. He had been dead wrong to assume she hadn't changed much. The Angelina Bertoli he'd believed he had known had been a sweet, compliant girl, a dimpled, smiling angel. Once upon a foolish time, he had believed that a cross word could not pass those lush kissable lips. He would have laughed and waved aside any suggestion that she might grow up to be snappish, waspish, or ill-tempered. At the same time he would have denied that he could ever feel this much bitterness toward a member of the fair sex. As recently as this morning, he'd assumed they would be cordially indifferent to each other.

Stepping away from her, he flagged down a passing wagon and offered the driver four bits to haul her luggage to his place. After a minute of haggling, he and Albie Morris settled on six bits. Neither the price nor Albie's curiosity improved Sam's mood.

Now the question became where to take her. They had to talk, but he didn't want to do it at home. None of the saloons were fit for decent women. And with so many people in town for the fight, even respectable places would be crowded.

"Now what?" she asked, watching Albie haul her luggage to his wagon, one piece at a time. "Be careful with the trunks!"

"There's a place on the way." Molly Johnson had mentioned the opening of a new bakery and pastry shop. If he was lucky few people would be in a pastry shop midway between lunch and supper. Of course, if he were lucky this problem with Angie would have been solved years ago. If he were lucky, he'd be a rich man with no legal difficulties, no worries, and no Angie.

But so far he hadn't been especially lucky. When they arrived at the pastry shop, without having spoken a single word during the downhill walk, he discovered Mrs. Finn owned the place, a detail Molly Johnson had neglected to mention. There was no question now. Tomorrow his name would flutter across a lot of tongues.

"Howdy," he said, lifting his hat. Through the back windows he spotted some outside tables. Taking Angie's arm, he started toward the French doors, but Mrs. Finn stepped in front of them.

" 'lo, Mr. Holland. Haven't seen you in an age." A bright smile grazed past him and settled expectantly on Angie.

Hope evaporated that Angie could depart Willow Creek before anyone learned who she was. Sam had known the Finns too long to insult Sarah Finn by refusing an introduction.

Anger burned in his chest. Whatever Angie had to say—and he hoped he knew what that was—could have been said in a letter. She didn't have to come to Willow Creek, didn't have to dredge up old pain and resentments, didn't have to place him in an awkward position in front of people he knew.

Grudging every word, he introduced Sarah to Angie, then clenched his teeth and hesitated before he said, "And this is Mrs. Holland, my wife."

Mrs. Finn's look of astonishment told Angie that no one in Willow Creek knew Sam was married. The information spoke volumes. Everyone in her life knew she was a wife without a spouse, but Sam had avoided that particular humiliation. She gripped her handbag so tightly that her knuckles whitened inside her gloves.

"My, my," Mrs. Finn breathed. Her startled expression turned to fascination as she studied Angie. "We have a wedding to celebrate."

"I'm afraid not. Our tenth anniversary was yesterday." If her reply embarrassed Sam, all the better.

Mrs. Finn's mouth dropped and her eyes widened to the size of saucers. Very satisfying. Angie hoped that Mrs. Finn was a gossip and that Sam's deceit would be widely broadcast.

"Bring Mrs. Holland a cup of coffee and one of those flaky things," Sam said gruffly, waving a hand toward the pastry counter. "We'll be outside."

His hand on her arm was none too gentle when he jerked her toward the doors. So he was angry. Good. So was she, angrier than she had imagined she would be.

In fact, shortly before her father died, she had told Peter De Groot that she never thought about Sam anymore, that she forgot about him for years at a time. And it was true. She only recalled Sam when he wrote her father a rare letter notifying them that he had changed his address.

Until she stepped on the train departing Chicago for

Denver, she had genuinely believed that her anger and pain had drowned in tears many years ago. But fresh resentment had grown with every click of the iron wheels, culminating in that appalling moment when she had drawn back her fist and hit him. That she had done such a thing scalded her cheeks with embarrassed heat.

She would have sworn on the family Bible that she had set aside that old promise long ago, that she would never humiliate herself by committing such an unthinkable act. She couldn't believe that she had actually struck him. In public. Or that she had enjoyed it so much and wished she could hit him again. Thank heaven her mother wasn't alive to hear about this.

"Was it necessary to tell Mrs. Finn our business?"

Oh yes. She wished she could hit him again. "Is our anniversary supposed to be a secret?"

Sam rocked back on the legs of his chair, staring out at the town, which sprawled steeply downhill in a ramshackle collection of small houses, shacks, and tents. Few trees shielded the buildings from the sun; most of the aspen and spruce had been cut to build houses and shore up mine shafts. The lack of trees and any attempt at prettification gave the place a raw new look of uncertainty as if permanency was by no means guaranteed. The surrounding mountain peaks also impressed Angie as daunting. She wasn't accustomed to seeing patches of snow in April. Dropping her gaze, she inspected Sam's stony profile.

Since he balanced his hat on his knees, she had a good look at his long dark hair. Men didn't wear long hair in Chicago, and she wasn't sure what to make of it. The single long curl at his neck made him look roguish and foreign. Adding to her feeling of meeting a stranger was the age in his eyes and lining his tanned face. He'd remained frozen in her mind at eighteen. Back then, he'd worn a mustache that she had thought very handsome. Now he was clean shaven and she could see the definition of his lips.

Oddly, she found this tanned, exotic-looking stranger secretly appealing. That thought was too disturbing to allow. She did not want to think about the shape of his mouth, or the width of his shoulders, or the chiseled angles of his profile, or the rich timbre of his voice, or anything else that might be remotely admirable or attractive.

Lowering her head, she pushed a finger at the croissant Mrs. Finn had placed before her. "I want a divorce, Sam."

He nodded, holding his gaze on the valley. "I figured. I've been expecting this for years." Not looking at her, he reached for his coffee cup. "You'll hear no argument from me. Go ahead and get one."

Blast his hide, he wasn't going to make this easy. She pressed her lips together and fought to control an outburst of temper and old grievances.

"I would have begun proceedings and then notified you by post, except I need your help. Actually, I need you to pay for everything." This was not the moment to let pride block her path. Still, begging assistance was so hard that she couldn't speak above a whisper. "I can't afford to hire an attorney, nor can I support myself while I'm awaiting the final resolution." Back in Chicago her father was rolling in his grave because she'd admitted her near destitution and made a plea for Sam's assistance.

When Sam finally looked at her, his eyes were hard. That's what she had remembered most, how blue his eyes were. Dark shining blue like the waters of Lake Michigan. Like twilight when the sky began to shade toward indigo. Or like blue ice, a comparison she'd never before had cause to notice.

When his silence began to unnerve her, she completed an explanation she had naively hoped not to make. She had foolishly expected Sam to step in and agree to do the right thing. She should have known better.

"My mother died a year ago, following a long and expensive illness. I didn't know how expensive until a few weeks ago." Letting a pause develop, she rolled a flake of croissant into a little ball, then carefully balanced the ball on the rim of her plate before she rolled another. "After Papa died, I discovered a basket of unpaid bills. Even our home was mortgaged."

First Papa had sold the gig and horses, then the silver began to disappear. But she hadn't suspected finances were a difficulty until Mrs. Dom stopped coming to clean. Once she had attempted to discuss the inconvenient changes, but Papa's pride erupted in shouts. She hadn't raised the subject again. Then Papa died and she experienced the shock of discovering herself nearly penniless.

"Do I understand this correctly? You want me to pay for the divorce and support you for—what?—a year until the divorce is final?"

"That doesn't strike me as unreasonable." Anger, swift and hot, scorched the back of her throat. Her head snapped up. "I'd hoped it wouldn't be necessary to remind you that you haven't contributed one single penny toward my support during the ten years that we've been married!"

His mouth thinned into a line as hard as his eyes. "Maybe you need a reminder that your father made it abundantly clear that he would care for you as he always had. He didn't want money from me. The only thing he wanted was for me to disappear. Or did he say that after you walked out on me?"

"Wait a minute." Stiffening, she stared hard, feeling her pulse pound in her ears. "You can't possibly be suggesting that *I* abandoned *you*?" It was unbelievable.

"You're saying that you didn't? We agreed we would tell your parents we'd gotten married, then we would go to the Grand Hotel. It was you who told me that your parents would be upset. I figured you would at least stand by me since you knew what to expect. Like a fool, I assumed we'd confront your father together, then leave. It never occurred to me that you'd run out of the room and vanish right in the middle of the worst of it."

"That isn't fair! I left the parlor because my father ordered me to my room!"

"For God's sake, Angie. You were a married woman with your husband standing next to you."

"I was sixteen and accustomed to obeying my father! You knew that. Why didn't you take my hand and support me? Why didn't you help me stand up to him? But you didn't ask me to stay. You let me go!"

"I would have welcomed some support myself. Your father accused me of seducing you, of destroying your innocence. He told me I wasn't good enough for his daughter and I would never amount to anything . . . and where were you through all that? Maybe he would have believed that I hadn't seduced you if you'd been the one to deny it."

"All you had to say was *Don't go*! That's all it would have taken!"

"How was I supposed to know that? You burst into tears and ran out of the room." He shrugged. "I expected you to come back. Why wouldn't I? We were married. We'd agreed to leave together and begin our lives.

Instead, you disappeared and your father ordered me out of his house." He leaned forward. "I waited outside for three hours. I thought for sure you would come."

"I wanted you to rescue me before you left the house. You should have," she said, her voice tight.

"Push past your father in his own house and invade his daughter's bedroom? That sounds reasonable to you?" Making a sound deep in his throat, Sam shook his head and dropped backward in his chair.

They sat in steely silence, too angry to talk. What surprised Angie was how immediate the emotions felt. As if he'd abandoned her yesterday, not ten years ago. The shock and hurt and devastation were right here, right now, aching behind her chest. She'd been crazy to believe she could be indifferent to him. Being with him again triggered all the bitterness and pain that she had felt on that terrible night when she realized he had left without her.

Striving for calm, she willed her hands to stop shaking, irritated that she was only partially successful.

"There's no point discussing that night." All this time she had assumed that of course he knew the outcome was his fault. Not once had it occurred to her that he might blame her. She had a few hundred things to say about that, now that she knew, but good sense warned nothing would come of it. She hadn't traveled all this distance to trade accusations. "I came to Willow Creek because I had just enough money to get here, meaning I had no choice. But it's time. We made a mistake by not divorcing years ago. We need to correct that mistake."

She waited for him to assure her that he would support her financially during the divorce waiting period. But he met her gaze and asked, "Why didn't you file years ago? I've been curious about that." When she didn't answer, he frowned and said, "Angie?"

"I heard you." Well, what difference did the reason make? "I thought my father would let me go west with you if he thought that we . . ." She hesitated, annoyed by how hard the words came. She wasn't a foolishly modest girl anymore. "I thought he'd accept the marriage if he believed I might be with child." In other words, without knowing what she'd done, she had let her father believe that Sam had indeed seduced her.

Nodding silently, Sam turned his gaze back to the valley.

"After a few months passed and it became obvious that I wasn't pregnant, my father wanted the marriage annulled. But by then people knew I was married." She might as well have worn a noose all these years instead of a simple gold ring. That's how the ring felt, like a rope around her neck instead of a band around her finger. "My mother was horrified by the idea of a divorce and the scandal that would result. It was easier to explain your absence by saying that I was waiting for you to send for me. Eventually people stopped asking about my husband." She placed another ball of rolled croissant on the rim of her plate. "Why didn't you file for divorce? Every time an envelope arrived with your name on it, I prayed it would contain divorce papers."

"A gentleman never files to dissolve a marriage. No matter what the circumstances, he allows his wife to request the divorce." Sam pushed a hand through his hair. "That's why I kept sending your father my address over the years. So he'd know where to mail the papers if I had to sign anything."

Once Angie had lived in fear that he would humiliate her by being the one to instigate a divorce. But as she began to understand that her life would be one of loneliness and boredom, of watching other people enjoy their lives while the years passed her by, humiliation and scandal had seemed a small price to pay for freedom and another chance at living.

"Well," she said finally. "So here we are, ten wasted years later." When he didn't say anything, she dropped the ball of croissant she was rolling between her fingers and wiped her hands on a napkin. "I imagine you're as eager as I am to get on with your life."

Sam looked toward the French doors. "This place would fare better if Mrs. Finn sold spirits." He cleared his throat. "All right. Just so we're clear, I want this divorce as badly as you do. In fact, I'm angry that you didn't file years ago." Finally he met her eyes. "We'll get a divorce, Angie, but it may take a while. I wish to hell I could prove your father wrong by telling you that I've succeeded beyond my wildest dreams. But that's not the case."

Sunlight struck him full in the face, etching golden lines on his forehead and at the corner of his eyes. It startled Angie to realize that for a fleeting second, she was as attracted to him as she had been ten years ago. The boy she had fallen in love with had been replaced by a man she didn't know, but this handsome stranger was hard enough, slightly dangerous enough, that something in her responded to his direct gaze.

Exasperated, she pulled her attention back to his voice and realized he was saying that he couldn't afford to support her and pay for a divorce. Turning her head, she gazed at the mountainsides and evidence of working mines.

"In ten years of trying, you haven't found any gold?"

"I wasn't looking. I've only been in Willow Creek for two years. Before that I prospected for silver, with only minimal success. And in between times I worked construction in Colorado Springs."

Try as she might, Angie couldn't help thinking that in the end, her father had been correct. Sam hadn't amounted to much.

His face colored slightly as if he'd guessed her thoughts. "I'll hit the jackpot and someday soon. I feel it in my bones. Meanwhile, I manage to put food on the table and a roof over my head."

"You don't need to sound so defensive. I didn't say anything." But she wanted to, because she wanted to hurt him as he had hurt her. Which was stupid after all this time. She drew a deep breath. "So when do you think you can afford a divorce?"

"I don't know. Even if I hit the jackpot tomorrow, there's another obligation that has to come first. Getting a divorce is not my first priority. In fact, you could say it's far down the list. I have other responsibilities, Angie. I'm sorry, but that's how it is."

Every small speech seemed to be followed by a lengthy silence. During this one, Angie thought about all the years of waiting for her life to begin. She'd been unrealistic to hope the waiting would end when she saw him again, to hope he'd readily agree and she could leave here tomorrow with enough money to start over.

Covering her eyes so he wouldn't see the tears of frustration and disappointment, she asked, "What am I supposed to do while I wait for you to find gold?" Gold that he'd already failed to find in two years of searching. "Where will I live? Where can I go?"

After another silence, he swore softly. And he avoided most of her questions. "I can't afford to set you up in a separate residence." Before she could protest or express the alarm she felt, he raised a hand. "Believe me, I wish I could. But I'm saving every cent I can. So—and I hate this as much as you're going to—I guess you'll have to live with me until I can afford to correct our mistake."

"That's appalling. Completely unacceptable."

"If you have a better solution, just say so."

She didn't. Neither of them had any money, and money was what they needed. The result was that she would have to delay beginning her new life. Battling tears, she struck the table with her fist, knocking the little balls of croissant off the rim of her plate. Angrily, she brushed them away from her lap.

"Do you know what it's like to be married but not a wife? To sit by and watch friends marry and have children and be happy?" Her eyes burned and her voice trembled. "Other women ran households and raised children while I sat in the parlor and embroidered endless numbers of pillowcases and napkins. I used to linger by the front window in late afternoon and watch the carriages drive past, carrying ladies home to their families and husbands home to dinner. I envied them so much it hurt. And it hurt to end an evening out by watching husbands and wives go home together while I left with my parents. I've waited so long, Sam. How much longer do I have to wait for a life worth living?"

"I can't answer that," he said, closing his eyes and rubbing his forehead. "I'm sorry how things worked out. If I could change everything I would."

Not for the first time, Angie wanted to twist the gold ring off her finger and fling it as far from her as possible. Her wedding ring had brought her one hour of happiness and ten years of misery.

"There's no other solution? None at all?" Despair trembled in her voice. "We have to live together for some unknown length of time, and there's no alternative whatsoever?"

Standing abruptly, he tossed some coins on the table. "I'll stay out of your way as much as possible. And don't worry. Your honor is safe with me."

That concern hadn't entered her mind. Now that he'd raised the subject, a rush of pink colored her cheeks. She didn't know whether to thank him for reassuring her or take offense that he thought it necessary to state something she trusted was a given.

He looked down at her while settling his hat. "I'm no happier about this than you are. I'd hoped you would arrive, announce you were seeking a divorce, then leave before anyone in town knew who you were. Instead I now have another mouth to feed, another person to support. I know that doesn't sound gentlemanly. I know you think I owe you, and maybe you're right. But your timing is off by several years and I can't help resenting that. It's also hard not to resent that I wasn't good enough ten years ago, but now when you need someone to feed and support you, you show up here expecting me to do it. Suddenly I'm good enough."

"I never said you weren't good enough! That was my father."

"But you believed him, or you would have come west with me."

There was no easy answer to his accusation, so she didn't attempt to offer one. She had plenty to cope with merely handling today's problems. Yesterday's unanswered questions would have to wait. She suspected the questions would come up again and again.

Not giving him a chance to hold her chair, she rose quickly and walked to the door, leaving him to follow. Mrs. Finn watched them curiously as they passed the pastry counter. Mrs. Finn couldn't have overheard anything they said, but she had lingered by the windows, observing angry expressions and gestures.

"Which way?" Angie asked, pausing in the street.

"Downhill."

All the streets ran downhill from the depot, she had already noticed that. And she had noticed this was Carr Street, one block off Bennet, which appeared to be the main thoroughfare. None of the streets were paved. There were no lamps at the corners of the side streets. And if Willow Creek had a street crew, they should be reprimanded. Flies buzzed around mounds of horse droppings that appeared to have accumulated over a long period. Someone nearby was burning trash, and the pungent fruity odor pinched Angie's nostrils.

Suddenly she missed Chicago with an intensity that was sharp and visceral. The small wooden houses on either side of Carr were shacks compared to the neat brick homes on the street where she'd grown to womanhood. Weeds and wildflowers ran rampant in yards where she was accustomed to seeing neatly trimmed grass and beds of cultivated flowers. In Chicago men didn't wear long hair that made them resemble pirates from a bygone era. Bakery shops carried a larger selection than only croissants and frosted buns. Chicago was civilized and it was home. Tears of homesickness glistened in her eyes, and she decided she hated it here.

"This is it," Sam announced in a flat voice.

They halted before a one-story structure smaller than the carriage house behind her home in Chicago. The only thing in the house's favor was that it looked sturdy and didn't appear quite as thrown together as the houses on either side. But the size dismayed her. They would be bumping into each other every time they turned around.

Slowly, she walked around the pile of luggage Albie Morris had dumped in the dirt yard and stood silently while Sam opened the door.

Outside, the planks ran vertically from ground to roof. Inside, the planks were placed horizontally. A pitched ceiling had been finished with canvas for weatherproofing.

A glance identified two bedrooms—thank heaven— opening off one main room that served as kitchen, dining room, and parlor. Leaving Sam to bring her things inside, Angie stood in the center of the room and looked around.

Flowered curtains at the window over the sink surprised her. As did a cloth on the table and the vase of dandelions. And the braided rug. These efforts to soften the bleak lines of stark necessity were unexpected, particularly in the residence of a bachelor as ruggedly male as Sam. Dust she would have expected; the tidiness she had not.

After fetching the last of her trunks, Sam walked past her to the sink. "This place isn't a tenth of what you're used to, but there's inside water." He indicated the pump handle at the sink. "And the walls are tight. There isn't a square foot that isn't insulated with newspaper this thick." He indicated half an inch. "The stove burns evenly, and there's a root cellar out back."

His expression indicated that he expected her to say something. But what? What could she say about a three-room house that had little more to offer than shelter from the elements? Where did one bathe? Where did one sit in the evenings? How did the occupants get away from each other to enjoy a little privacy? She doubted he wanted to hear that if she had to live in this tiny primitive place very long, she'd go crazy.

The back door slammed open and two small girls spun

into the room like miniature whirlwinds, their soiled and shapeless dresses flying around dirty, sagging stockings. They flung themselves at Sam.

"You're home early!"

"A man left a pile of baggage outside but Mrs. Molly said we couldn't touch anything."

"Girls?" Sam smiled at them, made an awkward attempt to smooth down their flyaway tangled hair. "Girls! We have a guest."

Now they spotted Angie and instantly went silent and shy, standing on either side of Sam, leaning against his legs. They inspected her with twin sets of gray eyes that had turned curious and wary.

"This is Angie. She'll be staying with us for a while." He lifted his head and met Angie's wide eyes. "These are my daughters."

Chapter 2

"This is Lucy. She's seven." Sam covered her golden head with his hand. "And this is Daisy, who is five."

Angie's mouth opened and closed, and she pressed a hand to her breast as if she couldn't breathe. Sam guessed her breathlessness would pass in about a minute and she would start to fizz like a geyser building steam. Kneeling, he gazed at his girls, wishing they didn't look so ragtag and flyaway today.

"What have you been doing since school let out?"

After sliding a look toward Angie, Lucy brushed at a stain on her dress, then whispered, "We had a rolling contest down Golden Avenue."

"Lucy won," Daisy solemnly announced.

"I rolled the fastest."

These were the moments that perplexed him and pointed up the difficulty of a man trying to raise daughters. Did he praise her for rolling down a hill faster than anyone else? Or chastise her for behaving like a young hoyden and getting her dress dirty?

"I'm glad you won," he said finally. "I need to speak to Angie a bit, so you two go back to Mrs. Molly's and ask if you can have supper there. I'll come for you after you've eaten and we'll talk then."

Lucy cupped her hand around her mouth and leaned to his ear. "How long is that lady going to stay with us?"

"We'll talk about it later. Off you go."

Before they banged out the door, they looked back at Angie, not sure what to make of her. Sam waited a beat then leaned outside and found them lingering beside the stoop. "Go," he commanded in a stern voice. "No eavesdropping." Giggling, they ran toward the house next door, but Sam didn't step back inside until he saw them talking to Molly Johnson.

Molly called across the yards. "Supper's fine. You come for them when you're ready." Her dark eyes gleamed with curiosity.

"Thank you."

Already Angie's presence was causing problems that radiated like circles spreading from a rock tossed in a pond. He'd have to tell the girls about her, and he guessed he'd have to explain things to Molly. Sure as sunset, someone had seen Angie sock him at the depot, and Mrs. Finn was undoubtedly out there right now spreading the word that Sam Holland had a wife and he'd had one for ten years.

When he returned inside, Angie was seated at the kitchen table staring at him with large shocked eyes and a white face.

"I can't believe this. I just cannot believe it! I guess the first question has to be, where is your daughters' mother?" Her cold gaze swept the curtains and other feminine touches. "Is that the next shock? A woman walks in here and announces that she's living with my husband?"

"Laura died of pneumonia over a year ago." Stepping to the stove, Sam stoked the coals and then slid the coffeepot over the heat.

"I don't know what to say." Her hands lifted, then fell back into her lap. "How could you do such a thing?"

There were a dozen answers, all of which would sidetrack the issue and lead to accusations and justifications. "Whatever you want to ask, do it now," he said, clenching his teeth. "I don't want to discuss Laura in front of my daughters, and they're usually here when I am. So let's finish the questions while the girls are next door."

"Did you love her?"

"Yes."

"You son of a bitch!" Her voice was low and shaking. "While I was wasting away in Chicago growing older and lonelier, you were living *your* life!" She reached for the vase of dandelions with a quick movement as if she intended to throw it at him, but she stopped, squeezed her eyes shut, then brought her fist back to her lap and drew a deep breath. "Did she know about me?"

"Yes," he said, staring at her.

All of his life he would regret that he hadn't been able to offer Laura marriage.

Because Mrs. Bertoli shrank from scandal and because Angie hadn't stood up to her parents, Angie had wasted a miserable ten years. And he hadn't done right by Laura. She'd become further estranged from her parents. Laura had deserved better. For as long as he lived, he would bitterly resent that he'd been unable to place a wedding ring on her finger.

"Laura didn't mind living in adultery with a married man? She just shrugged off the fact that you had a wife?" Angie spat the questions in a scathing tone hot with condemnation.

Reaching behind, Sam gripped the edges of the sink until he felt his knuckles whiten.

"Laura Govenor was a decent and good woman. Don't judge her because you didn't know her. Of course she minded that I couldn't marry her. And of course she would have preferred that my situation was resolved. But she also had the courage to follow her heart," he said, his gaze burning on a woman who had lacked that courage. "She said if we couldn't be happy with a ring, we'd be happy without one. She said she didn't care." But he had.

"Did you ever once think that I might care?" Her eyes flamed and snapped. "For that matter, did you ever think of me at all?"

"During the week after your father threw me out of his house, I wrote you six letters begging you to come west with me. And I know you received them. I gave those letters to Mrs. Dom, your mother's cleaning lady, and she promised that she delivered them to you. You wrote back once. You said your father would never permit you to leave Chicago. You made your choice, Angie. So, no. I didn't think you'd care what I did out here. Why would you? You'd made it clear as glass that you didn't care about me or us."

His anger surprised him. It reached beyond not doing right by Laura, reached back into the realm of first love and first betrayal and the first pain of the heart. Grinding his teeth, he turned his back to her and fetched two coffee cups from the shelf above the stove. After filling and placing them on the table, he took a seat across from her.

She was so different from Laura. Where Laura had been pale and delicate, Angie was vivid and strong featured. Laura had been a tiny wisp of a thing. Angie was tall and threw a punch like a man, as he had cause to know, he thought, feeling his jaw.

"I never believed I would ever hate anyone," Angie said in a whisper. "But I think I hate you." She shook her head and gazed at a point in space. "All those years . . . I was as chaste and unwanted as a spinster, and all the while you were—"

"What do you want me to say? That I was wrong? All right, I was wrong about everything. I should have walked away when your father refused me permission to court you. I should have talked you out of seeing me on the sly. I shouldn't have asked you to marry me. I shouldn't have suggested we elope that Sunday afternoon. I should have dragged you out of your father's house. Is that what you want to hear?"

Accusation glittered in her eyes. "You lived with someone as man and wife and had children."

"I won't apologize for that. The one thing in this whole mess that I don't regret is Laura. I do regret that I couldn't marry her. I do regret that I couldn't give her more. But Laura brought sunshine to this house and to me. She gave me Lucy and Daisy and they're the best things that ever happened in my life. If I had it to do again, Angie, I'd do it the same way. I'd take the good years with Laura."

In the ensuing silence he fought the anger clenching his jaw and watched Angie slowly withdraw her hat pins, then remove her hat. She placed the hat and pins in a row on the table.

"I suppose you already know how selfish and wrong you are, so there's no need for me to point it out," she said, pointing it out. "More important, a thought occurred while you were trying to justify your unforgivable behavior."

Sam stared at her.

"Are you expecting me to care for your daughters while I have to be here?"

Until this minute he hadn't thought ahead to consider

their everyday arrangements. "That seems reasonable," he said finally. "It doesn't make sense to continue paying Molly Johnson to watch the girls, do the laundry, and cook an occasional meal while you're living here. God knows I can use the money I'd save by not having to pay Molly."

"That's what I thought," she said unhappily. "Well, there's something you need to know. Unlike you, I haven't had children and I don't know anything about them. It's a good thing our situation is only temporary because I'm sure to make mistakes."

"If you have questions, Molly Johnson is right next door."

Angie lifted an eyebrow. "Does the woman who watches after your children know about me? What kind of person is *she*? Does she care that you and Laura lived together without benefit of marriage?"

"Molly Johnson is the salt of the earth." His eyes narrowed, but he managed to keep his voice level. "I'll explain who you are to Molly."

Every other word set a torch to his anger. Laura's parents knew why Sam hadn't been free to marry their daughter, and that's why they hated him. He supposed everyone else had assumed that he and Laura were married. For Laura's sake, that's what he had hoped. Now Mrs. Finn knew that he and Laura had lived in sin. He'd have to admit the same to Molly. Soon everyone who had known Laura would decide she wasn't the respectable woman they had believed she was. Laura didn't deserve that. Her only crime had been loving him.

And as much as he disliked Laura's parents, they, too, didn't deserve the shame they would experience when Angie's identity became known and it was publicly obvious that their daughter had involved herself in an adulterous liaison. Fortunately, once the initial gossip died down, most of Willow Creek wouldn't give a damn. The basic philosophy in mining towns was live and let live. But the Govenors cared about such things. They already believed he had corrupted their daughter; now they would blame him for shaming Laura and them and for heaping disgrace on their family name. They would use Angie against him.

"I wish to Christ that you had never come," he said, staring at her as if she was a devil who had popped out of the floor. He didn't spare himself. He was absolutely to blame for all of his difficulties and for what would happen to Laura's reputation. Angie's part was a small one. Or had been until she showed up on his doorstep. In a day or so he'd calm down and put the blame back where it belonged, on himself. But right now he detested the fact that Angie's appearance would tarnish a good woman's memory.

They finished their coffee in rocky silence, watching the sun fade to pink and orange against the window glass.

Eventually Sam cleared his throat and focused his mind on the present. "Are you hungry? I could go to town and buy something to eat."

And maybe take a minute to find out if the fight had started. He'd wagered five dollars that he couldn't afford to lose on Mad Morgan. But if he won, the return would be well worth the risk. He was always looking for ways to make extra money. For one crazy minute, he considered leaving the girls with Molly tonight, as he'd planned. But no, that wouldn't be right. This situation was getting off to a bad enough beginning without adding to the problems. He needed to talk to Lucy and

Daisy, and there was still a lot of ground he hadn't covered with Angie.

"I couldn't swallow a bite." She hesitated, then removed her cape and folded it across Lucy's chair, as if she'd finally accepted the inevitable: that she had to stay. A long sigh collapsed her shoulders. "Tell me about her. What was she like?"

"Laura?"

"Of course, Laura. Who else?" Muttering, she raised a hand and pressed her palm to her forehead.

Sam wasn't good at grasping situations from another person's viewpoint, but he could understand that she'd undergone a few shocks today. Maybe that accounted for her consistent bad temper. He could hope.

"Laura wasn't especially pretty like you are, but she had a natural sweetness that made her lovely," he said, after thinking about the question for a minute. "She was always smiling, always finding joy in little things no matter how hard life got." His gaze touched the dandelions wilting in the vase. Daisy had put them there, but it was something Laura might have done. She would have seen beauty in the weeds just as she'd seen goodness in him.

"She was a tiny thing. Looked like the wind could blow her away. But she had courage. She stood up to her parents and went her own way." He gave Angie what he hoped was a meaningful look. "She was not argumentative, she was always supportive.

"I never heard a cross word pass her lips. I never heard her swear or throw a temper. God knows I gave her reason to complain, but she never did."

"In short," Angie said with another sigh when he stopped talking, "she was everything that I'm not."

The gallant response would have been to remain silent.

But too many resentments simmered on his tongue. "You could say that." His answer didn't seem to surprise her, and that made him angry, too.

"There was a time, way back when, when I might have tried to be a gentle, compliant wife," she said after a moment, studying her empty coffee cup. "But that time is gone. I grew up. I learned men aren't the infallible creatures you'd like us to believe you are. Plus, I'm Italian."

"What does being Italian have to do with anything?"

"Mama came from English stock, like you." She glanced at him and then away, as if looking at him offended her. "She always said that Italians wore their emotions on their sleeves. Italians get as volatile and crazy over a worm in an apple as they would at finding an assassin at the door. Every upset is major. Papa was like that. Maybe I am, too. At least sometimes." She glanced at him. "I've never been to the old country, I don't know a word of Italian. But I've got the blood. That means I'm not likely to be gentle or compliant."

He hadn't guessed this ten years ago, but he certainly knew it now.

She watched him touch his sore jaw. "Maybe I'm a little sorry that I hit you, Sam, but you deserved it. To my way of thinking, you'd deserve it if I shot you."

"The way I see it, there's blame on both sides. More blame on your side than mine if you want my whole entire opinion."

Her nostrils flared before she closed her eyes for a long moment. "And that's a problem, but I'm too tired to discuss it anymore tonight." Suddenly she straightened and looked toward the bedroom doors with an expression of alarm. "One of the bedrooms must belong to the girls."

Instantly he saw the reason for her anxiety. "You take my bedroom. I'll set up my old tent in the backyard."

When she agreed that his solution sounded reasonable, he stared at her. Being displaced from his own house didn't strike him as anywhere close to reasonable. Necessary. Expedient. Considerate. But it wasn't reasonable to sleep outside on the ground when he had a house and a bed a few feet away. Already he could see another thing that he'd overlooked. His life was going to change, rapidly and not for the better.

"Well, since this has to be." Placing her palms flat on the table, she stood and looked down at him, her face carefully expressionless. "Get what you need out of your bedroom. I'll unpack what I require for tonight, then I'll put everything else away tomorrow." She shook her head. "I cannot tell you how much I hate this."

So did he. Ten years ago he had wanted her with all his heart and soul, but he couldn't have her. Now he didn't want her anywhere near, but he was stuck with her.

Angie felt small-minded and childish about eavesdropping on Sam's conversation with his daughters, but she managed to overcome the feeling enough to do it anyway. They sat on the steps just outside the kitchen door, and she could overhear by standing unseen near the big black stove.

"She's your wife?" Lucy asked in surprise.

Daisy's lighter tone followed. "Did you have a real wedding? Why didn't we get to go?"

"The wedding took place a long time ago," Sam explained in a grim voice.

He was telling them in a roundabout way that he and their mother had not been married. When the implication made no impression, Sam must have realized at the same time as Angie that the girls were too young to understand that he'd just blackened their mother's reputation and exposed them as illegitimate.

Lucy had concerns more in keeping with the moment. "If she's your wife, does that mean she's our new mama?"

"Do we have to call her Mama?" Daisy sounded worried.

Sam cleared his throat. "I don't think she'd mind if you call her Angie. The thing is, I don't know how long Angie will stay with us. I suspect it could be for quite a while, until we can afford to get a divorce. Do you know what a divorce is?"

"No."

"It's when a husband and wife decide they don't want to be married anymore. They go before a court judge and ask the judge to set aside the marriage. Then they go their separate ways. Angie and I don't want to be married, so eventually we'll get divorced."

"Good," Lucy said firmly. "We don't need a wife or a new mama. But I don't think we should wait for eventually. We should get our divorce right now."

"It takes a lot of money to get a divorce. Right now we're saving our money to fix Daisy's foot. Daisy's operation has to come first, before a divorce or anything else."

Daisy's foot? Angie blinked. Seeing the girls rush inside and throw themselves on Sam had been such a shock that she hadn't concentrated on details. Now she reviewed the scene in her mind and she did seem to recall that the smaller one had appeared to stumble. In retrospect, maybe Daisy hadn't stumbled. Maybe one leg was shorter than the other. Could that be the problem?

"I don't mind waiting for the operation, Papa. We could get the divorce first."

"No, honey, you've waited too long already. In fact, I feel a lucky strike coming, and we'll use the money to fix your foot. So. Are there any more questions about Angie?"

"Is she going to boss us around?" Lucy again.

"Probably no more than Mrs. Molly. I want both of you to behave yourselves. No sass. It would be nice if you did your chores without being asked." The girls giggled. "I want you to help me make this situation as easy as possible."

A stretch of silence ensued during which Angie heard cheers and shouts from the distance. The crowd noise puzzled her until she recalled the fight of the decade. Which Sam had undoubtedly wanted to attend.

Grudgingly, she granted him a thimbleful of credit for not dumping her and the girls on one another and leaving for the fight.

"She's pretty," Daisy remarked, yawning audibly.

"I suppose she is." No hint of expression betrayed Sam's feelings one way or another.

"She's not as pretty as Mama!"

Hearing Lucy's tone, Angie wondered if Lucy would be a problem. What was she thinking? Definitely Lucy would be a problem. Daisy, too. They didn't want her here, and she didn't want to be here. Of course there would be problems.

"I didn't say Angie was prettier than Mama!"

"Well, she's not!"

"Stop bickering. Your mama was pretty in her way, and Angie is pretty in her way," Sam said, surprising Angie with his diplomacy. "Just as you're pretty in your way, and you are pretty in your way. There's no rule that says there can't be a lot of pretty ladies in this world."

"Mrs. Molly isn't pretty," Lucy said in a low voice. "But I don't care. She's nice."

"I like Mrs. Molly, too."

Angie heard Sam plant his boots on the step and stand. "That's because Mrs. Molly is pretty on the inside. That's the best kind of pretty there is. Now in you go. It's time for bed."

Hastily Angie returned to the box she'd set on the table and began sorting her toiletries. When the girls came inside, she straightened her shoulders and pasted a bright smile on her lips.

"Hello there."

They said hello, but neither of them smiled. Thanks to Mrs. Molly no doubt, their faces were scrubbed and shiny clean, their hair brushed, and the dust had been sponged from their dresses.

Angie drew a breath and reminded herself they were just children; there was no reason to feel intimidated by their silence or solemn stares. "It's been a long day full of surprises," she said pleasantly, aware that Sam watched. "If it's agreeable to you, we could wait until tomorrow to get acquainted."

They didn't indicate one way or another whether her suggestion was agreeable. They simply stared with un-abashed curiosity and suspicion, as if she were an inter-esting novelty whose nature couldn't be discerned at a glance. She might turn out to be good or bad. They would wait and see.

Sam stepped into the breach. "No dawdling. Wash your faces—"

"We washed our faces at Mrs. Molly's."

"And clean your teeth. Then into your nightgowns." The pump handle squealed as he filled a basin, then hooked his boot around a small wooden step and pulled it close so they could climb up to reach the water and the soap he laid out.

Lucy was first. "Aren't you going to heat the water?"

"Not tonight." Sam glanced at Angie. "A splash will do," he said, handing Lucy a towel. "Daisy? Your turn."

Pretending not to, Angie observed the routine from beneath her lashes while she sorted her hairbrushes. Both girls were the spitting image of their mother, that was easy to guess. They certainly hadn't inherited their whitish gold hair or gray eyes from Sam. Already she could tell that Lucy would be tall like Sam, while Daisy would probably be petite as Sam had said Laura was.

Clearly something was definitely and seriously wrong with one of Daisy's feet. So wrong that Angie was astonished she hadn't noticed at once. When Daisy stepped on her right foot, her shoulder sank a good two, maybe three inches. She walked with a lurching, rolling gait.

At the finish of the nightly preparations, Sam followed his daughters into their bedroom and listened to their prayers. Then Angie heard the squeak of bedsprings, shouted laughter and gasps and bogus pleas from the girls begging Sam not to tickle them. After a few minutes, Sam pretended to get angry when they wouldn't sit still for their goodnight kiss, which finished the routine.

When he finally emerged, he closed the bedroom door, considered Angie a minute, then raised the lid of the ice box. "Do you drink beer?"

"Not usually, but tonight . . . yes, please."

He opened two dark bottles of ale and beckoned her toward the kitchen door.

"Should we blow out the lamps?" Immediately the suggestion impressed her as foolish. The girls' door was closed. The lamplight wouldn't keep them awake.

"No. It scares Daisy if she has to get up for some reason and the house is dark."

"You burn the lamps all night long?"

"Lamp oil is one of the few things that's cheap." He shrugged. "Before you go to bed, put one of the lamps in the sink and blow out the rest."

The ease and understanding that he demonstrated with his daughters was a side of Sam Holland that Angie had never seen or thought to imagine. This morning, when she had stepped off the train, she wouldn't have conceded Sam a single good quality or one admirable trait. But she reluctantly admitted that he seemed to possess a natural instinct for dealing with children. What a pity that his instincts didn't extend to women.

After dropping a shawl around her shoulders, she followed him outside into the darkness and sat on a step below him so they would not accidentally touch. Down the hill and to the left, she saw the glow of gas lamps outlining Bennet Street; heard music from the saloons on Myers Street, an occasional shout that burst from the noise of traffic, and a low hum of people talking at too great a distance to be heard distinctly. The crowd noise had dissipated, so the fight of the decade must have been decided.

Tilting her head, Angie gazed up at a miracle-work of stars, suppressing a gasp of wonder. In Chicago the lights of the city blotted all but the brightest planets. But here in the mountains, with less space and light between man and heaven, millions of tiny stars winked and sparkled, strewn thick across a field of black satin.

"Tell me about Daisy," she said quietly.

"She was born with a clubfoot."

Angie nodded. One of her friend's babies had been born with two clubbed feet. Now she understood Daisy's gait. A clubbed foot twisted inward and up, forcing the victim to walk on her ankle and the side of the foot.

"It's my understanding that the longer the condition goes untreated, the harder it is to correct," Angie commented. "Also, I've heard that the skin on the ankle can break down since it wasn't meant to be walked on. Is there some reason why Daisy didn't have corrective surgery earlier?"

"The doctor wanted to wait until she was a year old. Wanted to try manipulating and casting the foot first. It was painful for Daisy, and twisting and casting didn't seem to be working, so Laura discontinued that option. Then, every damned time I've saved enough money for the surgery, something has happened and I've had to spend it on other things." He paused. "Daisy's surgery is what I was talking about when I told you I had an obligation that had to come before the divorce."

She would have guessed even if she hadn't eavesdropped on his conversation with the girls.

"Daisy's surgery is my number-one priority. This time nothing is going to get in the way. Absolutely nothing."

From the corner of her eye, she saw his arm move, raising the beer bottle, then heard him swallow.

"Is there a qualified doctor in Willow Creek?"

"The doctor who treated her and agreed to do the surgery is in Colorado Springs. The bastard wants fifteen hundred dollars for the operation."

Angie sucked in a breath. "That's a lot of money."

"A king's ransom."

"How close are you to saving that amount?"

"I've got almost six hundred dollars put aside," he said after a lengthy period of angry silence. "Every time I get my hands on a little extra, there are forty other places demanding payment. The grocer, the iceman, the coal man, my attorney, my tab at the saloon, Molly, the laundry, the stables, and a half dozen other bills in arrears. Last week, all I could add to my savings was twenty dollars." Frustration shook his voice.

Angie hesitated then blurted what leapt to her mind. "I have about a hundred and thirty-two dollars."

Instantly she felt a scald of anger directed at her back. "The day I take money from a woman is the day I might as well shoot myself because I've ceased to be a man. Whatever money you have, it's yours and I don't want it."

"I'm not offering it to you," she said, stiffening. "I'm offering it for Daisy."

"I'll pay for Daisy's operation."

Hurtful words stung her tongue. It would have been easy to point out that Daisy was five and he hadn't yet managed to save enough for the operation. And she could have mentioned that Daisy was still young, but eventually the bones in her foot would become permanently misshapen and set in a position difficult to correct. But there was enough ill-feeling between them without emphasizing painful facts that he already knew.

At least not tonight. Not while she saw so clearly that her misfortune had compounded his misfortune. When Sam had resented her for adding another mouth to feed, she hadn't understood. Now she did.

"All right," she said, studying the dark silhouette of the tent he had pitched in the backyard. "We're agreed that we won't get the divorce until after Daisy's operation."

"That's how it has to be."

"I'm not arguing." She hoped she possessed the patience to put up with him during the time they were forced to remain together. He might be good with children, but when it came to communicating with wives, he stank. "I'll do everything I can to hold down the household expenses and save money."

"I hope so."

Angie ground her teeth and glared at the stars. Laura—undemanding, uncomplaining, that flawless paragon who was everything Angie was not—must have been a saint. It said a lot for the woman that Sam was still alive.

Chapter 3

To give her the benefit of doubt, Sam reminded himself that Angie had no reason to be an early riser. The Bertolis had employed household help to see to breakfast and the morning chores. She hadn't had children to get off to school or the responsibility of arriving at a job site. Still, he glanced at her closed bedroom door with annoyance. If nothing else, how could she continue to sleep through the girls' chatter and the noise they made setting the table?

On the other hand, breakfast was one of the few meals he could cook with confidence that the result would be eatable.

"How do you want your eggs?" he called over his shoulder.

Both girls said scrambled.

"They're going to be fried."

"Every morning we say scrambled, but every morning you give us fried. Why do you ask how we want them?"

"My dear Lucy," he said grandly. "Fried eggs are a work of art. The yoke has to be set, but not too hard. Absolutely it cannot be broken. And the whites must be butter-crisped but not scorched. It's an art. Scrambled eggs, on the other hand, require no talent. It's just stir together, then pour in the skillet."

The girls laughed and pushed each other. "Scrambled eggs are more work. You have to add milk and stir."

"That too," he said, grinning at them.

In the mornings his daughters looked like proper miniature young ladies. Combed hair neatly tied at their necks. Clean faces and hands. Fresh dresses with the sashes tied prettily. That reminded him. Had he paid the seamstress last week? Her bill had been in his ledger for a long time.

Angie's door flew open and she rushed into the room, hastily tying a wrapper around her waist. A long, dark braid swung down her back and her face glowed rosy from sleep.

Shock rooted Sam's boots to the floor. A man seldom saw a woman in her nightclothes or wearing her hair down, which made Angie seem as erotic as a French postcard. When he realized what he was thinking, he almost laughed. She wasn't showing a spare inch of exposed flesh. The high collar of her nightgown circled her neck up to her chin. The wrapper sleeves covered her wrists. All he could see at the bottom were the tips of her house slippers. It wasn't the actuality of her attire that aroused him, but the idea of it. A woman stood in his kitchen wearing a wrapper tied over her nightgown and with her hair still braided for bed. Such an amazing event was enough to put ideas in any man's head.

After calling good morning to the girls, she hurried up next to him at the stove, clearly dismayed to discover him sliding eggs onto the plates.

"I overslept. I'm sorry. What do you want me to do?"

"You can be forgiven for shirking your duty on your first day at work," he said, making it sound like a joke. He couldn't think straight with her standing beside him in her wrapper. Ten years ago, he had fantasized about seeing her with her hair down, wearing her nightgown. In the fantasy she had slowly raised her nightgown, revealing milky legs and thighs and . . . His hand shook and he almost dropped a plate of eggs on the floor. "Sit down," he said after clearing his throat. "Lucy, please pour Angie a cup of coffee. And be careful with the pot. It's hot."

Obviously flustered, she watched him add thick strips of bacon to each of the plates. "Maybe I should get dressed," she said, waving a hand toward the bedroom door. "You know, before I sit down. It won't take too long."

"If that's what you want to do. But cold fried eggs aren't the tastiest thing I can think of," he said, striving to keep his voice light.

He told himself that he'd be relieved if she put on some clothing. It wasn't decent for him to be thinking arousing thoughts in front of his girls. On the other hand, a long time had passed since he'd had the pleasure of sitting at a table with a woman whose hair was down. Seeing her this way was a sweet form of torture.

Angie shot him one of those narrow-eyed argumentative looks that he was starting to recognize and dislike. In this case, he could almost see her weighing her instinct to get dressed against his implication that letting the eggs get cold would be stupid.

Last night, after he finally crawled into his tent, he'd given some thought to their new arrangement. And he'd made a vow that no matter how bad-tempered, incompetent, and hard to get along with she was, he would not argue or be rude or sarcastic to her in front of his girls. This would be a hard vow to keep, and he knew it. But he was determined not to upset Lucy and Daisy. In fact, the situation with Angie could teach them some good lessons.

Such as making the best of a bad situation. Such as not shirking your responsibilities no matter how repugnant they may be. Such as getting along with others.

Remembering his vow, he amended his previous statement. "I suppose getting dressed is a good idea. I could leave your plate on the stove. The eggs might still be warm when you're ready."

"No, I think you were right before," she said, deciding. Chewing her lip, she stood beside the table and watched the girls open napkins across their laps. Sam felt a tiny burst of pride that they'd remembered about the napkins. "The thing is, if I'm going to be part of the household, we should eat our meals together."

"Then sit down," he said reasonably, carrying the girls' plates to the table. "All right. Whose job is it to fetch and pour the milk?"

"I'll do it," Angie volunteered quickly.

"No, I think it's Daisy's job this week." When he saw Angie's eyes widen, he added, "Daisy's very good at pouring milk, aren't you, Daisy?"

"I'm good at carrying milk, too."

Daisy's hint of defensiveness suggested she, too, had sensed Angie's surprise that she was expected to do chores.

"Daisy manages very well," Sam said, meeting Angie's gaze. "She can do everything Lucy can except walk upright." To his way of thinking, coddling did a child a disservice. Even a child that was disadvantaged. Moreover, he wanted both of his girls to think in terms of what they could do instead of what they couldn't.

Bright color stained Angie's cheeks. "I didn't mean to imply that—"

"I know you didn't. I'm only saying this so you don't get the wool pulled over your eyes. For weeks this imp had Mrs. Molly believing she couldn't carry anything, couldn't climb up to the counter, couldn't run errands, and a host of other *couldn't*s that excused her from a long list of chores."

Daisy turned bright red with embarrassment, but she smiled down at her plate.

"She even told Mrs. Molly that she couldn't brush her hair," Lucy said, laughing.

Sam glanced at the schoolhouse clock above the table. "Are you going to eat those eggs or just look at them? Get a move on. You don't want to be late."

"Did you pack our lunches?" Lucy asked, carefully separating her eggs and bacon before she punctured the yolks with her fork.

"Yes."

Daisy ate her eggs from the edge toward the middle. "Papa, did you give us bacon sandwiches again?"

"There's nothing wrong with bacon sandwiches. That's what I have in my lunch bucket."

"I hope we get something better when *you* start packing our lunches," Lucy said, giving Angie a stare.

"What would you like?"

"Fried chicken. The Saunders twins always get fried chicken in their buckets, and it smells so good."

"I'd like cake," Daisy said. "Lemon cake with frosting this thick." She held her thumb and index fingers an inch apart.

"You want Sunday dinner in your lunch buckets," Sam observed, shaking his head. "Well, I don't think you're going to get it."

Angie lowered her fork. "Lunch buckets . . . Sunday dinner . . ." Her gaze swung to the stove and cupboards, then settled on Sam with an overwhelmed expression.

"You do cook, don't you?" He'd simply assumed she would take over the cooking. But when it came to his unwanted wife, he hadn't yet guessed correctly.

"I can," she said, dragging out the words. "It's just that I've never had to cook every day, three times a day."

And she probably hadn't done more than hand laundry and hadn't cleaned a house on a daily basis. She'd probably never filled a coal shuttle or shopped for weekly provisions or established a budget.

Because Sam had vowed to get along with her, and because she sat at his table in her wrapper with her braid hanging down, looking soft and rosy, he decided he could bend a little.

"I've been cooking breakfast long enough that it's a habit," he said, checking to make sure the girls were listening to an example of compromise. "I'll continue doing breakfast. Then you'll only be responsible for the lunch boxes and supper."

He had every reason to expect an effusive eruption of gratitude since he'd just offered a huge concession. Men didn't cook for women. If word leaked out, he'd be a laughingstock. He was willing to make things easier for her only because he knew it had to be difficult, getting thrown into real life after living in pampered ease.

That was the difference between brick masons like her father and carpenters like him. At some point in historical times, brick masons had convinced themselves and the world at large that they were fricking artists, while the rest of the tradesmen were mere laborers. And, as artists, bricklayers naturally deserved higher pay than mere laborers. They were entitled to support their families in comfort and ease while carpenters, for instance, struggled to make ends meet and had to make do without hired cooks, cleaning ladies, and privately owned covered carriages. Brick masons raised daughters who embroidered, while carpenters raised daughters who mended. That said it all.

And one particular brick mason had raised a daughter who did not say *Thank you* when a man replaced his tool belt with an apron. She didn't even seem to recognize the magnitude of his sacrifice.

He stared, suddenly angry that she was who she was. He'd been a fool to reach above himself and pursue a mason's daughter. In his world women carried their own weight without complaint. In her world women had time for music and painting lessons and slept past sunrise and maybe learned to be grateful to those who performed the tasks they wouldn't dream of doing.

"Why are you staring at me?" Angie asked.

"No reason." He inspected her plate. "What's the purpose of serving you a perfectly cooked egg with an unbroken yolk when the first thing you do is cut up the eggs?" A mess of white and yellow mixed together on her plate.

"I beg your pardon? You object to the way I eat my eggs?"

She gave him that narrowed look again, the one he didn't like. "A lot of skill and effort goes into cooking the perfect egg. Those were perfect eggs."

"At some point," she said in a steely, level voice, "a person must nick the yolk, and then the yellow and white mix together. So what does it matter if I chose to mix everything immediately by cutting the eggs at once?"

"Well, just look at your plate. That's disgusting." He made a stirring motion with his finger. "It's all mixed together."

Leaning forward, she examined his plate. He'd eaten

the yolks first while they were nice and hot, sopping up the yellow with his bread. Now he was ready to eat the whites.

"Oh oh. You missed a tiny speck of yellow." She pointed at his eggs. "Right there. Quick, wipe it away with your bread. Heaven knows what might happen if you eat a dot of yolk with the whites. Wouldn't want to mix the two, now would you?"

If the girls hadn't giggled, he would have put down his fork and stormed out of the house. Their giggles reminded him that he was straying from his vow of cordiality. But Lord A'mighty. She had more annoying characteristics than any woman he'd ever met.

"Look, eat your eggs any way you want to, all right?"

"Well, thank you." She beamed at him and then at the girls. "I'm overcome with gratitude that you'll permit me to eat my breakfast in my own disgusting way."

He glared at his daughters to silence any giggles that might encourage Angie's sarcasm. They didn't giggle, but their eyes danced and sparkled brightly. They gazed at him expectantly, as if it were his turn to say something to further their breakfast-table entertainment. He swore he wouldn't say a word.

"I didn't say you were disgusting. I said your plate is disgusting."

She rolled her eyes. "Then don't look at my plate."

So calmly that it infuriated him, she spooned up a revolting mixture of yellow and white and put it in her mouth.

Sam threw down his napkin. Pounding nails was going to feel good today. "Girls, it's time to go. Don't forget your books and your tablets. I put your lunch buckets beside the door." To Angie he said coldly, "They'll be back about three o'clock. I don't know what time I'll get home. If the weather holds, I'll go up to my claims after work and prospect until dark."

She nodded and took a sip from her coffee cup, washing down the godawful mess she'd just swallowed.

"Are you going to walk us to the schoolhouse?" Lucy asked.

"Don't I always?"

"Papa?" Daisy tugged at his belt loops. "Are you mad at us, too?"

That stopped him in his tracks. He drew a breath, then kneeled beside her. "I'm not mad at anyone," he lied. "I'm sorry if I sound peevish. Sleeping on the ground is something I haven't done in a long time, and I didn't sleep well."

In fact, he hadn't slept much at all. After Angie went inside, he'd given her an hour in case she needed something and called to him, then he'd walked to town to discover who won the fight of the decade. The way his luck was running, it hadn't surprised him to learn that he'd lost his five-dollar wager.

So he'd gone to the Gold Slipper for a few beers to lift his spirits, but the mayor asked if it was true that a good-looking lady had flattened him up at the depot. Then Otto Finn said he'd heard Sam had a wife staying at his place. Both men seemed to think his situation was hilarious and the story worth repeating to everyone in the Gold Slipper. Rather than stick around and make himself the butt of embarrassing jokes, Sam came home and crawled inside his tent to brood.

After he made sure the girls were outside and out of earshot, he leaned back into the house. "Are you going to be here when I get home?"

She had her back to him, her coffee cup halfway to her lips. "I don't have anyplace to go. I'll be here."

"I was afraid of that," he said, banging the door shut behind him. Wishful thinking had prompted him to hope that she'd come up with a different solution to their problem.

He wondered how long it would take before Laura's parents learned that Angie was living in his house. Damn it anyway.

After Sam ducked outside, Lucy rushed back into the house to fetch the pencils she'd left on the table. Before she ran back to the door, she leaned close to Angie's ear and said, "My mama never came to the table in her nightclothes!"

Angie waited until she heard the door slam before she sighed, then swallowed another taste of coffee and scanned the table. Already smears of egg were drying on the plates. Spilled milk soaked into the tablecloth in front of Daisy's place. Bread crumbs and scattered bits of bacon marked where Lucy had sat. In the end, Sam hadn't eaten the whites of his eggs. And she decided her own plate of un-eaten breakfast did indeed look disgusting.

Rather than stare at the table, Angie sipped her coffee and gazed out the back door, which Sam had left open to clear the bacon smoke.

The scent of other breakfasts infused the morning air. Angie could identify scorched oatmeal, ham, bacon, the scent of bread fried in grease. From where she sat, she could see the top of Sam's tent and a clear, cloudless spring blue sky.

At home on a fine day like this, she might have donned her floppy gardening hat and an old dress and worked in the vegetable garden out behind the kitchen. Or maybe she would have gone downtown to shop and enjoy luncheon at the Victoria Tearoom. Or perhaps she would have felt like dressing up in a light-colored spring ensemble and repaying a few calls.

Her reverie was so complete that she was startled to abruptly realize she'd been staring for a full minute at a woman peering inside the back door.

"I know it's early," the woman said uncertainly, pointedly noting Angie's wrapper and undressed hair. "I'll just come back later." She glanced down at a covered pan in her hand. "I'll leave this and be on my way."

"No, no. Please."

Eyebrows rising, the woman straightened from bending to set the pan in the doorway. "It's just bread. I thought you might not feel up to baking, this being your first day and all."

"I didn't mean that I didn't want the bread. I meant, please don't go." Standing, Angie ran her hands over her wrapper and sighed. Her state of dishabille couldn't be helped. She was making a bad impression on everyone today. "I'm Mrs. Sam Holland. And I'd guess you are Mrs. Molly."

The woman smiled. "The very same. Mrs. Cannady Johnson."

Molly Johnson looked to be in her early forties. As Lucy and Daisy had agreed, Molly was no beauty, but she was handsome in a way that drew attention. Lively, intelligent eyes were her best feature, Angie decided. She also had an erect carriage, well-shaped brows, and a wide smiling mouth. Anywhere else Molly's cropped silver hair would have provoked a scandal, but the short no-nonsense style seemed to suit her.

"I apologize for still being in my wrapper, and the table . . ." Angie waved a hand. "And I apologize for daydreaming and not inviting you inside at once. The truth is, I'm not making a good beginning at much of anything."

Molly laughed. "You don't need to apologize on my account. I'm not one to stand on ceremony. I came over to say welcome and to help myself to a cup of your coffee if there's any left. Now don't trouble yourself, I know where the cups are."

Quickly, Angie stacked the plates and put them in the sink. She would have pulled off the crumb-and-milk-stained cloth, but she couldn't guess what shape the actual table was in. Meeting Molly flustered her because everything felt upside down. Molly should have called at the front door, and Angie should have had a parlor in which to receive her. Sitting at the family table with Angie in her bedclothes was excruciatingly improper and uncomfortable. But she noticed immediately that the situation also created a strange and immediate sense of intimacy.

Molly reinforced the feeling when she insisted that Angie call her by her first name rather than address her as Mrs. Johnson. As Angie could do no less, she, too, offered her first name. In a leap of etiquette that took her breath away, they jumped instantly from being strangers to being intimates.

"We're neighbors," Molly said, dismissing Angie's discomfort. "Have been for a long time and will be for a long time more. So, the way I see it, there's no sense being formal. That doesn't fit my notion of neighborliness." Molly dropped three lumps of sugar into her coffee cup. "Now. Here's what I know already. Sam said you two ran off and got married ten years ago, but your father objected, didn't think a carpenter was good enough for you, so Sam begged you to come west with him and make a fresh start, but you wouldn't do it because you were young and under your father's thumb. Do I have it right so far?"

Fascinated, Angie nodded.

"Now your family's gone and you're dead broke, so you came here looking to Sam to pay for a divorce but he can't, so you got mad and walloped him up at the depot and had a big fight with him at the new pastry shop, and here you are. Stuck, as I figure it, both of you. Waiting for a divorce that ain't going to happen anytime soon."

"That's the gist of it."

"Here's my story, the parts I'm willing to tell anyway. I was raised in Wisconsin, spent some time in Chicago, likely before you were born, and then spent some more time in Denver. That's where I met Cannady Johnson and married him fifteen years ago. We came here a little before Sam did, about three years ago, so Can could do some prospecting. He ain't found anything to speak of, but he's too stubborn to give up, so I reckon we'll be here until they plant us in the Mount Piscah cemetery. I've done things I'm not proud of, but my only real regret is that I never had children. There." She beamed at Angie. "Now we know each other."

Angie blinked, then laughed. "Well, it's a beginning."

"Actually, I came to answer any questions you might have about Willow Creek. The town's only about three years old. Has more saloons and parlor houses than churches or schools. If you live above Bennet Street you're respectable or trying to be. If you live below Bennet, you're either stone broke or no better than you ought. Same with Poverty Gulch up behind the depot. That's the one place 'round here that you never want to go. There's nothing up there but tents and cribs. The high-end parlor houses are on Myers Street, but you can walk there; lots of respectable women do. One thing you'll appreciate, being from Chicago and all, a woman doesn't need an escort here. You can walk alone anywhere you like with no fear of insult. Our men are proud of the fact that women are safe and revered in this district."

Answering Angie's occasional question, Molly continued talking, recommending the best grocer, the most reliable seamstress, the most meticulous butcher. In short order, Angie had a list of the merchants and deliverymen who would ensure that her new life ran smoothly and as cheaply as possible.

But the questions she wanted to ask had nothing to do with the town. Besides, it was too soon in her acquaintance with Molly to inquire about things that were none of her business. But a burning curiosity overcame any practical arguments.

"I guess you knew Laura."

"I knew her well enough that you could have knocked me down with a whisper when Sam told me about you. I would have sworn to the Almighty himself that Laura Govenor was not the type of woman to set up residence with a married man. Even a married man with a wife who didn't want him and refused to live with him."

Pink heated Angie's cheeks. Molly had only stated the truth, but it sounded so bald and stark and cold.

She let the moment pass and then said, "I regret that my presence is going to reveal that Sam and Laura weren't respectably married." Was that true? Not when it came to Sam. But for Laura? No, she decided that she didn't care about Laura's reputation either. But she did care that Lucy and Daisy would be exposed as illegitimate. They were innocent of wrongdoing and didn't deserve the label they would now wear.

Thinking about it swamped Angie under a wave of guilt. The girls would never have been branded as bastards if she hadn't popped up in Willow Creek. No, that wasn't the way to look at it. Sam and Laura had flouted convention and now their sins were coming home to roost. Still, she felt bad about the girls.

"There'll be talk for a few days, just because it's interesting, then something else will come along. Someone else will get shot, get in bed, or get rich." Molly shrugged. "In the end, no one cares about anyone but themselves."

"Sam said much the same thing. But it's hard to believe."

"Up here your life is your own business and you can mess it up any way you want to." Molly laughed. " 'Course they'll always be a few folks, like Laura's parents, who hit a jackpot, then turn into hoity-toity society with a whole new way of looking at things. They aren't going to be happy about you."

"Laura has parents?" It hadn't occurred to Angie to wonder if Laura might have family in the area.

"They live in Colorado Springs, in a house about the size of a palace." Molly made a face. "Can knew Herb and Winnie Govenor when Herb drove a freight wagon and Winnie was selling pies out her back door. Now they live in a mansion and rub elbows with the swells down there in the Springs. The last time Winnie and Herb came to Willow Creek, Winnie walked right past Can without a nod or a fare-thee-well, like those days of selling pies never happened."

"Wait." Angie frowned. "If the Govenors are wealthy, then why haven't they offered to pay for Daisy's operation?"

Molly blinked as if shutters had come down over her gaze, then she stared at the schoolhouse clock and jumped to her feet. "Glory be, the morning is half over and I haven't even made the bed yet." Walking toward the back door, she offered the obligatory comments about meeting Angie—*so nice* and et cetera—and Angie returned the same polite remarks. At the door, Molly patted the sleeve of Angie's wrapper. "I don't mean to dodge your question . . . well, I guess I do. The thing is, it's better if you hear about the Govenors from Sam."

Later, after Angie had tidied herself and the house and had set about mixing, rolling out, and cutting strips of noodles, she thought about what she'd learned from Molly.

Lucy and Daisy had grandparents nearby. Which meant that Angie would probably meet the Govenors eventually. Dread made her stomach cramp. If the Govenors hadn't known that Sam was married, they were in for a terrible shock. If they had known, they had kept the secret. Judging by Molly's comments they would be horrified and scandalized to learn of Angie's appearance, which exposed their daughter's shameful choices.

She was still thinking about Herbert and Winnie Govenor at half past three, when Lucy and Daisy ran in the front door and then stopped short when they saw the noodles Angie had hung to dry on every surface.

"We're going down to the Old Homestead," Lucy announced, picking up a noodle. She sniffed the strip of dough, then dropped it back on the curve of the chair top.

"Not yet," Angie said pleasantly. "Before you run off to play, I want you both to clean up your room. I know this morning was a bit chaotic, but from now on I want you to make your bed before you leave for school." She smiled at two sullen faces. "I'm sure that's what you usually do anyway, isn't it?"

"We don't have to make our bed every day."

As Angie had suspected, Lucy took the lead while

Daisy hung back, standing on her twisted foot so that her hem dragged and covered the specially made shoe she wore. Her left hip jutted and her spine tilted awkwardly in a way that made Angie wonder if the stance was painful.

"No, you don't have to, but proper young ladies do," Angie said, holding her voice level. "And I seem to recall your father mentioning other chores, too."

"We can't dust. Not with noodles hanging on everything." Lucy started toward the back door, pausing only to dump her books and tablet on the floor beside the coal shuttle. "Come on, Daisy. Let's go."

Frantically, Angie tried to think of the best way to handle outright disobedience. Give Lucy a smack as she was itching to do? Grab them before they dashed out the door and lock them inside?

"If you leave without cleaning your room, you will regret it." Even to her own ears the threat sounded hollow. "You'll be punished." Better, but too vague. However, to threaten anything specific would send her skittering out on thin ice since she didn't know Sam's policies regarding punishment. Moreover, she could easily imagine herself striking a man, like Sam, but she couldn't picture herself striking a child.

A burst of giggles suggested punishment was nothing to be feared in this house. They were out the back door before Angie darted forward and shouted, "Wait! I need to know where you're going!"

Lucy looked back at her. "I told you. We're going down to the Old Homestead."

That sounded harmless enough. "All right," Angie said angrily. "But be home in time for supper." The first skirmish had gone to the general, Miss Lucy, who best knew the rule book. By tomorrow Angie would also know the rules, and next time they would engage on a level field. "Lucy? What exactly is the Old Homestead?"

"It's the fanciest parlor house on Myers Street," Lucy shouted before their golden heads dropped below the crest that sheared off sharply toward Bennet Street. "It's where the prettiest whores work."

Chapter 4

Three pairs of furious eyes shot daggers at him. Sam felt as if he had walked through his front door to face a firing squad.

"Where have you been?" Angie enunciated emphatically as if each angry word were followed by an exclamation point.

"I told you I'd be late." Passing the table where Angie and the girls sat, he walked to the stove and lifted the lid off a tall pot. The fragrance of beef stew and homemade noodles made his knees go weak. He couldn't recall the last time a decent meal had been cooked on this stove. "After work I rode up to Gold Hill and checked a couple of my claims. One might have promise. We'll see."

"Papa, I have to talk to you!"

"So do I, Papa."

"And so do I." The exclamation points again.

"I figured. Can all this talking wait until I've had my supper?" Interpreting the collective silence as a yes, he ladled stew and noodles and a thick, rich gravy into a deep bowl. By rights, Angie should have served him as good wives did. But one glance at her arms clamped tightly across her breast, her pinched mouth and scowling eyes, and he'd known she wasn't going to be doing any serving tonight. He sliced some bread, then carried his supper to the table.

Three grim faces watched him flick a napkin across his lap and salt his stew. Watched him spread butter across his bread. Watched him sink a spoon into the thick gravy. When he swallowed his first bite, his audience intently watched his Adam's apple bob up and down.

He lowered his fork and suppressed a sigh. "All right. Who's first?"

"We are," Lucy insisted, shooting Angie a glare.

Daisy gazed up at him with solemn gray eyes. "We're innocent, Papa." She sounded suspiciously more like Lucy than herself.

"Do we have to talk in front of *her*?"

Angie unclamped one of her arms long enough to make a sweeping dismissive gesture. "I'm not budging. If you want privacy, you'll have to go outside."

The girls shoved away from the table.

April evenings were warm in some parts of the country, but not at an altitude of 9,500 feet. On the other hand, the cold night air would tend to limit the length of these talks, and Sam could get back to his stew and noodles sooner. Angie hadn't given herself enough credit. She could cook. He could forgive a lot in a woman who was beautiful and who could cook.

"Get your shawls, girls." Reluctantly he traded his napkin for a heavy denim jacket and opened the back door. Having learned a thing or two, he chose the top step and let the girls sit on the next step down. That way, when they turned to present their case, their faces would be illuminated by the lantern light spilling out of the doorway behind him.

"She started right out bossing us around!" Lucy began, indignation flashing in her eyes.

What Sam didn't understand was how his daughters began the day as proper, neat young ladies and ended the same day by looking like homeless street urchins who lived in a packing box. He'd always assumed that girl children emerged from the cradle with a deep abhorrence of stained, untidy clothing and mussed hair. But his daughters were never happier than when playing in the dirt with their skirts and tresses in a dusty tangle.

"The very minute we got home from school, she ordered us to make our bed and clean our room!"

"Is that what this upset is all about?" His shoulders relaxed. "I would have instructed you to make your bed and keep up your room myself except you've had so many other chores. But now that we have Angie to share the load, I think you should make your bed in the mornings."

"He's siding with *her*," Lucy said sadly. "Didn't I tell you?"

Sam ground his teeth together. "Well? Did you make your bed when Angie told you?"

"We'll do it from now on since you say we have to, but we don't take orders from her. Isn't that right, Daisy?"

"That's right. Angie's not our mama, she can't order us around."

"If all she did was ask you to make your bed and clean your room . . . that doesn't sound like an excessive amount of ordering you around. You should have done it. Did you do your regular chores?"

"We couldn't dust because she had noodles hanging on everything. We didn't have to bring in coal or fire up the stove because she'd already done it. And there was no sense sweeping because every time a breeze wiggled the noodles, flour sifted on the floor."

Daisy nodded. "We didn't have any home assignments from school. So we asked if we could go out and play."

"You asked?" When children looked the most innocent—that's when you needed to be the most suspicious. Sam had learned this parental lesson the hard way.

Daisy frowned at Lucy. "Well . . ."

"Like we said, there weren't any chores or school assignments so maybe we were in a hurry and didn't ask. Maybe we just said that we were going outside. But *she* said that was all right. She gave us permission to go."

"She did, Papa. Lucy told her where we were going and she said it was all right."

"Then she got mad because we weren't home one minute after the six o'clock whistle. And then she got mad because we didn't like her noodles and picked them out of the stew. She's mad at us all the time. She hates us."

His eyebrows lifted. "The noodles are delicious. Why wouldn't you eat them?"

"I don't like noodles."

"Since when? You've always liked noodles in the past." He looked at Daisy. "How about you?"

"Well, I liked some of the noodles." Daisy darted a glance at Lucy. "But not all of them. Most of them I didn't like."

"So you didn't eat your suppers."

"She didn't give us a chance! You'll never believe what she did! She took our plates away and scraped them back into the stew pot! She wants to starve us!"

"It's true," Daisy confirmed. "We're starving, Papa."

"All right, let's see what we've got here." He held up his hand and ticked down his fingers. "Angie did all your chores, but she wanted you to make your bed and clean your room. She expected you to come home on time after she'd worked all day to make your supper. And she wanted you to eat what was on your plates, which is probably the rule at every table in this country."

"It doesn't sound right when you say it," Lucy said, pushing her mouth into a pout.

"You didn't say the one about her starving us."

"If the two of you hadn't suddenly turned into picky eaters, your stomachs would be full now." Angie was starving them. Heaven help him. He pulled a hand down his face. "From now on you'll make your bed in the morning and keep your room picked up. And I want you here for supper no later than five minutes after the six o'clock whistle."

"You don't come home until it's dark."

"That's different. I have to check my claims."

"And then you stop by the Gold Slipper," Lucy said.

"We can smell the beer and the cigar smoke."

"A man's entitled to wet his whistle after a long day." That's where he caught up on the daily news, who'd made a strike, who was waiting for an assay report, who'd gone bust.

"What about her ordering us around?"

"Keep in mind that Angie won't be with us forever. While she's here, let's all try to get along. That's going to mean some compromise on everyone's part."

They groaned and fell on each other's shoulders.

"Angie's responsible for you when I'm not here, so you do as she says. And I don't want to hear any more about you refusing to eat what's set before you."

"We'll eat it if we have to, but she can't make us like it!"

"You don't have to like it. But you do have to eat your supper." Golden-haired, gray-eyed, their faces ravaged by his betrayal, they made him feel guilty about doing what he knew was fair and right. That was another thing he didn't understand. How did they do that? How did two small girls manage to make him feel so damned guilty when he was absolutely right and they were absolutely wrong? "I don't know about you two, but I'm getting cold. If we've covered everything, let's go inside and get warm."

"Papa?" In the glow of the lantern light, Daisy looked like Sam's vision of an angel. "What about how we're starving? Are you going to send us to bed starving?"

He kissed the top of her head. "Yes."

Everything in him objected to sending a child to bed hungry. His inclination was to give them another lecture about eating their supper, then offer them some bread and butter and jelly. But if he did, he would undermine Angie. If he expected the girls to respect her, then he had to support her decisions.

He placed a hand on two small shoulders. "Look at it this way. You'll really enjoy breakfast tomorrow." He gave them a little push inside.

While he was out in the cold talking to the girls, Angie had whisked away his supper plate. The girls weren't the only ones who would be going to bed hungry tonight. "It's your turn," he said in a tight voice, holding the back door open.

"I'd prefer that we settle these matters with everyone present so we all know where we stand." Rising from the table, Angie faced him, not dropping her gaze to the girls at his side. "First. In your opinion, is it reasonable to expect Lucy and Daisy to make their bed and keep their room clean?"

"Absolutely. We talked about it and they agree."

"What other chores do they usually do?"

"They dust, sweep the floors and porches, wash the dishes from breakfast, clean out their lunch buckets, keep the stove going, help Mrs. Molly if Mrs. Molly is doing any of our laundry on laundry days. What else? It feels like I'm missing something."

"That's a lot." Some of the anger faded from Angie's brow when she finally looked at the girls. "Most of what you've been doing, I'll do from now on. We all agree that you'll make your bed and keep your room clean. I'd like you to continue cleaning your lunch buckets. You'll take turns setting the table and helping with meals and the cleanup. Those are your regular chores. There may be special chores on occasion, and it's possible that I've overlooked something. If so it will be added later."

All right, her manner was a tad high-handed. And the snapping eyes and clipped words didn't make anyone happy. But what she said impressed Sam as reasonable, so he didn't interrupt.

"Apparently I'm the only person who believed that six o'clock was supper time." She pointed to the clock. In fact, she was doing a lot of arm waving. Sam figured it might be the Italian thing she'd told him about. "So what is supper time in this house?"

"The girls don't have pocket watches, so the six o'clock whistle is their only signal that it's getting close to supper. To give them a chance to get home and get washed, let's say six-thirty is the girls' supper time." He looked down at them. "I don't care what you're doing when the whistle blows, you head for home right then."

"The girls' supper time? And what about you?"

"With summer coming on, the light's going to last longer and I can get some work done on my best claim. I'll get home around sundown."

"This is not a restaurant." The fizz and snap returned to her eyes and she punctuated every word with a jabbing finger. "I serve supper once and once only. At six-thirty. If you're here you get hot food and you get a plate put in front of you. If you don't show up until after six-thirty, you can feed yourself with whatever is left over."

He blinked.

"Now. On to the next thing. Do you allow your daughters to loiter around the Old Homestead hoping for a glimpse of a fancy-dressed whore?" Narrowed eyes met his. "Whore is their word, not mine."

He stared down at his daughters.

"I told her we were going to the Old Homestead, and she said we could!"

"Lucy, you knew perfectly well that Angie wouldn't know about the Old Homestead. How the hell do you know about it?"

"Sam, you will not use profanity in front of the girls."

Now she was correcting him? He gave her a scowl that promised they would talk later. "Lucy? Daisy? How do you know about the Old Homestead?"

They looked at each other with incredulity. The stupidest question in the world had just been asked and they were amazed. Sam bit down on his back teeth and waited.

"Papa, *everyone* knows about the Old Homestead. That's where the prettiest, fanciest whores live," Lucy explained with great patience. This was a given, a fact. Lucy implied that only an imbecile could live in Willow Creek without knowing where to go if he had a two-hundred-dollar itch. And hell, maybe she was right. If five- and seven-year-olds knew about the Old Homestead, then who was left who didn't? "We like to watch Miss Lily ride."

Daisy nodded. "She rides a shiny black horse with a braided tail. And she wears pretty hats with long feathers. I like the red feather best."

"But the best thing of all is the way Miss Lily doesn't

look to the left or the right. She looks straight ahead like she doesn't know or care if anyone's watching. She rides like this." Planting her hands on her hips, Lucy lifted her chin, put her nose in the air, and glided forward with an air of haughty disdain. "We've seen her out walking, too. She has the most beautiful clothes!"

To say that Sam was flabbergasted would be to understate his reaction by a mile. He couldn't believe this. His daughters were ardent admirers of Willow Creek's most celebrated whore, but they didn't have a kind word for the respectable woman standing in front of them.

"Well," he said after a minute, feeling at a loss. He wasn't sure where to begin. "I don't want you going anywhere near the Old Homestead, do you hear me?"

They both stared at him. Then Lucy said, "We have to walk past the Old Homestead on the way to school."

Damn. In the mornings, the Old Homestead was as quiet as a tomb and he never paid it a lick of attention. Not one time had he imagined what might be happening there at three-thirty in the afternoon when they walked home without him.

"All right. You have to walk past the place." He would fix that problem if it was the last thing he did. "But you don't come home, say hello to Angie, then go back to the Old Homestead. You don't loiter around any of the parlor houses. And if I ever hear about either of you saying the word *whore*, I'll wash your mouth out with soap. Decent little girls don't say words like that."

Daisy frowned at him. "Well, what should we call them, Papa?"

The question planted a stake in his heart. Children this age shouldn't know about whores or parlor houses, shouldn't need to know how to refer to prostitutes. One glance at Angie's expression told him she felt the same.

But saloons, faro parlors, gambling dens, parlor houses, cribs, beer halls—they were the first buildings erected in a mining camp. The whores and saloon girls arrived long before the wives and mothers. In Willow Creek the sporting ladies had outnumbered the Mrs. Finns and the Molly Johnsons until very recently. Of course his daughters knew about the Old Homestead and Miss Lily. How many other prostitutes did they recognize on sight and know by name?

Sam clenched his fists. He was going to find his jackpot. Then Daisy would get her operation. And then he would move his daughters as far from the mining camps as he could.

"If you must refer to the ladies living at the Old Homestead, and I can't think why you would," he said, speaking through clenched teeth, "then refer to them as sporting ladies."

Somehow the phrase *sporting ladies* made the whores sound adventurous and athletic. A sporting lady sounded rather like a desirable person to be.

Angie shook her head. She also spoke through clenched teeth. "A better way is to refer to them as *those poor unfortunates.*"

"They're fallen angels." At once he saw that he had erred again. Both of his daughters stared up at him with stricken expressions.

Daisy wrung her hands together. "Did Miss Lily get hurt when she fell out of heaven? Is that why she doesn't turn her head to look at us? Did she hurt her neck when she fell?"

There were times when the responsibilities of fatherhood overwhelmed him. When he felt that every word he spoke painted him further into a problem corner. He glanced at Angie, hoping she would jump in and say something to rescue the situation. But she clamped her arms over her breast and lifted an expectant eyebrow as if she, too, wanted to know if Miss Lily had sustained any injuries as a result of her fall.

"Actually, Miss Lily didn't really fall out of heaven," Sam began. "*Fallen angel* is just an expression that some people use meaning that all women are angels, but some have fallen from grace. Do you understand?"

"Who said all women are angels? We're not angels. And *she's* not an angel."

"But Mama is an angel." Sudden tears welled in Daisy's eyes. "Oh no! Is Mama going to fall out of heaven?"

Lucy gasped and instant tears spilled over her lashes. "Oh! I don't want Mama to be a fallen angel like Miss Lily!"

Horror and disbelief slackened Sam's jaw. How on earth had this gone so badly? He lifted his gaze to Angie. "You can step in here anytime you like. I'd appreciate it."

"I wouldn't dream of interfering," she said, backing up a step. "I warned you that I don't know about these things. You got into this, you'll have to get out of it." She fanned her face with the edge of her shawl. "In fact, I think I'll . . . I'll just step outside for some air."

Wasn't that like her? To abandon him when he needed her the most?

Trying to be fair, he reminded himself that this was only Angie's second day. He knelt in front of his crying daughters. "Let's start over. . . ."

In the mornings, when John Avril was airing out the place, the Gold Slipper didn't smell as smoky and beer-soaked as it did during the rest of the day. In the mornings, with clean sawdust freshly laid down and the spittoons emptied, the Slipper smelled like coffee and Mrs. Avril's famous cheese bread.

"What I'm saying is our children shouldn't have to walk past the Old Homestead on the way to school."

One of the town councilmen that Sam had summoned swallowed a wedge of cheese bread, then shook his head. "No help for it, Sam. The Old Homestead is here to stay."

"I'm not suggesting that we shut down the ladies or that we force the Old Homestead to move. I'm saying let's build another school on the uphill side of Bennet where there aren't any saloons or whorehouses."

"There's already a school up there," the mayor reminded everyone at the table.

"I have to agree with Sam," one of the councilmen stated, lighting a cigar. "The Eaton Street school has thirty kids crammed into one room."

Sam nodded. "If that school could hold two more children, my daughters would be there, too. If we build another, we could put the lower grades in one school and the upper grades in the second."

"That's all fine and dandy, but where's the money coming from? Schools don't grow on trees. And frankly, Sam, there are things this town needs more than another school. We need a bigger jail for one thing. Now that we've got the railroad and important visitors arriving on a regular basis, we should pave Bennet Street. Install more streetlamps. Clean up Poverty Gulch." The mayor shrugged. "Now you want another school."

"Suppose I could get another school without it costing the town anything except the land underneath it?"

"How are you going to do that?"

Sam thought a minute. "I'll build it, and I won't charge for labor. I'm willing to bet my crew will donate their labor, too. We could ask that new fellow who owns the sawmill if he'd donate the lumber. We take up a collection for the materials."

"Well . . . that might work."

"Your enthusiasm isn't exactly overwhelming," Sam remarked. "Is there a problem that I'm not seeing?"

One of the councilmen leaned forward and propped his elbows on the table. "There's been some talk, Sam. I guess you know about it."

A flush of dark anger stained Sam's throat. "I didn't have anything to do with those fires."

"Nobody's saying you did. So far, all anyone's saying is that it's a strange coincidence that your last two projects burned to the ground."

"You're damned right it's a coincidence," Sam said in a low, hard voice. "What else could it be?"

"Well, no one's making any accusations, mind, but the only things those two fires have in common is that they were set deliberately, they were set before the building was completed, and you were the foreman on both jobs."

Striving to remain calm, Sam stared at the men around the table. "The first project was the union hall." He leaned forward, angry that he felt a need to defend himself. "There's no lack of anti-union sentiment around here." Last year had seen deadly riots between union and non-union supporters. "Maybe someone wanted to send an anti-union message."

"Wouldn't surprise anybody. There's still a lot of friction and hard feelings."

"The second project was the Whittier house. Eighty percent of the people in this county hate Homer Whittier, including several seated at this table." Homer Whittier had made a fortune cheating careless men out of their share of producing mines. Whittier operated within the gray areas of the law and boasted that he'd never done anything illegal. The loopholes he found allowed him to steal with the weight of the law behind him. "I'd say there are a couple hundred people who hate Whittier enough to burn down his new house."

"What you're suggesting is possible. I'm not arguing, Sam. I'll even go you one better by saying that no one believes you started the fires. Why would you? So don't go thinking that folks blame you."

Sam swore. "Then what's the problem here?"

"The problem is you being the foreman on both jobs. Now me and the police chief and everybody else thinks this is just coincidence." The mayor gave Sam a thoughtful look. "But if another of your projects burns, it's no longer coincidence. You follow?"

Sam dropped back in his chair. "So you don't believe I started the fires, but I might have, and you're waiting to see if I'm stupid enough to burn down another project. Is that what you're saying?"

"I'm saying if another of your projects burns, then we need to look harder at you. Maybe someone is sending you a message, Sam. On the face of it that sounds ridiculous, but who knows?"

Sam's eyes narrowed. "We've covered this subject. The fires don't have anything to do with a new school. The question here is, will you give me the land to build a school or won't you?"

By some silent process that Sam didn't see even though he was watching, the men at the table reached a consensus without speaking a word. Glances were exchanged, throats were cleared, cigars lit or extinguished.

At the end of the fidgeting the mayor said, "For the

time being, let's leave the question open. We'll talk again after you finish building Reverend Dryfus's house."

Sam stared in anger and disbelief. "You'll wait and see if someone torches the reverend's house?"

Clem waved a fat cigar. "You got to admit, Sam. Nobody's mad at the reverend. There's no reason in the world to burn down his new house."

"So if the place goes up, then you figure the culprit is me." Stiff with insult, he flattened his hands on the table and started to rise.

"Don't be an ass, Sam. Sit down. How many times do you have to hear this? Nobody believes you're burning down your buildings. All's we're saying is you might be the target. That's one reason on a long list of possible causes."

"We're drying-in the Dryfus place today," Sam snapped. "The day the reverend and his wife move into the house, I'm coming back to the council and I expect you to give me the land for a new school."

"Would you be willing to let someone else be the builder if it meant the school could get started sooner?" The mayor watched Sam's reaction with a raised eyebrow.

The new school was Sam's idea; he wanted to build it for his daughters, and he said so. "There's no rush. School's almost over for this session. We have until fall to build the new one." He was going to build it, no one else. The mayor nodded.

Throughout the remainder of the day, Sam considered what materials he'd need for the school and how much of everything and what kind of roofing he wanted and where he might buy a potbellied stove cheap. They'd need desks and a chalkboard.

When the noon whistle blew, he remained up on the Dryfus roof to eat his lunch. Angie had packed him a glass jar filled with the beef stew and noodles and gravy that he'd missed last night. The meal wouldn't be hot now, but he anticipated it would be delicious. He also had bread and a generous pat of butter wrapped in a scrap of oilcloth. The apple must have come from the root cellar and then from the bottom of the basket. But the skin wasn't wrinkled too badly, and it still tasted sweet when he bit into it.

While he sat in the sunlight on Reverend Dryfus's half-shingled roof eating his lunch, Sam gazed out at the low hills rolling down the valley. Willow Creek was growing by leaps and bounds, spreading down and out over ground that cattle had recently grazed.

His gaze settled on two blackened ruins, not far from each other. The burned-out Union Hall, and down three blocks and over two blocks, the charred remains of the Whittier house.

There was no doubt about the destruction being deliberate. The arsonist hadn't bothered to make the fires appear accidental or a result of natural causes.

As Sam had told the mayor and the councilmen, there were reasons why the new Union Hall and the Whittier mansion might have been torched. His guesses could be correct. Certainly it was possible.

But Sam's gut said otherwise. Frowning, he sent his apple core sailing off the roof toward the scrap heap.

Following the noon break he assembled his crew. "From now until the reverend and his missus move in, I want a watchman on duty every night. I'll pay time and half." The extra pay would come out of his pocket. "Any volunteers?" The added expense made him inwardly cringe. But another fire could destroy his livelihood.

If the mayor and the sheriff were correct that Sam might be the reason for the fires and if the Dryfus place burned, then he'd be in real trouble, because he agreed that three fires exceeded coincidence.

Worse, if the fires were not coincidence then he had a gut feeling that he might know who was behind them and why. If he was right, then he also understood the message.

Chapter 5

By Saturday Angie was grateful that Sam's house wasn't any larger, and she had developed a new appreciation for Mrs. Dom, who had cleaned the Bertoli residence for so many years. After Sam and the girls left in the morning, she allowed herself another cup of coffee, often with Molly Johnson, then she launched herself into an exhausting day of dusting, polishing, washing, sweeping, scrubbing, shopping for provisions, and cooking.

Everything revolved around cooking. When Angie wasn't actually cooking, she was preparing to cook, cleaning up after cooking, or thinking about what to cook next. All her other tasks were sandwiched between the unrelenting demands of cooking.

This morning, while her bread loaves were rising, she had rushed up to the grocer on Bennet Street and bought carrots and potatoes since there weren't any more vegetables in the root cellar. The items cost the Earth, which irritated her since she used her own money to buy them.

From there, she hurried to the butcher shop, where she purchased two chickens, one for tonight and one for Sunday dinner. Which she also paid for with her own money.

When she arrived back at the house, the iceman was at

the door with the weekly block of ice and demanding payment on delivery. There went another fifty cents.

After she put away her hat and gloves, she punched down the dough for rolls and let the dough rest while she shook out the floor rugs. Then she shaped the dough and covered the balls with a towel for the second rise.

Next she sat outside on the kitchen stoop and plucked the feathers off the chickens, saving the feathers in an old pillowcase. She hated plucking feathers, but it was pleasant to sit in the thin mountain sunshine, listening to the traffic spinning along Bennet Street and the dynamite blasts in the hills, which had taken a little getting used to.

Many of the mines had coal-fueled pumps to keep water out of the shafts. Plumes of smoke curled from the stacks, sulfurous and dark, drifting south along the mountain ridges. The ore trains also added smoke to the valley haze, as well as contributing the noise of whistles and squealing wheels. Dust hung above the streets dividing rows of houses and shacks and tents.

Loud and boisterous and energetic, Willow Creek was nothing like Angie's old neighborhood in Chicago. She could remember summer days so quiet and still that she would believe she was alone in the world. That could never happen here. The mines operated twenty-four hours a day and so did the town. A miner coming off shift at midnight could buy a meal at a chophouse or a restaurant or, if he stopped by the bathhouse first, he could dine at one of the hotels. He could drop by a saloon for a drink and a game of poker, or he could find a polka at the dance halls. Whatever a man's vice, he could find it in Willow Creek at any hour of the day or night.

This thought made her wonder where Sam went and what he did every evening. Usually he didn't come home until well after dark. Last night the girls had been in bed asleep by the time he quietly sneaked into the kitchen to see if Angie had left him any supper on the stove. She hadn't.

Tonight, however, she planned to wait up for him. They needed to talk, and she doubted the encounter would be pleasant for either of them.

While she baked bread, she cut up the chicken and reviewed the items she needed to discuss with Sam. And it occurred to her that she had thought more about Sam in the last five days than she'd thought about him in ten years.

Being aware of him began even before breakfast when Sam came into the kitchen to wash up and shave. From the first day, the routine of shaving had fascinated Angie. First he put a pot of water on the stove. Then he took the mirror off the wall and propped it over the sink. Next he washed his face and groped for the towel he had forgotten to lay out.

After Angie had observed the procedure a couple of times, she started heating the water and laying out a towel as soon as she was up and dressed. It was a mistake, of course. Once a woman did a chore, the chore became hers forever after. Now Sam expected hot water and a towel. He did thank her, but even so.

After washing, he stropped his razor. Years of habit made his movements so easy and efficient that he hardly paid attention to what he was doing. Finally he soaped his face and leaned to the mirror, pulling his skin tight before he drew the razor across his jaw. When he finished shaving, he combed his hair and tied it at his neck where it fell naturally into a long curl.

Watching Sam perform his morning toilette almost seemed an invasion of privacy. Maybe that's why observing gave Angie a delicious forbidden thrill. She had never before watched a man shave or comb his hair. Hadn't considered that such a simple everyday act might create an odd sense of intimacy.

She wondered if Sam had felt something similar that first morning when she'd rushed into the kitchen dressed in her wrapper with her night braid hanging down her back. For her the incident had been embarrassing and excruciatingly uncomfortable. But what had it been for him? A moment of intimacy? A reminder of Laura?

She didn't like thinking about Laura, but it was hard not to. This was Laura's house. Laura's curtains hung at the windows. Her tablecloth covered the table. Laura had either purchased or made the braided rugs; she'd chosen the chairs and side table in the parlor half of the big room. The dishes and utensils were Laura's. Angie slept in Laura's bed, cooked on Laura's stove, fed Laura's children, and spent many hours every day being angry at the man Laura had loved.

And being intrigued by him as well. Sam Holland was a handsome man whom Angie had once dreamed about and longed for. When she looked at his mouth, she remembered all the girlhood hours she had spent, dreamily speculating about kissing him. To her shock, she'd wondered about that recently as well.

Irritated by this unwanted line of thought, Angie put the pieces of chicken into a hot skillet, then went into the bedroom and brushed the spring suit she planned to wear to church tomorrow. She had time to change the ribbon on her hat before the chicken finished cooking. Before she peeled potatoes, she finished unpacking the last of her trunks.

Inside, carefully wrapped and padded, she found her mother's favorite teacup. For a moment Angie sat on the side of the bed, holding the cup and saucer and remembering her mother. In the afternoons, her mother had composed letters at her writing desk with this cup and a teapot beside her. One of Angie's last memories was of her mother sitting in bed, gazing into the teacup as if she glimpsed eternity there.

Angie turned the teacup between her fingers, examining the tiny rosebuds painted on the china. The roses were as delicate and serene as her mother had been. Angie hadn't understood her mother's serenity, and she supposed her mother hadn't understood the emotional outbursts of her husband and daughter. Angie hadn't thought like her mother or looked like her. She didn't have her mother's stillness or grace, and she wasn't delicate. She must have disappointed her mother in many ways.

"Oh, Mama. I miss you. There are so many things I wish we could have talked about."

Sighing, Angie turned the cup between her fingers.

When she had packed for this trip, she hadn't imagined she would stay in Willow Creek longer than overnight. She had pictured herself settled in a small house waiting for the divorce to be final. She had brought the teacup as a piece of home and history to comfort her when the days were lonely and the wait seemed long. She had wanted the teacup as a reminder of family and of her mother.

What on earth would Emily Bertoli have thought if she'd seen where Angie was living now, still waiting for her life to begin?

Deciding she needed something to see and touch that had not belonged to Laura, Angie placed the cup and saucer on the windowsill above the sink where she would see them every time she washed dishes or prepared a meal. The cup and saucer would remind her that this situation was temporary. Eventually she'd go home again, this time as a free woman.

The rest of the day passed in a blur of cooking and chores and cooking and cleaning and cooking and thinking about what she would say to Sam when he finally came home.

But first there was supper with the girls. As usual they rolled their eyes and turned sullen when they ran inside and found her waiting instead of Sam.

Angie had warmed wash water for them and watched diligently as they scrubbed their faces and hands, then brushed dust off their dresses before they sat down to supper.

"What did you do all day?" She hadn't seen them since lunch and that made her uneasy. "I thought we agreed that you would tell me where you were."

"We got busy," Lucy said. Her eyes brightened when she saw the fried chicken, but heaven forbid that she should admit she was pleased.

"You didn't go to Myers Street, did you?"

"No," Daisy said solemnly. "Papa told us not to."

Angie passed the mashed potatoes. "So where were you?"

Closing her eyes, Lucy held the bowl of mashed potatoes under her chin and let the steam bathe her face. Angie had no idea why she would do such a thing. "We played kickball with the Mueller children for a while, then we went to the site and watched Papa work." She considered Angie through a sweep of pale lashes. "I want to be a carpenter when I grow up."

Daisy's mouth rounded in surprise. "I thought you wanted to be like Miss Lily."

"I want to look like Miss Lily when I'm not being a carpenter."

"Girls can't be carpenters." Daisy looked to Angie for confirmation.

"Well, I've never heard of a female building a house," Angie said slowly, "but there's no reason why a woman can't hit a nail with a hammer. I've done that myself."

"Was Papa a builder back when you knew him?" Lucy asked.

Angie touched her napkin to her lips and nodded. "My father hired your papa and his father to build new cabinets for our kitchen. That's how I met your father."

The first time she'd seen Sam, she had stopped abruptly as if she'd run into an invisible wall. She'd never seen a man as handsome or as natural. He took her breath away and made her heart race even before he looked at her and before she heard his voice. He stood in the backyard beneath the big elm measuring a length of wood balanced across two sawhorses. His expression was intent and focused, his hands sure and quick with the yardstick.

The young men of Angie's acquaintance, brothers or cousins of friends, wore stiff-looking suits and polished shoes and slicked their hair with pomade. She knew boys didn't dress as formally at home, but she didn't often see them in their private casual mode. It was strange to observe a man without a jacket and with his shirtsleeves rolled up. She could see the hair on Sam's arms, which seemed shockingly scandalous and made her feel warm and strange inside.

Eventually he'd looked up and smiled, and her heart stopped. Dark hair and dark mustache. Blue eyes. Sun bronzed skin on his hands and face and throat.

At age sixteen, she had believed in heaven and happy endings and love at first sight. And she had seen all three in Sam Holland that first day, that first minute.

"Angie?" Daisy tugged at her sleeve.

"What?"

"You have a funny look on your face."

"I was just . . ." She looked around, her gaze settled on the three pots of water heating on the stove. "I was wondering where you keep the bathtub. It's Saturday night. Bath night."

Daisy lowered a drumstick to her plate and her face tightened. "I don't need a bath."

"We use the laundry tub for baths," Lucy said, wiping grease from her fingers. "Daisy doesn't want to take a bath because she doesn't want you to see her foot."

"That isn't true," Daisy said hotly, her face turning red. Then her chin came up and her mouth turned down. "But I'm not going to take a bath!"

"If Daisy doesn't have to take a bath, then I don't either," Lucy said, measuring Angie with a challenging gaze.

She might have guessed that it wouldn't be as easy as Sam instructing them to mind her and them doing it. All along she had suspected they would defy her at some point, if for no other reason than to see what would happen.

"You don't want to go to church tomorrow wearing a week's worth of dust and grime," she said in a pleasant tone, letting her gaze touch meaningfully on their evening-wild hair.

"We have to go to church?"

Lucy's tone suggested that church was not a regular occurrence. A while had elapsed since Angie had last attended church herself. But she wasn't five or seven years old and in need of spiritual and moral guidance. In her opinion, anyone who wanted to grow up and become Miss Lily required some serious pew-time.

"If I'm too dirty to go to church then I'll stay home,"

Daisy stated, staring down at her plate. "I'm not going to take a bath."

Angie didn't spot any compromise. Either they obeyed and got into the bathtub, or they learned that their will was stronger than hers.

"Where is the laundry tub?" Angie asked Lucy.

Daisy's small fingers curled into fists. "I won't do it."

"It's outside, under the kitchen stoop."

"Would you fetch it, please?"

"You can't make me!" Daisy whispered.

Usually Daisy looked to Lucy for guidance and loyally agreed with whatever Lucy proposed. That her refusal came with no reference to Lucy told Angie this was a serious situation. Daisy's defiance went beyond a test of wills.

"Would it make you feel better if I promise not to look at your foot?" she asked while Lucy was outside.

A tear quivered on Daisy's eyelash, then spilled down her cheek. "Please don't make me."

Although Daisy managed very well, there were signs of self-consciousness. Walking on the side of her foot, on her ankle, had the effect of making her shorter on the right side by about two inches. Daisy placed her weight on the short side when she stood still so her hem would drop and cover the special shoe she wore. Although Lucy pattered about in bare feet after supper, Daisy never did. Twice she had come home from school with reddened eyes as if she'd been crying, and Angie had wondered if other children teased or tormented her. But Daisy had refused to explain.

On the other hand, Daisy didn't let her awkward lurching gait slow her down. She ran after Lucy without hesitation. She didn't appear to avoid people. And there was no sense that Daisy expected special treatment or consideration.

Huffing and puffing, Lucy rolled the laundry tub into the kitchen. And then both of the girls stared at Angie with blanked expressions, waiting to see what she would do. Angie was curious about that, too.

"You both need a bath," she said slowly, desperately hoping for sudden inspiration. "And you're too young to shampoo your own hair." She had to be here.

Daisy stared up at her with large pleading eyes, as if she wanted Angie to find a solution but didn't believe there was one. This could end badly.

"All right. Here's what we'll do." She drew a breath and wondered how a real mother would solve the problem. Probably not the way she was about to. "Tonight— this time only—we will each leave on one article of clothing. It can be whatever you chose. I'm going to leave on my shimmy." The idea was appealing, actually. She wasn't overjoyed at the thought of appearing naked in front of them either. Especially since she would have to sit in the tub with her knees upraised and that meant her top would be exposed.

When neither of the girls spoke, Angie summoned a bright voice and smiled at Daisy. "I suppose you'll leave on your stockings." She turned the smile on Lucy. "What will you leave on?"

"I think I'll leave on my petticoat," Lucy said finally.

"Excellent choice." Going to the stove, she tested the water. Not too hot, not too cool. "I have some bath salts on the dresser in the bedroom. Daisy, will you fetch the bottle, please?"

"We get bath salts?" Lucy brightened at once. "Mrs. Molly says bath salts are too expensive to waste on little girls, so she never lets us have any."

Angie wiped out the laundry tub, then filled it halfway with warm water. "Occasionally a small extravagance makes a woman feel better. I suspect we can all use a little feeling better tonight. As soon as you're undressed down to your stockings and your petticoat, you can stir the bath salts into the water."

She made a point of not watching them undress and didn't turn around until the scent of roses filled the kitchen. They had used a lot of her bath salts. "Who's going first?"

"I am." Daisy lifted her good leg over the rim and climbed into the water. "Oh, it smells so good!"

Angie gave her a washcloth and a cake of rose-scented soap. Molly was correct about the expense. But if Sam could afford beer and cigars, then she and the girls could afford bath salts and scented soap. She would explain that to him when the time came to replace her supplies.

Lucy kneeled beside the tub and wiggled her fingers in the water. "You look so funny wearing stockings in the tub."

"You look funny wearing your petticoat and nothing else!"

Only minutes ago Angie would have wagered everything she owned that tonight would not end in giggles. Smiling, almost enjoying the moment, she asked if Daisy was ready for a hair wash. When Daisy seemed reluctant to get down to business, Angie reminded her that the water was getting cool and two other people were waiting for their turn.

Daisy ducked her head underwater and came up sputtering, rosy, and laughing. Her fine golden hair felt like silk beneath Angie's fingers, and so did Lucy's hair when it was Lucy's turn to be shampooed.

Angie wrapped their hair in towels and sent them to

their room to finish drying and get into their nightgowns while she popped into the cool water for a hasty wash. After toweling off and slipping into her wrapper, she ducked her head into the tub and reached for the shampoo.

When she was finished they sat beside the open oven door, letting the heat dry their hair.

Angie had seen Daisy's poor twisted foot, of course. Her wet stocking had clearly revealed the inner and upward twist. And Angie had examined Daisy's custom-made shoe. She'd felt her heart wrench in her chest, and she'd experienced a burst of hot anger.

How was it possible that Sam hadn't saved enough for Daisy's operation in five years? He could have sold his horse and his house and anything else of value that he owned. He could have robbed a bank. He could have done *something*.

The bath and the heat from the oven almost put the girls to sleep before their hair dried. Eventually Angie led them into their bedroom and pulled the covers up to their chins. For one uncomfortable moment they lay in bed staring up at her and she suddenly wondered if they expected her to kiss them goodnight. Before she could decide what to do, Daisy crawled out of the blankets, stood up, and threw her arms around Angie's neck.

"Thank you," Daisy whispered against her ear.

Angie had never been a mother or an aunt. Rose-scented hugs from a child were a new experience. Pleasant, but odd, too. Small arms around a person's neck did strange things to the heart.

She forgot to have them say their prayers, but all in all she thought the evening had gone well. Disaster had been averted.

After draping the wet stockings, petticoat, and shimmy

on the backs of the kitchen chairs, she put on a skirt and shirtwaist, pinned up her hair, and washed the supper dishes while she waited for Sam to come home.

Chapter 6

Two lamps burned inside the house, which meant either that Angie had forgotten to put Daisy's night-light in the sink and blow out the other lamp, or she was waiting for him. On the off chance that she was waiting, Sam didn't know whether to be pleased or worried.

Quietly, he opened the kitchen door, looked inside, and stopped short. Angie sat at the table, looking as fine as a woman could look and smelling like summer roses. She wore a dark skirt and a crisp white shirtwaist that curved over her breasts and made him wonder why he hadn't noticed her magnificent figure before. Actually, he had noticed. Not that he wanted to. Thinking about Angie's body, which he did far too often, was as futile an exercise as wishing he could change the past.

"Sit down," she said, starting to rise. "I'll fix you a plate."

Now he noticed that she'd set a place for him at the table. He covered his eyes, drew a breath, then looked at her. "I ate supper at the Bon Ton." After almost a week of going to bed hungry, he'd figured she was never going to leave him any food, so, resenting it, he'd spent fifty cents he hated to spend and he'd bought himself a big meal. Naturally, this would be the night she decided to relent and feed him.

That was the thing about women. The minute a man believed he could predict their behavior, they changed their way of doing things and cut the ground out from under him.

"We need to talk, Sam."

That was another bad sign. Nothing good ever came out of a conversation that began: We need to talk.

"Is that coffee still hot?"

"Warm."

She didn't look as if she intended to pour him a cup, so he helped himself, then returned to the table, concentrating on the scent of the coffee instead of roses. "What's on your mind?"

"Do you know what time it is?"

Her hair was glossy brown in the lamplight and looked as silky as a child's. A few tendrils floated loose around her face, softening her strong features. He tried not to think of her as beautiful. He thought of her as irritating. But, in fact, there were moments when he glanced at her and felt his breath catch. Moments when he realized that he missed making love to a woman, having a woman in his life.

"It's almost eleven," he said, frowning at the schoolhouse clock.

"Since I've been here, you've come home in time to say goodnight to your daughters only twice." Disapproval furrowed her brow. "Do you think it's right that you spend only an hour at breakfast with your children?"

"Are you tired of taking care of them?" Just once, he wished they could have a conversation that wasn't adversarial.

"That isn't fair," she said stiffening. "It isn't me they want to see at the end of the day."

She had a point. "If I could, I'd spend more time with

them, but I work ten hours on the job, then work on my claim. Afterward I go to the Slipper or one of the other saloons to catch up on the news."

"You think sitting in a saloon is more important than your children?"

Anger flushed his face. "Nothing is more important than my daughters. Everything I do is focused on making money to get Daisy the surgery she needs. Even sitting in the saloon. That's where I learn about new strikes, if any are near my claims, and where costs are heading, and which syndicates are buying, and if claim jumpers are in the area. You don't know mining, so you'll have to take my word for it. This information is vital."

"Your daughters need you," she said, as if she hadn't heard a word he said. "Isn't that vital?"

"Damn it, Angie, I'm doing the best I can. I can't be in two places at once. And I'm never going to find my jackpot if I keep banker's hours. As much as I wish things were otherwise, that's how it is."

"Molly Johnson says you used to get home earlier than you do now."

"Did Molly also mention that until recently the days were shorter and darker than they are now?" He returned her steady stare. "I can work later because it stays light longer. Plus, with you here, I don't have to get home before the girls' bedtime." He didn't like having to explain himself or having to account for how he spent his time. That was one of the many negatives about having a wife. He would do well to remember more of the negatives.

"I don't mind taking care of your daughters. I'm willing to earn my keep while I'm here. But I don't like paying for the privilege. That wasn't our agreement."

"What are you talking about?"

She told him about buying provisions and paying the iceman with her own money. Earlier in the week she had offered him every cent she had toward Daisy's surgery. Now she resented spending a couple of dollars for food and ice. If he lived to be a hundred, Sam would never understand the female mind.

"All right," he said, speaking between his teeth, "I certainly don't want you to spend any of *your* money." Reaching into his back pocket, he withdrew his Saturday pay packet. "What do I owe you?"

"Nothing. This time." Leaning back in the chair, she studied his pay envelope with a thoughtful expression. "Would it be fair to guess that you don't handle money well?"

"What?" The woman was a font of insults.

She shrugged. "I'm basing this observation on how little you've saved toward Daisy's operation."

The comment stung, and badly. She didn't need to remind him how far he was from the amount he needed. Her father's words echoed in a dark corner of his mind. *You'll never amount to anything.* In a manner of speaking, she'd just said the same thing. Pride and fury stomped across his chest and pinched his expression.

A dozen acid responses burned on his tongue, but he held himself to saying, "Where is this leading, Angie?"

"I *am* good with finances." The color had risen in her face, too. "Judging from what I've seen so far, I think we might save faster if I managed the money."

The sheer gall of her suggestion flabbergasted him. Yes, he knew men who handed their pay packets to their wives. But he didn't know his wife, had no idea if she was frugal or extravagant. Couldn't guess if she'd pay some debts and ignore others. Or waste a week's wages on a hat from Paris, France.

"I managed the household after my mother died, even after Papa reduced the funds several times. And I did it well." When he didn't say anything, she rushed on. "Here's how I'd manage our money."

"*Our* money?" He flat could not believe what she was saying. Since when had his money become her money, too? From what she'd said in the last minutes, she appeared to think there was her money and "our money." He hadn't heard any reference to his money. By God, she had brass.

"I'd set up a ledger with a list of creditors and see that everyone got paid. Then I'd portion out what was left. I'd put aside funds for provisions, emergencies, saloon money for you, a bit for me and the girls, some toward Daisy's operation, and a little for the divorce."

She had thought about this, and she had worked out a reasonable-sounding plan. That halted his furious response and gave him pause.

Sam pulled a hand through his hair then down across his jaw. If he stripped out his pride, if he took a long, hard, honest look at his strengths and his weaknesses, if he really didn't care whether she respected or approved of him—then he had to concede that he probably didn't manage money as well as some did.

The thought that tipped the balance was: If allowing Angie to manage the money hastened Daisy's operation, then he should hand over his pay packet and be grateful. No matter how much he hated the idea. And he hated it.

He turned the envelope between his fingers, reluctant to give it up. Laura had never asked for his pay packet. But Angie was as different from Laura as peas from pudding.

"I don't know about this," he said finally.

"The only way you'll know is if we give it a try."

It wasn't like he'd be surrendering his manhood. With one or two exceptions, all the married men he knew gave their pay packets to their wives. Women had a knack for managing money. At least most of them seemed to. Or their husbands believed they did. Of course he didn't know about Angie, except for what she claimed.

"I suppose we could try your plan," he conceded slowly, grudgingly. He reminded himself that he would do it for Daisy. "For a week or two. See how it works."

"Good!" Her dark eyes narrowed and flashed in the lamplight. "You won't regret this."

Hell, he regretted it already.

"You should probably pay your crew. I wouldn't be comfortable doing that."

He managed not to roll his eyes. "I'd be a laughing-stock if my wife paid my men. I should tell you though, I'm paying a lot of overtime right now and will be for several weeks."

She held out her hand and reluctantly he placed his pay packet on her palm. Damn. In less than a week she'd taken over his house, his daughters, and now his money. What he had left was a tent in the backyard. And a lot of heated thoughts about a woman who detested him that kept him from sleeping.

"Are we finished?" he asked, scowling.

She tucked the envelope in her skirt pocket. "Every morning, you interrogate the girls. You ask them questions designed to discover how I'm treating them." Her chin came up. "I feel like you're looking over my shoulder, judging everything I do or say to them."

"You're damned right I am. I don't have much choice; I have to leave my daughters in your care. But the fact is, until I know you well enough to know you aren't going to mistreat my girls, you're right. I'm looking over your shoulder and judging everything you do."

Offense stiffened her shoulders. "I've never been a mother, but I certainly know enough not to mistreat a child!"

"Then we won't have a problem." To be fair, she hadn't done anything to make him think she might treat his girls harshly. "Look," he said in a softer voice. "I'm all the family that Lucy and Daisy have. I'm their father and their champion. I stand between them and the rest of the world. It's my job to protect them. I'd be remiss if I wasn't looking over your shoulder." A vision of a soft rounded shoulder flashed through his mind. Pale smooth skin leading to . . . Sam gave his head an impatient shake. These thoughts tended to take him completely by surprise.

She frowned. "They have grandparents, don't they?"

Stiffening abruptly, he stared. "How do you know about that?"

"Molly said Laura's parents live in Colorado Springs."

He swore. "Like I said, I'm all the family they have." Standing, he looked down at her, his gaze suddenly cold. "I didn't realize Molly Johnson talked so much."

"Molly's become a friend. She's only trying to help."

She stood, too, and suddenly they were only a foot apart. He inhaled the scent of roses on her skin and the starch on her shirtwaist. If he had lowered his eyes, he would have seen the rise and fall of her breasts and the narrowness of her waist.

Out of nowhere came the memory that he had kissed her three times. Twice on their wedding day. Once before then. Hard, passionate, closed-mouth kisses. The kisses of two inexperienced people scarcely out of childhood.

"Have you ever kissed anyone besides me?" he asked suddenly.

Scarlet flooded her cheeks. "Of course not!"

"That's too bad."

Discovering that he was the only man she had kissed drove home the wasted years. She was a twenty-six-year-old married virgin who'd never really been kissed. No wonder she was angry 90 percent of the time.

"Angie, I'm sorry." He'd said it before, but this time he meant it. Life hadn't treated her fairly. He shook his head. "We were so young, all those years ago. So damned young."

The fight went out of her eyes, and she sat down abruptly. "How could we have believed that we were old enough to make a marriage?" A sigh lifted her breast and briefly she closed her eyes. "It's late, Sam. Let's not talk about the past. We'll just get angry."

He nodded and fought an urge to wonder what might have happened if she had come west with him all those years ago. Would they have been happy? On a night like tonight, would they have cast eager glances toward the bedroom door? Wasted thoughts. "Good night, Angie." He'd reached the kitchen door before she called to him.

"Oh. I should remind you. Be ready to leave at ten-thirty."

"Leave for where?"

"Church." Looking over her shoulder, she lifted an eyebrow and ran her gaze over his denims and work shirt. "I imagine you'll want to stop by the bathhouse first."

Molly usually took the girls to church. When they went. But he could hardly beg off, not after Angie had all but accused him of neglecting his daughters. Immediately he understood there was no way he could spend

Sunday morning up on Gold Hill working his claims. Cursing beneath his breath, he let the kitchen door bang shut behind him. And then turned around and went inside again.

"My suit and my good shoes are in your closet." His closet.

She nodded. "I'll set them out in the morning."

"You're changing things," he said after a minute. He wondered if her hair smelled like roses, too. Wondered if the dimples on either side of her mouth deepened when she smiled. In fact, he was beginning to wonder if she ever smiled.

"I don't mean to change anything." He could swear that she was staring at his mouth with an odd expression. "I don't like the idea of Laura and I'll never respect her. I want to be clear about that. But when I look at the girls, I ask myself what she would have done, what she would have wanted. I think she would have wanted them to spend time with their father. I think she would have wanted them to go to church."

He didn't argue. Just turned around and went outside.

Sleeping in a tent was no hardship. Sam had lived in his tent during the years he'd wandered the west, seeking his fortune and his future. The musty canvas odor was familiar, a reminder of a lot of hopes and disappointments.

But he hadn't had a house nearby during those years. Hadn't owned a featherbed. Which his wife was enjoying without him.

Folding his hands behind his head, he stared up at the tent ceiling. He didn't like having Angie back in his life, didn't like the feelings of desire she aroused or the sense of inadequacy that he had believed he'd long ago overcome.

At odd times, he found himself conducting a silent dialogue with her father in which he explained that he might have prospered if he had settled down instead of seeking his fortune in the mining camps. But with his wife refusing to leave Chicago, he'd seen no reason to settle down. He'd been free to prospect for silver first, and now for gold. With nothing tying him down, he'd dreamed big dreams and he'd had the opportunity to chase them. He'd done well enough that he hadn't lacked for necessities, but unfortunately he hadn't prospered.

People said Gold Hill had already divulged most of its treasures, but Sam didn't believe it. And the naysayers claimed the days of huge strikes were over. Sam didn't believe that either. Only last month Mort Jablonski had sold his claim to one of the syndicates for eighty thousand dollars. It wasn't a million, but the figure wasn't to be sneezed at either, especially considering Jablonski's ore didn't assay at a high concentration.

He rolled on his side and closed his eyes. During most of his prospecting years, he'd wanted to find his fortune. Now he needed to find it. Needing made a big difference. There were nights he couldn't sleep because he heard the summer ticking away.

And there were nights like tonight when he couldn't sleep because the scent of roses filled his nostrils and his mind teased him with flashing black eyes and dimpled cheeks and lips just begging for a real kiss.

The girls came out their room looking neat and tidy but wearing calico dresses and untrimmed straw hats. Both girls wore their scuffed everyday shoes.

Angie narrowed her eyes, drawing her gloves through her hand. Was this another challenge? Or a rebellion? They had made their reluctance plain; they were not enthusiastic about attending church. And they resisted doing whatever she wanted them to do.

While she was considering, Sam entered the back door, muttering and tugging at his necktie. For an instant, Angie forgot about Lucy and Daisy and stared at him. Lord A'mighty, he was a handsome man. She'd thought he couldn't look much better than he did wearing his denims and the flannel shirts that made his shoulders look a yard wide. But seeing him in his Sunday suit reminded her of the man she had married.

Except he didn't wear a mustache now, and the maturity in his face made him more interesting. Time had exaggerated the stubbornness firming his jawline, had deepened the intensity of his gaze. He carried himself with confidence, as if he didn't expect to encounter anything he hadn't seen before or couldn't handle. If Angie had met him today, she would have guessed he was a successful businessman, a bit ruthless, a bit calculating. And in need of a haircut.

When she realized they were staring at each other, she cleared her throat self-consciously and touched a hand to the brim of her hat before she returned her attention to the girls.

"Please go back and put on your Sunday dresses," she said pleasantly but firmly.

"We don't have Sunday dresses," Lucy answered, looking more offended than Angie would have believed a seven-year-old could look.

"I'm sure you won't mind if I check." Marching past them, she entered their room, not believing Lucy's claim for a minute. Jerking open an old armoire, she peered inside, then scanned the room. Angry, she rushed back to the kitchen and planted her fists on her hips. "They do not have Sunday dresses!"

Sam blinked, then studied his daughters. "They look fine to me." Lucy and Daisy beamed at him.

"Aside from the hats, they look like they're dressed for school! It's outrageous! Unacceptable."

Finally Sam appeared to register that Angie was wearing her navy spring suit and enough petticoats to give the skirt a fashionable drape. She was not wearing one of her everyday dresses. A frown pleated his brow, and he turned to his daughters. "Why didn't you tell me that you needed Sunday dresses?"

Angie noticed Lucy wringing her hands, and tears welled in Daisy's eyes. She rounded on Sam. "This is not their fault!"

His eyes narrowed into slits of cold blue. "I'm not implying that anyone is at fault. Merely that I wish I'd known they needed new dresses."

"All you had to do was—" Angie stopped the accusation. Her father had never noticed her clothes. That had been her mother's responsibility. But Lucy and Daisy had no mother. And clearly Sam hadn't given a minute's thought to the difference between everyday dresses and Sunday dresses. Part of her blamed him for sending his daughters off to church in their school clothes, but the larger part of her grudgingly understood how it could happen.

"Well," she said, tight-lipped. She beckoned the girls into her bedroom. "Let's see if we can find something to spruce you up a little."

"We look fine," Lucy said, lifting her chin. "Papa said so."

"Yes, you do," Angie responded after a minute. "But for church you want to look extra-special nice."

She rummaged in her accessory drawer, hoping to find something suitable for children.

"Here. This lace collar will look very smart with your

dress." To her gratification, Lucy's eyes widened and she stroked a finger over the lace. "Tie it around your neck."

Daisy gazed at her with damp eyes. "Are you fighting with Papa? I don't like it when you fight."

It hadn't occurred to Angie that the tensions simmering between her and Sam might upset the girls. Guiltily she considered the tears floating in Daisy's gray eyes.

"It's just that I forgot that men don't know about women's clothes," she said, patting Daisy's small shoulder. Her reassurance was awkward because she was a novice at dealing with children. But every day she learned something new. Today's lesson was to save any disagreements with Sam for a private moment. "Let me have your hat."

After five minutes with a needle and thread, a bright blue ribbon circled Daisy's hatband, and a spray of tiny pink silk rosebuds adorned the brim. Silently, the girls sat on the bed beside Angie and watched her transform the hat.

"I can sew, too," Daisy offered shyly. "But not as good as you."

Lucy nodded. "I made a sampler last year."

"I'm glad to hear it," Angie said, placing the newly trimmed hat on Daisy's head. "Sewing is a useful skill."

The girls stood on the bed and examined themselves in the bureau mirror.

Lucy touched the lace collar. Which, Angie decided, looked ridiculous on the calico dress. "Miss Lily wears lace collars sometimes."

"Well, if the fabulous Miss Lily wears lace collars then we know we're in fashion." They didn't appear to notice the sarcasm in her tone. Angie sighed, something she'd been doing a lot of lately. As a final treat, she dabbed a tiny bit of rose cologne behind the girls' ears and her own. "I think we're finally ready."

They were ready except for their calico dresses and their scruffy everyday shoes. And the white gloves they were outgrowing. And the little drawstring purses that didn't match anything else they wore.

"Your hair looks especially nice," Angie offered as they scrambled down off the bed. They had brushed out any tangles. Sheets of white gold rippled almost to their calico sashes.

"Thank you," Lucy said, sounding surprised.

Pressing her lips together, Angie led the way into the kitchen where Sam waited impatiently. Did she make so few pleasant or complimentary remarks that Lucy had to thank her? At the moment she felt harassed and over-whelmed. A little pew-time would do her as much good as she hoped it did the girls. Miss Lily, indeed.

"You'll need your coats," Sam said, giving Angie a narrowed glance that said See, I'm doing my duty by my daughters. But even he frowned when he saw that Lucy's coat was too short at the hem and sleeves. "It snowed last night."

"Snow? In April?" Angie's mouth dropped.

"Just a light skiff. It'll melt before noon."

Daisy took his hand. "Papa, smell me! Angie let us have real perfume!"

"Snow?" When Angie opened the front door, she stared at the ground in disbelief. This was a barbaric place. She couldn't wait to get out of here. In Chicago the weather would be warm and mild. The tulips and daf-fodils would have come and gone, and the perennials would be up in her garden. Except it wasn't her garden anymore. The house she'd grown up in belonged to strangers now.

But no, she couldn't allow herself to think of that, or

homesickness would make her chest ache and bring tears to her eyes.

Squaring her shoulders, she strode through the thin sugary layer of snow and waited for the others in the road. A bank of clouds floated south, leaving clear, crisp sky behind. To be positive about it, the cold air felt good and bracing on her cheeks.

Doors opened up and down Carr Street and families emerged, dressed in their Sunday best. The people across the street smiled and studied Angie curiously as did several others along the block. Angie returned the smiles, wondering if everyone was comparing her to Laura. Probably. And they probably knew that Sam slept in the backyard and wondered what that was about.

She slid a look toward him as he stepped up beside her and gingerly took her arm. This was the first time he had touched her since they entered the pastry shop on the day she arrived. Her impulse was to jerk away because his hand on her arm was vaguely disturbing. By the time they had climbed two streets to the church, all she could think about was the heat of Sam's fingers burning through her sleeve.

And then, when they were seated inside, all she could think about was his shoulder touching hers and the scent of him, a soapy bathhouse scent beneath the spicy fragrance of bay rum and the light tang of his hair tonic. There were few things she admired more than a good-smelling man. But Sam didn't need bay rum and hair tonic to smell good. He always smelled slightly like soap, a lot like a man.

Sighing softly, she noticed his hands on his thighs. Strong, square hands with long fingers. Oddly, she had never noticed what artistic hands Sam had. He could have been a brickmason with those hands. Or a poet.

Leaning close and feeling a bit foolish, she whispered, "Do you play the piano?"

His dark eyebrows soared and he smiled. "The fiddle."

Good heavens. She'd had no idea. Their eyes met and held, and Sam's smile widened before he looked toward the preacher as if he knew exactly what she was thinking. They knew so little about each other.

Flustered, Angie edged away and frowned at the girls, who were swinging their feet and craning their necks to see who was coming down the aisle. Hoping to spot Miss Lily, no doubt.

"Stop fidgeting and pay attention," Angie admonished them. And she recalled her mother saying the same thing to her.

She turned her own face forward as the choir took their seats and silently chided herself as well. What kind of woman was she to sit in church and be distracted by artistic hands and warm shoulders and the scent of bay rum and the thought of intense blue eyes? It was disturbing that physical thoughts intruded so frequently on what was nothing more than an unwanted but necessary arrangement between her and Sam.

After the service Angie joined the women and Sam joined Cannady Johnson, the mayor, his attorney, and a half dozen other men near the big spruce at the edge of the churchyard. The men lit cigars and talked about the prizefight scheduled for later in the summer.

Sam smoked and listened, watching the women congregate near the church doors. Molly Johnson had taken Angie in hand and introduced her to the group. All the women wore Sunday clothing, Sam noticed with a grimace. So did the children chasing and skipping around the churchyard. Except his. Damn it. Well, Angie would take care of that. He didn't doubt for a minute.

Ten years ago he wouldn't have guessed that she'd mature into the kind of woman who would stand up to a man and demand this or that. And back then he couldn't have imagined how inadequate her demands would make him feel. Until Angie Bertoli reappeared in his life he had believed he was succeeding with his daughters. Now he felt guilty that he couldn't spend more time with them and appalled that they didn't own Sunday dresses. He was no closer to Daisy's operation than he had been a year ago. That was his biggest inadequacy.

Exhaling, he squinted and stared at Angie through a stream of smoke. How many times a day did she remember her father shouting at Sam: *You'll never amount to anything.* Did she think of that prediction as often as he did? Did she look at him and thank her stars that she'd spent ten years alone in Chicago instead of wasting her time with him?

Cannady Johnson rocked back on his heels and studied Sam with a twinkle in his eye. "That's a mighty fine-looking wife you got yourself, Holland." The men shifted to study Angie.

"Eye-talian, isn't she? I've heard that Eye-talian women are—"

Whatever Peak Jamison had been about to say died when he saw Sam's cold eyes.

Cole Krieder stepped into the silence. "My first wife was Italian. Best cook who ever stirred up a tomato sauce, God rest her soul."

"Speaking of your new wife, Sam, we should talk." Marsh Collins, Sam's attorney, walked away from the men and beckoned Sam to follow. Sam guessed he'd known they would have to discuss Angie sooner or later. A churchyard was as good a place to talk business as the Gold Slipper, he supposed.

"Is it true that she isn't a new wife, but a wife you've had for several years?"

He wished someone else would involve themselves in a scandal so the gossips could occupy themselves with problems other than his. "It's a long story, but yes."

Marsh nodded. "It was a good idea to bring her here. Might help. Just in case."

"In case I miss the deadline for Daisy's surgery." His gaze swung to the children and he concealed a wince. Daisy ran after a half dozen little girls, her lurching gait painful to observe. She bravely insisted that it didn't hurt to walk or run on her ankle bone, but it was hard to watch and believe her.

His chest tightened and he bit through his cigar, spitting out the piece with a swear word. Sometimes it felt as if the powers that be conspired against him. Three times he'd had the money saved for Daisy's operation. The first time, a low-down no-good thieving bastard had stolen his nest egg. The second time he'd saved enough, one of his men had fallen off the roof of a project, landed on a pile of bricks, and died. Sam had given his savings to the man's widow. His last nest egg had gone to pay for a decent funeral for Laura. He'd bought her a silk dress to be buried in, and the best casket Mel Jackson carried, the one with brass fittings and handles. A granite headstone would have cost less, but he bought marble. He didn't regret his choices; he only wished he could manage Daisy's surgery, too. And he would, damn his hide.

"If things don't work out like we hope," Marsh Collins said, phrasing the possibility with uncharacteristic delicacy, "we aren't giving up. Having a wife will help. Looks like a stable home and all that. Plus, everyone in this town will stick up for you."

"Unless the Dryfus house burns down," Sam said. He ground his cigar under his boot heel.

Marsh nodded. "Unless the Dryfus house burns down. We'll assume that won't happen."

So far everything was quiet enough that Sam suspected he was paying a fortune in overtime for nothing. Well, better safe than sorry. Tonight was his turn to patrol the site after midnight. It didn't cost him when he took a turn.

Clovis Petry came up to them without a by-your-leave for interrupting a legal consultation. "Would the name of your long lost wife happen to be Angelina Bertoli?"

There was only one reason why the postmaster would know his wife's name. Before he answered Clovis, he turned to Marsh. "If you're charging me for this brief basically useless conversation, turn off the clock because we're finished."

Marsh smiled. "I'll add today's consultation to your bill."

"Why do you want to know my wife's name?" he asked Clovis.

"If she's Angelina Bertoli, then I got a letter for her from Chicago. Came general delivery. I've been holding it for three days."

"I'll pick it up tomorrow on my way to the site."

"It's from a man."

Marsh Collins laughed. "What's the letter say, Clovis?"

"I don't read people's mail!" Offended, he stamped away.

Sam looked across the yard at Angie. She was the best-looking woman in the bunch. A fact he was becoming more and more aware of, to the extent that he'd experienced the warmth and fragrance of her next to him in the pew and he'd spent most of the sermon thinking decidedly unchurchlike thoughts.

This was becoming a problem. But he couldn't get it out of his mind that she was a grown woman, a wife, who had never been kissed by a mature man.

Chapter 7

Monday dawned bright and clear. The crisp air was dry and cool, a perfect wash-day, according to Molly Johnson. As this was the first time Angie had put up a full wash, she was no expert on the subject.

But she would be after today. In short order she learned that doing major laundry was a far cry from washing a few delicate items by hand. Laundry was hard, back-breaking work.

She'd filled all her large pots at the pump, hefted them up on the stove, heated the water to boiling, then lifted down the pots and filled the laundry tubs. One tub for scrubbing, one tub for rinsing, one tub for soaking the whites in bluing. After getting down on her knees and scrubbing clothes on the washboard, she carried heavy wet laundry out to the line, pinned the clean items to the rope, and returned to the kitchen to wash the next batch.

Stepping back from the line, Angie waved at Molly, who was hanging clothing in her backyard, then she placed her hands against the small of her back and pressed aching muscles. Her whites looked as white as Molly's, she thought with pleasure, judging Molly's wash against her own. Of course, she hadn't tackled Sam's clothing yet. And hadn't decided if she would.

Looking down the valley, she noticed that all across

Willow Creek clotheslines sprouted brightly colored clothing that waved in the light breeze like tattered petals.

There was something satisfying about knowing that all over the district women worked in hot sudsy kitchens, cursing stubborn stains, putting up the weekly family laundry. Tomorrow, the same women would spend the day sprinkling and ironing. And Angie was connected by gender and history to all the women past and present who cooked and cleaned, washed and mended for their men and families.

Of course, this wasn't her family, she thought with a tiny pang. The small petticoats and calico dresses fluttering on the line had nothing to do with her. Lucy and Daisy were the fruit of another woman's womb. If Sam had been able to afford a divorce, Angie wouldn't have known that Lucy's drawers needed mending or that Daisy's blue sash had faded nearly to white. If Sam had been able to afford a divorce, Angie would have been living alone and sending her washing to the nearest Chinese laundry as she always had.

Turning abruptly from the clothesline, she strode toward the flap of Sam's tent and flung it open to peer inside.

His crumpled sleeping bag lay on a cot. There was a low, beautifully built side table holding a lantern and a book about geologic formations. He'd made a clothes tree with enough branches to support several sets of clothing.

Feeling like a trespasser, Angie glanced over her shoulder then bent and stepped inside to examine his clothing. Everything needed washing. There wasn't a pair of pants that didn't look as if he'd crawled around in heavy dirt while wearing them. Which she supposed he had, up at his claims.

An odd impulse made her lift one of his soft flannel work shirts to her face and press the material to her cheek, then to her nose where she inhaled the exotic male scent of him. Bath soap. Shaving soap. A whiff of perspiration. A hint of cigar smoke. The earthy outdoors scent that was Sam: partly sunshine, partly pine, partly wood shavings and roof tar.

A wave of dizziness overcame her and she stumbled, almost pulling down the clothes tree. Heat infused her face and her stomach tightened abruptly. She would have sat down but the only place to sit was on his cot. Where he slept.

Good heavens, what was happening to her? Steadying herself against the clothes tree, she blinked hard. A minute ago she'd been standing in the high mountain sunshine thinking lofty thoughts about the sisterhood of women and being connected to past generations through family tasks. Now she suddenly felt strange and shaky. Sam's scent lingered in her nostrils and a slow-burning fire had kindled between her thighs.

Appalled, she backed out of his tent and threw down the flap, shutting out the sight of his clothing and his pillow. Skirts billowing, she spun on her heels and fled to the kitchen. After pouring coffee into her mother's teacup, she dropped into a chair at the table.

This was so peculiar. Her fingers shook. Simply touching Sam's clothing and examining his bed had made her hands shake. She couldn't believe it.

That settled her indecision about doing his wash. Grimly she concluded if merely sniffing his shirt and inspecting his cot sent her into a near swoon like some silly yearning spinster, heaven knew what scrubbing his underwear would do to her. She didn't want to find out.

"Angie?"

The unexpected sound of Sam's voice made her twitch and guiltily thank her stars that he hadn't appeared five minutes ago to catch her inside his tent.

Jumping to her feet, she glared at him, instantly furious for no good reason. "What are you doing here?"

"I live here, remember? This used to be my house." After glancing at her pinned-up skirts and wet apron, he walked to the stove, dodging the laundry tubs. "I forgot my lunch bucket this morning."

"I am not going to do your laundry!"

Seething, her eyes snapping with resentment, she suddenly felt very sorry for herself. She hadn't come here to be Sam's drudge. Hadn't asked to feed, wash, and worry about the children he'd had while she was withering on the vine in her parents' house. While she'd remained as chaste as a nun, he'd explored, probably reveled in pleasures that were still a mystery to her. It wasn't right and it wasn't fair.

Sam paused at the sink and frowned. "Did something happen that I should know about?"

She planted her fists on her hips and ground her teeth. "How could you! We were married! Damn you, Sam." The fire that had started between her legs flamed up to her throat. Whirling, she paced to the front door, then back to the table. "You just set up housekeeping as if I didn't exist! Created a cozy little nest for yourself and someone who wasn't me. And you had children! I wanted children. Did you ever think of that?"

He watched her kick the bluing tub, sending a slosh of liquid over the side and onto the floor. She didn't care.

She wanted to kick things, throw things, and scream at the injustice of her life.

"No woman should have to wash a man's underwear unless he's a *real* husband! And hankies! Underwear and hankies are not things a woman should have to scrub unless she's utterly destitute, insane, or crazy in love!"

"Excuse me, would it be out of line to ask what brought this on?" He watched her with narrowed, wary eyes, the way a man would watch a burning fuse.

"Isn't it obvious? Here I am taking care of some other woman's children!" Heat pulsed in her face, choked her. "Another woman that you loved and held and . . . and while you were doing all that I was embroidering hundreds of stupid pillowcases, remembering three kisses and wondering if I'd go to my grave without ever . . . without ever . . ." She threw a hand past her face. "You know what I mean. Of course you know. Being married to me didn't stop you from—"

He crossed between the laundry tubs so swiftly that she had no time to grasp his intention. She wouldn't have guessed his intent anyway.

His hands caught her waist and pulled her hard against his body, and the good male scents she'd smelled in his tent enveloped her and reeled through her senses. The heat of his hands and the hard, muscular power of his body stopped the words in her mouth and the breath in her chest.

A gasp broke from her lips. "What are you—"

Then his mouth came down hard on hers, hot, demanding, almost angry. This wasn't the kiss of an inexperienced youth. His tongue forced her lips apart, shocking her, shooting a searing current of electricity down her spine and through her limbs.

Eyes wide, Angie raised her hands to shove him away,

but to her astonishment, her arms circled his neck instead and her knees collapsed. She sagged against him in complete surrender, giving in to the electric tingling that burned away resistance and willpower.

Heaven help her, she tasted him. Pushed her tongue against his and felt him stiffen against her. Felt his arms tighten and his hands cup her buttocks and mold her into his body. He touched her backside. Nothing like this had ever happened to her. It was shocking, amazing, stupefying. And the heat of his hands on her buttocks made her feel strange and hot and wild inside.

Her hands slipped to his cheeks and for the first time Angie felt the texture of her husband's face beneath her palms. His skin was firm, warm, slightly whiskery. And she discovered the exciting, almost salty taste of him. This wasn't the careful chaste kiss of so many years ago, not the gentle embrace that had made her feel as cherished as porcelain.

This was a man's kiss and a man's need that explored her mouth and pressed her hard against an iron body that set her mind and flesh on fire.

When Sam finally released her lips, they were both breathing hard, and Angie would have fallen if he hadn't kept his hands on her waist. Her knees had turned to porridge. Staring into her eyes, he said, "Now you've been kissed."

But all her jumbled brain could think of was that she was wearing her oldest dress, pinned up so her snarliest stockings showed, and her hair was a flyaway mess. Wasn't a kiss like she'd just experienced supposed to happen when a woman was at her most seductive and alluring? She didn't understand anything.

Sam's gaze cleared and he dropped his hands as if her

waist scorched his palms. Walking to the sink, he leaned on the edge and stared out the window.

"I apologize. I swore I wouldn't touch you." He shoved a hand through his long hair, then dropped his fist to the sink.

Dazed and trembling, Angie sank into a chair. The Earth had just shifted on its axis. The world could not be the same place. A man had tasted the inside of her mouth and it had been the most exciting thing that ever happened to her. She had never imagined such an act. Would mistakenly have been repelled if she had.

Lifting a hand, she touched the quivering corners of her lips. They felt swollen and hot. At least her heart had begun to quiet and was no longer slamming against her rib cage.

Lord save her, she wished he'd do it again.

"Well." Sam cleared his throat and tilted his head back. He noticed the jars Angie had placed on the top shelf over the stove. "What's all that?"

"Just what the labels say." Her voice sounded husky and breathless. She cleared her throat too. "I started late on the wash because I went to town and paid a little on all your debts. I portioned out the remainder into the jars." They were labeled SAM (for saloon, bathhouse, and now laundry money), ANGIE AND GIRLS (for school supplies, clothing, and incidentals), FOOD, HOUSEHOLD, SURGERY, DIVORCE.

"I don't see a treat jar. Little girls need treats every now and then. An ice cream cone, a pretty ribbon." He shrugged.

"I've allowed for incidentals."

He rattled the surgery and divorce jars, then looked inside. "Fifty cents in each jar?"

"You were behind on most of your debts, so there

wasn't much left over." Her mind stuck on his previous comment. When had he become the kind of man who believed that little girls needed treats? When he said such things, the breath ran out of her body. On the one hand, Sam worked too much to spend the time with his daughters that Angie believed he should. But he was a natural-born father.

He replaced the jars above the stove. "Winter is a lean time for builders. Jobs should pick up now."

Surprisingly, he made a good wage. Unfortunately, she hadn't been able to keep much as he'd held out a large chunk to pay his men overtime, and he was behind on so many debts.

"I couldn't locate Marsh Collins, whoever he is. I wanted to pay something on that debt because it's the largest. The grocer told me I might find Mr. Collins in the Gold Slipper, but of course I wouldn't go into a saloon. Who is Marsh Collins?"

He nodded but it wasn't until later that Angie realized he didn't explain Marsh Collins. "Is there enough money to buy the girls new clothes?"

She had to ask him to repeat the question because her thoughts had swerved and stuck on the way his flannel shirt pulled across his wide shoulders. Her throat burned with the memory of his solid muscular chest against her breasts, and she hastily averted her gaze from the tightness of his denims around his buttocks and thighs.

"New clothes. Yes. I've been thinking about that." She wished her voice didn't sound so embarrassingly breathy and strange. "We can save money by cutting down a couple of my dresses for the girls." She had enough clothing that she'd left much of it unpacked. "Then we'd only have the cost of a seamstress. And shoes. And a few incidentals."

Turning from the sink, he frowned. "You don't need to sacrifice your things. Buy new material."

"I don't mind. The dresses are just—"

"Your father dressed my wife for ten years, I don't want my daughters dressed by him, too. Buy new material."

Silently, she watched him grab his lunch bucket and stride toward the door. "Buying new is a waste of money we could use in a dozen other places," she said, keeping her back to him. "It's penny-wise and pound-foolish."

"I don't want them to have castoffs."

Had she known how stubborn and prideful he was? She didn't think so. Realizing he was about to leave, she stood and faced him, and her chin came up.

"I am still not going to wash your clothes."

If he thought kissing her and getting her all riled up would make her welcome the drudgery of a real wife, he was wrong. In fact, instead of softening her, his kiss had demonstrated what she'd been missing all these years and the loss made her furious.

He stood with his hand on the doorknob. "I almost forgot. Who is Peter De Groot?"

Angie's mouth dropped. This was a morning for shocks. "How on earth could you possibly know Peter's name?" She couldn't have been more startled if he'd begun speaking in tongues.

Reaching inside his shirt, Sam withdrew a letter, which he placed on the small table beside the door. "I'm guessing he must be your father's attorney. Is that correct?"

Color heated her cheeks. "No," she admitted slowly. "Mr. De Groot is a friend. A good friend."

"I see." Sam stared at her across the tiny parlor section, across the cooling laundry tubs. "Just how good a friend is he?"

Uncomfortable, she brushed a strand of loose hair off

her forehead. "We . . . Mr. De Groot and I intend to, well, marry perhaps. After you and I obtain our divorce."

Sam's eyebrows soared and his stare intensified. "Are you saying right to my face that some son of a bitch is courting my wife?"

She blinked. "Well, I suppose you could say that." Sudden fury boiled up inside. "How dare you object?" She threw out her hands, indicating the house, the curtains, the rugs, the furnishings. "You lived here with another woman! You didn't just court someone, you moved her in with you and had children!"

"It's not the same thing."

"It sure isn't!"

"I wasn't courting a woman who's living with her legally wedded husband! You tell that bastard not to contact you again."

Her mouth opened and closed like a fish gasping for air. "I certainly will not!" This was unbelievable. "Once you and I are divorced, I hope to marry Mr. De Groot!"

"Well, we aren't divorced yet. Until we are, you're my wife and I won't stand for you carrying on with another man."

"I have every right to my future!" She was sputtering.

Sam jabbed a finger in her direction. "You tell him, Angie. He is not to write to you again. What you do once we're divorced is your business. While you're living in my house, it's my business. So take care of it. I don't want to see any more letters from this arrogant back-stabbing son of a bitch!"

Astonished and speechless, she watched him stomp through the door and outside. Needing to do something, anything, she looked around, then grabbed the salt shaker off the table and threw it at his back. The shaker bounced off the wall beside the door and crashed to the floor. Running outside after him, she hurled a vase at the curl on his neck. The vase sailed past his head and shattered in the road ahead of him.

He stopped and glared back at her. "You can be as Italian as you want, but I'm not changing my mind. No sneaky bastard is going to court my wife while she's living in my house, eating my food, and managing my money. You tell him that."

"I'm never going to wash your dirty underwear!" she shouted after him. "Never! Do you hear me?"

He pretended he didn't. But all the neighbors did.

When Sam heard Cannady Johnson's "hello," he climbed out of the pit he was digging and knocked the dirt off his hat brim before he shook hands.

"Having any luck?" Can inquired, standing at the edge of the hole. He squinted down inside where Sam had left a lantern burning.

"I have hopes for this one. I followed a float trail that as near as I can figure ends somewhere on this claim." He'd believed the same thing before and he'd been wrong. Someday he'd be right, and he believed he was this time.

Already the sun had sunk beneath the range to the west. Orange and pink lit a fan of billowing clouds. Down below, Sam noticed the electric lamps along Bennet and Myers Streets, and lantern light glowed in the windows of most of the houses and cabins. He imagined mothers calling children inside, and fathers digesting their suppers while reading the newspaper. Or maybe the fathers were having a few drinks in one of the sporting houses and the mothers were figuring out how to slip rat poison into their husband's morning eggs.

With a sour expression, Sam leaned against a boulder

and wiped sweat from his forehead. He'd been swinging a hammer all day, and now his pick and shovel seemed to weigh about a hundred pounds each.

"Brought you a sandwich and some pickled eggs from the Slipper." Can handed him a wax-paper package. "The way I hear it, you ain't likely to find supper waiting when you get home. Or clean clothes either." Can's blue eyes twinkled in the fading light.

Sam's stomach told him to accept the packet. He lifted an edge of the bread. "Beef. Thank you." He took a bite, his gaze fixed on hints of indigo fringing the edges of the pink and orange. "I didn't do a damned thing. I just walked in the house and she started shouting how she wasn't going to do my laundry." He shook his head. "I didn't appreciate Laura enough."

"Reminds me of a time when Molly chased me down Fourteenth Street in Denver. If she'da caught me, she would have beat me half-dead with that broom she was swinging." He laughed.

Sam slid him a look. "Did you know why she went after you?"

"She thought I was seeing some doxy at Matty Silks's. I didn't know at the time that was the reason. Found out later."

Molly wasn't a woman to put up with much guff. Sam smiled, seeing the scene in his mind.

"And no, I wasn't involved with any whore."

"Didn't think you were."

"Thing is, I'd rather have me a woman with spirit. She might embarrass me, delight the gossips, make me mad as a wet hen. But Molly keeps me on my toes, and she ain't boring. Don't know if you've noticed, but there's a lot of dull and boring women in this old world."

"Laura wasn't boring," Sam said after a minute. She'd

been quiet and she didn't stand up to him much, but she'd had opinions. She wasn't a shouter or a thrower like Angie, but a lot of hidden strength had resided in that small frame.

"I didn't say she was. I am saying you shouldn't get too het up about your real wife chasing you down Carr Street and refusing to do your wash. If you want some good unasked-for advice, I'd say your wife's telling you in her own way that you got some home work to do, boy."

The unasked-for advice made him recall kissing Angie, which had been a big mistake. If he'd thought sleeping was hard before, now he had the memory of her body in his arms, the scent of her hair, the soft crush of her breasts, her trembling palms on his face, and the sweet taste of her in his mouth. He didn't need those thoughts in his mind and didn't want them.

"As soon as I hit my jackpot Angie and I will get a divorce." And then Peter De Groot would step forward, the son of a bitch. "Until then, I guess I can take my laundry to Su Yung's."

Frowning, he glanced at the mouth of the shaft he was digging. Somewhere down there the future waited. He felt it in his gut. But his unreliable gut had told him the same thing at a dozen other pits, and his gut had always been wrong. Giving his head a shake, he reminded himself that he'd sworn to think positively. Every hole was new and every hole could be the one.

"Heard you got your crew standing watch over Dryfus's place every night." Cannady lit one of the cheap cigars that the Gold Slipper sold for two cents. "Anybody seen anything?"

"I thought I heard something the other night, but it turned out to be only a couple of deer."

"I did some checking, Sam. Bill Haversham, Jason Todd, and Jack Hudson worked on the other sites, too. Wasn't just you."

He knew that. "There's no sense placing anyone else under suspicion."

"Thing is, none of those boys have any more reason to start the fires than you do. Unless someone paid them to do it."

"I haven't noticed any of them spending any extra money."

"Me either," Can agreed with a sigh. "Are the union people still talking about suing you?"

Sam shrugged. "Marsh Collins says they don't have a case. You can't punish a man because a crime happens on his watch. I'm hoping the union lawyers see it the same way and the suit doesn't materialize." Meanwhile, it was costing him a bloody fortune in attorney's fees. Every time Collins received a letter about the matter, he and Sam had to confer. Then Collins sent him another bill. "Are you having any luck with your claims?" he asked, changing the subject.

"I've got one that's starting to look interesting. But the vein I'm following could peter out. Who knows?"

Can's response was vague and Sam expected no less. Only a fool would broadcast a rich strike before everything was confirmed and his next move solidly protected.

"So, what's going on?" he asked after a minute.

"Easy Effie, up in Poverty Gulch, overdosed on morphine last night. Third whore this month who's killed herself. Another assay office opened up near the depot—that's forty-two assay offices now. There's strike talk up at the Vindicator. The mayor is threatening to ride up to Victor and kick their mayor's butt because Victor's mayor said our mayor couldn't manage a sewing bee, let alone a town." Can laughed. "That English syndicate is still nosing around, looking for promising sites they can steal for a song. Some damned fool shot himself in the foot while he was chasing another damned fool down Myers Street, claiming the second damned fool stole his money and grabbed his woman. The only other items of interest are that Mrs. Finn scalded her arm in hot grease, and Mrs. Leland finally died of whatever was ailing her."

Sam nodded. "You just saved me several hours at the Slipper. Guess I'll work here until late and then take my watch at the Dryfus place." Every watch he took saved him the cost of paying someone else overtime. Wadding the wax paper into a ball, he tossed it toward his lunch bucket and tool belt. "Thanks for the sandwich and the news."

"One thing." Can peered at him through the darkness. "Are you getting close to what you need for Daisy's surgery?"

"Not yet."

Standing abruptly, he walked to the pit and descended the ladder. Lifting his pick, he hefted the weight in his hand and stared at the sylvanite he was following. Sylvanite was pay dirt. Occasionally a lucky miner accidentally opened a vug that contained gold as most people pictured it. But the district's fortunes had been made by extracting gold from sylvanite. The frustrating fact was that sylvanite could contain little gold, some gold, or a rich concentration. It wasn't enough to locate the sylvanite. A man had to find the rich concentration. After next payday, he'd take in another sample of his ore and have the gold content assayed.

Sam swung tired arms over his head, felt the jolt as the pick bit into solid rock, then he jerked and twisted the handle, bringing down a shower of loose dirt and rock that covered his boots to the ankle. And then again. And again, over and over into the night.

He had Daisy's surgery to motivate him. And the divorce he and Angie wanted. Riches. There was plenty to think about as the moon climbed in the sky. So it irritated him that he spent most of the night thinking about Angie.

And wishing he could pound Peter De Groot into the dirt.

Chapter 8

Nibbling on the end of the pen, Angie tapped her fingertips on a half-covered sheet of stationery and stared into space. What to say and how to say it, that was her dilemma. Peter would be disappointed to learn that her divorce could not happen in the foreseeable future. So was she.

On the other hand, Peter was a patient man. His interest and affection were of long standing, although she hadn't suspected until a few months ago. Because he was an honorable man, not once in all those years had he behaved in a manner that indicated he viewed her as other than a casual friend. Not until the terrible aftermath of her father's death, not until she announced that she was selling her home and leaving at once for Willow Creek to speak to Sam about a divorce, had Peter declared himself. Only then did Angie suddenly and thrillingly see him as a suitor and possible husband.

The idea of Peter as the future she was trying to reach was still new and exciting. One of the many things she had missed was a genuine courtship, but it appeared she would have one. When she thought of Peter, she daydreamed about flowers and lacy boxes of candy and lovely dinners in elegant restaurants. He had promised those things lay ahead for them.

And she would enjoy a comfortable life as Peter's wife. Peter's age and maturity represented an established law practice, success, and financial security.

Well, she concluded unhappily, a man who had already waited a number of years could wait a while longer. And so could she, since they had to.

Frowning, she ticked the tip of the pen against her teeth. For reasons she couldn't pin down, she resisted informing Peter that Sam could not afford a divorce. To reveal Sam's lack of prosperity felt disloyal. Which was foolish on her part, since she had no reason to exhibit any loyalty toward a man who had abandoned her and who had gone on with his life as if she didn't exist. But there it was: a niggling sense of obligation to protect Sam's pride.

She also preferred not to tell Peter about Lucy and Daisy, partly because she didn't want Peter to feel distressed about her tending to someone else's family, and partly because she didn't want Sam to appear utterly lacking in morals and character—even though Sam's morals and character were in dire need of improvement. But the more incorrigible Sam seemed, the worse her own judgment appeared for marrying him in the first place.

And if she mentioned living with Sam, she would have to explain their sleeping arrangements. As her future husband, Peter would want to know who slept where and unquestionably he had a right. But would he believe that Sam slept in a tent in the backyard? That would sound far-fetched to an urbane man like Peter.

Setting down the pen, Angie rubbed her temples. Truly she was in the midst of an impossible situation. Her new life seemed tantalizingly within grasp, but she couldn't reach it. Every day when Sam finished breakfast and left the house, she hoped and prayed that today would be the day he hit his jackpot. But her prayers were accompanied by a sinking conviction that a rich strike wouldn't happen.

At the back of her mind grew a fear that spring would melt into summer and summer would fade, then the snow would fall, and she would still be here.

Yesterday several of the neighborhood ladies had gathered at Molly Johnson's house to do their mending. Tilly Morgan had made a reference to last winter, when the temperature had remained at fifteen below zero for a week. If Angie were here when winter descended, would Sam continue to be willing to sleep outside in sub-zero weather? Or would he demand to come inside? And then what?

As much as she resisted, these questions circled her back to his kiss. In fact, everything conspired to make her remember his kiss. She went to sleep reliving his kiss and woke up thinking about his kiss. She wished he had never taken her into his arms. She should have shared her first real kiss with Peter. Even worse was a tiny suspicion that she wouldn't have enjoyed Peter's kiss as much.

Irritated, she crumpled the page of stationery in her fist and glanced at the clock. The girls would be home from school soon. She would answer Peter's letter tomorrow. In her heart, she knew she would end by revealing everything. But one thing she knew she would not tell him. She would not tell him the things Sam had said. And their correspondence would continue. Sam had said he didn't want to see another letter from Peter, and he wouldn't. The day after she had thrown the vase at him, she'd marched down to the post office and arranged to rent her own postal box. Which she saw no reason to mention.

When the girls came home, she stood tall and tried to

look authoritative so they would obey when she instructed them to do their homework. Abby Mueller had informed her yesterday that her son attended the same school and he usually had homework every day. Mrs. Mueller had lifted her eyebrows in surprise that Angie didn't know this.

"If you lie to me again," she said to Lucy, placing two glasses of milk on the table, "I'll have to punish you. I can't abide lying." She had to threaten and she would have to follow through, but the thought of actually meting out punishment terrified her. If necessary, she'd start small by confining them to their room. But first, she'd drop the problem in Sam's lap.

"I didn't lie," Lucy insisted, her chin coming up. "You asked if we had home assignments."

"That's not the same as homework," Daisy explained.

Two pairs of solemn gray eyes challenged her.

"I think you were both aware that I meant homework."

Children were more clever than she had ever imagined. And utterly literal. They identified and exploited loopholes in ordinary speech. She thought about that for a minute. Maybe she did the same thing. Maybe everyone did when they were searching for wiggle room.

Lucy turned a longing gaze toward the open kitchen door. The scent of lilacs wafted in from outside. "Are you going to sit here and watch us do our homework?" she asked sullenly.

"Yes."

The minutes seemed like days. The following hour stretched out like a week.

"Now can we go out to play?" Lucy demanded, throwing down her pencil.

"Let's talk first." Angie drew a breath and folded her

hands in her lap. "I've been here awhile now, and the three of us aren't making much progress."

They regarded her suspiciously.

"I'd like to be your friend."

"We don't need another friend," Lucy said. Following her lead, Daisy nodded.

"I found the snake in my bed last night," Angie said in a level voice. "If you know who put it there, tell them I'm not afraid of snakes. And tell them I'm not going away."

They glanced at each other, then looked down at their tablets.

"Did you tell Papa about the snake?" Daisy asked.

"For the moment, the snake incident will remain between the three of us. And whoever hid the snake in my bed."

She had recognized at once that the creature was harmless, a simple garden snake. But finding it had hurt her feelings and discouraged her. No one wanted her here. Not Sam, not his daughters. She didn't want to be here either, but that was beside the point.

She drew another deep breath. "I'm not trying to replace your mother, if that's what you're thinking. My mother also died, and I know no one can replace her."

"Your mama died, too?" Daisy's eyes widened and she leaned forward, clasping her hands around the milk glass.

"Yes."

Daisy was a sweet little thing, or would have been if she hadn't tried so hard to emulate Lucy. Lucy might also have been a sweet child, for all Angie knew, but she hid behind a wall of sullenness that bordered on defiance. Sam was the only person who stepped through Lucy's wall, and Angie doubted Sam realized that Lucy didn't let anyone close but him.

"Did you cry and cry?"

"Yes, I did."

Even Lucy paid attention. "Do you remember what your mama looked like?"

Oh dear. The conversation was taking an unexpected turn. "Not as well as I wish I could," she admitted slowly.

Daisy's eyes filled with silvery tears. "I try and try, but I can't remember what Mama looked like."

The small whisper tugged Angie's heart. Swiftly she did the arithmetic and realized Daisy had been about three and a half when Laura died. Daisy wouldn't have understood about dying, only that her mama suddenly disappeared.

"I think God helps us forget things that pain our hearts. And it isn't important to remember the details of our mothers' appearance," she said, speaking off the top of her head. "What's important is to remember that your mother loved you."

Lucy wiped at her milk mustache. "Does it hurt to die?"

Lordy. How did they get into this? "I think dying is the end of hurting." Her answer didn't satisfy anyone.

"Do you believe that people go to heaven when they die?" Lucy stared at her.

Angie floundered, feeling as if she were out of her depth. Talking about death with an adult was difficult enough. The responsibility of discussing death with children overwhelmed her. "I'm sure people like your mother do," she said carefully.

That was a lie. Laura Govenor had lived with another woman's husband and had borne him two illegitimate children. If Laura could get into heaven, so could Miss Lily. For that matter if Laura Govenor could get into heaven, then Angie had wasted a lot of time and guilt and misery trying to atone for small sins that now seemed minuscule in the grand scheme of things.

"The Sanders twins told us that people make a horrible rattling sound when they die," Lucy informed her. "Like this." She grabbed her throat, rolled her eyes, and made a long drawn out sound. "*Aaaaach! Aaaaach!*" And another one for good measure. "Is that true?"

That did it. Standing abruptly, Angie dusted her hands together. "I wouldn't know. So. Come into the bedroom, please. I've laid out two dresses and I want you to pick which you like best."

"Why?"

"Because we're going to take the dresses to the seamstress and have them remade into Sunday ensembles for you."

Immediately, both girls hopped down from the table and skipped toward Angie's bedroom as if they hadn't been having a serious discussion about death and dying. Angie blinked. Were all children this mercurial?

"I like the rose-colored one," Daisy decided, stroking the bright folds draped over the bed.

"I want the blue one." Lucy gazed up at her. "Can we go out and play now?"

She had imagined an animated discussion of design, trim, and accessories. But already they were moving toward the door, making their escape from her.

"After school tomorrow we'll take the dresses to the seamstress and have you both measured." They didn't regard the comment as interesting enough to merit further conversation.

"We'll be home after the whistle."

Angie followed them to the kitchen door and watched them run across several backyards toward a group of children playing behind the Koblers' house. Raising a hand, she opened her mouth to call them back to wash out their lunch buckets. Instead, she waved when Lucy looked back, and said nothing.

She simply wasn't skilled with children. Their interests shocked her. They didn't like her. She wasn't sure that she liked them. She'd expected them to thank her for donating two perfectly good dresses to their needs. But gratitude had not entered their minds. Or maybe they disliked her too much to express a word of thanks.

When Sam came home only an hour after full darkness, she looked at him in surprise and arched an eyebrow.

"I decided I was coming home to put the girls to bed when Molly watched them," he said, passing her on the way to the girls' room. "I'll go to the saloon for the news afterward."

Standing beside the stove, Angie listened to the girls' squeals of delight, then the giggles and happy shouts of the tickling routine. Finally Sam heard their prayers.

"God bless Mama and Papa and Gramma and Grandpa," Daisy said loudly enough that Angie could overhear in the kitchen. "And Angie," she added in a defensive tone. Angie could picture her sliding Lucy a defiant glance.

Lucy's prayer pointedly did not include Angie. Well, one small step at a time. She felt ridiculously pleased that she had made a few inroads with Daisy.

After Sam closed the bedroom door behind him, he took a bottle of beer from the icebox and gave Angie a questioning glance. After a brief hesitation, she nodded and he opened two bottles.

As if they had discussed what to do next, Angie lifted her shawl off the hook and they headed out the kitchen door and sat on the steps. The evening was cool and fragrant with the scent of lilacs and wood smoke. A glow radiated above Bennet and Myers Streets and occasionally Angie heard a shout from that direction. Usually the sounds of evening revelry didn't reach this far. A comfortable quiet prevailed in the neighborhood, disturbed only by the buzz of insects and quiet murmurs from nearby houses.

"I'm glad you came home," Angie said when the silence between them began to feel awkward. "I know it means a lot to the girls." It was nice for her, too, to end the day with adult conversation.

"I'm not coming to see the girls before bed because you suggested I should," he said, raising the beer bottle to his lips.

"Certainly not. Heaven forbid you should accept one of my suggestions." She rolled her eyes at the dark shape of his tent.

"I had an additional reason for coming home early. To give you this." He tapped an envelope on her shoulder.

"What is it?" The envelope felt padded.

"It's a hundred dollars. I hit a small strike last week and sold some high-grade ore. I just got the money. I held back ten."

She twisted on the step to frown at him, her face lit by the soft lantern light falling from the kitchen. "Why did you hold out ten dollars?"

"For a celebration down at the Slipper." His features were in shadow, but she saw the movement of his eyebrows coming together, heard justification deepen his tone. "A man's entitled to a little celebrating when he hits a jackpot, even a small one."

"Sam, we have fifty cents in the surgery jar, and only fifty cents in the divorce jar."

"No, we have six hundred and fifty dollars in the surgery jar. I added my savings."

"Ten dollars in the divorce jar would be a start."

"I just gave you a hundred dollars," he said sharply. "You can put it in any damned jar you want to."

She thought about the money, tilting her head back to gaze at the stars. "There's the seamstress, and both girls need Sunday shoes and gloves and new hats and purses. Or I could put most of the amount in the surgery jar. Or I could pay down a few of your debts." She would have loved to put the hundred dollars in the divorce jar, but she wouldn't.

"It's your decision. So. What did you do today?" he asked, as if she had a lot of choice about how she spent her days, as if her routine might be interesting.

"The usual." Cooking, scrubbing, cleaning, cooking, a trip to town to buy lamp oil and butter, cooking. "Abby Mueller stopped by to offer me a few columbines and wild lupin to plant in the front yard."

"Good." He dangled the beer bottle between his fingers. "The front yard's going to weeds."

"Look," she said sharply, twisting on the step to face him again. "There have been a lot of adjustments to make. I can't do everything at once. I'll get to the front yard when I can."

"Damn it, Angie, I wasn't criticizing. I know it hasn't been easy stepping into a family and a life you're not used to." He hesitated then added, "And you're doing a good job."

Her angry retort died in a glow of surprise. This was the first compliment he'd offered since her arrival, and it made her speechless. As with Daisy's blessing, the depth of her gratitude was embarrassing and annoying.

"Thank you," she said finally. Then she straightened

her shoulders and told him about her conversation with his daughters and Lucy's death-rattle performance.

Sam laughed, a deep rumbling sound that made Angie smile to hear it. "That girl should be an actress."

Her smile faded to concern. "Do you think it's natural for young children to be so interested in such matters?"

"Sure." He shrugged. "Weren't you when you were their age?"

"I don't know," she said slowly. "I don't remember. But I know they're thinking about Laura, and I'm afraid I'll say the wrong thing."

"Maybe they aren't. Two miners died in a cave-in a few days ago. It's a safe bet the girls heard about the deaths at school."

"I'm certain they were thinking about Laura."

"It's hard to lose a mother at their age," Sam said after a moment, his voice soft in the darkness. "When they ask me questions, I try to answer honestly. I don't paint a halo on their mother; I don't want them to make a saint out of her. But I don't want them to forget her either."

In Angie's mind, *saint, halo,* and *Laura* were not words that went together. She tasted the cold beer and tried to will the tension out of her shoulders. Being with Sam made everything inside tighten into a state of waiting. Waiting for what she couldn't have said because she didn't know. Waiting for the next argument? The next sharp difference of opinion? The next touch? The next kiss?

Not the next kiss, she told herself firmly. There would be no more kissing. Neither of them wanted that.

"Is it a good sign that you hit a small jackpot?" she asked at length. "Does that mean you'll hit a big jackpot?"

When he shrugged, the scent of earth and soap stirred

around him. She became aware of the warmth of his knee near her shoulder, and she edged away. Never in her life had she been so constantly or so acutely aware of a man. Sometimes at the end of the day, she felt exhausted from thinking about Sam Holland. Wondering. Speculating. About things that shouldn't have been in her mind in the first place.

"Finding a pocket of high-grade might mean nothing at all," he explained. "That's the frustrating part. Or it could mean I'm close." After finishing his beer, he set the bottle on the step. "The syndicates are snapping up claims right and left, but they aren't interested unless the ore is a sure thing with long-term prospects and assays out at five hundred dollars a ton or more."

"I don't know anything about mining," Angie said with a frown, trying to follow what he was saying. "What do the syndicates have to do with anything?"

"If I found a jackpot, I'd sell it to a development syndicate."

That shocked her. "Wouldn't you be giving up your riches? Why wouldn't you keep your mine?"

"It takes a fortune to develop a working mine. The sylvanite—that's the ore—isn't lying around on the surface. You have to go deep. That means shafts with access elevators. That means a crew of hard-rock miners. Then you have to buy lumber to shore up the stopes. And pumps and coal to run them to keep water out of the mine. And expensive equipment. Then you have to pay transport to the mill and pay mill fees to extract the ore. An ordinary man like me can't afford the development costs."

She'd had no idea. "What kind of price would a development syndicate pay?"

"It depends. Al Jordan got over a hundred thousand

for his Nobby Hill claim. But Al was down two hundred feet and had dug several drifts. The ore he brought up was top grade. Clink Williams, on the other hand, sold his claim for six hundred dollars. All he had was a dry pit and a pocket that had the assayer shouting *eureka.* Highest-grade ore anyone's seen in a year."

"Then why did he sell for only six hundred?"

"Because no one knows what's beyond the pocket. The syndicate figures it can afford to lose six hundred dollars if the sylvanite peters out. Clink Williams figures this is six hundred in hand versus nothing if the pocket is an anomaly." Sam shrugged again. "Clink's wife wants to go home to Ohio. The six hundred will get them there."

Angie thought about what he was saying. It wasn't what she'd expected. "What are you hoping for, Sam? What do you want from the future?"

"I want a house in Denver near good schools for my girls," he said without hesitation. "I want them in a place where schoolchildren don't discuss what fashions the whores are wearing. And I want our house to be bigger than your father's house."

That surprised her but she supposed it shouldn't have. The past reverberated for both of them.

"What about the house Laura's parents live in? I have an idea from Molly that they live in a mansion. Does your house of the future have to be a mansion?"

Sam shook his head. "Herb Govenor struck it rich a couple of years ago, back in the days when millionaires were as common as deer ticks. But Laura was already grown and out of the house before the Govenors moved to Colorado Springs and built their mansion." He looked down into Angie's upturned face. "Herb Govenor hates me for some damned good reasons, but he's never held it against me that I'm not rich."

Heat burned Angie's throat. "My father's dead, Sam. You don't have to best him. You don't have to prove anything for his sake."

"That's only part of it. Most of all, I need to succeed for me. I've failed two women—I don't want to fail two little girls." Lowering his head, he rubbed his forehead. "I want them to live in a house with a real parlor, go to decent schools and then to college if that's what they want. I want them to have an armoire stuffed with Sunday dresses," he said, opening his eyes to stare at her. "I want them to grow up a hundred miles from the nearest mine. When the time comes for beaus, I don't want to see any miners lining up at the door. Living in a mining camp is too hard a life for a woman."

"And what about you? Will you marry again?" she asked softly.

He laughed, a short harsh sound. "I've had my fill of in-laws. And you of all people should know that I'm not good husband material. I never do or say the right thing."

In fact, she didn't know what kind of husband he could be since they'd never had a real marriage. From what he'd said, and the hints Molly had dropped, Laura had been happy enough. But Sam as a real husband didn't bear thinking about.

She poured the last drops of her beer over the side of the steps. "There's something that puzzles me. If the Govenors are rich, why haven't they offered to pay for Daisy's surgery?"

Instantly she felt him stiffen and pull his shoulders back. Anger rolled off of him in waves.

"They told Laura they'd pay to fix Daisy's leg if Laura

would leave me," he said bitterly. "I don't blame them for not wanting their daughter to live with a married man. But I blame them for using Daisy and their fortune to manipulate their daughter. I blame them for being unwilling to help their granddaughter unless certain conditions are met."

Angie stared, peering through the darkness, trying to see his expression. "That's not fair," she agreed. And Laura must have loved him very much to choose him over fixing Daisy's foot. Or maybe that was an unjust thought. More likely Laura had believed that Sam would find the funds, and she could have both the man she loved and the operation for her daughter. "But Laura's gone. Why aren't the Govenors stepping forward now?"

"The new demand is that I give them custody of my girls and then they'll fix Daisy's foot." Standing, he stepped past her and halted in the yard beside the clothesline. He tilted his head to glare at the stars. "There isn't a single day that I don't feel guilty. Daisy could have her operation next week. All I have to do is pack them up and deliver them to the Govenors in Colorado Springs."

"Oh, Sam."

"I can't do that. I won't give them up until I have to."

She watched him pace, losing his silhouette against the blackness of the tent, picking him up again when he emerged near the lilac bush. "What does that mean? Until you have to?"

"Remember you asked about Marsh Collins? Marsh is my attorney. After Laura died, Herb and Winnie demanded custody of the girls. They were estranged from Laura, hadn't been in contact with her for over a year, hadn't come when she was dying, hardly knew the girls.

Yet here they came after Laura's death, demanding her daughters."

"Go on," Angie urged when he stopped speaking.

"I wouldn't agree so the Govenors filed suit. Marsh Collins isn't a big-city attorney—hell, he isn't even the best attorney in Willow Creek. But he was willing to let me pay as I could. And just when it looked like I was going to lose the girls, Marsh came up with a plan both sides could agree to."

Angie clutched the shawl to her throat and strained to see him through the darkness. "Which was?"

"The whole outcome depends on Daisy's operation. The Govenors argued that I wasn't fit because I couldn't provide for her surgery and they could. Marsh argued that winter was almost upon us, the worst time for someone in the building trades, but once spring came I'd be able to save money for Daisy's expenses. So the Govenors finally agreed to give me a year. They figure they'll get the girls anyway. And I figure I'll be able to fix Daisy's foot before October first."

Angie sucked in a breath. "This coming October first?" Immediately she decided to pay for the girl's new Sunday clothing, then put the rest of the hundred dollars into the surgery jar.

"One way or another, Daisy will get her surgery. That's the only good thing in this mess, the most important thing."

"Is it, Sam?" Leaning forward on the step, she struggled to see through the deepening darkness. "Yes, it's important that Daisy has her foot straightened. But it's also important that the girls remain with their father. If the Govenors could let that little girl . . . if they could tie her health and happiness to Laura leaving you . . . if they can withhold the operation she so desperately needs . . ."

Anger shook her. "Then they cannot be allowed to raise your girls! It's all control and manipulation with them."

She sensed surprise in his silence. "That's what I think, too," he said finally. "They'd twist my girls in knots of guilt just like they did Laura. Maybe they didn't mean to. Maybe that's what they think all parents do. But Laura believed she couldn't please them, couldn't do anything right. Usually because she wanted something they didn't approve of. After a while she quit trying to make them happy, but she never quit feeling guilty about it. I don't want my girls to feel guilty about living their lives in whatever way makes them happy."

October. A hard weight descended on her shoulders. "Sam, can you earn enough from your wages between now and October to pay for the operation?"

"It's possible," he said, his voice a harsh sound floating out of the night. "Just barely. If we eat beans for a few months, if my creditors would suspend payment demands, if I didn't have to pay overtime . . . Hell, Angie, I don't know. Every time I get ahead something happens to set me back." Frustration shook his voice.

Like a wife showing up on his doorstep. No wonder he was upset by the idea of supporting her.

"My best hope is to find gold."

"There's something else I've wondered about. . . ." she said, drawing a breath. "About this overtime you're paying. Do you own a construction company? Do these men work for you?" If he didn't have to pay the overtime wages, they could put more money into the surgery jar. She waited. "Sam?"

"I'll explain, but not right now, okay? Right now I need to go back up to Gold Hill and swing a pick for a few hours."

"Now?" She blinked. "It must be nearly ten o'clock."

"Don't start."

"Don't start?" Her eyebrows lifted, then came down hard. "What are you talking about?"

"Don't come up with fourteen reasons why I shouldn't go to the saloon or shouldn't work on my claims until all hours or why I should be here instead of taking a watch at the Dryfus place."

"Taking a watch at the Dryfus place? I don't know what you're talking about." She also hadn't known there were nights that he wasn't sleeping in his tent. Standing, she clutched her shawl and watched him walk into the light spilling from the kitchen. "If you're not going to be here at night, you should tell me!"

"Why? What do you care where I am at night?" He stared up at her, his eyes in shadow.

On some level Angie understood that he was angry at the Govenors, at fate, at himself. But the anger spilled over onto her. And his anger triggered hers.

"I don't care where you are," she said sharply. "You could spend your nights at the Old Homestead frolicking with Miss Lily and her companions and I wouldn't care this much." She snapped her fingers. "But I would like to know when you plan to be gone all night. In case something happens. An emergency." He owed her that much.

Suddenly it occurred to her that anger lay very close to arousal. She felt the same heat on her cheeks, the same tightness in her stomach, the same tension drawing taut between them that she had felt when he kissed her. Her gaze dropped to his mouth and she swallowed, feeling a great weakness spread through her knees. Following the direction of his gaze, she realized that she stood silhouetted in the light, her waist and hips in sharp relief. She told herself to move, but she didn't.

Knots ran up Sam's clenched jaw. "You know, sometimes this feels like a real marriage," he said quietly,
speaking through his teeth. "We see each other every
day, we argue all the time, and we don't have sex."

Turning, he strode away from her and disappeared
into the darkness.

Chapter 9

"May I speak frankly, Mrs. Holland?"

"Please do," Angie said coolly. She objected to the frown the cobbler had continued to direct at Daisy's hem since they entered his shop. While she understood Mr. Kravitz's professional interest, his thoughtless stare had cast Daisy into an anguished state of self-consciousness. She hid behind Angie's skirts.

"For the smallest young lady, patent heels and top-grade kid uppers are a waste of my skill and your money." Because Daisy would walk on her ankle and scuff the patent and wear through the soft uppers. "A better choice would be a tough, thicker-grade leather."

Angie drew herself up as she felt Daisy press against her side, trying to disappear. "We want everyday shoes, Mr. Kravitz, and we also want Sunday shoes."

"I understand. But the little miss is going to scratch the patent and—"

"And I understand *that*." She leveled a flat, cold look at a point midway between Mr. Kravitz's eyes. Her tone, posture, and icy expression all stated the offensive discussion had ended. How dare he suggest that Daisy should make do with everyday boots for Sunday wear?

"It's your money," Kravitz said with a shrug.

"How gratifying to discover you realize that. Now may we get on with it?"

After sizing her up with a sharp glance, Kravitz beckoned to Lucy, who stood before the window peering out at the traffic congesting Bennet Street. "If you young ladies will take a seat, we'll measure your feet."

Daisy tugged Angie's sleeve and gazed up with imploring eyes. "I don't want new shoes. Please don't make me." Tears of humiliation choked her voice.

The right answer didn't come instinctively when Angie faced a problem with the girls. Certainly she understood Daisy's abhorrence and why she shrank from allowing a stranger to examine her twisted foot. Daisy still hadn't allowed Angie to see. But how was Daisy to get new shoes if the cobbler couldn't measure her feet?

"Measure Lucy first," she instructed Mr. Kravitz, then walked to the big display window facing the street.

Bennet Street baked in the sun beneath a cloud of dust and powdered horse droppings kicked up by a constant stream of wagons, carriages, and riders. Angie could barely read the shop signs on the far side of the street through the traffic and haze.

Unlike the shops in Chicago, businesses were not grouped by commonality in Willow Creek. A saddler's storefront and a hotel rose on either side of the cobbler's shop. The grocer conducted business next to the stables. Assay offices dotted the landscape like widely spaced weeds. Saloons had sprung up willy-nilly, here beside a medical office, there beside the lady's notions emporium. One tack shop was on Golden Avenue, another lay across town below Myers Street. Angie could identify no rhyme or reason to the town's layout.

"Angie?" Daisy whispered at her side.

"I'm thinking about it."

"I'll do anything you say if you don't make me do this."

She sighed and pushed at the fingers of her gloves. "Do you have another pair of shoes at home?"

Daisy nodded. "Old ones."

"All right. Take off your shoe." Kneeling, she gazed into Daisy's moist gray eyes. "We'll leave the shoe with Mr. Kravitz."

"Why?"

"Instead of measuring your foot, we'll tell him to use your shoe as a pattern. But you'll have to walk home in your stocking feet." Smiling, she tucked a strand of ashy gold hair behind Daisy's ear. "Are you comfortable with that plan?"

Daisy closed her eyes and leaned her forehead against Angie's shoulder. "Oh, thank you."

Angie took the twisted battered shoe to Mr. Kravitz. "I want the patent and good kid shoes and a set of everyday shoes for both girls. For Daisy, use this shoe as your pattern. Only make the new one a bit larger."

Kravitz looked up from noting Lucy's measurements and frowned. "A bit larger? That won't do, Mrs. Holland. I need exact measurements. Particularly in her case."

"That's not how we're going to do it," she said pleasantly but firmly. "If the new shoes don't fit correctly, I'll bring them back and we'll continue making adjustments until they do fit properly."

Kravitz held her gaze for a full minute, then threw up his hands. Angie knew capitulation when she saw it.

"Now then. What will the charge be for two pairs of good shoes and two pairs of everyday shoes?"

He studied the odd-shaped, scarred shoe in her hand. "The special-made shoes will be five dollars a pair. This young lady's shoes will be two dollars and fifty cents a pair." His stony expression dared her to object.

"That's robbery," she snapped, scowling. "Come along, girls." At the door she glared back with eyes as hard as black rock. "And when will the shoes be ready?"

"A week from tomorrow."

"That is not acceptable," she said. "The shoes will be ready the day after tomorrow."

"I couldn't possibly—"

"For the price I'm paying, you will have them ready when I say they should be ready. And that's the day after tomorrow!" Her eyes narrowed and flashed, and her earrings swung in indignation. "I'm giving you a day longer than I would like to." Her stubborn expression added an unspoken addendum: Meet the deadline or there will be hell to pay.

Chin in the air, she sailed outside onto the boardwalk and turned toward the notions emporium.

"This is so embarrassing," Lucy murmured, her head down. "First you argued with the seamstress, then with Mr. Kravitz, and now Daisy is walking down Bennet in her stocking feet. Is she going barefoot to school tomorrow? I'll just die."

"Daisy has an old pair of shoes that she can wear to school." She glared at Lucy, out of patience. "I'm sorry it embarrasses you to see someone refuse to be trampled by shop people. I'd think you especially would understand standing up for oneself."

Lucy's head lifted and her mouth formed into a pout. "You still had to pay Mrs. Hooten in advance, and you had to pay Mr. Kravitz's price."

"But Mrs. Hooten agreed to include buttons and trim, and Mr. Kravitz will have your shoes ready the day after tomorrow. I expect and will by heaven receive service for my money. If that embarrasses you, then I hope you marry a wealthy man." She'd cut her shopping teeth on Chicago merchants, and she'd learned a few universal truths. Timidity and politeness got one exactly nowhere with shopkeepers.

And long ago she had run out of a room instead of standing up for herself and what she wanted. She'd had ten endless years to think about that.

She watched Lucy while they shopped for gloves, bags, stockings, and new handkerchiefs. If Angie approved or suggested a particular item, Lucy immediately rejected that choice. If Angie gravitated toward one display, Lucy headed in the other direction. Worse, they seemed to wage a subtle tug-of-war for Daisy's attention. Doubtful and confused, Daisy followed after Angie and then responded to Lucy's call, then she returned to Angie before Lucy pulled her away again. Finally she covered her eyes and burst into tears.

Lucy shot a gaze down the aisle that said: Now look what you've caused.

"We're finished here," Angie announced grimly. She gathered the items she thought they needed, making the choices for them, and carried her selections to the counter. She left Lucy to comfort Daisy, not knowing if that was a wise decision or simply the quickest way to get out of here.

No one spoke a word until they arrived home.

Angie placed their parcels on the kitchen table. "I'd hoped this would be a pleasant and enjoyable excursion. I'm sorry it wasn't." Worse, she didn't know why the outing had turned sour. What had she done or said?

"Put on your old shoes, then we'll go outside," Lucy instructed Daisy. While she waited, she watched Angie

remove her hat and gloves, then fold her summer cape.
"Daddy loved my mama," she said suddenly.

Angie glanced at her out-thrust chin and angry mouth,
then untied the string on the packages. "I'm sure he did."

"I saw them kiss. Lots of times."

Her fingers fumbled in the string, then steadied.
"That's nice."

"He doesn't kiss you." Turning away, she shouted
toward the bedroom door. "Are you ready yet?"

Daisy ran out of the bedroom toward the front door,
lurching from side to side in her awkward dipping gait.
"Wait a minute," she called to Lucy.

She returned with a fistful of columbines which she
shyly pushed into Angie's hands without a word. Then
she ran out the back door, shouting at Lucy to hurry up.

Angie blinked at the columbines she had planted in the
front yard only this morning. An odd ache opened inside
her chest.

Every third night, Sam took the midnight-to-morning
watch at the Dryfus job. The difficulty was trying to stay
awake during the wee quiet hours, particularly as he was
beginning to feel the long hours and lack of sleep.

Smothering a yawn, he raised his lantern to examine
the plasterwork on the reverend's new parlor walls. Rafe
had done a superior job. Neither Sam nor his men lived
in splendid houses, but they knew how to build one, he
thought proudly. And the reverend's parsonage was
quality all the way. It even had baseboards and rose-
carved lintels capping the interior doors. Best of all, the
finish work was nearly done. They'd start painting and
complete the site cleanup early next week.

Relief made his shoulders slump, followed by a glim-
mer of optimism. After he handed the key to Reverend

Dryfus, he'd call on three maybes and turn them into you've-got-the-job. Perhaps his fortunes had turned, and the worst of his troubles lay behind him.

Cheered, he stepped outside and walked around the house, moving carefully in the inky darkness. At this hour, no lights burned in the windows of nearby residences, and heavy clouds blotted the moon. He saw nothing suspicious near the house, heard no sounds out of the ordinary.

Reassured, he sat on the ground to eat a sandwich of butter and cheese. He propped his back against the rough bark of a cottonwood tree. Angie and the girls would be asleep, resting sweetly in their beds. Angie's thick braid would lie on the pillow. Maybe she'd opened the top buttons of her nightgown. . . .

Sam woke with a start, blinking hard and cursing beneath his breath. Damn it all, he would have fired any man who fell asleep on watch, and now here he'd gone and done it himself. One minute he was listening to the quiet rustle of the leaves overhead and thinking about Angie, and the next thing he knew, he was pulling himself out of a sound sleep.

Lifting his pocket watch close to his nose, he tried to make out the time, but the darkness was too thick beneath the cottonwood. Cussing softly, he walked toward the window of the parlor where the light was better.

His eyes snapped open and a yawn died in his throat. Son of a bitch.

In three seconds flat he was through the front door and into the parlor. Smoke drifted near the ceiling, curled down to sting his eyes. Rags and paper and scrap lumber blazed in a pile in the center of the room.

Tearing off his denim jacket, Sam beat at the flames, scattering burning pieces across the bare parlor floor.

Thank God the planks hadn't yet been oiled. After ten long minutes, he had stamped or smothered all the flames. Coughing, he opened the windows and leaned his head outside to gulp deep breaths of cool night air while the smoke streamed past him.

The fire hadn't been burning long. He couldn't have missed the arsonist by more than a few minutes. His fist came down hard on the windowsill. If he'd been awake. If he'd caught the perpetrator. Then the worry and anxiety would have ended. No more wondering if anyone else would hire him. No more fear that he wouldn't be able to feed his family. The girls would get a school far from the Old Homestead. The night watches would end and he'd have more money for Angie's jars.

But he'd been asleep, dreaming about a kiss that wouldn't be repeated. Damn, damn.

Furious and disgusted, he swept up the ash and debris and got down on his knees in the lamplight to examine the floor for damage. Then he climbed a ladder and inspected the smoke stains darkening the ceiling before he opened his watch beside the lantern.

If he worked like a demon, he could paint out the smoke stains before first light. He couldn't repair the floor before his crew arrived, but he could remove the charred planks and make sure no evidence remained. No one needed to know the Dryfus place would have burned if he hadn't awakened when he did.

Grimly, he assembled paint, brushes, and a cloth to catch any splatters. He positioned the lantern, then climbed up his ladder. Beginning tomorrow, he'd assign two men to the night watches.

But now he had an answer. He'd made discreet inquiries and not a single soul in the district held a grudge

against Reverend Dryfus. In fact, one of the town councilmen had insisted, "The reverend is as universally liked
and respected as you are, Sam."

Well, someone out there did not like or respect Sam
Holland. And Sam suspected he knew who it had to be.
He couldn't think of anyone else or any other reason.
The question now was what to do about it.

Angie had the laundry down to a routine. First she put
a large pot of ham and beans on the back of the stove,
enough for two suppers, which would carry her through
wash-day and ironing day. Then she began washing,
rinsing, bluing, starching, and hanging clothes in the sun
to dry. If not for the guilt, wash-day would have gone
smoothly.

Standing in the sunlight near the clothesline, wiping
her hands in her apron, she narrowed her eyes on the flap
of Sam's tent. All right, she could admit that he was
doing everything he could to help Daisy. He worked ten
hours on the Dryfus site, then several more hours at his
claim, and every third night he stood watch from midnight until morning. Why, she didn't yet know, but he
did it. Circles of fatigue had appeared beneath his eyes
and lately he'd seemed distracted. It didn't seem right
that she was adding to his problems by refusing to do his
laundry. Plus, sending out his laundry cost money they
could put into Daisy's jar.

Muttering, she entered his tent, sighed, then collected
his work clothes and, yes, his damned underwear, socks,
and hankies. Deliberately she made her mind go blank
while she washed his intimate items and then hung them
out so the neighbors could see that she'd changed her
mind. They would also see a mistake that would cause

them laughter and Sam grief. Sighing again, she returned to the kitchen to scrub his work clothing.

She saved his denim jacket for last because the front was covered with black spots and would require heavy scrubbing on the washboard. But when she got to it, she discovered the spots were holes. Taking the jacket to the window, she examined the holes in stronger light. Charred at the edges. Large scorched areas. Most of the holes were too large and ragged to be mended.

Frowning, she tried to imagine what circumstances could account for the ruin of Sam's jacket. A fire, obviously. But the ladies talked town gossip in the churchyard after services, and no one had mentioned a fire. Sam hadn't said anything either.

After thinking a minute, she untied her apron, tidied her hair, then donned her hat, gloves, and everyday cape. She had planned to run a few errands if she finished the laundry before the girls got home from school. If she hurried through paying the creditors and didn't linger to visit, she could pay the weekly bills, post her letter to Peter, pick up the girl's new shoes, and still have twenty minutes to stop by the Dryfus site.

Golden Avenue was a steep climb from Bennet and she was slightly winded when she arrived at the site. Stopping to catch her breath, Angie shaded her eyes and examined the reverend's new two-story parsonage.

Her first impression was that the reverend's wife would be delighted with the intricate fretwork along the eaves and with the wide veranda shaded by a stand of cottonwoods. Her second sobering impression was that Sam was a gifted builder. The house was elegant, snug, and tight, every detail a lesson in perfection.

One of the men painting the exterior climbed down a

ladder and crossed the street. "Angie? What are you doing here?" Sam smiled, pleased and surprised.

"I brought you some ham and beans," she said, pulling the jar out of her cloth shopping bag. "For tonight. When you go up to your claims," she added when he looked puzzled. "Oh. I almost forgot to give you the spoon. Here."

"That's very thoughtful." He accepted his supper, but his gaze narrowed warily.

"I just thought . . . Well, by the time you get home, I've put away the supper things." She spread her hands, feeling her face blaze crimson. "I know you must get hungry. It's a long time between dinner and supper."

A sparkle of amusement chased the suspicion. "You don't have to explain doing something thoughtful."

"You had an odd look on your face. Like maybe you thought the beans were tainted or something."

"I was surprised, that's all."

Surely there was something wrong with a woman who felt a weakness for a man wearing a work shirt rolled to the elbows, Angie thought helplessly, fighting an urge to fan her face. She glanced at the light gold–tipped hair on his arms and the thick muscle turning brown in the sun. Then she lifted her gaze to a strand of long dark hair that had pulled out of the twine tying the curl on the back of his neck. When the strand of hair lying against his cheek began to seem bafflingly disturbing, she lowered her gaze to the hammer hanging from a loop on his denims near his thighs.

Oh Lord. What was happening to her? Images she'd seen only in secretly obtained medical tomes teased her mind and left her feeling light-headed.

"Angie? Are you all right?" Catching her elbow, he steadied her.

But his strong fingers on her arm only made things worse. A hot electric jolt ran toward her shoulder and made her twitch.

"I shouldn't have washed your underwear," she whispered. Handling a man's underwear did strange things to a woman's mind. But how could she have known?

"What?"

"I washed your clothes," she said, pulling away from his hand. Her chin came up and her eyes turned defiant, daring him to comment.

For a long moment, he didn't. He stood in front of her, tall, handsome, the muscles flexing along his forearms. The intensity in his gaze shot another bolt of lightning along Angie's spine and she wondered frantically if she were coming down with an early summer ague. Standing this close to him made her feel feverish one minute and shivery the next.

She gave her head a shake, scattering images that made her feel as if she'd eaten something about to go bad.

"I came to ask about your jacket." A quick glance didn't reveal any burns on his arms or along the arrow of tanned skin at his throat. "I was going to wash it, but the jacket is ruined beyond mending." Turning away from her, he gazed across the street at the reverend's house. "Sam? It appears to be fire damage. Were you in some kind of danger?"

"We'll talk about it tonight. Would you like to see the house?"

Frustration tugged her lips. She wanted to talk about the fire *now*. But the stubborn way he spread his legs and folded his arms over his chest told her the mystery would remain unsolved until he was good and ready to answer questions.

"I'd like that," she said, letting him take her packages.

The painters on the ladders tipped their caps to her and smiled. One of them grinned and gave Sam a thumbs-up sign, which made Angie blush.

The house was wonderful, a house Angie could have happily lived in herself. Silently, she considered wallpaper patterns for the parlor, dining room, and bedrooms, and furnished the windows and floors with draperies and carpets. A large, leafy fern would have finished the bay window to perfection.

The large, airy kitchen had room for a worktable and a separate laundry area. "It's a marvelous house, Sam," she said with genuine admiration. She knew just enough about construction to know the structure was well built with a keen eye for detail.

Sam leaned against the doorjamb, watching her inspect the kitchen cabinets and shelves. "Maybe you heard about the new hotel down by the depot. There's a grand opening Wednesday night."

He seldom said what she expected him to, but she followed his lead. "One of the ladies mentioned the grand opening last week when we got together to do our mending. The event is by invitation only."

"I've been invited. Would you like to go?" He cleared his throat and scuffed his boot tip at a paint speckle on the floor. "There's a dance and a late supper."

Her mouth dropped and she stared. "Tilly Morgan said people were coming up from Denver and Colorado Springs. She said the only locals invited were town dignitaries."

"Turns out I've served on enough town committees that someone or other thinks I'm a dignitary." A grin curved his lips. "Maybe you don't know, but you have me and one of my committees to thank for the public toilet beside the bathhouse. Do you want to go to the grand opening?"

Already her mind raced through the trunk she hadn't unpacked, discarding one gown, considering another. Then her eyes sharpened on Sam. "Do you have proper attire for a dance?"

He looked pained. "I can pull myself together when I have to."

Her hand fluttered in an embarrassed little wave. "Of course you can. I just . . . I have to leave. The girls will be home by now, and I should be there." A dance.

She had never attended a dance with a male escort or without her parents as chaperons. She had never danced with the same man twice, except her father. Or flirted during a waltz. Her frozen state as a married woman without a husband had made her a wallflower. During those rare times when the husband or brother of a friend had requested a duty dance, Angie's behavior had been tediously circumspect.

He laughed at the excitement growing in her eyes. "I take it that you want to go?"

"Oh yes," she said softly. "But wait. The girls." For a moment she'd forgotten them. They were too young to leave alone. "Maybe Molly . . . I don't think she and Mr. Johnson were invited."

Sam walked her through the house and back to the street where they turned to face each other.

"I'm glad you came by."

For some reason she had a tendency to forget how tall he was until she stood next to him. He was taller than Peter De Groot. And better looking, too, a traitorous little voice whispered in her mind. And he built won-derful houses that would be standing long after they were both gone. There was something remarkable about men who created enduring legacies.

"I wanted to see your house." Surprise lifted her eyebrows as she recognized the truth in her admission. Now she understood she hadn't needed an excuse. He'd enjoyed showing her his work. His pride had been palpable. She touched his arm and looked into his eyes. "You're a gifted builder, Sam." Even her father would have had to concede the truth if he'd seen this house.

A subtle shift occurred in his expression. Her compliment embarrassed and pleased him. He cleared his throat. "Well. I'll see you later. At home."

"Yes." She took her packages from his hands, careful not to brush her gloved fingers across his wrist. But she was aware of the smell of paint and sunshine, of his solid warmth and the sheer maleness of him. Aware that he looked at her with a slightly puzzled tilt to his eyebrows, as if he'd seen something in her that he hadn't noticed before.

"The girls' new shoes," she explained, taking the heavy package.

"I'll look at them later."

"Oh, I didn't mean that. . . ." Stopping, she shook her head and smiled. The conversation felt as it had ten years ago when they couldn't quite say good-bye to each other. "Will you be home to tuck the girls in?"

He nodded, studying her upturned face. "We'll talk then."

Once he was halfway across the street, Angie realized how late she was running. The twenty minutes she had allowed for this detour had long since expired, Lucy and Daisy would be wondering where she was as this was the first time she hadn't been home when they returned from school. On the positive side, her hurried walk was downhill.

She rushed into the house, relieved to discover both girls sitting at the kitchen table. "I have your new shoes," she said triumphantly. "Let's . . ." Then she noticed they were not alone.

The woman sitting with them stiffened, but did not turn. Angie noted a rigid set of shoulders, a white coil of hair beneath an expensive gray hat.

Lucy raised an expressionless face.

"Gramma Govenor came to visit us."

Laura's mother. The air ran out of Angie's chest.

Chapter 10

"That's Angie. She's Papa's wife."

Mrs. Govenor's silk-clad spine straightened until only her shoulder blades touched the back of the chair. "Lucy, I should think a young lady of your age would know by now how to perform a proper introduction."

Discovering a stranger in her house, particularly this stranger, threw Angie off balance. What could she possibly say to Laura's mother? Surprise and dismay tumbled her mind in equal measure as she walked around the table to stand behind the girls and face Winnie Govenor.

Familiar gray eyes returned her examination. Very likely Winnie Govenor had never been as pretty as her granddaughters would be, but strong features and a determined jaw created a presence that assured she would not be overlooked. In middle age, she wore a mantle of dignity, acquired when Herbert Govenor hit pay dirt (according to Molly Johnson), that suited her well. If Angie hadn't heard the story of Winnie selling pies out of her door during Mr. Govenor's prospecting days, she would have believed that Winnie Govenor had been born into wealth and ease. But no amount of newly acquired dignity could conceal this woman's iron will and fierce pride. Her determined mouth and steely gaze stated plainly she was no soft society creature.

"We're drinking tea," Daisy announced into the silence. "Like grown-ups."

The girls cradled two steaming coffee cups. Mrs. Govenor drank her tea from Angie's mother's rose-painted teacup. Seeing that Winnie Govenor had appropriated her mother's cup lit a small fire in Angie's stomach. Mrs. Govenor didn't know the cup belonged to Angie or that it was her only connection to her mother and to the civilized life she longed to restore, but still.

"Can we try on our new shoes?"

"*May* we try on our new shoes. Truly, Lucy. Are they teaching you nothing in your school?" Mrs. Govenor cast Angie a sidelong glance. "That's the problem with schools in this kind of town. Skilled teachers are not attracted to rough mining camps."

The implication found its target. If Mrs. Govenor had custody, her granddaughters would attend a larger, better school in Colorado Springs. They would have the benefit of top-notch teachers and they wouldn't have to walk past a brothel to reach their desks.

"We'll try on shoes later," Angie said, slowly removing her gloves. A shaft of sunlight gleamed along her wedding ring, creating a glow like a halo encircling her finger. She had a feeling she would deserve a halo if she survived this encounter with Laura's mother.

Suddenly she realized Lucy and Daisy were not chattering as they usually did after school. They behaved more like they had on first meeting Angie, shyly and awkwardly. Curious, she examined their faces and discovered they had both twisted in their seats to stare up at her. Nothing in their expressions revealed what they might be thinking, but their eyes spoke volumes.

"Oh my, look at the time." If Angie was mistaken in her quick assumption, they would correct her. "You have five minutes to get to Mrs. Hooten's for your next fitting."

Immediately the girls dabbed napkins at their lips then slid from their chairs. "We're getting new dresses, Gramma."

Lucy nodded. "Angie bought us new hats, gloves, and bags, too. We're getting everything new."

"That's an expensive undertaking," Winnie observed, lifting an eyebrow. She waved the comment aside for one of more importance. "I think you can postpone your fittings. I don't see you often. I'd like you to stay."

"We can't." Lucy's posture reflected regret. She looked as if she genuinely longed to stay, even though Angie knew Lucy was perfectly aware the fitting wasn't scheduled until tomorrow afternoon. Sam was right. That girl should grow up to be an actress. "Angie says shop people work hard and are entitled to respect. It wouldn't be respectful to ignore our appointment with Mrs. Hooten."

Angie pursed her lips and narrowed her eyes. She didn't recall saying any such thing. But it was just barely possible that she had. Certainly she agreed with the sentiment. But then, how could she object to Lucy's lie—if it was a lie—when she had just reminded the girls of an appointment that three of the four people present knew did not exist?

This incident served further depressing evidence of how ill-suited she was for motherhood. She hadn't the knack for setting a good example.

"I expect you home for supper at the usual time," she said before the girls threw her a hasty look of gratitude and ran out the back door. Leaving her alone with Winnie Govenor.

And she wasn't making the best impression, she realized, skimming a glance over the laundry tubs she'd left on the kitchen floor. The water in the wash and rinse tubs had gone cold, flat, and gray. A pair of Sam's long underwear floated in the bluing tub. The burned jacket that had sent her flying off to see Sam lay beside the sink beneath Lucy and Daisy's lunch buckets. Her apron was still hanging over the pump handle where she'd carelessly tossed it. Breakfast dishes filled the drying rack; she hadn't taken the time to put them away. Even with the back door open to the sunshine and air, the house smelled of beans and ham.

Well, she wouldn't apologize. She hadn't invited Mrs. Govenor to come calling on wash day.

"Perhaps it's just as well that my granddaughters ran off," Mrs. Govenor said. She frowned at the teacup she jiggled against the saucer, but Angie suspected she didn't really see it. "I have some things to say to you."

Angie removed her hat and cape and placed them with her gloves on the seat Lucy had vacated. A cup of tea would have suited her, perhaps calmed her nerves, but she'd be switched before she sipped tea out of a thick coffee cup while the mother of her rival sipped from the only teacup in the house.

She couldn't think of a single word to say to the woman who was trying to take her husband's children away from him.

"I want you to know that my husband and I were horrified when our daughter took up housekeeping with Sam Holland. I assure you, she wasn't raised to be a trollop or to steal another woman's husband. I can't explain her shocking behavior and I heartily condemn it. You have my deepest apologies for the grievous wrong my daughter inflicted on you."

Angie blinked. She hadn't expected such blunt talk,

would have supposed that Mrs. Govenor would tactfully avoid a subject as delicate and scandalous as her daughter's relationship with Sam. Obviously the words cost Mrs. Govenor dearly. This woman detested being placed in a position where an apology was necessary. Yet she'd done the right thing as she believed it to be. She had made the apology.

Angie decided she could be equally generous. "Your daughter wasn't entirely to blame."

Mrs. Govenor's head snapped up and fire blazed behind those fine gray eyes. "We are well aware who was to blame, don't doubt that for a minute. But we can't ignore the fact that Laura was too weak-willed and lacking in moral character to do what she knew was right. She allowed herself to be seduced into an adulterous liaison, and now, with your arrival, her sin is exposed! If it were only Laura paying for her lack of moral fiber, one could say she has reaped what she sowed. But a public stain has now blackened the Govenor name."

And that was unforgivable. Dropping her glance, Angie looked at the rose-painted teacup and tried to imagine her mother ever referring to Angie as weak-willed and lacking moral character. No matter what sin Angie might have committed, no matter what her mother thought privately, Emily Bertoli would have leaped from a three-story building before a disloyal word passed her lips.

"And Lucy and Daisy! The shame they must feel!"

"The girls are young," Angie said slowly. "I don't think they grasp the stigma of—"

Mrs. Govenor leaned forward. "I tried to warn Laura. I told her that she was throwing away her reputation, her life, her family. I warned her that her children would grow up in shame."

While Mrs. Govenor continued to list the warnings

she'd given Laura, Angie wondered how her parents would have reacted if she had defied their wishes and gone West with Sam. Would they have disowned her as the Govenors had done? Because they disapproved of her choice? Or would they have come around eventually and wished her well?

And it suddenly and shockingly occurred to her that it was just barely possible that Sam was not entirely to blame for her wasted years. An argument could be made that her need for her parents' approval had been stronger than her love for her new husband.

She shifted uncomfortably in her seat. "I don't know if you're aware of the situation between Mr. Holland and myself."

Mrs. Govenor sat back with a look of disgust. "Mr. Holland called on us shortly before Laura broke our hearts and ruined our good name. He explained that the two of you never had a real marriage. That you remained in Chicago by choice, and that he expected you to seek a divorce at some point."

"That's true," Angie said, nodding. "Your daughter didn't steal my husband, as you put it." Angie had thrown him away. If she could have figured a way to mention that Sam was an unused husband when Laura got him, she would have said so. He had been as good as new in that regard. But Sam's ring was and always had been on Angie's finger, and that was all Mrs. Govenor cared about. "Sam and I were never really husband and wife. We should have divorced years ago."

"Then why did you come here?" Mrs. Govenor stared at her with undisguised dislike. "If you hadn't come to Willow Creek, no one would ever have known that Laura wasn't an honest, decent woman. Our name would be untarnished."

Angie felt her gorge rising with an odd sympathy for Laura. "From everything I've heard, your daughter was an honest, decent woman. She made an unfortunate choice, but that doesn't change who she was. From all accounts, she was a good person." What had the world come to? Now Angie was defending a woman she had loathed up till this minute. In fact, as recently as this morning, she had agreed with Mrs. Govenor's assessment of her daughter's character. But it pained her that Laura's mother could no longer recognize any admirable qualities in her daughter.

"Your defense of a woman who lived openly with your husband shocks me, Mrs. Holland. Your sentiments confirm my opinion that you're totally unsuitable to care for my granddaughters."

Angie's spine snapped to attention and her eyes widened. "I beg your pardon."

"If you believe a woman who chooses to live in adultery can retain any honesty or decency, then you clearly should not be acting as a mother to my granddaughters. May heaven protect them from your influence!"

Sputtering, Angie fell backward in her chair.

"And don't think you're fooling anyone. Mr. Govenor and I know why you came here."

"I came in hopes of obtaining a long-overdue divorce."

"We know the real reason. And I promise you this ploy will come to nothing. When Sam fails to provide Daisy's much-needed operation, the court will award custody to us. If Sam thinks bringing his wife into this house will alter the court's ruling—it won't. Your presence and the implication of forgiveness and acceptance means nothing. Underneath, Sam Holland is still an immoral man."

Angie's pulse pounded at the base of her throat. "Sam

has made his share of mistakes, maybe more than his share, but he is not immoral! I haven't been here long, but I've talked to enough shopkeepers and townspeople to know that Sam is well liked and respected."

"This pretense of creating a stable household is only that. A pretense. I wasn't in Willow Creek more than three hours before I knew Sam was sleeping in your backyard."

"I will not discuss our sleeping arrangements with you or anyone else." Outrage flamed on her cheeks. "But I can assure you that I did not come to Willow Creek because of your custody suit." Anger shook her voice. "I didn't know about Laura or the girls until I arrived."

"I doubt the judge will find that explanation any more convincing than I do."

"Will the judge believe your contention that Sam and I had no communication for ten years and then Sam suddenly requested my help to beat his lover's parents in court and I said Of course I'll help you? That's ridiculous!"

"It doesn't matter because Mr. Holland will never find the wherewithal to provide Daisy's surgery within the time granted by the court. And we will not tolerate an appeal based on the questionable appearance of a wife and a cozy family charade."

Angie stood. She was not Laura and she didn't care about this woman's approval. If Mrs. Govenor wanted blunt talk, that's what she would get.

"I didn't come to Willow Creek as a ploy to influence the court if the need arose. But now that I'm here, I'll help Sam in every way I can to retain custody of his daughters. He's a good father, and he loves those girls. It would be a miscarriage of justice if he loses them and if they lose him. Lucy and Daisy should be with their father."

"*We* are their blood relatives and *we* should raise them!" Mrs. Govenor rose also. They faced each other across the kitchen table. "Look around you, Mrs. Holland. My granddaughters are living in a shack. They attend a third-rate school. Every day of their lives, they are exposed to drunks, brawls, and women of ill repute. Their father, as you call him, is a known adulterer. Mr. Govenor and I can give them a decent life."

"Your blindness and narrow-mindedness take my breath away!" Angie stared. "If you care so much about your granddaughters, then why didn't you offer to pay for Daisy's operation with no strings attached? Pay for her surgery simply because she needs it. Pay for it because her life will be better with a straightened foot!"

"How dare you!"

"Do you know that other children laugh at her and tease her? Do you know that people stare at her? Can you even guess what agony it is for her to buy new shoes? Have you ever seen her foot? She tries to hide it, you know." Full fury overcame her. Her eyes blazed; her hands flew; she fizzed. "I don't think you really care about Daisy. I think you use her and your money in an attempt to control. First Laura, and now Sam. If you cared about Daisy, Daisy would have had that operation years ago!"

White-faced and trembling, Mrs. Govenor drew herself rigid. "You don't know what you're talking about. Daisy would have had her operation years ago if Laura had come home. That's all she had to do. Just come home."

"So you punished Daisy because Laura wanted to be happy." Angie's lip curled. "And you dare to question my qualifications to be a mother."

Now it was Mrs. Govenor who sputtered in fury. "I

actually felt sorry for you. I lowered myself to apologize." A shudder convulsed her shoulders. "I see now that you and Mr. Holland are of the same bad ilk."

"I want you to leave. Right now. And don't return to this house again."

Spinning in a swirl of gray silk, Mrs. Govenor marched to the front door, her head held high. She paused with her hand on the latch and shot a venomous look back at Angie. "You are not in control here, Mrs. Holland. Mr. Govenor and I are granted access to our granddaughters by the court. I shall return if and when I please, as often as I please, and you have nothing to say about the matter."

Angie expected her to slam the door, and perhaps she wanted to, but Mrs. Govenor's dignity reappeared and the door closed softly behind her.

Dignity was not Angie's long suit. Throwing back her head, she shouted "damn" at the ceiling, then ran outside and yanked the laundry off the line, scattering clothespins all over the ground. She threw the clean clothing on her bed, then sat on top of it and covered her face with her hands.

With all her heart, she wished she could turn back the clock and have five more minutes with her mother. She longed to tell her mother that she had never doubted that she was loved. Had Angie made the same choices as Laura, her mother would have been as shocked and horrified as Mrs. Govenor. But Emily Bertoli would never have disowned her daughter. She would have wept, prayed, and blamed herself for raising Angie wrong, and in the end she would have fought to understand.

Throwing back her head, Angie stared at the ceiling. Mrs. Govenor could not be allowed to raise Lucy and

Daisy. The wrong things were important to Laura's mother.

Right now, feeling as she did, if she had believed it would help, Angie would have joined Sam at his diggings every night and would have swung a pick until dawn looking for gold. They had to find the money for Daisy's operation. And soon.

The minute Sam heard that Herb Govenor was in town, he nodded slowly and abandoned his usual routine. He wouldn't be going up to his claim tonight. He'd been awaiting the Govenors' arrival, taking for granted that they would be among the out-of-town dignitaries invited to the hotel's grand opening.

After the six o'clock whistle, he gave his tools to Rafe for safekeeping, then washed at the rain barrel and slicked back his hair. The Govenors might be staying at the new hotel, but he guessed it more likely that they would stop at the Congress as they usually did. If so, at this hour Herb would be in the bar off the lobby.

The Miners' Bar smelled of polished oak, soft leather, and rich cigar smoke. There were no wood shavings on the floor in here, no painted women competing for a quick trip upstairs. Men in evening dress relaxed in deep club chairs, discussing investments and the syndicates that many of them headed.

In his denims and work shirt, his paint-spattered boots and worn hat, Sam stuck out like a penny in a pile of gold coins. A few years ago most of the men in the bar had looked like Sam and had dreamed Sam's dreams. The scowls directed his way said these men resented an echo from the past invading their sanctuary. Most didn't welcome a reminder of the hard days before mansions and fancy carriages.

Herbert Govenor shared a table with two other newly minted moguls, only one of whom was worth a damn in Sam's opinion. That was Marcus Applebee, a man who hadn't forgotten where he came from.

Applebee stood and shook Sam's hand with a smile of pleasure. "I was thinking about you not long ago. The mayor tells me you're going to build a new school on the upside of Bennet. It's a good idea that's long overdue. When you're ready to put together the financing, come see me."

"I'll do that, Marcus." Sam watched Herb Govenor push to his feet, and his face went flat. "It's time we talked."

"You and I have nothing to say to each other."

"We can talk here, or we can talk privately."

Clamping his cigar between his teeth, Govenor studied Sam's hard eyes before he nodded shortly and dropped his cigar in an ashtray. Sam followed him to the door of the bar, feeling the stares of curiosity that trailed him.

In the light of the marble-floored lobby, he got his first good look at Herb Govenor since he'd seen him in court months before. It seemed that Govenor had added a few pounds to his tall wiry frame. His hairline had receded another inch. But the arrogance and hatred hadn't changed. Both were starkly evident.

"What do you want, Holland?"

Other than a desk clerk at the far end of the room, they were alone in the lobby. Still, Sam lowered his voice. "I want the fires to stop." Govenor stared at him. "I know what you're doing. If the jobs dry up, I won't be able to afford Daisy's surgery, and then you'll take my daughters."

"You're accusing me of starting the fires on your sites?"

"I'm accusing you of hiring it done." They squared off, facing each other. "So far no one has been injured, and the places you burned are owned by people who can afford the loss. But it ends now or I go to the authorities."

"You can't prove a damned thing."

The lack of denial solidified Sam's suspicions into fact, and fury boiled in his chest. "You son of a bitch!"

Govenor leaned close, his eyes glittering. "I'm going to ruin you like you ruined my daughter."

He hit Govenor hard enough that Govenor went down and slid sprawling on the marble floor, and Sam wondered if he'd broken his knuckles. Govenor regained his feet quickly for a man twice Sam's age, and they fell on each other, punching and gouging with no regard to where they were, with no thought but to inflict damage and punishment.

By the time the men in the Miners' Bar had rushed into the lobby and pulled them apart, bright blood soaked Govenor's shirt front and waistcoat, and the front of Sam's shirt was equally red. Both had aching jaws and ribs, and both had swollen eyes that would turn blue-black by morning.

None of the men crowding around the combatants considered sending for the law, and none thought of inquiring into the cause of the fight. Most knew and respected Sam Holland and Herb Govenor, and most knew an explosive family situation existed between them.

Marcus Applebee placed an arm around Sam's shoulders and turned him toward the street door. "It's over now, son."

"Not by a long shot," Sam muttered, testing his jaw and checking for loose teeth. He ached all over. Herb might be getting old, but he could still throw a mean punch. All Sam could hope was that he'd given as good as he got.

Marcus grinned. "Best fight I've seen in a while. Another two minutes and you would have had him." They stepped outside and offered a token glance toward the sinking sun.

Sam pressed his handkerchief against the blood dripping from his nose. "Are you still buying?"

"I'm always interested in making money. What have you got?"

"Not me. Not yet. Cannady Johnson. I've got a feeling Can's about to pop. If so, he'll get a fairer shake from you than from most of them in there." He jerked his head toward the hotel and immediately regretted the abrupt movement.

"I've got some contacts. I'll check out the assays and if things look promising, I'll talk to Johnson."

"Good." He looked at his bloody handkerchief and damned if he didn't picture Angie kneeling over the scrub board and having a fit about bloodstains. He almost laughed.

"Sam. If I told you how much money per day my company is taking out of the Moose Jaw Mine, your mouth would fall open. If you ever need—"

Pride reared past the pain in his nose and ribs and his shoulders stiffened. He stuck out his hand and gripped Marcus Applebee's palm firmly. "I hope it works out for Cannady. He's close. Goodnight, Marcus."

"The problem with being stubborn as a mule is that it turns a man into a jackass."

"Could be," Sam said with a smile and a wave.

He'd hoped he could go directly to his tent and clean up a bit before he faced Angie. But she and Molly Johnson were sitting on the back steps enjoying the sunset and eating bowls of wild raspberries with the girls.

Angie looked at his battered face and the blood on his shirt and screamed. Lucy and Daisy dropped their bowls and burst into tears.

Chapter 11

"Sometimes you just got to wonder what God was thinking when he created men," Molly said, staring at Sam through the fading light. Short waves of silver swung against her cheeks as she shook her head and stood. "Damn fools."

Angie leaped off the steps and ran forward. Her hands flew around Sam's face and chest, but she was afraid to touch him because she wasn't sure where he was injured.

"Now, girls." Molly frowned down at them. "Stop that caterwauling." Lucy and Daisy sat frozen on the stairs, peering at Sam through their fingers and sobbing in fear and panic. "Head wounds gush like a leak in a dam, especially when the leak's in the nose, but it's over now. Your pa is standing on his own two feet, no bones are sticking out, and the bleeding's almost stopped."

"Sam! What *happened*?"

"Molly's right," he called to the girls. "I'm fine."

He was a long way from fine. "You're covered in blood and one of your eyes is almost swollen shut!" She had to get water and an eye wash. Alum to stop the blood trickling from his nose. There was nothing she could do for the bruise spreading on his jaw. She started to touch his nose then jerked her hand back. His nose didn't look broken, but it had started to swell. "Oh my heavens. Oh my heavens."

Sam gripped her shoulders and peered into her eyes. "Angie, it's all right. I'm going to be sore as hell, but nothing's busted."

Her heart was going to pound through her chest, she just knew it, and her hands shook.

Paralysis broken, Lucy and Daisy raced past her and threw themselves around Sam's legs, hanging on and crying. Sam patted their backs and threw Molly a glance.

Striding through the twilight, Molly pried the girls loose. "Come along now. You come to my place and we'll have another bowl of raspberries. If you ask nice, I'll bet you can persuade Mr. Johnson to tell you a story." She lifted her head. "I'll keep 'em overnight. Looks like you two have some catching up to do."

Sam knelt and placed his arms around both girls. "You go with Mrs. Molly. I'll fetch you in the morning."

Daisy wiped a sleeve across her eyes. "Are you going to die, Papa?"

"It takes more than a nosebleed to kill me, honey."

"Your eye is all swollen." Lucy stared at him, her face as white as paper. "You look scary."

"I ran into a bit of trouble, but I'll be right as rain in a few days." Standing, he gave the girls a little push. "Molly? Thank you."

As soon as he'd waved his daughters inside Molly's house, Sam gingerly placed a hand against his ribs and groaned. "Damn."

"Come inside," Angie said, picking up her skirts. "I'll heat some water. No, I already have hot water on the stove." But where were her medical supplies? Under the sink. But there wasn't much she could do. The only injuries she could doctor were his eye and his nose. "Sit there," she said, pointing to a kitchen chair. "I need a rag." Thank heaven it was laundry day. Everything was clean and at hand.

She dipped a laundered rag in the hot water on the back of the stove, wrung it out over the sink, then folded the cloth into a pad. "Put this on your eye. If we've caught it soon enough, the heat will prevent further discoloration."

He drew back. "It's hot."

"It's supposed to be."

Swearing and grinding his teeth, he let her dab alum on his nose. Stepping back, Angie nodded with satisfaction when the bleeding stopped. Now to clean him up.

"Can you get out of that shirt by yourself or do you need help?" At once she saw that he couldn't hold the hot pad to his eye and take off his shirt.

Even anxious and feeling squeamish about the blood, stripping off his shirt made her face flame. His bare skin felt firm and warm beneath her fingers, and she was very aware that she was touching bare parts of his body that she'd never touched before. Once she had his shirt off, she wet another rag and bathed blood smears off his throat.

"Stop looking at me," she said in an odd voice. She stood close beside him and his naked chest. Close enough to feel the warmth of his body, to feel his breath on the back of her hand. Close enough to sense the speculation behind his steady gaze. Flustered, she lowered her eyes.

Silky dark hair covered his chest. That was a surprise. As was her sudden longing to run her palms over the strands. The color in her face intensified, annoying her no end, especially since he watched her. She was no longer a romantic, dreamy maiden. She was a no-nonsense adult who could doctor a grown man without swooning. Surely.

When she realized she was washing the same spot on his throat over and over, she made a sound of disgust and tossed the bloody rag into the sink on her way to the pile of folded laundry awaiting tomorrow's iron.

Determined not to respond to bare skin and twitching muscle, she helped him into a clean work shirt, rolled up the sleeves for him, then took two beers from the icebox. Despite her conviction that beer was not a lady's beverage, she was beginning to enjoy the taste. And right now she needed something to calm her thoughts. She kept seeing Sam in her mind, walking out of the gloaming covered in blood. Her heart had stopped and the world had gone black in front of her eyes. As for taut bare skin and muscles so defined she could have traced them with her fingertip—those disturbing images could wait to be considered later.

"All right," she said, sitting down at the table and drawing a deep breath. "What happened?"

"How long do I have to hold this heat on my eye?"

"At least twenty minutes. What happened?"

"A piece of steak works better."

"We don't have a piece of steak. Sam, if you don't tell me what happened, I'm going to black your other eye!"

He took a deep pull from the beer bottle and exhaled slowly. "It's a long story."

Angie threw up her hands and glowered. "I'm not going anywhere. We have all night." Which was another unnerving thought that didn't bear close examination.

First he explored his ribs with his fingertips. Then he felt along his jaw. Examined his bruised knuckles. "The trouble started last autumn," he said finally. "After the court ruled that I had a year to fix Daisy's foot. That's when the first fire occurred, at the new Union Hall I was building. The hall was almost complete. My crew and I had it dried in; we were halfway through the finish work. Then one night it burned to the ground. Nothing left standing except the chimney chases."

Angie started to protest. What did an event last autumn have to do with a bloody fight tonight? But the word *fire* flashed her mind backward to his burned jacket. Best to let him tell it in his own way.

"The cause of the fire was arson." Sam placed the beer bottle on the table and turned it between his fingers. "While the police and the union people sorted it out, my crew and I moved on to the Whittier job. Mick Kelly was the original contractor and he'd gotten the shell of the house up before his horse fell and crushed him. Whittier hired me and my crew to dry it in before the snow and then to return and finish the house this spring."

" 'Dry it in' means getting the roof on, right?"

He nodded and ran his free hand through his hair. At some point he'd lost the twine that tied his hair back, and waves of dark hair hung over his shoulders. With his hair loose and his collar open, with his nose and eye swollen, he made Angie think of a pirate fresh from battle. Wildly handsome, powerful, and slightly dangerous. A soft breath stuck in her throat.

"We got the roof on, and then Whittier's place burned down. Nothing was left standing but the stonework around the foundation. The arsonist didn't try to make it look like an accident."

Angie's eyes sharpened and her mind focused. At once she understood that Sam had been carrying a heavier burden than she'd guessed.

"That's when the talk started. Everyone says the fires

aren't my fault." His gaze met hers. "But there's a hint of doubt when they say it."

"That's ridiculous," Angie stated flatly. "Why would you burn down a structure you're being paid to build?"

He shrugged and winced at the movement. "Maybe I don't agree with the union's politics. Maybe I hate Homer Whittier as much as most people do. Maybe I want to extend the job and get paid again to rebuild the place. Maybe I'm just crazy. The one fact that no one disputes is that it's a strange coincidence that my last two jobs have burned down."

Frowning, she let her thoughts jump ahead. "So that's why you put a night watch on the reverend's house." A third fire would not be coincidence. "Your jacket . . ." Her eyes widened. "There was a fire on this job site!"

"It happened on my watch. I caught it early before any real damage occurred." Removing the pad from his eye, he looked at her. "No one knows about it."

But he'd told her. His trust surprised and touched her, and made her want to perform some act to demonstrate that she was worthy. Jumping up, she took the folded rag from his hand and replaced it with another that was hot. It frustrated her that she could think of nothing noble or heroic to prove herself.

And suddenly it occurred to her that Sam had demonstrated confidence in her from the first. He trusted her with his children and his home. Trusted her with his money. And now he had entrusted a secret to her safekeeping.

She, on the other hand, had a secret postal box, spent hours seething and brooding about Sam and Laura, and she didn't entirely believe that Sam would succeed in putting together the funds for Daisy's operation. Feeling guilty, she lowered her head and chewed at her bottom lip. Suspecting that Sam might be a better person than she was a very new thought and not a comfortable one.

"You've had time to think about it," she said after a minute. "Who's setting your job sites on fire, and why?"

"I'm one hundred percent sure that Herb Govenor is behind the fires. I think he hired some thug to set them."

The answer was so unexpected that Angie gasped. "Mr. Govenor would do something like that?"

Sam nodded and finished his beer. "I believe he wants to destroy my livelihood. If all my projects burn down then no one will hire me. If I can't work, I can't set aside money for Daisy's operation."

"You could find gold."

"I've been searching for gold for a lot of years, Angie." He closed his eyes and tilted his head back, and she saw how exhausted he was. "All I've found are small pockets. Realistically, how probable is it that I'll hit my jackpot in time to meet the court's deadline?"

She leaned forward, staring at him. "It could happen. You can't give up now, Sam."

His eyes snapped open. "I didn't say I was giving up. Never. I'm saying I can't depend on finding gold to solve my problems. I have to assume that what I earn on the job is the only money we're going to have for Daisy."

Angie glanced at the row of jars above the stove. At the rate she was adding money to Daisy's jar, Daisy wouldn't have her surgery for a year or longer. By then, Daisy and Lucy would be living with the Govenors.

She rubbed at the headache forming behind her temples. "So you're paying your crew overtime wages so they'll watch for someone trying to start a fire on the site." At least that mystery was now solved. "What if one of them is the arsonist?" she asked, lifting her head.

"I've worked with these men for two years. I trust them."

"We can't save money because of the overtime you're paying, but if you don't pay it, there might be another fire, and then no one would hire you because they'd be afraid that their place would burn down, and if there are no new jobs then there isn't any money at all. Sam, isn't there anything you can do?"

"Which brings us to tonight," he said, carefully touching his nose and grimacing.

Angie listened as he described the fight with Herb Govenor, getting angrier with every word he spoke. "There must be a way to stop him," she said when Sam fell silent.

"Govenor's right. There's no proof."

Unable to sit still, Angie stood and paced in front of the stove. "These people are unbelievable! What kind of grandparents would go to such lengths to take children away from their own father?" She threw out her hands. "Their focus should be on what makes their grandchildren the happiest. By the way, Winnie Govenor was here when I returned from seeing you at the site."

Sam's shoulders shifted and he gave her a grim smile. "How did that meeting go?"

"Let's just say that both of us got beat up by a Govenor today."

Sam laughed. "That bad?"

"You're an immoral father, and I'm an unfit example for children."

Instantly, his expression sobered. "No, you're not. Through no fault of your own, you've been tossed into a situation you didn't ask for and didn't want. I know it hasn't been easy, going from being a rich man's daughter to a poor man's wife. But you haven't complained, you do what you have to do, and you keep trying. And Angie, you're doing just fine with the girls."

Compliments cut the ground out from under her. Especially from Sam, knowing that he blamed her for the collapse of their marriage and for the ruined reputation of a woman he had loved. Yet he found things to admire about her and possessed the generosity to say so.

"I burned the beans," she said in a small voice, staring at him.

"Hell, I like burned beans," he said, smiling.

"You don't know this yet, but some of your underwear has a pinkish cast. Daisy's red sash fell into the rinse tub." She'd scrubbed like a demon to get his underwear from rose to light pink. Left the items soaking in bluing until she'd started to worry the strong solution would eat through the material.

"I won't claim I like pink underwear," he said, tilting his head back, "but I guess I can think of worse mistakes."

"And Lucy hates me."

His head came down and he fixed her with a level gaze. "Lucy was the lady of the house before you came, a seven-year-old trying to be a grown woman. Give her time to realize that now she can be a child again."

Just like that, she understood. She had displaced Lucy and had become Lucy's rival. Angie blinked. Lucy and Sam had been the grown-ups. At least that's how it must have seemed to Lucy. Now it was Sam and Angie. Lucy had been responsible for the care of the house; now the house was Angie's obligation. Lucy had tried to mother Daisy; now Angie did. Sam had belonged solely to the girls; now they shared him with Angie.

She covered her eyes and shook her head. "Sometimes I feel so inadequate."

Sam's arms came around her, startling her because she hadn't heard him rise or walk toward her. "So do I," he said in a tired voice, speaking against her hair.

Leaning backward, she rested against his chest, lightly so she wouldn't put pressure on his bruised ribs. And she placed her hands over his at her waist.

The window over the sink reflected something Angie had never expected to see. She and Sam leaning on each other, depending on each other, finding comfort in touching. A moment ago she had felt as if the world were closing around her, as if the mountain of problems rearing before them was insurmountable. But with Sam's arms around her, she felt protected and hopeful that together they could chew a few pieces out of that mountain.

All she had to do was turn in his arms and his mouth would be mere inches from hers.

Her breath accelerated and a spreading warmth flowed down her limbs.

"Angie?"

Wetting her lips, she answered in a husky voice. "Yes?"

"If I don't lie down, I'm going to fall down." His arms dropped away from her waist, and he rested his weight against the edge of the sink. "I hope that son of a bitch is as bruised and aching as I am."

What a silly idiotic creature I am, she thought before she turned around. He was bruised, battered, and reeling with fatigue. Kissing was the last thing on his mind. On hers either, she hastily assured herself.

She dusted her hands together and tried to look brisk and efficient, like a person one could entrust with secrets, money, and children. Tried to look like a woman who had never entertained a single thought about kissing.

"I think you should sleep inside tonight, in your own

bed. You'll rest better." When Sam's gaze flickered, she added quickly, "I'll sleep in the girls' bed."

"Of course."

Blushing was a trait that she hated, hated, hated. "It wasn't necessary for me to mention that," she said, angry that she had.

"No."

"I mean about me sleeping in the girls' bed."

"I know."

"I don't know why . . . it's just . . ." To occupy her hands, which dangled uselessly by her sides, she stepped to the sink, edged Sam aside, and started scrubbing furiously at the bloody rags. "I know you aren't thinking about . . ." She was digging herself deeper into a hole. "About dishonorable things."

"Like sleeping in a bed recently occupied by a beautiful and desirable woman? Like the scent of your hair and how good you feel in my arms? Are those the dishonorable things you mean?" When her head snapped up, he was staring at her with his good eye. "Don't give me too much credit, Angie," he said softly. His gaze dropped to her throat and the soft beat of her pulse.

She froze with her hands deep in soapy water and her breath hot in her chest. If he had taken a single step in her direction, she would have disgraced herself by flying into his arms.

"I accept your invitation to sleep in a bed tonight," he said instead, turning away from her and walking toward the bedroom. At the door, he looked back and his expression suggested he wanted to say more, but he wouldn't. "Goodnight."

After the door closed, Angie gazed at her blurred reflection in the window panes above the sink. Confusion tossed her thoughts like bits of paper before a spring gust. In the span of two hours, she had raced from a debilitating fear that something terrible had befallen Sam, to the secret thrill of touching his skin, then to feelings of pleasure and unworthiness that he trusted her, and on to fury at the Govenors, followed by the comfort of Sam's arms around her, and finally to longing for his kiss.

The emotional tide left her exhausted and bewildered. After she tidied the kitchen, she entered the girls' bedroom and took down her hair. Sitting before the mirror, she used Lucy's brush for the requisite one hundred strokes before she braided her hair for sleeping.

Today's events offered much to think about and ponder. But her mind stuck on what was surely the least important item of all. Her growing cognizance of Sam as a virile, exciting man.

In a few short weeks Angie had changed from an adult woman who never thought of sexuality at all into an adolescent whose mind and body were awakening into an intense awareness of deep restless longings and previously unknown desires.

Not a day passed that she didn't recall every sensation of Sam's kiss, reliving that moment until her face burned and her heart pounded.

Everything he did fascinated her. From the shaving ritual in the morning to the way he held his knife and fork. She found it intensely interesting that he flipped his hammer before he dropped it through the loop on his denims. And that he was right-handed but drank beer and coffee with his left hand. He always sat closest to the aisle in their Sunday pew.

The deep baritone of his voice could send shivers down her spine. Sometimes he looked at her in a certain way and her mouth went dry. The night before last, she'd seen him standing in the back yard smoking a cigar, hip-shot, preoccupied, his face bronzed by a setting sun, and her hands had trembled.

Ten years ago Angie had been too young, too innocent of the world to understand why she went weak and shaky inside when Sam stood close. And then came the lonely years during which she had shut a door between herself and any hint of sexual awareness. Now that door was edging open.

Disturbed, she threw down the hairbrush and covered her face with her hands. She absolutely did not want to respond to Sam as a man. She wanted a divorce.

Desperate to push the memory of his naked chest out of her mind, she tried to think about Peter De Groot. Peter, whom she admired and respected. Her friend, Peter. Peter, her future. Peter was the man who would unveil for her the mysterious acts between men and women. It was Peter who would eventually satisfy her strange new longings.

But it was Sam Holland who slept in the bed she had vacated this morning. Sam, who would not leave her thoughts no matter how hard she tried to shove him away. Sam, whose mouth and hands inflamed her dreams.

Near dawn Sam awoke and couldn't fall back asleep. Mounding the pillows behind him, he sat in the darkness, surrounded by Angie's scent. Eventually he closed his mind to arousing thoughts and concentrated on the fight with Herb Govenor.

He'd gone to the Miners' Bar intending to pound Govenor into pulp and he'd done his damnedest to carry through. There was satisfaction in that.

But whatever damage he'd inflicted wouldn't change

anything. Anyone who hired Sam was in danger of watching his new house go up in flames.

Frowning, he edged toward the only conclusion possible. No man with a conscience would expose his clients to the possibility, maybe the probability, of financial loss.

Next week, after he handed Reverend Dryfus the key to his new home, Sam Holland would be out of business.

Which meant that Govenor had accomplished what he set out to do: deprive Sam of his livelihood.

Brooding, he got out of bed and stood before the window, watching the lights wink out along Bennet Street as the sky turned pale and opalescent. And he asked himself if Herb Govenor would burn down a schoolhouse. Despite his opinion of the Govenors, he didn't think Herb was the kind of man who would punish children to get what he wanted. But then, he would have said that Herb wasn't the kind of man to burn down a preacher's house either.

When the sky had brightened to a milky blue, he entered the kitchen, intending to start the coffee and heat water for shaving. But first, he paused outside the door of his daughters' bedroom.

Even from here he imagined he could smell the same seductive rosy scent that he'd inhaled on Angie's pillow. He pictured her sleeping, curled on her side, her lips slightly parted, her lashes long on her cheeks. And his stomach tightened.

Angie had played no role in his life for so long that he'd naively assumed his indifference would continue with her living in his house. But seeing her every day in all her moods and all her womanly ways, watching her step into his life and share the burdens he was accustomed to carrying alone . . . being exposed to her dimpled beauty and his growing need for her was changing something deep inside him.

He wanted her to respect him. He wanted her to admire him.

He wanted her.

Chapter 12

The Wednesday mending circle helped Angie decide between the two ball gowns she'd brought from Chicago. After an hour of heated discussion and vacillation, the satin-and-brocade was chosen over the faille-and-velvet.

Abby Mueller carefully ironed the lace ruffles that flared over puffed sleeves and repeated in a lacy outline framing a deeply pointed waist, while Tilly Morgan worked at the kitchen table, creating a hair ornament out of bits and scraps.

"Eardrops, but nothing at the neck," Molly advised.

Dorothy Church nodded. "Bare throats are fashionable. Bracelets are good though."

"Bracelets look so silly worn over long evening gloves, don't you agree?" Frowning, Tilly tried to choose among the sprays of rosebuds she'd placed in a row for comparison.

Stepping back, Molly eyed Angie's hair. "You tuck the hand and fingers of the glove inside the wrist, as you would for dinner, then shake the bracelet down," she explained absently.

Abby stopped ironing. "Molly Johnson! How would you know about ball gloves and formal dining?"

Molly laughed. "I know more tidbits of useless information than anyone you've met."

"But you've obviously been to balls and social suppers," Abby said to Angie. "Is Molly correct?"

"I believe she is. Molly, stop looking at me like that. I don't want some outlandish hairstyle. Just a simple upsweep."

Bending to rummage in the trunk she had dragged into the kitchen, Angie located slippers, a bag to match the white satin-and-brocade, and a lacy white evening fan.

Molly snapped open the fan and peeked over the top. "Remember when ladies used to send gentlemen messages through the secret language of the fan? Here's the come-hither look."

"My mama was too busy raising eight children to teach me any language of the fan," Tilly said, rolling her eyes.

Dorothy smiled. "Your come-hither look isn't too subtle, Molly. Give me the fan. Now watch. You're supposed to appear disinterested and let the fan speak for you."

They all burst into laughter. Shaking her head, Abby exchanged the cool iron for a hot one. "You don't look indifferent, Dorothy, you look madder than a wet cat. Maybe that fan says come-hither, but you look like you'd stomp any man who dared try."

While Molly brushed out her hair, Angie listened and enjoyed the easy banter of the women in her kitchen. It touched her that they wanted to share in the preparations and the excitement of the hotel's grand opening. And there was not a hint of envy or resentment that Angie would attend, but they would not.

Right at this moment, she decided there was no place on Earth she would rather be than here in her crowded kitchen with these women and the smell of coffee and the sound of laughter and the warmth of the afternoon sunshine falling through the back door.

"If you'll pin up the back of her hair," Dorothy said to Molly, "I'll crimp her bangs. As soon as the iron is hot."

Abby glanced up from pressing Angie's gown. "Did I see Winnie Govenor coming out of here not long ago? Are the Govenors in town for the grand opening?"

"Good heavens." Tilly looked up from the table. "You have to be the only person who didn't hear about Sam Holland and Herb Govenor getting into it over at—" Abruptly she stopped speaking and turned a stricken look toward Angie.

Angie drew a breath and folded her hands in her lap. "There was a fight." To her relief no one inquired as to the cause. No one spoke at all until Molly stepped into the silence.

"Angie's a grown woman. She isn't going to swoon at the mention of the Govenors." Impatient hands tugged at Angie's hair. "Everyone here knows what's going on. And everyone here dislikes the Govenors because of it. But if you ask me, Winnie Govenor isn't all that bad. She's just cold and distant and misguided."

"Other than that, she's a swell person," Tilly murmured sarcastically. A splendid creation, fashioned from rosebuds, dried leaves, and a broken strand of pearls, was taking shape beneath her nimble fingers.

Dorothy wet a finger and tested the crimping iron to see if it was hot. "I think Mrs. Govenor would like to be more social and pleasant. She just doesn't know how."

"I don't know why you'd say anything nice about her after the way she treated . . ." Abby swung a look toward Angie, who pretended to be lost in private reverie. "She wouldn't visit her daughter even when Laura was dying."

"In fairness," Molly said briskly, "none of us believed

Laura was dying until very close to the end. It's possible the Govenors weren't aware how grave the situation was."

Everyone looked at Angie and she abandoned the silly pretense that she wasn't avidly listening. "I know about Laura," she said, stating the obvious. She cleared her throat. "Her name is going to arise on occasion. Please don't feel awkward on my account." The words sounded stiff even to her ears.

"It's hard not to, now that we know Laura was living with your husband," Dorothy said tartly.

"Now just hush," Molly said in a sharp tone. "We liked Laura, so let's remember who she was, not what she did. And the same goes for Sam." She frowned at the top of Angie's head. "We don't have to judge and we don't have to take sides."

"Do you hate Laura?" Abby asked curiously.

"I thought I did," Angie admitted after a moment. "But I'm not so sure anymore." How could she hate a woman whose children hugged her before they went to sleep? Even Lucy had given her a quick clumsy hug last night.

As if on cue, Lucy and Daisy ran in the back door, bringing the scent of fresh air and licorice sticks. Immediately the women stopped talking, but the girls didn't notice. They bounced around the kitchen, waving Angie's fan, pulling on her long gloves, holding her pearl eardrops to their ears.

"When do I have to wear a corset?" Lucy asked, fascinated by Angie's heavily boned evening corset.

"I believe thirteen is the usual age," Tilly answered.

"Well . . . that depends," Abby said with a discreet cough.

Daisy touched the ribbon hemming Angie's corset. "Mabel Hooser wears a corset and she's only eight."

Abby nodded. "My point exactly. Poor little Mabel already needs a corset." She sighed.

"Will Gramma and Grampa be at the party?" Daisy asked Angie.

"I suppose so, but I don't know for certain." The possibility of running into the Govenors horrified her.

"I think you and Gramma will be the prettiest ladies at the party," Daisy said, leaning close to inspect the hairdo Molly and Dorothy were arranging.

The comment gave Angie pause and surprised her. Because the girls had seemed eager to escape Winnie Govenor's company, Angie had assumed they disliked their grandmother. But suddenly she saw another possibility. Maybe they'd just been tired of sitting in school all day and had wanted to play outside, where they could run and skip and work off the day's energy.

Lucy met Angie's uncertain frown. "Miss Lily is having a ball tonight, too. She ordered a gown from Paris especially for her party. I wish we could see her in it."

"How on Earth do you learn about such things?"

Lucy shrugged. "Germaine Jablonski heard about the gown from her second cousin, who heard it from someone who knows the daughter of Miss Lily's second cook."

"I don't think your grandmother would approve of this talk about Miss Lily," Angie said, watching both girls carefully.

They laughed. "Gramma doesn't approve of anything." Daisy smiled with obvious affection. "That's the way she is."

"She wants us to be ladies." Lucy raised an imaginary cup and extended her little finger, managing to look graceful and ridiculous at the same moment. "Gramma said it's easier to learn the rules of etiquette at our age than later when we're grown."

Lucy's simple statement revealed a crack in Winnie Govenor's armor. The woman who had sold pies out of her back door had not made an easy transition to wealth or to the tangle of etiquette that accompanied social elevation.

"We don't mind. Gramma corrects us because she loves us," Daisy said confidently. Not a hint of doubt shadowed her smile.

"She wants it to be easier for us than it was for her," Lucy added. The fascinated silence of the women in the kitchen clearly puzzled her.

Studying a point in space, Angie slowly nodded. She had made a very wrong assumption. Lucy and Daisy did not dislike their grandmother. They didn't resent Winnie Govenor's reprimands, and they believed their grand-mother loved them.

None of the women spoke after the girls ran outside again.

Finally Tilly went to the door and leaned out to make sure the girls weren't eavesdropping. "It sounds like Winnie makes a better grandmother than a mother."

Dorothy Church blew on the smoking crimping iron. "Maybe she wants a second chance. She can't change the estrangement between herself and Laura, but maybe she hopes to correct her mistakes with Laura's children."

Molly made a snorting sound. "If Winnie really wanted to do right by those girls, then Daisy wouldn't be lurching around here like a drunken miner. Her foot would have been straightened years ago."

Angie was glad someone shared her opinion about Winnie Govenor.

Tilly stood at the door and smiled back into the kitchen.

"You know, I wish I could see Miss Lily's Paris gown, too."

And suddenly they were laughing and chattering again and everything was all right.

But underneath the banter and the bustle of preparation, Angie's thoughts circled around a disturbing new way of looking at things. She had believed the Govenors wanted Lucy and Daisy only to punish Sam for ruining their daughter. But maybe, in their own strange way, the Govenors truly cared about their granddaughters. Lucy and Daisy thought so. And children had a gift for spotting hypocrisy and deceit.

Nothing would change her opinion that Lucy and Daisy belonged with their father. But the situation had seemed more clear cut when the Govenors could be condemned as black-hearted villains on every level. Now a troubling gray area had appeared.

Everything was ready. Angie's cape lay folded over the back of a kitchen chair. She'd packed her evening bag with a fresh handkerchief, a small bottle of eau de cologne, and a puff to blot the shine from her nose and forehead after the dancing began. Her satin gown glowed in the lamplight. She had checked the mirror a dozen times to admire her fashionably crimped bangs and the single tease of a curl at the back of her neck. Tilly's lovely hair ornament was well anchored at the crown of her head and completed her ensemble to perfection.

Wetting her lips in nervous anticipation, Angie stood in the center of the kitchen, afraid to sit lest she crush her gown, afraid to touch anything lest she soil her gloves. Her gaze flew to the schoolhouse clock over the table just as Sam came in the back door, followed by the girls.

Angie's breath caught in the back of her throat, and

her heart stopped. Sam wore a dark cutaway over a silver-shot waistcoat. His white shirt was one of the new pleated soft shirts, but the high butterfly collar was starched and as stiff as it should be. His dark hair was brushed to a glossy sheen, and he'd tied it back with a length of black ribbon.

Stunned, Angie spread her hands. "You look . . ." Handsome didn't begin to describe his appearance tonight. He might have stepped from the pages of a gentlemen's magazine. Except for the black eye, of course. Astonishingly, Sam appeared as comfortable and at ease in formal wear as he did in his denims and flannels.

He smiled but his gaze narrowed in intensity as he slowly scanned her gown, letting his interest linger at her small cinched waist, and again at the curve of breasts swelling above her neckline. When her cheeks started to burn and she thought her nerves would fly apart, he finally met her eyes.

"You look beautiful," he said in a low, gruff voice.

Suddenly they were shy with each other, strangers again. If the girls hadn't been present as a buffer, neither would have found anything to say.

Lucy and Daisy gazed back and forth between them, eyes wide with awe and admiration.

"You don't look like you," Lucy said to Sam.

Laughing, he knelt in front of her. "Because of the black eye or because of the fancy rig I'm wearing?"

"I don't know." Puckering her lips, Lucy glanced at Angie. "And Angie looks like a fairy princess."

Daisy ran her fingertips lightly across Angie's satin skirt. "When I grow up, I want a dress just like this one." She lifted shining gray eyes. "You're as beautiful as Miss Lily tonight!"

"Now that's high praise indeed." Angie could never

have imagined that she would be pleased by a favorable comparison to a sporting lady.

Molly came up the back steps, smiling broadly. "My, my, don't you two make a picture!" She placed a hand on top of Lucy's and Daisy's heads and turned them toward the door. "Don't forget to bring me a souvenir. And we'll be here first thing in the morning to hear all the details."

"Thank you for keeping the girls."

"It's my pleasure, Sam. You know that. If I'd had children, I'd have wanted girls as smart and sassy as these two imps."

The girls looked back. "I wish we could go, too," Lucy said wistfully. Something in her expression flickered and changed, and Angie predicted that she would be more interested the next time clothing and fashion were topics of discussion.

Angie tilted her head and her brow puckered. She had a feeling she had just witnessed a landmark step on the journey to womanhood. Oddly, her first thought was for Laura. It should have been Laura whose beauty and finery raised longing in her daughter's heart. And Laura should have been the one to observe and recognize this significant moment.

"There are many balls and late suppers ahead for you," Angie promised softly. "Your time will come."

"Me, too," Daisy said brightly. "After my operation."

"Yes. You, too." Angie did not let her gaze drop to Daisy's twisted foot.

Sam lifted her evening cape from the back of the chair and dropped it lightly around her shoulders. "Well, Mrs. Holland. Now that we have universal approval, shall we go?" He extended his arm and Angie hesitated then wrapped her glove around his sleeve.

"If there's cake, please bring us some," Daisy called before Molly closed the back door.

They looked at each other and laughed, then Sam touched his fingertips to her cheek. "This is your first grown-up party, isn't it?"

"You always surprise me," she whispered, her throat suddenly tight and hot. "This will be the only formal event I've attended without my father as escort and chaperon. So, yes, I suppose you could say that tonight is my first grown-up party."

"I thought so." Leading her forward, he opened the front door and stepped back with a broad smile.

"Sam!" Her hands flew to her mouth and her eyes widened. "Is that a carriage? For us?" The liveried driver saw her step forward and touched his fingers to his cap. "But . . ." she turned back to Sam. "Can we afford a carriage? And we're only going six blocks." She twisted her hands together. "This really isn't sensible. Renting a carriage must be outrageously expensive."

He placed a finger across her lips. "Listen to me. I bartered a day's work for this finery." He touched his cutaway. "But Angie, an occasional extravagance like the carriage is as necessary as paying bills and saving. It's the occasional extravagance that makes life worth living. Without an extravagance here and there along the way, life is just a drudgery. And sometimes an event is special enough that it will become a memory. I want the memory of your first real party to be everything it can be. You've waited a long time for tonight."

"Oh Sam." She looked up, blinking hard and searching his eyes. "You told me once that you don't often see things from another person's viewpoint. That isn't true." Oh heavens. She was going to embarrass herself by getting teary. Why was it that she never cried when the sky fell on her but usually turned weepy over a compliment or a kindness?

Sam raised an eyebrow when he saw the moisture glistening behind her lashes. "Tears? That's not what I had in mind for tonight. This reminds me. I have a question of the utmost importance that requires an immediate answer."

"What is it?" she asked, fumbling in her bag for her handkerchief.

He looked from side to side, up and down the street, then leaned in to whisper, his breath warm in her ear, "Do you think anyone will suspect that I'm wearing pink underwear?"

"What?" Her head jerked up and the threat of tears vanished in a burst of helpless laughter.

"Because if they do, my manhood will never recover from such a blow." Taking her arm, he led her out the door and toward the carriage. "I'll have to leave the county in disgrace."

"Sam Holland, sometimes you are just the most amazing—" He handed her into the carriage and swung into the seat beside her.

"You're evading the question." A grin hovered at his lips. His eyes sparkled in the twilight.

He had turned her mood around, and Angie decided he was right. This was not the time to worry about the evening's expense. What was done was done. And Angie had dreamed of a night like tonight for so many years, had tried to imagine a party she could attend on the arm of a man who was not a relative, had longed for the time when no one would gaze at her with pity as they had when she left a party early with her parents.

She wanted tonight to be everything she had imagined so many times. And Sam, she thought with a strange ache in her heart, wanted to give her an evening to remember.

Snapping open her fan, she drew a breath and followed his lead. Peeking over the top of the fan, she fluttered her eyelashes in a parody of bottomless pity.

"Oh my dear Mr. Holland. I'm afraid I have the most terrible news."

He took her gloved hand in his and pressed her fingers. "And what would this terrible news be, Mrs. Holland?"

"It's so dreadful, so distressing that I can hardly bring myself to tell you."

"Will I have to leave the county?"

She nodded, eyes sparkling above the lace edge of her fan. "You'd better go home at once and start packing, because your pink underwear spent an afternoon on the clothesline flapping in the breeze for all the neighbors to see."

"I'm destroyed." He buried his face in his hands. "I'll be a laughingstock. Men will sneer when I pass. Women will snicker."

They were both laughing when Sam handed her out of the carriage and onto a red carpet that ran from the street to the frosted glass doors of the new hotel. Pausing a moment, Sam tucked her arm in his and gazed into her eyes before leading her forward. Anyone watching would have assumed they were lovers.

Enormous gilt-framed mirrors, lit by immense crystal chandeliers, reflected gleaming cherry wood and columns and floors of polished marble. Fountains of greenery filled every niche; magnificent bouquets perfumed the air.

Angie and Sam passed through the receiving line. They congratulated Stratton Miles, the hotel's owner, and murmured a word to his flushed, jewel-bedecked wife. Then someone took Angie's cape, and they were free to join the crush of people thronging every room off the shining lobby.

"Oh my," Angie breathed, her eyes bright.

A string quartet played near the grand staircase, and music from a larger ensemble could be heard wafting from the ballroom.

"Champagne?" Sam asked, lifting two flutes from the tray of a passing waiter.

"Champagne!" Almost giddy with a surfeit of sensation, Angie tasted the champagne, then wrinkled her nose and laughed at the tickle of bubbles in her mouth.

What a strange and wonderful world it was. A few days ago she had been down on her knees bent over a washboard scrubbing Sam's underwear, and now here she was surrounded by silks and satins and flashing earrings and stickpins, and sipping champagne while a handsome and exciting man with an interesting black eye smiled down at her.

"Shall we tour the premises?" Sam inquired, extending his arm. "I'm told the upstairs gallery has paintings all the way from Europe."

"While we're touring, keep an eye out for things we can take back as souvenirs for Molly and the girls."

They were interrupted a dozen times on the way to the grand staircase. Sam introduced her to wealthy mine owners, to powerful men who operated far-flung syndicates, to the mayor of Willow Creek, and to the governor of Colorado. It was almost a relief when he introduced her to Marsh Collins, his lawyer and an ordinary citizen.

After Collins bowed over Angie's gloved hand, Sam raised a suspicious eyebrow. "How much is this encounter going to cost me?"

Collins smiled. "Well, we do have one small item of business."

"Which is?"

"Whittier's attorney says Whittier won't sue if you agree to rebuild his house at no charge."

Sam swore and turned aside to stare across the lobby. "Tell him to sue. The fire was not my doing, and damned if I'll go into debt for something that wasn't my fault."

Collins nodded and Angie caught a whiff of the pomade slicking back his hair. "The good news is that the union is not going to sue you."

"Excellent!"

"And so far Herb Govenor isn't clamoring to have you arrested for assault and battery, and so far we haven't heard from his attorneys." Marsh Collins smiled at Angie. "Surely this charming lady isn't the wife you intend to divorce?"

Pink flooded Angie's cheeks and throat, and she covered the lower part of her face with her fan.

"Marsh, you ass. This is not the time to discuss a divorce."

Collins's eyebrows rose. "Your plans have changed?"

Anger stretched Sam's jacket across his shoulders. "As I told you before, the divorce won't happen until after Daisy's surgery." He took Angie's arm and led her to the stairs. "You wanted to know who Marsh Collins is? He's a lawyer with no office and no sense of timing." At the landing, he placed his hands on her shoulders and turned her to face him. "Is talk about lawsuits and divorce going to spoil our evening?"

Being reminded that she shared this special night with a husband she wanted to be rid of certainly did nothing to elevate her spirits. But Marsh Collins had only been tactless. Angie hadn't sensed any harmful intent.

"No," she said in a determined voice. "Nothing is going to spoil this evening." She lifted her chin and made her fingers relax on Sam's sleeve. "Let's view those European pictures."

They rolled their eyes over some of the paintings, nudged each other while they stood before one by Monet. Most of the paintings impressed them as blurry and a waste of Stratton Miles's money.

It delighted Angie and restored her good humor to discover that she and Sam disliked the same smudgy paintings and admired the same realistic portraits. They would never purchase artwork for a shared home, but it pleased her to know they would have agreed on what to buy.

Feeling a bit superior and pleased with themselves, they descended the staircase, vaguely aware that they made a handsome couple and pleased by that, too.

"Would you care to dance, Mrs. Holland?" Earlier, Sam had filled her dance card, writing his name beside every set.

"It would be a pleasure, Mr. Holland. But first I'd like to freshen my appearance." She leaned to his ear. "I'm dying to see if the powder room is as ornate as everything else."

Entering the powder room was like stepping into a woman's most lavish fantasy. The carpet, wall hangings, upholstered chairs, little footstools, and towels were all in shades of rose ranging from a deep rich maroon to the most delicate pale pink silk. Gilt-edged mirrors reflected lamplight positioned to be the most flattering to a lady. A half dozen rose-clad attendants saw to the ladies' needs, providing hairpins here, stitching up a fallen hem there, scurrying to fetch this or that.

Smiling and nodding to the ladies resting their feet in the luxurious parlor area, Angie glided toward an arch leading to the hand-painted sinks that someone had told her were imported from Italy.

She was marveling at the wallcovering, wondering if it was silk or paper painted to look like silk, when she almost collided with Winnie Govenor.

Tonight Winnie wore satin and tulle in a richly gleaming gray that complemented her eyes and hair. Diamonds glittered at her ears and wrist, and an arrangement of gray pearls ornamented her hair. She was as imposing and coldly distant as an ice queen.

One glance told Angie that Winnie was about to serve up a crushing humiliation by cutting her dead before a roomful of watching women. Her face flamed scarlet and her heart sank.

Chapter 13

While Angie stood paralyzed, wide-eyed with dread, Winnie's mouth thinned into an expression of contempt. She pulled her skirts to one side as if brushing Angie's gown would soil or contaminate her. Then she swept past, eyes forward, icily aloof.

A dozen women inhaled sharply, creating a hissing sound. One seldom witnessed a deliberate snub, not in the tight-knit mining district. The incident would be repeated and dissected at length over the next several days.

Shock tingled along Angie's spine. Never in her life had she been cut. Fire burned in her cheeks and she could hear her pulse thundering in her ears. The utter humiliation of being publicly insulted made her shrivel inside, made her wish the floor would open and swallow her. When she darted a quick glance toward the other women, most averted their eyes, but two or three gazed back with pity and embarrassment.

The pity made her wild inside. She had to do something or explode.

Lifting her skirts, she strode toward the exit, catching Winnie Govenor's arm as she reached for the latch.

"Mrs. Govenor, it's Angie Holland. I don't think you recognized me." Anger flashed in her dark eyes, but she kept her voice bright and pleasant as she pretended to misunderstand. "I'm not surprised. I looked quite different when we had tea together."

Winnie directed a cold gaze toward Angie's fingers on her glove. "Remove your hand."

"In case we don't have an opportunity to chat later, I wonder if you intend to visit your granddaughters before you and Mr. Govenor return to Colorado Springs." Behind her, the parlor was so silent that Angie could hear the music outside the door. "If I know when you wish to see the girls, I can have them ready and waiting. I know how much they enjoy spending time with their grandparents."

With those words, she reminded everyone present that she was caring for Winnie's granddaughters, and she made Winnie Govenor appear small and petty. Winnie understood at once. Now it was her turn to flush crimson with embarrassment.

"We intend to take our granddaughters to lunch on Saturday," she said, her voice trembling with anger.

"I'll see that the girls are ready and dressed appropriately."

Both women nodded, then Winnie left the parlor and Angie passed through a wall of silence to enter the water closet. When she was certain she was alone, she pressed her fingertips to her forehead and let her shoulders slump.

There had been no winner in her encounter with Winnie Govenor. Each had been publicly embarrassed. On the other hand, it must have shocked the daylights out of Winnie when Angie chased after her. A deep sigh expanded her chest. Her mother would have said such an unseemly response was due to the Italian half of her heritage. And maybe it was. The Italian side of her temperament prompted her to do things that the English side later regretted.

Sam was waiting when she emerged from the powder room, a frown drawing his handsome face. "Winnie Govenor came out of there a minute ago looking as if she could spit nails. What happened?" A humorless smile curved his lips after he'd heard the story. "We've spoken to Marsh Collins and we've faced down the Govenors. Now the worst is behind us and we can enjoy ourselves."

Gratefully, she accepted his arm and let him escort her toward the ballroom. "You had a word with Herb Govenor?"

"If I'd gotten close enough to have a word with Herb Govenor, there would have been another fight." Sam's eyes glittered. "We exchanged glares from a distance. I'm happy to say he looks as bad as I do."

If Sam believed he looked bad, then he was oblivious to the sidelong glances directed his way by the women they passed. There was something exotic about a tall, formally dressed man with a black eye and long shining hair tied at his neck. Angie considered calling Sam's attention to the interest he garnered from the ladies—then decided against it.

The ballroom blazed with mirrors and lights. Tall French doors had been thrown open to the cool evening breeze. Graceful couples circled the room to the sweetness of a lilting waltz, the ladies' skirts swirling, diamonds flashing beneath the chandeliers.

"Oh Sam. This is the grandest party I've ever attended!"

His dark eyebrows rose. "I would have said you had attended dozens of affairs as grand as this one."

"Sam, my father wasn't a robber baron. He was a bricklayer. My parents and I attended the masons' ball and various fund-raising soirees; there were social evenings at the homes of friends, musical events or lectures hosted by my mother's club ladies. But never anything as lavish or opulent as this." To underscore her point, she added softly, "Despite what you insist on thinking, I grew up comfortably but in an ordinary household with ordinary parents."

"It didn't look that way to me," he said, gazing down into her eyes. "You were a beautiful princess living in a brick palace. One day I heard you playing the piano. And I promised myself that someday I would have a palace and a piano."

"And a beautiful princess?" she whispered.

His eyes searched hers. "Do you miss having a piano?"

"Sometimes. Pounding on piano keys is a better way to soothe a temper than chasing someone down the street throwing things at him."

Sam laughed and offered his arm. "Enough of the past. Shall we explore the terrace?"

"If you like. But aren't we going to dance?" The musicians were superb. Angie turned a longing gaze to the ballroom floor and the couples whirling in a kaleidoscope of music, color, and movement.

"I have a confession to make." Sam pressed her arm to his chest as they skirted the floor. "I'm a terrible dancer. I'd only embarrass you."

"But you filled my dance card!"

"I didn't want you to dance with anyone else." He gave her a lopsided grin before he stopped a waiter serving champagne. "I know. That was unforgivably selfish."

Carrying flutes of champagne, they strolled through the French doors onto a stone terrace romantically lit by strings of Chinese lanterns. The perfume of carnations and dianthus wafted from dozens of pottery urns, and ornately carved benches invited one to sit and enjoy the music and a velvety evening sky.

Angie smiled over the rim of the champagne flute. "So we've come to a dance with no intention of dancing?"

"We're going to dance," he said, taking her champagne glass and his and placing them on one of the benches. "But not in front of a roomful of people."

"I have a feeling you're being modest. You're probably a wonderful dancer," she said as he slipped his arm around her waist and took her hand in his.

He paused, waited a beat, then frowned in concentration and stepped forward. "*One* two three, *one* two three, *one* two three."

Angie's father had excelled at dancing, and so did Peter De Groot. Both men moved from set to set with seemingly effortless grace. In fact, it had been during a waltz that Angie first suspected that Peter viewed her as more than a friend. She had seen something in his gaze that made her suddenly and acutely aware of his arm around her waist and his hand holding hers.

She wanted that tingly awareness with Sam. In a perfect world they would have executed a flawless waltz across the flower-scented terrace, gazing dreamily into each other's eyes, lost in a private reverie of enchantment. Her cheeks would flush with the intimacy of his touch; his gaze would soften with tenderness as he held her in his arms.

"*One* two three, *one* two three."

"Sam, wait. Your one-two-three isn't lining up with the music's one-two-three."

They stopped moving and he tilted his head to scowl at the stars. "Why don't they play a polka? No one cares if a man misses a step during a polka."

He hadn't been modest. He was truly an awful dancer. "Let's begin again," Angie suggested. They adjusted their grips on shoulder and waist. "All right, *one* two three, *one* two three."

Sam trod hard on the toe of her slipper, which made her stumble and groan. Apologies spilled from his lips.

"It's all right, no harm done," Angie lied, wiggling her toes inside her slipper. Very likely none of her toes were broken, but they hurt. "Let's try one more time."

They paused for a beat then set out again. This time Angie tripped on the rough stones of the terrace floor. If Sam hadn't caught her to his chest she would have toppled backward and fallen flat.

"Damn it, I'm just not good at this."

Put a hammer in his hand and Sam could build anything. Give him a pick and shovel and he could dig a mine halfway to China. He could fight, he could cook, he knew how to tickle little girls and make them laugh. He could kiss a woman and make her knees melt. But when it came to dancing, he was hopeless.

There was something charming about discovering a confident man's weakness. Something appealing about his rare helplessness.

Angie didn't have time to explore these thoughts as she was clasped against Sam's body, her heart beating against his chest, her breath mingling with his. The moment might have been romantic except her toes throbbed painfully and she was lopsided, still trying to find her footing on the rough stone floor. The clumsy results of their blundering attempt to waltz struck her as funny and she giggled, then laughed.

Sam set her firmly on her feet then stepped back and raised an eyebrow over his black eye. "Are you laughing at me?"

"Yes!" And she couldn't stop. *One* two three, *one* two

three. His grim count rang in her mind, sounding hilarious. "You were right. You're absolutely the worst dancer that I ever—"

"Well, here's something I am good at."

Catching her by the waist, he swung her into his body and his mouth came down hard on hers.

She tasted champagne and heat. She was less innocent than she'd been the last time he kissed her. Her lips parted and she leaned into the solid power of his muscled chest and tight thighs. Her hands slid up his chest and around his neck, and she gave herself to the sensations his lips and tongue aroused in her.

Kissing Sam was like . . . like being electrified by a golden tingle that tightened her scalp and raced through her body, awakening every nerve ending. Time slowed, allowing her an acute awareness of each small adjustment, every tiny nibble and taste. His kiss made her aware of her own body in a way she had never experienced before. She felt the breathless rise and fall of her breasts, felt a moist weakness spread between her thighs. His kiss created an odd sense of urgency that made her crave something more.

They broke apart only when a man cleared his throat followed by a woman's soft laugh. Blushing furiously, Angie turned her face aside and brushed at her skirts. Ridiculously, she felt as if they'd been caught doing something shameful and wrong.

When she slid a look toward Sam, he was grinning and his blue eyes twinkled in the light of the Chinese lanterns. And then they were both laughing helplessly, leaning on each other, laughing and wiping their eyes. They had jumped apart like illicit lovers caught in the most damning of guilty circumstances. But the couple who interrupted them would only have seen a man stealing a kiss beneath the starry skies.

But Sam was right. He was very, very good at kissing.

So good that the party lost focus and all Angie could think about was the man by her side. They toured the rest of the hotel but afterward all she could remember was the light from the chandeliers sliding through Sam's hair. She could scarcely recall what they dined on at the midnight supper, but she remembered Sam's sure hands on the silverware. She remembered the shape of his lips and the way he couldn't seem to look away from her. It was as if she and Sam inhabited a private space that excluded all others. The musicians played for them alone, the midnight banquet was only for them. The spell wasn't broken until dessert appeared before them.

"Stop," Angie said, returning to reality with a jolt. "Sam, don't eat that."

Puzzled, he glanced down at his fork hovering above a wedge of fudge cake. "Why not?"

"Daisy."

"Daisy?"

"We promised we'd bring her cake if cake was served." But how would they get it home?

"We promised?"

Angie leaned to his ear and cupped a hand around her mouth. "We have to steal our napkins." Sam drew back to stare at her, but she pulled him close again. "Wrap your piece of cake in your napkin for Lucy. I'll wrap mine for Daisy."

"Angelina. Exactly how much champagne have you drunk?"

"A lot," she said after considering the question. She gazed into his eyes and decided she had never seen a bluer blue. "I'll be your lookout." The dining room was crowded with chattering guests, but she didn't think anyone was watching them. "Quick. Put your plate in your lap and wrap the cake in your napkin. I'll do mine now, too."

Sam glanced around the room, then sighed and put his cake plate in his lap. But that was as far as he went. Angie had to wrap both pieces of cake and hide them in her bag. She put their empty plates back on the table and reached for her champagne glass.

"So far, so good."

"Maybe you've had enough champagne."

"Now then. See the favors?" Before each place setting was a three-inch-tall sculpture of the hotel's facade, molded out of colored sugar. "We need four of those. Our two and two more."

"Angie . . ."

"For Molly, Tilly, Abby, and Dorothy." She gave him a conspiratorial wink and leaned into his ear again. "We'll each have to steal our neighbor's favor."

"And then what? We steal the silver and a plate or two?"

"Just the cake and the favors. When Mrs. Finn is talking to her husband, snatch her favor. Or wait. Maybe all we have to do is ask." To test the idea, she turned to the man on her right and tapped his arm with her fan. When he shifted to look at her, she gave him a dazzling dimpled smile. "I'd like to have your favor please. The little sugar hotel front? I need it, so please give it to me."

The man blinked, then his eyebrows lifted and he glanced beyond her at Sam. But he gave Angie his favor. She thanked him then turned her back and added the favor to the two in her bulging bag. "You see?" Now she gave Sam the dazzling dimpled smile.

He stared, then laughed and pushed back from the

table. "My dear Mrs. Holland, I think it's time we got you home and away from waiters pouring champagne."

"No, no. Not yet." Distress widened her eyes. "We need one more favor!"

Sam opened his hand below the table level and smiled.

"You got it! Excellent." She tucked the fourth favor into her bag then let him help her to her feet. "We must find our host and hostess and thank them for a lovely evening."

Sam cupped her elbow and led her to the cloakroom off the lobby. "We'll send a note." He dropped her evening cape over her shoulders. "I'm glad I didn't keep the carriage. Walking home in the fresh air will do us both good."

Before they left, Angie took a last admiring look at the hotel lobby. "It's truly magnificent! I don't want to forget a single detail."

Sam studied her shining eyes and flushed cheeks. Tonight she had been incandescent, luminous. Radiant with happiness, she'd drawn every eye. Even trying her best to appear formally serene and dignified, Angie projected a charming exuberance. She couldn't stay still. She clapped her gloves together when something pleased or amazed her. She tapped her foot to the music and her shoulders swayed slightly. Her dimples flashed and winked.

Taking her arm, he led her outside and assisted her with the steep climb to Carr Street, listening as she asked if he had seen this or overheard that. Did he think the flower vases were Chinese porcelain as someone had said? Was it true there was a penthouse suite on the top floor? What color, exactly, were the marble tiles in the lobby, and how many musicians had been on the ballroom dais?

She threw out her arms and spun in a circle while he opened the front door. "Oh Sam! It was a wonderful evening!"

"I still hear bubbles in your voice." Laughing, he went inside and lit the lamp on the kitchen table, then grinned when she danced inside, her arms lifted to an imaginary partner. For the first time in his life, Sam wished he could dance. When she twirled past him, he caught her cape from her shoulders and dropped it across the back of a chair. On her next pass, she tossed him her bag and he set it on the table.

"I think I'll make you some coffee."

"I don't want this evening to end," she said, standing in the center of the kitchen, her eyes closed, swaying to remembered music. A smile played around her lips. Lamplight glowed golden on the swell of her breasts above her neckline.

There was no creature on earth as beautiful as a happy woman. She took his breath away. And when she opened her eyes and smiled at him, his arousal was immediate and powerful.

"Kiss me again, Sam," she said in a husky voice that resonated through his body.

He placed his hands on her shoulders, crushing the poofy little sleeves of her gown. "I don't want to take advantage of you, Angie," he said gruffly, trying to ignore his rampant desire. "We've both had a lot of champagne. It would be easy to do something that we'll regret in the morning."

Stepping close, she raised her arms and reached around his neck to open the ribbon tying back his hair. The scent of powder and rose water enveloped his senses and a low groan rumbled in his throat. His hands dropped to her waist and slid lower, and he pressed her to him, feeling the heat and length of her thighs beneath the layers of skirts and petticoats.

She raised her face and gazed at him with black eyes that became seductive when she looked at his mouth, and Sam knew without a doubt where a kiss would take them.

Staring into her eyes, he recognized the moment when she, too, understood that another kiss would be a beginning. A flame had ignited on the hotel terrace when he kissed her and every glance since, every touch, every smile, every small movement had wound the tension a little tighter, had made the fire a little hotter, and had swept them closer to this moment of decision.

She wound her fingers through his loose hair. "At first I didn't like your long hair. I thought it made you look like a pirate."

His fingers found the satin-covered buttons running from the nape of her neck to her waist. He pressed his lips to her forehead and murmured against her skin. "Say no, Angie, and it stops right here."

"Yes." Her arms went around him and she turned her head to rest her cheek on his chest beneath his chin. "Yes, yes, yes."

"Do you know what you're saying? What you're deciding?"

The back of the gown was opened almost to her waist, and he felt her shudder as his fingers brushed warm, bare skin.

Then her head fell backward and she gazed at him from half-closed eyes. "Sam?"

He bent to kiss her throat, inhaled the scented powder on her breasts, felt her tremble beneath his lips. "Hmmm?"

"If you can't say something romantic or nice, don't say anything at all."

He jerked upright to stare at the smile on her parted lips. "I just want to be sure that you know that we're about to—"

She pressed a finger across his lips. "Sam? Hush." Raising on tiptoe, she bit him lightly on the chin. "I'm a grown woman in full possession of my faculties. I know what we're doing."

He wasn't so sure about the last. Her faculties were soaked in champagne, and she couldn't really know what they were doing because she hadn't done it before. But he'd satisfied the laws of decency and gentlemanly behavior; he'd acted as honorably as a man could given the circumstances. Now he could give in to his own champagne-soaked desires.

This time when he kissed her, he didn't hold back. The passion he'd first felt ten years ago shook him with his need for her. When he released her mouth, they were both breathing raggedly, and Angie was wide-eyed and gasping.

He pushed down the top of her gown and she drew her arms out of the sleeves, then he slid the satin over her hips and let her gown and petticoats puddle around her ankles on the kitchen floor.

She stood before him with the hair ornament trembling on her head, wearing long gloves, a lace-edged French corset, white pantaloons, and white stockings. The lamplight made her eyes shine and her skin glow.

Slowly Sam removed his jacket and pulled the studs from his shirtfront and cuffs, not taking his eyes off of her. She raised her arms and removed the hair ornament, then pulled the pins from her coiffure. A rich wave of reddish brown tumbled down her back and around her shoulders, and Sam sucked in a breath.

She wet her lips and watched him tear off his shirt and throw it behind him. Then she wiggled out of her pantaloons.

He would have liked to finish undressing her in the lamplight, but this was her first experience. She would find comfort in darkness. Crossing to her, he swept her into his arms and carried her into his bedroom. After he pulled off his trousers, he knelt before her, rolled her garters down her legs, and peeled off her stockings, then sat beside her on the bed and unlaced her corset.

"I can't move," she whispered. "I feel weak and heavy."

"I know." He kissed her eyelids, her temples, her mouth. When his hands found her breasts and cupped them gently, she stirred and her breath quickened.

"Can you see me? Please don't look at me."

"You're beautiful, Angie. So beautiful." He jerked the blankets back, then gently drew her to the pillows. "Just lie there."

His touch was light but his hands were callused and rough on her skin. The roughness made her shiver with pleasure and twist beneath his caresses, offering herself like a wanton. She had imagined this so many times, and she had been so wrong. She had imagined something gentle and dreamy with tenderness, but it wasn't like that, and she didn't want it to be.

His mouth burned on her skin, and his hands moved on her body, teasing, coaxing, touching, withdrawing only to approach again, tease again, until she was panting and twisting to follow his fingers. He kissed her mouth, her breasts, her belly. Her head thrashed from side to side on the pillow, and she whispered a mindless, "Please,

please, please," not knowing what she begged for but needing whatever it was, needing him.

When she was bathed in sweat and wild with wanting more than his mouth and hands could give, when she thought she would surely die if he didn't come to her, Sam rose above her and thrust forward. A sharp pain caused her eyes to fly open and her fingers dug into his damp shoulders.

The pain was fleeting and swiftly forgotten, swept aside by a tide of passion that overwhelmed thought and mind. Her hands flew over his chest, his back, his hips, then to his lips and mouth. Her body lifted with the rhythm of his thrusts, and a great joy burst through her.

This was the mystery that had hovered beyond reach for so many years. Now she knew. Now she had felt a man's heartbeat pounding next to hers, had felt his breath hot on her lips and bare skin. She had discovered an unsuspected emptiness and known the astonishment and bliss of fulfillment.

Angie fell asleep in Sam's arms with a smile on her lips.

At first light she awoke with a start and bolted up in bed. Good Lord, she was as naked as the day she was born. Snatching the sheet, she held it over her breasts and stared at Sam, appalled. She gave his shoulder a rough shake.

"You're still here! You've spent two nights in the house this week and both times the girls were gone. What will the neighbors think!"

Sam opened one eye. "They'll think Sam Holland slept in his own bed with his own wife. That bastard. He should be tarred and feathered and run out of town on a rail."

"I'm serious." Angie jumped out of bed, pulling the

sheet with her. "Get out of that bed. . . . Oh!" He was naked, too. Spinning around, she faced the bureau, struggling to pull the sheet behind her to cover her exposed fanny. Fire blazed on her cheeks. He was *very* naked, and now she'd seen his very nakedness in the daylight. Lordy. "Sam, get up right now and get out of here. Molly and the girls could arrive any minute."

If he got out of bed as she was demanding, he would walk naked past her and walk naked into the kitchen to find his trousers. "Wait." Swallowing hard, she clutched the sheet to her breasts. "Stay there for a minute. I'll fetch your trousers."

When she saw the kitchen she groaned aloud. Pieces of clothing were strewn everywhere. After tossing several items aside, she found his trousers. Rushing back to the bedroom, nailing her gaze firmly to his face and nowhere else, she threw the trousers across his lap and spun again to face the bureau.

Her reflection in the mirror made her sigh. Wild loose hair curled down her back and over the slope of her breasts. Her lips were still swollen from passionate kisses, and recalling those kisses caused her nipples to bud and stand out beneath the sheet as plain as day.

In less than twenty-four hours she'd fallen from dull respectability to a state of disheveled wantonness. Narrowing her eyes, she studied her image, wondering if Miss Lily looked like this in the mornings.

Sam appeared behind her and met her gaze in the glass. "Having regrets?" he asked softly.

"I don't know," she said after a minute. "Are you?"

"Me?" He laughed and kissed the top of her head. "Can a man regret heaven? No."

"What happened between us . . ." She hated the violent pink burning on her cheeks. "It was a one-time event, Sam. I guess I don't regret what we did. I always wondered about, well, you know. But this can't happen again."

"I understand." He placed his hands on her bare shoulders and spoke to her reflection in the mirror. "Well actually, maybe I don't understand."

"How can you not understand?" She threw out her hands, then grabbed the falling sheet and yanked it up over her breasts. "We can't share a bed again. It wouldn't be decent. As soon as we can, we're going to get a divorce!"

His hands caressed her arms, and the long strokes made her shiver. Gently he pulled her long hair back and gazed into the mirror at the thrust of her nipples against the sheet. "Remind me. Why are we getting a divorce?"

For one fevered moment she couldn't remember, couldn't think. Then she jerked away from him. "Why? For one thing, we ruined each other's lives. For another thing you betrayed me with Laura, and for the last thing, I'm going to marry Peter De Groot!"

Oh Lord. Peter. The room spun around her. No, she wouldn't think about Peter. Later she would flog herself with thoughts about Peter, but not now. How on earth had a simple thing like a divorce gotten so complicated?

She'd have to sort that out at another time because right now she had a more urgent problem. Molly called her name and knocked on the back door. "Yoohoo, Angie. Are you awake?"

Wide-eyed, she whirled toward Sam. "Quick, quick. I'll pick up the clothes in the kitchen, you jump out the window."

"What?"

"Out. Go." She made a shooing motion with her

hands, then she dropped the sheet and grabbed her wrapper from the hook on the back of the door. "We don't want Molly and the girls to know you spent the night in my bed."

"It's *my* bed."

"I don't care whose bed it is, you and I shouldn't have been in it together," Angie hissed. "Go!" She looked down, then clapped a hand over her eyes. "First, put on your pants."

"You really are beautiful," he said as she turned aside to tie the belt of the wrapper.

"Damn it, Sam. Go." Dashing past him, she ran into the kitchen, bending and grabbing clothes off the floor and chairs. "I'll just be a minute," she said to the door.

"Did you bring us something?" Lucy called.

"Is it cake?" Daisy shouted.

"You'll find out in about one minute."

Rushing into the bedroom, she flung their evening clothes on the bed, then gasped and put a hand over her heart when Sam's head and naked shoulders appeared outside the window.

He scratched his jaw and gave her a thoughtful look. "When you have a minute, I'd like you to explain why I'm sneaking out of my own house."

"Think about your daughters!" She jerked the curtains together, shutting him out of sight. She could only hope he had the sense to wait until Molly and the girls were inside before he made a dash for his tent.

Damn, damn. There wasn't a thing to do about her wild hair, swollen lips, bare feet, or a certain knowing look that she could swear had not been there yesterday.

"Angie?"

"I'm coming!"

After Angie opened the door, Molly looked her up and

down and raised her eyebrows, but she didn't say anything. And she didn't say anything a few minutes later
when she pushed aside two shirt studs before she set
down plates for the cake.

When the coffee was ready, Molly settled back in her
chair. "Well. Tell us all the details that are fit to tell." Her
gaze was steady, but her mouth twitched at the corners.

Daisy sighed happily. "Cake for breakfast. Wait til
Papa hears."

"Was there music?" Lucy asked. "And pretty dresses?
Did Papa dance with you? I wish I knew how to dance."

Angie cupped her hands around the coffee mug, gave
Molly a long look, then told the details that were fit
to tell.

Chapter 14

Walking away from a soapy pan of breakfast dishes, Angie dried her hands, then sat at the kitchen table and pulled Peter's letter out of her apron pocket.

My dearest Angelina,

I've delayed a reply to your last letter in hope of receiving further news that your appalling circumstances have changed. As I've heard nothing, I assume the worst: that you are still forced to live with Mr. Holland and his illegitimate children.

My dear, this situation cannot be allowed to continue.

Your compassionate nature is to your credit and I wouldn't wish you otherwise. Truly I understand why you would agree to delay the divorce and make the child's surgery the primary financial priority. However, your letters seem to suggest the surgery will not occur anytime soon and therefore the divorce is indefinitely postponed.

I've given our situation careful thought, seeking a solution that will permit us to be together sooner than Mr. Holland's circumstances allow. As both you and Mr. Holland have agreed to dissolve your marriage, and the only impediment is monetary, I wish to offer you the financial wherewithal to accomplish the dissolution sought by everyone involved.

I want you to return to Chicago, Angelina. I'll lease a house where you can live comfortably during the waiting period until the divorce is final. Naturally, I will handle all legal matters. I foresee no difficulty with your case.

My darling, I beg you not to let pride or propriety stand in the way of accepting assistance. Remember, what matters is our future.

Now I must chide you. Surely you can guess the torment and questions that arise between your letters. Take pity on one who loves you and write more frequently, I beg of you.

I miss you more than I can express and long to see your dear face and press you in my arms.

> *Faithfully yours,*
> *Peter Markam De Groot*

Oh, the guilt. Guilt for not writing more frequently. Guilt for being too busy to think of Peter as often as she should. Guilt, guilt and more guilt for giving herself to Sam. Angie pressed her fingertips to her temples. Each time she read the letter her agitation and confusion increased.

What should she do? If she accepted Peter's generous and astonishing offer, her life could begin much sooner than she had dreamed.

But of course she couldn't accept. No decent woman would take money from one man while married to another. She couldn't ignore a lifetime of proper behavior, no matter what Peter advised.

Her gaze lifted to the row of jars above the stove and

settled on the last jar, the empty jar. A sigh dropped her shoulders. If, and it was a big if, she and Sam saved enough to pay for Daisy's surgery before the court's deadline, then afterward they could start saving for the divorce. They would need enough money to support Angie in a separate residence for a year, plus attorney's fees.

Even if she lived as frugally as possible, the amount they needed to save was equal to or greater than the amount required for Daisy's surgery. Assuming everything went smoothly with no setbacks, she might be free to begin her life with Peter two years from the time of Daisy's surgery.

Or . . . she could accept Peter's generosity and begin her life a year sooner. She could leave Willow Creek almost immediately and spend the year of waiting in Chicago being courted and fussed over.

Her conscience twisted sharply, and she covered her eyes. How could she even think of letting Peter spend well over a thousand dollars on her behalf after she had betrayed him?

No, she couldn't accept his offer. Such a thing just wasn't done. But there was no harm in daydreaming, in pretending that she had a choice.

"Angie?" Lucy's blond head leaned into the back door. "We're through snapping the beans. Are you ready to pick up our new dresses?"

Hastily she stuffed Peter's letter back into her apron pocket and returned to the pan in the sink. "Let me finish up here, then I'll find my hat and gloves. Ask Daisy if she is absolutely sure her new shoes fit. We could drop them off at the cobbler's while we're in town."

"They fit," Daisy said, bringing the bowl of string beans inside. "Where shall I put these?"

"In the ice chest. Mr. Kravitz agreed to work on your

shoes again." The process was slow, but gradually the fit was improving.

"My shoes are just right." A small silence opened behind Angie then Daisy said in a small voice, "Do you want to see?"

Angie's head jerked up and she bit down on her back teeth. Please, please, she thought. Don't let me mess this up. "I believe I would feel reassured if I saw for myself. Sit down. I'll be there as soon as I wipe out the dishpan. Lucy? Here's a towel; will you dry the dishes, please?"

"Why do I always have to dry the dishes?"

"Because you're good at it. You do a thorough job, and you're careful not to chip or break anything."

"Oh."

After drying her hands, Angie knelt in front of Daisy and gazed into her steady eyes. Since the girls were having lunch with the Govenors today, Angie had insisted on baths last night. Daisy had worn her stockings as she had since Angie arrived, but she'd taken them off in the washtub, which she hadn't done before. Angie had made a point of not looking when Daisy climbed out of the water.

Now Daisy regarded her with uneasiness, but Angie also saw the beginnings of trust in those large gray eyes. She drew a deep breath, then rested Daisy's clubfoot in her lap and pressed the everyday shoes above Daisy's twisted toes. "There's room, but not too much." Mr. Kravitz had reinforced the heel so Angie couldn't pinch the leather to check for fit. "The heel isn't too tight, is it?"

"No."

"Good." Already the outer leather and the area of the ankle bone showed wear because Daisy walked on the side of her foot. But now that Angie could examine the fit up close, she realized Mr. Kravitz had built this shoe taller than the other to protect Daisy's ankle and had added padding where Daisy walked on the bone. Bless the man. She would take Mr. Kravitz a jar of noodles and gravy next week, and she'd pay him first thing when she next paid bills.

She held Daisy's small twisted foot between her hands, and raged in her heart at a fate that had let this happen. Tears lay close to the surface and she felt like weeping.

Instead she blinked hard and reached deep for a smile. "Do your good Sunday shoes fit as well as these?"

Daisy nodded, studying Angie's expression for any hint of revulsion or pity.

And in that moment Angie knew she had to be present for Daisy's operation whether Sam arranged the surgery or the Govenors did.

When she answered Peter's letter, she would tell him that she couldn't accept his money. He would protest and attempt to persuade her. Then she would answer that she couldn't make any decisions about the divorce until after Daisy's operation. If she explained carefully, surely he would understand.

"Excellent. I'm glad they fit." Standing, Angie removed her apron and hung it on the hook beside the back door, hoping nothing in her demeanor suggested that something momentous had just occurred. "If we don't dawdle, we have just enough time to pick up this batch of new dresses, then hurry back and get you dressed before your grandparents arrive to fetch you."

While the girls were having lunch with the Govenors, she would do her baking for Sunday, return a cup of cornmeal she'd borrowed from Molly, and scrub the floors. If she had any extra time, she'd pull the weeds in the front yard around her struggling columbines before she started supper. As she worked through her list of chores, she'd think about what to say when she answered Peter's letter.

But something else lay heavy on her mind. After they married—would Peter be shocked to discover that she wasn't a virgin? Or would he assume that she and Sam had consummated their marriage all those years ago? She decided Peter most likely believed the marriage had been consummated. Therefore she could stop worrying about not being virginal when she married him.

That didn't make her betrayal any less reprehensible, she told herself sternly.

Nevertheless, her mood improved and her conscience relaxed, as consciences often did when assured that a wrongdoing would not be found out.

"Come along, girls," she said briskly. "It's a grand day. School is out for the summer, you have new dresses, and you're going someplace nice for lunch."

They skipped down the road in front of her, kicking up puffs of dust that made Angie sneeze. But nothing could spoil the day.

She had waited ten long years for her life to begin. Now Peter had appeared like a fairy godfather to grant her fondest wish. It was a lovely gesture even if she couldn't accept.

An odd thought occurred while Mrs. Hooten folded the girls' new dresses into packages. Was obtaining a divorce truly her fondest wish? Well, of course it was.

Except for having to leave Sam. And the girls.

After Sam walked through the new parsonage with the Reverend and Mrs. Dryfus, accepting their compliments, he presented them with the house keys, then headed downtown to spread the word that the job was finished. With a little luck, the information would reach Herb Govenor before the Govenors caught the train for Colorado Springs. As far as the Dryfus project was concerned, the fire danger would end and Sam could relax.

"Sam Holland. You're just the man I'm looking for." The mayor slid onto the barstool next to Sam and signaled Maxie for a beer.

"I've been looking for you too. It's time we discussed building the school."

"There's been some developments."

Sam turned his head. "I'm ready to start work as soon as you and the council decide on the land and start soliciting the donations we need."

"We've decided on the lot, but there's a problem with the current owner. He wants twice what the ground is worth. We'll handle things, but it's going to take a few weeks." The mayor slid Sam a look, then concentrated on his beer mug. "As for donations, it turns out that a single donor has stepped forward. He'll pay for everything."

Marcus Applebee, it had to be. Sam nodded. "The delay on the lot will give me time to work my claims and put aside a little money to tide me over."

The mayor wiped a hand across his mouth after a long swallow of beer. "I'm glad the Dryfus place went up with no incident. People are saying all that talk about you and the fires was just talk. Nothing to it."

Any niggling leftover doubt would vanish when the word got out that the mayor and town council had approved Sam to build the new school.

"But we have a problem." Lifting his head, the mayor met Sam's gaze in the mirror above the back bar. "Herb

Govenor is the man who's paying for the new school. It won't cost the town a red cent. Govenor will pay for the building lot, hell, he'll pay for everything right down to chalk for the blackboard and enough firewood to get through next winter. He'll even furnish housing for a new teacher."

Sam's mouth thinned and his eyes went flat. He could guess what was coming.

"The condition is, he doesn't want you as the builder. If you're the builder, the deal's off."

"The new school was my idea."

"It's a good idea, and it's going to happen. Isn't that the important thing?" The mayor slid off the stool. "We can spend the next few months soliciting donations, hoping we get what we need. Or we can accept Govenor's offer and start immediately."

"You already agreed, didn't you?"

"Taking Govenor's offer makes sense." He shrugged. "There was no way to justify turning him down." The mayor placed a hand on Sam's shoulder. "Come fall, your girls won't have to walk past the Old Homestead to get to school. That's what matters, Sam."

After the mayor left the saloon, Sam frowned at his beer mug and told himself the mayor was right. It didn't matter who built the new school. If Herb Govenor wanted to pay for the entire package just to deny Sam the pleasure of being the builder, he couldn't blame the town for accepting the offer. The project would go faster and smoother with only one donor to deal with instead of dozens.

But he had wanted to build the school.

Well, hell. There were a lot of things he wanted that he would never have. And now nothing stood in the way of doing what he wanted to do, which was devote all his effort to his best claim. Building the school would have required at least a month. That was a month he desperately needed up on his claim. Maybe losing the school project was a good thing. He flipped some coins on the bar and left the saloon.

He spent the afternoon digging in his mine shaft and thinking about Herb Govenor. He didn't fault Govenor for hating him. Sam figured he'd hate any man who took advantage of Lucy or Daisy, and that's how Govenor saw the situation. It was easier for Govenor to believe that Sam had seduced his daughter rather than to accept that Laura was willing. And now Govenor believed that Sam was trying to steal his granddaughters.

For those reasons, Govenor had promised to destroy Sam, and he was doing his best to accomplish that goal. The thought returned Sam's mind to the fires.

He didn't kid himself that he'd prevented Herb Govenor from burning down the Dryfus place. A determined arsonist would have gotten the job done no matter how many men Sam posted on watch. What he didn't understand was why such a feeble attempt had been made instead of an all-out effort. What was different about the Dryfus project?

The only answer that sprang to mind was that Whittier and the union could afford a loss, but Reverend Dryfus could not. Sam frowned. He didn't like attributing a conscience to Herb Govenor. Didn't like thinking that Govenor might set aside his personal agenda out of consideration for the reverend's sparse pocketbook. He didn't like thinking about Herb Govenor at all. He would far rather have devoted his thoughts to Angie.

She wouldn't discuss the night of the grand opening. If Sam alluded to the amazing conclusion of the evening,

Angie would blush violently and a little smile would play around her lips, but she wouldn't acknowledge his comment or offer any response of her own. Last night, when they were sitting outside on the kitchen steps, he'd told her that he'd thought about everything, and she was right. Enormous complications would have resulted if Molly and the girls had caught them in bed together.

And he'd meant what he said. His daughters shouldn't see him taking advantage of a woman he planned to send packing as soon as he could afford to do so.

Throwing down his pick, he pushed back his hat and wiped his forehead. The sun was sweating out the beer he'd had earlier.

What if he didn't send Angie packing? Or, to phrase it more realistically, what if he somehow managed to convince her not to walk out on him again? This was a new idea and it surprised him. Maybe it shouldn't have.

Most of the time they got on well. His daughters were gradually accepting her. And she was good with the girls. She was a wonderful cook, appeared to manage money well. She was settling into the community. He enjoyed her company. And Lordy, he wanted to take her to bed again, wanted that in the worst way.

On the downside . . . he couldn't offer her any more than he'd been able to offer her ten years ago. It hadn't been good enough then; why would it be good enough now? Moreover, she intended to marry that bastard De Groot. Worse, he had an idea that De Groot could give Angie all the comforts she deserved. Sam couldn't compete unless he found his jackpot.

Keeping his daughters and possibly keeping his wife depended on finding gold. Frowning, he peered into the pit he was digging. This was a hell of a way to live—depending on luck to solve his problems.

*   *   *

Angie stood in the front doorway while the Govenors' driver escorted Lucy and Daisy from the house to a polished black vis-à-vis. The Govenors faced forward. Neither gave her a glance.

But when the carriage returned, the only occupants were Winnie and the girls. The girls jumped to the ground and ran to the bed of columbines, their eyes bright with excitement.

"We could order anything we wanted to eat," Lucy said. "I had clam chowder and I liked it, and baked chicken that I didn't like as much as fried like we do it here at home."

"We had ice cream for dessert!" Daisy's eyes widened in thrilled amazement. "And the ice cream had strawberries in it, and strawberry jam on top!"

"I want to hear every detail," Angie said, standing and pulling off her gardening gloves. "But first, run inside and put on your everyday dresses and shoes." Her gaze flicked to the vis-à-vis. "Is your grandmother waiting for something?"

"Oh, she wants to talk to you," Lucy called over her shoulder before she and Daisy banged into the house.

Angie's heart sank. She couldn't imagine what she and Winnie Govenor might have to say to each other. Resisting an urge to remove her apron and smooth back her hair, she reluctantly approached the carriage.

"Step inside, if you please," Winnie said, skimming an eye over Angie's everyday work dress and utilitarian hairstyle.

"Yes?" Angie asked warily once she was seated across from Winnie Govenor. Winnie wore a dark summerweight traveling suit trimmed with blue and cream.

"I'll come straight to the point. Mr. Govenor and I

would like Lucy and Daisy to spend the summer with us in Colorado Springs. This request should more properly be put to Mr. Holland or his attorney, but Mr. Holland has shown no inclination to listen to reason. It is my hope that by making the approach through you, Mr. Holland will consider our wishes."

Angie stared in disbelief. "Mrs. Govenor, Sam will never give up his girls. He'll never agree to this proposal."

"Mr. Holland will lose the girls in any case. It's obvious to all that he won't be able to arrange for Daisy's surgery before October. When he defaults on his commitment, custody will revert to Mr. Govenor and me. All parties have agreed to this resolution."

"We still have three months."

"There is no reason to prolong this. Since we will receive custody anyway, we would like to have the summer with our granddaughters. We'd like to spend time with them before they leave for school."

"Leave for school?" Angie frowned. "In the unlikely event that you receive custody, wouldn't Lucy and Daisy attend school in Colorado Springs?"

"We have enrolled both girls in Miss Washington's School for Young Women. Miss Washington prefers that her young ladies board on premises. As the school is indeed in Colorado Springs, Lucy and Daisy would come home for holidays and selected weekends."

Angie threw up her hands. "Why do you want custody at all if you're only going to send them off to live somewhere else?"

"I assure you that Miss Washington's School for Young Women is the best of its kind in the West. Miss Washington is extremely selective and accepts only young ladies from families of quality and standing. Attending

Miss Washington's is a fine opportunity for Lucy and Daisy."

Angie fell backward against the seat cushion. She wasn't sure where to begin, but she had to try. "Mrs. Govenor, Lucy and Daisy are seven and five years old. Miss Washington's school might be a wonderful opportunity when they're older, but not now. Right now they need the stability and security of a home and family."

Winnie's face tightened. "Clearly you have no appreciation for how difficult it will be for Mr. Govenor and myself to raise children at this time in our lives. But we're willing, even eager to assume our duty. However, the situation will be easier on all concerned with the girls at Miss Washington's during the school year."

"The girls don't need more upheaval and change. They need to be with their father, not sent away." Anger flashed in her eyes and she clenched her hands in the lap of her apron.

"It grates to hear you continually refer to Mr. Holland as my granddaughters' father. If the court wasn't so blind, we wouldn't be having this conversation in the first place." Winnie raised a trembling hand to her forehead. "If Mr. Holland wants children, then he should have his own instead of stealing Laura's! This is not right."

Angie's gaze narrowed. "What are you talking about?"

Winnie made a sound of exasperation and annoyance. "You know perfectly well. Lucy and Daisy should be raised by blood relatives, not by Sam Holland. He can call himself their father until the cows come home, but that doesn't make it true."

"Wait." Angie raised a hand. "I don't understand your meaning."

"You really don't know?" Winnie said after studying

Angie's flushed face. She shook her head, then released a long low breath. "Laura eloped when she was seventeen. The man was unsuitable, of course. Laura chose unsuitable men." Winnie twisted her hands together in her lap. "Mr. Payton owned a feed store on Myers Street, down near the stables. He had consumption when Laura married him, and that's what finally killed him. We asked her to come live with us, but she said this was her home, where her friends were and where her children had been born. A year later she met Mr. Holland and you know the rest."

"Lucy and Daisy are not Sam's children," Angie whispered. Shock stopped her breath.

"Of course they're not," Winnie said, her voice hardening again. "Adoption is just a piece of paper. Adoption doesn't make Mr. Holland their real father. It doesn't make him a blood relation."

"They aren't Sam's children." He'd adopted them, but they weren't his natural children. Angie shook her head, then stared.

"That is exactly my point."

She would deal with the shock later. If she could. "Tell me something. If Sam was their true father, would you fight so hard to take the girls away from him?"

"Why can't you understand this? Mr. Holland has no blood tie to my granddaughters."

"I see." Suddenly the Govenors' position made a lot more sense. "Mrs. Govenor, do you really want to raise Lucy and Daisy, or is it that you don't want Sam to raise them?"

"We have a family obligation to our granddaughters. Mr. Holland does not. And it isn't just him. We have to consider who he brings into their lives, what woman he takes up with next. Who do you think a skirt-crazy man like him would put first? My granddaughters or his next woman?"

"He'd choose his daughters," Angie said without hesitation. There was no doubt in her mind. "Sam loves his girls. He'll never neglect them or put them second to anyone."

"What if he someday has a child of his own?"

"That's an insulting implication. Sam wouldn't stop loving his daughters if he had another child. If he can love two children, I think he can love three or four, don't you?"

"You're shockingly naive, Mrs. Holland. Either that, or you're as besotted by that man as my daughter was."

Angie climbed out of the vis-à-vis and looked up at Winnie Govenor. "You're trying to force something that no one wants, not even you, not really. I wish you'd stop thinking about obligation and ask yourself where the girls will be happiest and where they will flourish. It's true that Sam can't give them the material comforts that you and your husband can. But will those comforts make them feel less lonely and less abandoned at Miss Washington's? Or would they be happier at home with a father who loves and wants them?" Angie's gaze hardened. "I'm not naive, and I'm not besotted. I'm also not blind to what's best for Daisy and Lucy."

Mrs. Govenor tossed her head and ordered her driver to drive on.

Angie stood in the street, watching until the vis-à-vis turned downhill toward Bennet Street. Then she raised a shaking hand to her forehead.

Lucy and Daisy didn't resemble Sam because they weren't his daughters. Angie's arrival hadn't exposed Lucy and Daisy as illegitimate because they weren't born out of wedlock. And Sam hadn't had five years to arrange Daisy's operation, Daisy had been born before Sam met Laura. Sam hadn't been with Laura for eight years as Angie had jealously assumed, hadn't been present for the miracle of his daughters' births as she had also assumed.

Later, after the girls were finally tucked into bed, Angie followed Sam out to the back steps and sat in the darkness looking at the silhouette of his tent while he told her that he wouldn't be building the school after all.

"I'm sorry. I know building the school was important to you." When he crawled into his tent at night, did he think of her? It was a silly thought that came out of nowhere, and she looked away from his tent. "I guess you'll be looking for a new project."

"I won't put any more clients at risk." Sam related his theory as to why the Dryfus place had not burned. "Govenor isn't totally lacking in principles, just almost. I don't think the Dryfus fire was intended to burn down the place. I think it was a warning to me."

"But the fire could have burned down the parsonage." The moonlight was bright enough that she saw him nod.

"If it had happened that way, I suspect Govenor might have made an anonymous donation to Reverend Dryfus so the reverend could rebuild. The point is, it's too risky to take on another client. Not until things are settled between Govenor and me." Sam turned his face toward town. "Or maybe I'm wrong. Maybe there won't be any more fires because time's running out. Maybe Herb believes he's already won."

Usually this was Angie's favorite part of the day. When the chores were finished and the girls tucked into bed, then she and Sam came outside to sit on the steps together and talk.

Sometimes they recalled growing up in Chicago and

spoke of how the city had grown and changed. Occasionally they filled in bits and pieces of the years they had spent apart. Often they talked about the day just passed, the girls, their neighbors, and the latest town gossip.

She felt so close to Sam sitting together listening to his voice in the darkness, sensing the solid warmth of him on the step above her. It was hard not to remember passionate kisses and the touch of his hands stroking her body. And his mouth. Oh heavens, his mouth teasing her breasts and exploring the inside of her thighs. Heat flooded her body at the memory.

But tonight the conversation had turned in a direction that chased away passionate thoughts. Her chest tightened and her mouth suddenly went dry.

"If you don't work, how will we pay the bills?" Panic swirled beneath the question. There was enough money in the jars over the stove to carry them for a week or two, but after that . . .

"I'm following a vein of sylvanite that looks like high grade. I'll know more in a couple of days, after I get the assayer's report. Selling small quantities of high grade won't put us ahead, but it'll pay the bills. If we're careful."

"I thought you'd already had the ore assayed." It seemed to Angie that she was continually shifting money around the jars to find enough funds for another assay.

"I wish one assay were enough, but the gold content can increase or diminish within a few yards. The assays are an ongoing necessity."

"Sam? What if the high grade runs out?"

He was silent for several minutes. "I won't let us starve, Angie. You don't know about ore and minerals and mining, so I won't ask you to believe in my diggings. But I'm asking you to believe in me. This is the claim I've been waiting for ever since I came west. The gold is there."

Ten years ago she'd had a choice, and she hadn't believed in him enough to follow him west. Now there was no choice. Whether she believed or not, their fate was tied to his claim. He wasn't going to seek another building job.

For a moment she watched the moonlight slide on her wedding ring, then she wrapped her arms around her legs and rested her chin on her raised knees. "Sam? Why didn't you tell me about the girls?"

"Tell you what?"

"That you adopted them. I thought you were their real father."

"I *am* their real father."

"You know what I mean."

"I'm the man who tucks them in at night, and I'm the man who cooks their breakfast and walks them to school. I'm the man who puts a roof over their heads and shoes on their feet. It's me who worries about their grades and what they eat and who they play with. It's me who's proud of Lucy and who hurts inside when I watch Daisy run. Me who's teaching them not to lie and not to steal and not to be rude and to use their napkins. Someday I'm going to be the man who chases off boys who aren't worthy of them. And someday I'll walk them down the aisle and give their hands to men who *are* worthy of them."

It was the longest speech Angie had heard him make.

"If that isn't a father, I don't know what the hell is."

"You don't need to get angry. I'm on your side."

"Really?" She felt his stare through the darkness. "I ran into the postmaster on the way home tonight. Do you want to explain why we're paying for two postal boxes?"

Angie's heart sank. "I'm paying for my box with my own money." His silence told her that was not the root of his objection. "I'm corresponding with several friends in Chicago," she said finally.

"Including Peter De Groot?"

"Yes." She wouldn't lie to him. "I won't apologize, Sam. You took the last ten years, but I won't let you take my future away."

"You still blame me for those ten years?"

"Maybe I see your side better than I did before." She hesitated. "Maybe we're both to blame. The point is, nothing has changed."

That wasn't true. Everything had changed the night they held each other in bed. Angie's world had forever altered. She couldn't look at Sam the way she had before, and couldn't look at herself the same way either. And to her dismay, Peter's face and features became more shadowy with every passing day.

But it was her world that had changed. She saw no evidence that Sam's world had altered.

"I won't throw away my future because a few letters scratch your pride."

She wanted Sam to tell her there was more than pride at stake. She wanted to hear that his world had changed, too. But he said nothing. In the silence Angie heard crickets strumming and the faint sounds of revelry drifting from town. A dog barked in the distance, and a nearby neighbor played a sad tune on a harmonica.

Sam stood. "You write to anyone you damned well want to." He strode past her down the steps and started toward his tent. "It doesn't matter to me what you do."

"Good. Because I'm going to keep writing to Peter."

The problem was, she wished Sam did care.

Tilting her head, she gazed up at the moon, blinking through a haze of tears. Everything had seemed so straightforward the day she arrived in Willow Creek. She'd known what she believed and what she wanted.

Now she didn't.

Chapter 15

Throughout the next ten days Sam left the house immediately after breakfast and didn't return from Gold Hill until sunset. That gave him an hour to enjoy his daughters' company before he tucked them into bed. During his time with his girls, Angie either went into her bedroom and shut the door, or she sat by the lamp at the kitchen table, sewing or writing letters. Ignoring him.

He didn't speak more than was necessary. If he'd sold a few bags of high grade, he put the money next to the sink before he headed back to town to have supper at one of the saloons. After he'd bypassed the pot on the stove for two nights in a row, Angie stopped leaving him anything. If she had asked, he would have told her there would be more money next week. This week he'd kept back a large percentage to buy lumber to shore up the drift he was digging. But she didn't ask.

He was behaving badly. And he knew it, damn it.

Everything Angie had said was correct. They were married, yes, but they weren't husband and wife. He had no right to tell her who she could write to and who she couldn't. And he had no right to place obstacles in the path to her future.

By now he also knew that she had wisely disobeyed him about buying material for the girls' new dresses.

He'd been angry about that, too, until he counted the money in the jars and realized that accommodating his pride meant doing without something else. Now she was cutting up more of her dresses to make Lucy and Daisy new school clothes for the fall.

Angie was holding up her end of the bargain, keeping his house, paying his bills, saving him money, caring for his children. And she was getting damned little in return.

Stepping back, Sam lowered his hammer and squinted at the braces he'd built to shore up the drift. His drift was discouragingly shallow, only about ten feet back from the main shaft. The digging progressed slowly when there was only one man working the pick and shovel, and then hauling the dirt up and out of the main shaft.

But he knew his mine was rich. He knew it like he knew the sky was blue, like he knew the dimples beside Angie's mouth. This was a fact.

This time the vein wouldn't peter out a few feet from his main shaft. This time the quality of the ore wouldn't deteriorate. The L&D mine would be one of the richest digs on Gold Hill. There wasn't a doubt in his mind.

The only real question was how long he would keep digging, hoping to find a vug where he could pick gold off the walls and ceiling like picking golden apples from a money tree. If he found a vug, he'd never have to worry about money again.

Daisy would get her operation. Angie would get her divorce.

Sam thought for a minute, then he locked his hammer in the toolbox, climbed out of the shaft, and headed toward town.

*   *   *

"I don't like that. I hate green," Lucy said, dismissing the pieces Angie was carefully cutting from a skirt she had taken apart. "I won't wear it."

Angie put down the scissors and straightened up from the table. It was hot today and her back ached from bending over for so long. This morning the last of the ice had melted in the icebox and a puddle of water had leaked across the kitchen floor. She'd noticed a tear in her favorite apron. And Lucy's attitude had steadily worsened since school let out for the summer.

"You picked this skirt. You said you liked dark green." She took a sip of tea, hoping it would soothe her nerves. She'd read somewhere that a hot drink on a hot day was actually cooling. But so far the theory wasn't working.

Daisy nodded over the sampler she was stitching. "You said you liked green, I heard you."

"Just shut up. I'm sick of you always taking her side!"

"Lucy, that's enough." Angie shoved back the heat-damp hair sticking to her forehead. "We don't tell each other to shut up in this family. It isn't nice."

Lucy's chin rose and she thrust out her lower lip. "You're not part of our family. I wish you'd go back where you came from!" Sudden tears glittered in her gray eyes. "Nobody wants you here."

Before Lucy's dress was ready to wear, Angie would spend a dozen or more hours stitching seams, then doing the finish work and trim. And for what? A dress that Lucy wouldn't wear? Because Lucy didn't like her and wished she'd go away?

Maybe it was the heat, maybe she was discouraged, or maybe she was just tired of trying, but something snapped.

"I will not permit you to speak to me like that," she

said angrily. "Go to your room and stay there until you're ready to apologize."

"I won't!"

This confrontation had been coming from the beginning. Angie realized she'd been a fool to think she could avoid it. And today she was in no mood for persuasion or diversion or any of the other ploys she'd used to evade escalating the friction between herself and Lucy. She was hot and tired and out of patience.

Planting her fists on her hips, she drew herself up and made no effort to disguise her temper. "You will go to your room. If I have to drag you in there—I promise you, I will!"

Neither of the girls had seen her really angry before, with the Italian side in full flare. Moreover, the incident that sparked her temper was a small one, as last straws often were.

The girls stared at her flushed face and hard eyes, and Angie recognized the instant that Lucy understood she would make good on her threat. One way or another Lucy was going to her room. She could go under her own power or Angie could drag her, but she was going.

Furious tears spilled down Lucy's cheeks. She stamped her foot then her gaze settled on the table. Snatching up the teacup and saucer, she hurled them to the floor. "I hate you!" Sobbing, she ran into the bedroom and slammed the door.

Shocked, Angie blinked down at the shattered pieces of her mother's teacup and saucer, then, throat tight, she sank to a chair and covered her eyes.

There was no escape. She couldn't run away. As she had known she would, she had refused Peter's proposition in no uncertain terms. Peter would not repeat his offer of financial assistance.

"Me and Papa want you here." Daisy knelt on the floor, collecting the broken pieces of china into the lap of her apron. "This was your mama's cup."

Angie nodded dully. "Be careful. Don't cut yourself."

"Maybe we can glue it back together."

"I don't think so."

Daisy wiped a hand across her eyes. "Lucy didn't mean what she said." She blinked up at Angie. "She thinks Mama is watching us."

"Hello, hello." Sam came in the back door, smiling and as cheerful as if ten days of silence had not occurred.

Angie's eyebrows rose. "What are you doing home in the middle of the day?"

"Get your hats and gloves, ladies. We're going to town for ice cream." Sam looked at the material bunched on the table, then at Daisy kneeling on the floor with the broken cup and saucer in her lap. "Where's Lucy?"

To her disgust and embarrassment, Angie burst into tears.

The ice cream excursion was not a success.

First Sam had to deal with Lucy, who wept in his arms and sobbed that she wished Angie had never come to live with them. Angie made her feel bad, and Angie ordered her around. She wanted her *real* mother. The best Sam could do was hold her, pat her small back, and murmur, "I know, I know."

He let that storm pass then approached the apology, which he agreed had to be made.

"Angie doesn't deserve the hurtful things you said. And I think you know it was mean and wrong to break Angie's mother's teacup."

"I do feel bad about the teacup," Lucy whispered miserably.

Sam dabbed at the tears on her cheeks with his handkerchief. "Angie's tried hard to take care of you and Daisy and do right by you both. Why won't you let her be your friend?"

Something in what he'd said must have been wrong because the result was a fresh onslaught of tears. In the end he resorted to a tactic he didn't like, but he couldn't think of anything else.

"Lucy, you were wrong in what you said and did, and you owe Angie an apology." He drew a breath and held out the bribe. "If you want ice cream, you'll have to apologize."

The apology was sullen and sounded a long way from sincere, but Lucy offered and Angie stiffly accepted.

No one said much during the walk to Stetson's Ice Cream Shoppe. Lucy was red-eyed and angry. Daisy didn't have anything to say. And Angie seemed mad at the world. Certainly she was mad at him. Two wash days had come and gone, and she'd let Sam's laundry pile up in his tent.

He was beginning to understand that the state of his underwear was a barometer of his wife's moods. At the moment most of his underwear was at Su Yung's Laundry, which meant that she was mad and ignoring him.

"Well," he said brightly when they were seated at a ridiculously small table glumly inspecting dishes of melting ice cream. "What have my favorite girls been doing since I saw you all at breakfast?" His favorite girls gave him venomous glances.

As he might have predicted, it was Daisy who finally answered. "We did the morning dishes, then helped clean up the mess from the icebox. Then we shelled some peas. And I started a sampler. Angie's showing me how to sew different stitches."

Usually Angie wore her summer straw hat slightly tilted at a stylish angle. Today her hat sat squarely on top of her head giving her a severe look. She also seemed tired. Maybe she wasn't sleeping any better than he was.

"Why did you come home in the middle of a workday, Sam?" she asked quietly.

"I'm putting in a lot of hours now that the days are long, and I miss all of you. It occurred to me that you three haven't really been anywhere since the Fourth of July parade. So I thought we all deserved a nice family outing."

Lucy pushed her empty dish forward. "Can we go now?"

Sam's small fantasy crumbled. He had imagined passersby glancing in the shop's window and admiring his fine-looking family. The admirers would see his beautiful daughters smartly turned out in their little hats and gloves, and his beautiful wife with bright dark eyes and smiling dimples. And there he would be with his hair slicked down and tied back, beaming proudly.

"You may go," Angie said. "Don't forget. You promised to help Mrs. Molly weed her kitchen garden."

The girls slid off their tall chairs and ran out of the shop, leaving Sam alone with Angie. He cleared his throat and tugged at his collar.

"I guess I owe you an apology, too."

"Yes, you do."

Angie had her gracious moments, he'd be the first to say so. But this wasn't one of them. The look in her eye reminded him of the day she'd arrived, right before she hit him. She had that fizzy look, like she was spoiling for a fight.

"The thing is, De Groot sticks in my craw. What kind

of man courts another man's wife?" Talking about it made him feel fizzy himself. "How could the bastard talk to you about marriage when you're wearing my ring? That isn't decent."

Her gaze was frosty. "Is this your idea of an apology?"

She had a point. "Well, surely you can see why I wouldn't want him writing to you, can't you? And what do you say when you write to him?" It drove him crazy wondering what they said to each other. Did De Groot call her *darling*? Did she call him *dearest*? Did they long for each other on paper?

"I'm going home."

He caught her arm. "Angie, wait. I'm sorry, all right?" She stared at him with those bottomless dark eyes, and he wished he were an eloquent man. Since he wasn't, he longed to kiss her and let his mouth and hands speak for him. "When I said I didn't care who you wrote to, that wasn't true. You'll say this isn't fair and you'll be right, but I hate it that De Groot is out there waiting for you. I hate it that you think about him and write to him. Call it pride, call it pettiness, call it selfishness. But I can't stand to think of you with another man, especially after . . ."

She looked around hastily, then lowered her gaze and blushed bright red.

"You know what I'm saying." And he was saying it badly. "Anyway. I apologize for . . ." Frowning, he tried to think of the right words.

"For trying to deny me my own postal box."

"Did I do that?" He recalled asking why they had two boxes. He didn't remember telling her that she couldn't have her own postal box.

"And for attempting to control and ruin my future."

"I just think you should wait until we're divorced before you get engaged to someone else." No matter what she said, he didn't think that was an unreasonable point of view.

"And for being sulky and childish."

"On that one I plead guilty, damn it." Ignoring propriety, he took her gloved hand in his and squeezed gently. "I'm sorry, Angie. I've missed you. I particularly miss talking to you at the end of the day."

He'd missed the light rose scent of her and the wink of dimples when she smiled. He'd missed the way her skirt crackled with purpose when she walked. And the pleasure in her eyes when he complimented her cooking or noticed a freshly scrubbed floor. He'd missed the undercurrent of tension between them and the possibility, even if remote, that she might step forward and into his arms, that she might hunger for him as he hungered for her.

The chill in her eyes gradually thawed, and she sighed. "I've missed you, too, Sam."

Well, that was something. It gave him an absurd burst of pleasure to hear her admit it.

"This probably isn't a good time to mention this, but there's never going to be a good time. I get so anxious and worried about everything." Closing her eyes, she withdrew her hand and raised it to her throat. "I worry that the high grade will play out and we won't be able to pay the grocer or the iceman or buy lamp oil or wood for the stove. I worry that we'll never have money in all the jars at the same time. And I worry most that you'll lose the girls and the Govenors will win. Then they'll be sent off to Miss Washington's school and they'll be lonely and unhappy, and—"

"I promise you, Angie. None of that will happen."

She stared. "How can you sound so certain? Did you find your jackpot?"

"No. But I'm following a solid vein and it isn't going

to play out. Someday the L&D Mine is going to be as famous as the Moose Jaw."

She looked away and he knew that she didn't believe
him. She thought he was presenting dreams and hope
as fact. That had always been the problem. She hadn't
believed in him ten years ago, and she didn't believe in
him now.

But he suddenly knew why he kept delaying doing
what he knew he had to do. It wasn't just the hope of
finding a vug and marvelous riches. It was knowing that
the joy of arranging Daisy's surgery would be balanced
by the devastation of losing Angie.

She stood on the boardwalk in front of Stetson's Ice
Cream Shoppe and watched Sam walk away from her.
Thank heaven the period of silence had ended. The days
had seemed so long when she didn't have their time together to look forward to. She didn't remember ever
feeling that way about Peter.

She had never wondered where Peter was or what he
was doing. Had never asked herself what Peter might be
thinking. She had never gazed into Peter's eyes and felt as
if she were drowning in heat and light, and she had never
longed to stroke Peter's skin or drink a hundred kisses
from his mouth. But she had thought all those things in
regard to Sam Holland.

Frowning and feeling confused, she lifted her hem off
the dusty street and climbed Fourth Avenue to the Carr
Street crossway where she halted abruptly.

Half a block ahead three boys circled Daisy, chanting,
"Gimp along, gimp along, look at Miss Limp-Along."

Horror filled Angie's eyes. She couldn't see Daisy's
face, but she saw her small rigid back and the way she

struggled to stand up straight. She saw the handfuls of skirt gripped in Daisy's shaking hands.

And she spotted Lucy farther up the block walking away from Daisy and the jeering boys.

"Gimp along, gimp along, look at—"

Angie charged forward and cuffed the boy's ear hard enough to knock the rest of the taunt out of his head.

"You should be ashamed of yourselves, all of you! What kind of low-down bully would ridicule a little girl for a condition she can't help?" The boys stared at Angie, then glanced toward Daisy and lowered their eyes to the ground. "What if it was you with the crippled foot?" Fury snapped in her gaze. "What if you were the one who was different?" None of the boys would look at her. "Is this how your parents taught you to treat girls? Is this how you treat people with afflictions? If I hear of any of you doing something like this again, I'll call on your parents and ask if they're proud of you for bullying and taunting defenseless little girls."

All three boys looked up with dread and alarm.

"Oh yes, I'll do it," she promised, letting them see her disgust. She grabbed the nearest boy by the collar and dragged him forward. "You apologize to her, you nasty little ruffian!"

One by one they muttered apologies while Daisy stood silently, tears running down her face.

The last boy threw a quick look at Angie, then shyly touched Daisy's sleeve. "I really am sorry," he said again. "You have pretty hair."

Angie gripped Daisy's hand. "Get out of our way," she said to the boys. Lifting her chin, she stepped forward. "Hold your head up, Daisy. It's them who bear the shame, not you." And there was someone else who should be ashamed, she thought, narrowing her gaze on the small figure ahead who walked into their house.

By the time Angie and Daisy arrived, Lucy had already put away her straw hat and white gloves. She waited beside the kitchen door.

Angie took Daisy's hat and gloves, then knelt and washed the tears from Daisy's cheeks with a cool, damp cloth. "I don't think they'll bother you again. But if they do, ignore them. Believe me, three boys like that aren't worth one little girl like you."

Daisy threw her arms around Angie's neck and held on so tightly that Angie couldn't breathe. Finally she drew back and looked into Angie's eyes and a faint smile brushed her lips.

"You really smacked Billy hard."

Immediately she thought about setting a good example, about teaching young girls the gentler, softer side of life. Undoubtedly a real mother would have handled this situation very differently and much better.

Angie stood and smoothed down her skirts. "A woman should never resort to violence," she said self-consciously. "It's unladylike and absolutely wrong to strike anyone." She gave each girl a long, sober look to show that she meant what she was saying. And she hoped they hadn't heard about her smacking Sam when she got off the train. "But . . . if you ever find yourself in an unusual circumstance—such as we just experienced—and violence is the only sensible recourse . . . and unfortunately, sometimes it is . . ." She threw up both hands and prayed her Italian temper wouldn't ruin them for life. "Then hit the bastard as hard as you can."

They gaped at her. "You said a bad word," Lucy gasped.

"I know and I apologize." Today was certainly the

day for apologies. "Now then. Daisy, you run over to Mrs. Molly's and ask her which part of her garden she wants you to weed. Tell her that Lucy will be along in a few minutes." She looked at Lucy over Daisy's head. "You and I need a few words."

Lucy dragged her feet to the table and sat down. A sulky pout stole across her eyes and mouth.

Angie pushed aside the green material and folded her hands on the table. "I'm disappointed in you," she said finally.

"I said I was sorry for breaking your mama's cup and saucer."

"If someone had asked, I would have sworn that you would never abandon your sister to a gang of bullies."

At once Angie saw that her instinct had been correct. A stricken expression erased any trace of a sulk, and Lucy looked down at her lap. "Daisy doesn't stick up for me."

"She sides with you whenever she can. Daisy idolizes you, Lucy. She tries to do everything just like you. She brushes her hair a hundred strokes because you do. She wants to go where you go and do what you do. Her new school dresses might be different colors than yours, but the pattern must be the same. I could give you a dozen other examples. When Daisy honestly cannot agree with something you say, it upsets her terribly. She loves you and looks up to you."

A tear welled over Lucy's lashes and plopped on her clasped hands. "She sticks up for you!"

"Is that a reason to punish her?" Angie asked gently. "Those boys frightened and humiliated her. Don't you think you should have helped her?"

"She doesn't think about Mama anymore." Lucy's tears came faster and she wiped the back of her hand across her eyes. "But Mama's watching from heaven and Mama feels bad because Daisy loves you!"

Angie blinked. Had she heard correctly? Leaning forward, she put a hand on Lucy's shoulder and bent to see the child's streaming face. "Lucy . . . do you think that you and Daisy betray your mother if you love someone else?" Oh my heavens. She dropped to her knees beside Lucy's chair.

"She's our mama and we should love her!"

"Of course you should. And I know you do."

"We shouldn't love anyone else!"

"Darling, you can love two people at the same time. If Daisy loves me, and I hope she does, that doesn't mean that Daisy no longer loves her mama. She can love us both." Gently, she pulled a tear-damp strand from Lucy's cheek and tucked it behind her ear, then she framed Lucy's face between her hands and gazed into wet gray eyes. "Think about all the people you love. Daisy, your papa, Mrs. Molly, your teacher, maybe even Miss Lily."

Lucy stared at her.

"Wouldn't it be a shame if we could only love one person? But my darling girl, we don't have to love someone at the expense of someone else." She peered into Lucy's eyes. "We have an endless supply of love, and isn't that wonderful? We don't have to stop loving one person in order to love another."

"Are you sure?" Lucy whispered.

"Oh yes. Daisy isn't betraying your mother if she loves me, too. There's room in Daisy's heart to love many people. That's true for you, too. I think of your mother a lot, did you know that? I didn't know her, but I think she and I would have liked each other because we have something important in common. We love the same people. I wish I could sit down with your mother over a cup of coffee and tell her how fast you're growing and ask her about your grandparents. There are so many things I'd like to tell her and ask her. I imagine you feel that way, too."

Lucy threw herself into Angie's arms. "I'm mad that she died! Then I feel bad for being mad at her! And sometimes I like you a lot, and then I feel bad about that, too."

"I know." Angie patted her back, felt Lucy's tears on her neck. "Sometimes I get mad at my mother for dying."

"Then do you feel bad?"

"Sometimes. But sometimes I think it's all right to be angry. Because that means I miss her and I'm sorry that she died." Gently she guided Lucy backward so she could look into her eyes. "We don't ever want to forget our mothers. But there's something else we shouldn't forget."

Lucy wiped her nose. "What?"

"Our mothers loved us, Lucy. And our mothers wouldn't want us to be unhappy. Our mothers would want us to go forward and to open our hearts and love and laugh and live our lives. Our mothers wouldn't want us to stop loving. Don't you agree?"

Fresh tears spilled down Lucy's cheeks, and she lowered her head. "I don't want to feel bad when you do something nice for me."

"You don't have to. Truly. Your mother knows you love her. And I think it would make her happy if you and I could love each other, too."

"Angie?" Miserable wet eyes looked into hers. "I really really really am sorry that I broke your cup."

"I won't say that what you did is all right, because it isn't." She wiped the tears from Lucy's eyes with a scrap

of green material. "But I can tell you that I think I understand, and I forgive you."

Daisy burst through the back door, her hair flying and
her eyes wide. "Angie, come quick! Mrs. Molly is crying!"

Chapter 16

Angie rushed up the porch steps and burst through the Johnsons' back door, the girls at her heels. Molly sat hunched over her kitchen table, a wet handkerchief pressed to her eyes.

Molly Johnson was so sturdy and indestructible that the sight of tears on her face constricted Angie's chest with dread. "Oh Molly. Has something happened to Cannady?"

"That crazy fool." Molly shoved back a wave of short silver hair, then blew her nose. She pointed at the table. "Look."

"Oh my heavens! Those can't be . . ." Angie gasped and her hands flew to her throat. Astonishment widened her eyes. "Molly, are those real diamonds?"

An array of jewelry glittered across Molly's oilcloth table covering. A hat pin, earrings, necklace, a brooch, two bracelets, three rings, and two shoe buckles. More diamonds than Angie had ever imagined seeing in one place. The gems drew the light like fire swallowing night, flashing, winking, sparkling.

Angie fanned her face. "My Lord! If those diamonds are real, you have a king's ransom sitting on your kitchen table!"

"They're real, all right." Fresh tears welled in Molly's

eyes. She made a face and shook her head. "That damned fool man. Bless his heart."

"Where . . . How did . . . ?" Angie sank to a chair, then snatched Daisy's hand away from the table. "Don't touch."

"If she wants a closer look, let her have it." Mustering a smile, Molly nodded to Lucy and Daisy. "I was in my teens before I saw a real diamond. And I never owned any until now. Take a good look, girls."

Angie pulled her gaze away from the stunning display and stared at Molly. The only thing she understood was that Molly's tears were the happy sort. "What happened?"

"Can always said he'd drape me in diamonds when he got rich." She pressed the handkerchief to her eyes. "I thought he was teasing. I mean look at me. Have you ever seen me wear jewelry? Just my jet earrings and my wedding ring." Which was a plain gold band, like Angie's. "We don't go anyplace where I'd wear diamonds. We never have, and I can't imagine we ever will."

Leaning forward, Angie gripped Molly's wrist. "Molly Johnson! Are you saying Cannady found his jackpot?"

"He told me last week, but I didn't believe it. Just didn't seem real, not after all these years." She waved a hand. "Well, I knew he was doing something up there after he put a half dozen men on picks and shovels. Some of those booms we've been hearing during the last weeks were up at Can's mine. He and his crew were dynamiting, following a web of gold veins as fast as they could dig drifts. Then he talked to one of the syndicates, and . . ." She waved a hand in front of her face and looked at Angie with amazed eyes. "Can went to Denver to sign the papers and he came home this morning with these."

They gaped at the diamonds sparkling on the faded old oilcloth.

Then Angie leaped from her chair and pulled Molly to her feet. They danced around and around the kitchen until they were both breathless and laughing. After they caught their breath, Angie danced with Lucy and Molly danced with Daisy. At the finish, the girls went outside to weed the garden, and Molly poured coffee into thick crockery mugs. She pinned the diamond brooch to the center of her apron front and insisted that Angie wear the diamond bracelets.

"My, aren't we grand."

"I can't even imagine what all this cost," Angie said, turning her wrist to admire the sparkle of afternoon sunlight flashing on the bracelets' gems. She figured this was the closest she'd ever get to real diamonds.

"Can won't tell me. All he'll say is that we're rich and there's plenty more where this came from."

Dazed, Angie studied the pieces shining on the table. "I was thinking it couldn't happen. Not to Sam, not to Cannady. That hitting the jackpot was just a dream. Wishful thinking."

"There were times when I thought so, too. Times when I thought all the mines were dug, all the gold had been found." Molly leaned to pat Angie's hand. "Don't give up believing."

Angie frowned and sipped her coffee, gazing at the diamond brooch pinned to Molly's apron. Had she ever believed? Ten years ago she hadn't believed in Sam enough to go with him on his quest for fortune and success. And he was still searching. But he hadn't given up. Still, every time she paid the bills, then portioned out what little was left into the jars over the stove, her heart sank further. And believing got harder.

They drank their coffee in contemplative silence, listening to the buzz of summer insects and the girls chattering outside in the garden. Angie had gotten used to the distant boom of dynamite exploding in the hills and seldom noticed the noise anymore. But she did today. The dynamite represented men's hopes of wresting the Earth's treasures out of the ground.

Suddenly she thought of something upsetting. "Oh Molly! You'll be moving!"

The dreamy half smile vanished from Molly's lips and she frowned. "We won't go to Colorado Springs like so many do. We already decided that. We'll move to Denver. Can and me could be as rich as Midas, and we still wouldn't fit into society." She shrugged. "But there must be other folks like us in a town the size of Denver. Folks with some money who don't care about the hoity-toity crowd." A smile curved her lips and the brooch twinkled and flashed as her bosom rose. "We'll buy two building lots and save one for you and Sam."

Standing abruptly, Angie walked to the stove. Instead of immediately pouring more coffee, she stood looking out the kitchen window at the haze of mill smoke overhanging the valley.

"If Sam is ever rich enough to buy a lot in Denver," she said quietly, "he'll be rich enough to afford a divorce."

Sam heard the news from Jim Richards, the contractor chosen by the town to build the new school. Jim rode up to the L&D to make sure Sam wasn't harboring any hard feelings and to ask him about his vision for the school.

When they finished discussing design and materials, Jim thumbed back his hat. "Have you heard about Cannady Johnson?"

The news was hardly out of Jim Richards's mouth before Sam was saddled up and riding toward town. He found Can at the third saloon he checked, smoking a hand-rolled Cuban cigar and buying drinks for every man in the place.

He slapped Can on the back. "Damn, Can. You son of a gun." They grinned at each other. "If you aren't tired of telling the story, I'd like to hear it."

During the next three hours, Sam heard the story a dozen times.

Can had lacked the money to develop the mine, so he'd gone out on a limb and borrowed a frighteningly large sum to hire eight men to dig enough drifts so that Can could follow and map the veins branching off the main lode. When he knew he could prove the worth of his claim, he'd hired a Denver attorney to pit two syndicates against each other in a bidding war.

"Worked just like we hoped it would," Can said, wonder roughening his voice. "It's hard to believe, but the Brits paid three hundred thousand up front, and I'll get a two percent royalty on every ounce of gold that comes out of the Johnson Mine." It was a sweet deal and strongly indicated that Can's strike was a rich one.

Sam thought about Can Johnson's good fortune as he walked home in the darkness. It wasn't going to be like that for him. Soon he would have to accept that no syndicates would enter a bidding war to gain control of the L&D. Even if a miracle occurred and he somehow put his hands on enough development money to hire a crew of miners, there wasn't enough time left to blast and clear a dozen drifts to map the ore branches. Even if he could prove beyond doubt that he had more trailing veins of rich ore than branches on a tree, he'd still need several weeks for Marsh Collins to contact the syndicates and nail down a buyer. But he didn't have several weeks.

The court hadn't decreed that he had to schedule

Daisy's surgery by the first of October. The court had decreed that Daisy's surgery had to be performed prior to October first. Therefore, he had to contact the surgeon at least by the middle of September. That was five weeks from tomorrow.

Angie's voice floated out of the darkness. "I've been waiting for you."

A lifetime had elapsed since he'd seen her in the ice cream parlor. It wasn't possible that had happened only hours ago.

He sank down on the bottom step of the kitchen stoop and leaned his back against her legs. She made a little movement as if he'd surprised her, but she didn't pull her legs away.

"I guess you know about Can," she said. He nodded. "You smell like whiskey and smoke."

"Do you want me to leave?" He hoped she didn't, because suddenly he felt too tired to move.

"No."

After a while she told him about Molly's diamonds and he smiled because buying Molly a fortune in diamonds sounded exactly like something Can would do. Then she told him about Lucy believing that she'd betray her mother if she let herself care for Angie.

"I'll speak to her."

"Lucy and I talked, and I think she feels better, but it would be reassuring if she also heard from you."

He was quiet a minute before saying, "It isn't going to work out the way I wanted it to, Angie." He'd dreamed such grand dreams. Had planned such grand plans. "For a time I thought it would."

The night was overcast and dark, chillier than the usual cool August nights. The only light came from Daisy's lamp shining through the kitchen window. The leaves of the lilac bush scattered the dim light and smothered the glow in shadow.

"I've been thinking about how we're going to manage." She touched the long curl tied at his neck, surprising and pleasing him. "If we sold everything . . . your horse and tack, my garnet earrings and pin, our wedding rings. And if we sold the house . . . how much money do you think we could put together?"

"Sell the house?"

"Just hear me out: I've been thinking about this. We could live in your tent, up on the claim. The girls and I could help you dig."

His impulse was to laugh, but her tone was too serious. Touched, he shifted on the step and took her hand.

"It means more than I can express that you'd willingly move into and live in a tent to help Daisy." He could no more imagine Angie cooking over a campfire or sleeping on the ground than he could imagine the surface of the moon. Sam suspected she couldn't imagine herself living in a tent either. But she was willing to do it. "It's not necessary to sell the house. I'll get the money for Daisy's operation."

"How?"

It depressed him to discover that Angie's hands were rough and chapped. Molly Johnson was dripping diamonds and Cannady was buying drinks for a hundred men tonight. While Sam's wife was sitting here with her chapped hands talking about selling the house and moving his family into a goddamned tent.

"I have a plan."

"Can you tell me about the plan?" she asked softly. "I don't mean to push, Sam, but I can hardly sleep for worrying. The days are flying past and there's only a few dollars more in the Daisy jar than we had a month ago."

"Not tonight, all right?" His plan would sound so paltry and disappointing after Can's big news.

Angie pulled her hand out of his and rubbed the side of her cheek. "There must be something I can do to help. Winnie Govenor sold pies to help Mr. Govenor get enough money to develop his mine. I could do something like that." She waved an insect away. "I could bottle my tomato sauce and sell it. Or noodles. Noodles take so long to make, I think women would buy them ready-made."

Anger, sudden and hot, tightened his chest. "Let's see. You want to sell everything we own, live in a tent, dig my claim, and sell noodles. And me? I guess I'll buy a hammock and take naps until my wife has scratched up the money we need, because I can't. Is that how you see it?"

"That's ridiculous!"

"I can do this, Angie. I can pay for Daisy's operation, and I will."

She drew a deep breath, audibly striving for patience. "Why are you angry? I just want to help."

The anger rushed out of him as quickly as it had come and he dragged a hand down his face. "You help most by doing what you're doing. By taking care of Lucy and Daisy so I don't have to worry and I have time to work on the L&D. By being here. By listening."

That's what he'd missed the most during his recent foolishness. These quiet talks at the end of the day. The nearness of her, the scent of her. The occasional accidental touches.

"Every time I look at the girls, I wonder if we'll still have them after October first." When he said nothing, she asked, "Are you going to borrow the money for Daisy's operation?"

"Assuming anyone would be foolhardy enough to lend money to an out-of-work contractor, how would I repay the loan? It could take years." He stared into the darkness. "And it would feel like a cheat. Borrowing the money is not an acceptable solution."

"Then tell me what is acceptable. Sam, please, I'm worried sick."

Discouragement weighed him down. The simple act of standing sapped his energy. "I don't want to talk about plans tonight," he said wearily. "I'd feel like a fool to lay out a plan that I hope and pray will net a few thousand dollars after we've just heard Can and Molly's good news about hundreds of thousands of dollars."

"Sam, I don't—"

"Can's been digging for his jackpot for years. He's worked hard; he never stopped believing. He and Molly deserve a wonderful future."

"But you wish it had been you," she added softly.

"I don't begrudge Can and Molly their jackpot. I just wish I could find mine, too." Pushing his hands deep in his pockets, he lowered his head and walked toward the entrance to his tent. "Goodnight, Angie."

Scowling toward the beckoning lights of town, he considered going back to the Gold Slipper and drowning his mood in a few mugs of beer. But he wasn't a man to brood over his troubles in public. Instead, he turned his face toward the lamp that Angie had set in the kitchen sink in case Daisy awoke and needed the reassurance of light in the darkness. After a few minutes, he sighed, then threw back the flap of his tent and walked inside.

Damned if the tent wasn't starting to feel like home.

Slowly, Angie pulled the brush through her hair, studying herself in the mirror. She looked as disheartened as Sam.

Like him, she didn't resent Can and Molly's good fortune. But it was hard not to want some of that good fortune for Sam and herself. Since she had arrived in Willow Creek at least a dozen men had celebrated a sudden rise to wealth. Such rewards could happen. So why didn't it happen to Sam?

If she was feeling this low and discouraged, what must he be feeling? Lowering the hairbrush, she tapped it absently against her palm.

Sam knew the men who had become instant millionaires, and he was always happy for them. There wasn't an envious bone in his body, Angie knew that. Sam's low mood after another man's good news wasn't based on resentment or rancor; he was just impatient, just wanted his turn to come.

Her gaze dropped to the top of the bureau and Peter's most recent letter. Peter was also an impatient man. Angie sighed again and tossed the hairbrush aside.

Peter was becoming annoyingly insistent. The letter on the bureau contained a well-reasoned argument in favor of her returning to Chicago immediately.

They no longer wrote of mutual acquaintances or items of common interest. Peter's letters had assumed an exasperated and imperious air, almost ordering her back to Chicago. This approach triggered Angie's independence and her Italian temper. Her responses had become short and clipped and repeated her oft-stated position with increasing annoyance.

A tiny suspicion had begun to form that the future was not as cut-and-dried as she had hoped. She tossed Peter's letter back on top of the bureau to answer tomorrow. If Peter truly cared for her, why couldn't he be patient? Or maybe she was being unfair.

An inner voice reminded her that not that long ago she

had felt wild with resentment that she had to wait to begin her life with Peter. Now delaying a life with him for a year or two seemed reasonable, perhaps prudent.

This circled her mind back to the husband she wished to rid herself of. And an odd thought burned color onto her cheeks. Given the annoying way Peter was behaving, it would serve him right if Sam kissed her again and if she enjoyed it. In fact, she thought, raising her chin, if Sam kissed her again she wouldn't feel guilty. It had occurred to her that really she should use their peculiar marital circumstances to learn a few things. At her age, her next husband, probably Peter but maybe not, would expect her to be at least somewhat experienced. The more she considered, the more she believed a case could be made that she owed it to her next husband to learn more about kissing . . . and maybe more about some other things as well.

She was out the back door and standing at the entrance of Sam's tent before she understood that she had intended all along to go to him.

Sam needed her tonight.

He rubbed his eyes, weary but not sleepy. Even a book discussing geologic formations in the mountainous West hadn't made his eyelids grow heavy. Swearing under his breath, Sam tossed the book on the low table beside his cot.

The day had been long and eventful, and parts of it ran through his mind over and over. The part that disturbed him most was his claim. Progress was so slow, and he hadn't discovered the vug that would solve all his problems. Closing his eyes, he raked his fingers through his hair and swore out loud.

A small sound made him blink, and for a moment he

thought he was staring at a vision conjured by wishful thinking.

Angie stood in the entrance of the tent, her long flowing hair shining like a halo behind her, outlined by the starry night. His breath caught in his throat. Silky curls of reddish brown curved over her breasts, tumbled down the back of her nightgown. Bare toes peeked from her hem.

"Has something happened?" Jumping to his feet, he faced her across the small space. And saw the midnight softness in her eyes and suddenly knew why she had come. "Angie." Her name rolled off his tongue, half whisper, half groan.

Stepping forward, he moved his hands up her arms to frame her face and tilt her mouth up to his. For a long moment he gazed into her eyes, trying to see into her heart and what she might be thinking and feeling. But no man could ever know a woman's heart, not completely. He would never understand her, and that was part of her fascination.

Slowly he lowered his head and lightly brushed his lips across hers, testing to make certain that he hadn't misread her intentions. She tasted of honey and biscuits and tooth powder and the sweetness that was hers alone. Her full breasts warmed his chest. He felt her tugging at the strip of rawhide at his neck, then she pushed her fingers into his loose hair.

"Angie."

The dreamlike state evaporated. She was here, not a wisp of imagination constructed out of his desire. She was solid and real. The faint rose scent of her hair and skin reeled through his senses, and he could feel the arousing shape of her body beneath the white drape of her gown.

Folding her in his arms, he crushed her against him. And this time when his mouth covered hers, his kiss was demanding, almost punishing in his need for her. Letting his hands drop, he cupped her buttocks and pulled her hard against his arousal, feeling the firm sweet curve of her through thin summer material.

"Sam . . ."

"If you didn't want this, you shouldn't have come here with your hair down and wearing your nightgown," he murmured hoarsely, kissing her again and again.

"It isn't that," she whispered, her breath hot and ragged.

His mind raced. Where? His cot was narrow, uncomfortable, and not sturdy enough to support the weight of two people. The floor of the tent was dirt. They couldn't go inside. Daisy occasionally awoke and stumbled into the kitchen to reassure herself at the light of the lamp in the sink. And if he and Angie went inside, they might make enough noise to wake both the girls. So where?

His hands moved over her with feverish desire, stroking, exploring, and he kissed her long and hard and deep, his palms cupping her breasts.

"Sam," she gasped, pulling back. "The light."

For an instant he didn't grasp her meaning. He wanted to see her magnificent full body. Then his mind cleared enough to comprehend that the canvas walls cast them in silhouette to any neighbor glancing their way.

"Wait." There was only one thing to do. Yanking the bedding off his cot, he spread the blankets over the dirt floor, then blew out the lamp and reached for her, sinking to the ground with Angie in his arms, her breath sweet and hot on his throat.

Kneeling on the blankets, their bodies pressed tightly together. He kissed her the way he had dreamed of kissing her from the first moment he saw her. But tonight was better than his boyish dreams. He held a woman in his arms, not a girl, with a woman's full lush body and a woman's desires. And tonight she knew what to expect.

Her fingers fumbled at the buttons on his shirt while he kissed her eyelids, her nose, her cheek, the trembling corners of her mouth. He caressed her breasts and felt her stiffen, then lean into his palms with a shudder of pleasure. His shirt parted and her hands, warm and eager, slid across his chest. She made a sound deep in her throat that made him feel wild inside.

Feverishly they tore at each other's clothing until they were naked in the darkness, discovering each other by touch and small gasps and murmurs of pleasure.

When Sam would have risen above her, she surprised him by pressing him flat on the ground. Then she kissed his throat and chest, and her lips burned nips and kisses down his body until he writhed beneath her attention and sweat slicked his brow.

"Angie. . . ," he whispered, then sucked in a hitching breath as her hand closed around him.

She lifted her head. "Shh. You did this to me."

A shudder of deep pleasure rippled down his body, and he stroked her naked back with his fingertips. In the darkness with innocence and anxiety no longer a factor, she shed all inhibitions in the delight of exploration and discovery. Using lips and hands, she found his greatest pleasure and her own power and reveled in both.

When he finally reared above her and plunged forward, she lifted to receive him and whispered his name. And it was as if they had been together always, attuned to each other's needs, to each other's rhythm. He knew the moist inner heat of her, the way her eyes would shine up at him, the way her lips parted and her breath emerged in small gasps. He knew her, and yet he had only begun to discover her.

One thing he understood without doubt. Afterward as she lay in the crook of his arm, panting to catch her breath, he knew he would never have enough of her.

Good Lord A'mighty. Sam's eyes widened in astonishment. He was falling in love with his wife. Correction. It had already happened. He loved her. Damn.

Closing his arms around her, he buried his nose and mouth in her tangled hair. He wanted to hold her forever, but it wouldn't happen.

When he awoke in the morning, lying on the ground next to his cot, Angie was gone. She came into the kitchen as briskly as always, with her hair pinned up, wearing an everyday skirt and a high-collared shirtwaist.

"Your shaving water is on the back of the stove," she said, as if nothing momentous had occurred between them.

Lucy poked her head out of the girls' bedroom. "Since there's no school, can we wear our wrappers to the table?"

Sam started to answer, then realized Lucy had addressed the question to Angie. His eyebrows rose and a smile of pleasure curved his lips.

"No," Angie said, an answering smile twitching her mouth. "Get dressed, please. Do either of you need help with your hair?" For summer play, the girls had been wearing braids.

"I can plait Daisy's hair, but I have trouble with mine." A shy, almost apologetic expression stole across Lucy's face. "Would you help me?"

In the past, Lucy had been more likely to reject Angie's help than to request it. Sam studied the long look the two exchanged. Something was happening here, something good.

"I'd love to do your hair," Angie said softly, walking toward their room.

Breakfast was Sam's favorite meal, even if he had to cook it himself. He liked starting a brand-new day where the dawn shimmered with promise and anything could happen. Most of all, he liked sitting down at the table with his wife and daughters. He'd rather eat bacon and eggs with Angie and his girls than dine with the crowned heads of Europe. He smiled at his daughters and realized the flyaway days had ended. Since Angie's arrival his girls looked neat and tidy, and their clothing fit.

Lucy and Daisy stared back at him with puzzled expressions.

"What?" he asked.

"You two keep looking at each other funny," Lucy said. Daisy nodded, swiveling her head between Sam to Angie.

"Funny? I don't know what you mean." But he had a suspicion.

Lucy gazed at Angie, who kept her gaze demurely downcast. "You both have, I don't know, soft eyes. Don't they, Daisy?" Daisy nodded. "And usually you complain about the way Angie eats her eggs, but you haven't said a word."

He stared at the godawful mess on Angie's plate, then she raised dancing eyes, and they both burst into laughter.

Sam couldn't have explained what was so wonderfully funny about Angie's stirred-up eggs and him forgetting to comment. He only knew he had loved ending yesterday with her in his arms, and he loved starting a new day looking at her across the table. He loved knowing she'd be here when he came home tonight, tired, dirty, thirsty, and longing for the softness of a woman's voice.

He had loved her ten years ago, and he loved her now.

Chapter 17

Everyone on Carr Street contributed to the success of Can and Molly Johnson's gala celebration and going-away party.

The neighborhood women baked for three days, vying to outdo one another with their cakes, fruit pies, cobblers, and bread puddings. Wonderful scents wafted from every kitchen as favorite potluck dishes simmered or bubbled or baked.

Abby Mueller's husband dug a fire pit in the Mueller backyard, lined the pit with rocks of similar size, and then chased everyone away while he laid a fire by his secret method, settled a pig in the coals to slow roast for two days, and covered the pit with a dome of rocks and dirt. Those who had savored Hugo Mueller's roast pork in the past wandered by to inspect the dome and lick their lips in anticipation.

Tilly Morgan's husband took up a collection for the kegs of beer that the men set up next to the bandstand Sam built. Days before the event Tilly started squeezing lemons, and her oldest girl went door to door soliciting sugar to make tubs of lemonade for the ladies and children.

Sam and Henry Church knocked together long tables to hold the food and built a dozen benches so folks could sit and rest their feet a spell during the dancing. They assembled sawhorses to barricade both ends of the block.

When the ladies weren't cooking or doing housework or inspecting the men's handiwork, they ran in and out of one another's houses borrowing a smidgeon of baking powder or returning a cup of flour, comparing notes and checking last-minute details.

"The hardest part was keeping our guests of honor from contributing like everyone else," Angie said, smiling at Sam as she tied his necktie. "I think Molly made Can a batch of molasses cookies just because she had to cook something or explode."

Standing this close, she felt Sam's warmth and the solid power of muscle and strength. She sensed the magnetic pull of his body and remembered the salty taste of his skin. For an instant she felt dizzy. Her fingers stumbled and she fought an impulse to step forward into his arms.

Sam gazed down with twinkling eyes as if he'd guessed what she was thinking. "It's been a week since you came to my tent," he murmured in a throaty voice. "I miss you."

"Hush. We agreed to be circumspect," she said, giving his tie a sharp tug.

"I miss kissing you and caressing you and licking that spot between your—"

"Sam Holland, you stop right now!" Then her eyes softened above fiery cheeks. "Soon."

Over and over again she promised herself that making love to him was a learning experience, nothing more. And how fortunate she was to have Sam as her teacher. He seemed to know a great deal about the subject.

"You're blushing," he said, grinning down at her. "Whatever might you be thinking, Mrs. Holland?"

"Nothing I can say aloud when the girls will be running in the front door any minute."

As if a mention became a summons, Lucy and Daisy ran inside, eyes bright with excitement. "We put our pies at the end of the table like you said. The table was one cloth short so we borrowed a table cloth from Dilly Crane's mother."

Daisy spun in a lurching circle, her golden hair flying like silk. "Are you really going to play the fiddle, Papa?"

"That I am. Will you fetch the case, please? But we have several fiddlers, so I won't be playing all evening. You ladies save me a dance."

Daisy's excited smile altered to distress. "I don't like to dance."

"Well, you're going to tonight," Sam promised. "You can dance at the party or you can dance here in our kitchen after the party. But I'm going to dance with the three prettiest ladies and that includes you, Miss Daisy Holland."

A smile of adoration lit her face and she laughed. "I'd rather dance after the party."

"Well then, I think we're ready. Shall we go see what good things there are to eat? I believe I'll start with Angie's famous beef noodle stew."

"Me, too," Lucy said loyally. Since the day she and Angie had talked, she'd developed a new attitude toward a lot of things.

"And me, too," Daisy said.

They stood smiling at her, her handsome husband and his beautiful daughters. And Angie's throat tightened at the thought of how amazingly different her life had become in so short a time.

There was no leisure in which to read a novel or compose long, amusing or informative letters home. A list of chores demanded every available minute; most of the time she felt she'd never catch up. And something always ached, either her knees from scrubbing the floor, or her back from bending over the sink and over her sewing, or her arms from carrying heavy baskets of wet clothing outside to the line.

She couldn't recall what she used to worry about, but now most of her concerns dealt with the children. Where were they? What were they doing? Were their good dresses ready for Sunday school? Had they cleaned their plates, done their chores? How old should they be before they stopped playing kickball? And how did they manage to create that tender ache in the chest at the end of the day when they knelt in their nightgowns, their faces scrubbed, their hair shining in the lamplight, and bowed their heads over small hands tented in prayer?

Her eyes lifted to Sam's tanned face and she frowned at her conflicted emotions. No one in Willow Creek thought of her as "the Bertolis' poor abandoned daughter." When she attended church or a grand opening or a farewell party or a backyard gathering of neighbors, she had an escort, a husband of her own. A man who opened doors for her, who saw her safely across a street, who went home with her at the end of the evening. A man whose tie she had tied, whose shirt she had washed and ironed. A man she fed and cursed and cheered, argued with and longed for.

Tonight she would sit with neighborhood friends and talk about ordinary things while scanning the crowd, looking for a tall, dark-haired man and keeping an eye peeled for two bright heads among the children. The Carr Street ladies wouldn't discuss elevating topics or current events. They would talk about quick recipes for wash day and how to bring down a fever and what brand of bluing worked best and where to buy the cheapest cuts of meat.

"Angie, are you crying? Your eyes are wet." Lucy came to her with a worried expression and clasped her hand. Daisy followed, peering up anxiously.

"What are you thinking about?" Sam asked curiously.

"I'm thinking there's no place I'd rather be tonight than right here. With the three of you." Turning her head, she scanned the kitchen-parlor area with the canvas ceiling, thickly painted walls, and pieces of mismatched furniture.

One man's shack was another man's castle. She had no idea where the phrase came from or why it suddenly popped into her mind. But she lived in a castle. "I don't know what's wrong with me tonight," she whispered, blinking hard.

"You feel bad because Mrs. Molly and Mr. Johnson are leaving, and we don't want them to," Lucy said promptly. She tugged Angie toward the front door.

"We don't like people to leave," Daisy added, taking Angie's other hand.

"We used to want people to leave," Lucy said, giving Angie a meaningful look, "but we don't anymore."

"That's right. We don't want you to leave," Daisy said.

And there it was, a problem in the making, one Angie had not considered. Already she knew it would hurt like a knife in her chest to say good-bye to Lucy and Daisy, but it hadn't occurred that her departure might hurt them, too.

Feeling Sam's stare, she lifted her head. They hadn't talked about divorce in weeks. Did he still want her to leave? Maybe he felt as confused as she did.

Sam picked up his fiddle case and opened the front

door. And the moment passed. He cleared his throat. "Looks like we're among the last to join the party."

Lucy and Daisy pulled her forward and out the door. The sun hadn't yet dipped below the peaks, but the western sky blossomed in rusty pinks and oranges and golds. Torches had been lined up along both sides of the block, awaiting twilight and the touch of a match. Already people crowded the long food tables, and a group of men talked and laughed around the beer kegs. Boys who had thrown off their jackets darted through front yards and over fences playing tag. Older girls chased along behind the boys while small girls ignored them.

"You have to see Mrs. Molly," Lucy said, excitement returning to her bright eyes.

"We made her a surprise."

Since Molly couldn't be kept away, Abby Mueller had positioned her at the table beside Hugo Mueller's splendid roast pig. Molly served slices of steaming pork as fast as Hugo could carve.

A calico apron protected Molly's best Sunday dress and she wore all her new diamonds. Diamonds flashed at her ears, throat, wrists, fingers. One sparkling brooch was pinned to her apron front and another had been attached to a tiara made out of colored ribbons twisted around wire shaped to resemble a crown.

"We made the crown," Daisy explained, clapping her hands in delight.

"Mrs. Molly hung the diamonds on it!"

Molly grinned and blew Lucy and Daisy a kiss across the table. "Unbelievable, isn't it? Can forgot to buy me a tiara. I would have been plum embarrassed to show my face tonight if it hadn't been for your girls." Lucy and Daisy smiled proudly and looked around to see who else had heard Molly's praise. Molly leaned across the table to Angie. "You and Sam come by the house after the party, will you? Me and Can have something we want to talk to you about."

Angie carried a plate of food toward a group of women talking about setting up a quilting bee. She listened for a while before joining a group who discussed the new school and where the new teacher might live. Then Mrs. Dryfus spotted her and asked if she had made a decision about singing in the choir.

An hour later, Angie slipped her plate into the dirty dishes tub, then wandered to a spot near the bandstand where she could see down the length of Carr Street. It surprised her that she knew everyone and knew them well, in fact. She had seen their laundry flapping on the line, had smelled their suppers. She had overheard a few arguments, had observed some hasty kisses. She knew who yelled at their children and who didn't. Who kept an immaculate house and who could tolerate a bit of dust and clutter. Sometimes she felt as if she had known these folks all of her life.

Molly had said, *Your girls.*

Her gaze swung toward the group of children following Andrew Morgan as he lit the torches up and down the street.

Your girls.

The simple words and not-so-simple emotions tightened Angie's throat and chest. What should have been a happy and relaxed, if bittersweet evening was turning into something else for her.

It was a relief to hear a burst of music from the bandstand. When she turned, she saw Sam standing under a line of swinging lanterns, sawing a bow across his fiddle strings. His tie and jacket had vanished, and he'd rolled up his sleeves. He stepped to the edge of the platform, winked at her, then bowed slightly and played a jig that she knew was just for her.

Amazed and delighted, Angie clapped her hands as others drifted toward the bandstand. Sam had told her he could play a fiddle, but she'd had no idea he meant he could play like this.

Molly appeared beside her. "Lordy, that man can make a fiddle sing, can't he?" She grabbed Angie and they dipped and skipped and twirled and danced in front of the bandstand until they were breathless and holding their sides. Then Reverend Dryfus and his missus spun past doing a polka step, while the audience clapped and toetapped and shouted encouragement.

On stage, Dick Juniper swung his fiddle under his chin and faced off with Sam, both of them playing furiously. At the end of the tune, both fiddlers lowered their instruments and grinned at each other, then bowed to the crowd who applauded wildly.

Before the evening ended, the composition had changed half a dozen times on the bandstand. Sometimes there was an accordion or a mouth harp or a banjo, sometimes only fiddles. The only time the music stopped was for a speech singing the praises of Cannady and Molly Johnson and wishing them well in their new wealthy life. Then Cannady stepped up on the bandstand and said how he and Molly would miss everyone and that everyone was invited to a party at their mansion in Denver as soon as it was built.

Along about midnight the torches began to sputter. All the desserts were gone, along with the beer and lemonade. People sought out Can and Molly for a few words, then drifted toward their homes, carrying empty potluck dishes and small sleeping children draped over shoulders.

Angie smothered a yawn and smiled at Lucy and Daisy, who could hardly keep their eyes open.

"Papa, can we dance tomorrow?" Daisy murmured, leaning against Sam's leg.

"If that isn't just like a pretty girl. Making a man wait."

"Let's tell Can and Molly that we'll talk to them in the morning. It's late," Angie suggested.

But Molly wouldn't hear of it. "You'll be busy cleaning up from the party tomorrow, and then Can and I are going to start packing. We aren't taking much with us, just some dishes, clothing, personal items." The diamond brooch swung from the homemade crown as she looked back and forth between Angie and Sam. "Please?"

They glanced at each other, then Angie nodded. "Let us get the girls to bed, then we'll run over for a few minutes."

"Good. I'll boil up some coffee."

By the time they went next door, the street was dark and only a few lights still glowed in the houses along Carr Street.

Sam yawned, then dropped an arm over Angie's shoulders. "Just one cup of coffee then we'll go, all right? Dawn is going to come awful early. Besides, I've said my good-byes to Can, and I imagine you've said your good-byes to Molly."

Angie and Molly had exchanged small mementos to remember each other by, had wept and promised to stay in touch. Denver wasn't too far to visit. And because of Can's continuing interest at the mine, he and Molly would return to Willow Creek from time to time. But

Molly's departure would leave a hole in Angie's mornings. Until very recently she hadn't realized how often she ran next door for a cup of coffee or a word of advice.

As they went in the back door, Molly gave them mugs of coffee and waved them to the kitchen table. She'd removed her apron and taken off her diamonds. Can had rolled up his shirt sleeves and loosened his suspenders.

"It was a nice party," Angie said. "I don't think there was a scrap of food left."

Sam blew on his coffee and nodded. "Hugo's pig sure went fast. Did the guests of honor get any before it was gone?"

"We certainly do appreciate everything," Can said, "but we didn't ask you here to talk about the party." He gave Molly a look. "You tell them."

Molly brushed imaginary crumbs off the oilcloth, then studied Sam and Angie's curious expressions. "You know how much we think of your girls. We couldn't care more for them if they was our own flesh and blood."

It was a nice thing to say, so Angie didn't understand why Sam suddenly sat up straight and stiffened.

"We know how hard you've struggled to meet the court's conditions, and the setbacks you've suffered. We know about the fires, and we have our suspicions as to who's responsible for that piece of trouble."

Now Angie sat up straighter. Something was going on here. She didn't know what it was, but she felt a prickle of tension that she'd never sensed with Can and Molly. Sam and Can held each other's gaze and a scowl had begun between Sam's eyes.

Molly also noticed the scowl, hesitated, then hurried on. "I had a little speech prepared, but . . . Well, the long and the short of it is this. We'd like to pay for Daisy's operation."

Angie started. Her mouth dropped open and her eyes widened then overflowed with tears. "Oh my God," she whispered. "Molly, you and Can are angels. You're a miracle."

"We can certainly afford to do it. We love those girls like our own. And we think it would be a travesty to yank Lucy and Daisy away from their parents and give them to the Govenors."

There it was again. Even in the midst of overwhelming joy, Angie noticed that Molly included her. She had said parents.

"I can't believe it. Bless you both. This is the most wonderful thing I ever heard of!"

"I got nothing against Winnie Govenor. She means well. But I don't think Winnie is particularly cut out for parenting. And I also think children should be raised by young people. We sure as shooting don't want to see those girls go to a man who'd start fires to ruin the father of his granddaughters."

Now Can leaned forward, his gaze holding Sam's. "We don't want you to lose your daughters."

"Thank you, thank you, thank you." Tears of joy and relief flooded Angie's cheeks. Her chest expanded as if an iron corset had fallen away, and a tremendous weight lifted from her shoulders. "You've saved us. You've solved everything." Gratefully, she accepted the handkerchief that Molly pushed into her hand. "Oh thank heaven. How can we ever repay you?"

"Then you'll accept our gift?" Can asked.

"Of course. A thousand times, yes," Angie gasped, sobbing with happiness.

Sam's voice was low and firm. "No."

Chapter 18

The coffee bubbling on Molly's stove sounded loud and cheerful, at odds with the tension at the table.

"Sam! What are you saying?" Angie stared in disbelief. It was as if she had never seen him before. "You can't mean that!"

Knots ran up Sam's jawline and his voice was as stiff as his spine. "Thank you, Can, Molly, but I can't accept your generous gift."

Can fell back in his chair and frowned at Molly. "What did I tell you?"

"Sam Holland, don't be a stubborn damned fool." Molly glared, then swung a stare to Angie. "Talk some sense to that man."

"Sam? Please. What are you doing?" Anguish thinned her voice. "We're going to lose the girls!"

"I told you I have a plan."

She didn't want to make a scene in front of Can and Molly, but she couldn't stop herself. Her voice spiraled sharply upward. "When do you intend to put this mysterious plan in motion? We're running out of time." Harsh, angry words scalded the back of her tongue, wanting to be said. But that would make the situation worse. She swallowed with difficulty and pleaded instead. "Sam, please, I'm begging you. We're all begging you. Let Can and Molly do this for Daisy. For heaven's sake, let them help us."

"Would help be more acceptable if we offered you a loan instead of a gift?" Molly's appeal was equally agitated.

Sam placed his hands on the table and slowly curled them into fists. "A gift or a loan wouldn't violate the letter of the law," he said finally, his voice expressionless. "But it violates the spirit of the law."

Angie didn't care about splitting hairs. She cared about keeping the girls. "Sam. In the name of heaven, think about this. Think about what's best for Lucy and Daisy."

Sam raised his head. "Laura gave me her daughters because she believed I would be a good and decent father. I would raise them and care for them and love them." Tilting his head back, he stared at the ceiling. "The court defined what makes a good and decent father. The definition is that a good and decent father would fix his daughter's crippled foot within a year's time."

"Oh Sam." The whispered words floated on a breath of despair. She knew how his mind worked, and what he was thinking.

"I agreed that definition was reasonable. I still do." Lowering his head, he examined the faces staring back at him. "If I can't pay for Daisy's operation myself . . . if I can't or won't do whatever is necessary to fix Daisy's foot . . . then I deserve to lose my daughters. Then they deserve better than me."

"Sam," Molly said after a minute, "you are full of horse manure."

A strained smile softened his expression for an instant. "Maybe. But if I were going to borrow money for Daisy's surgery, I would have done it last October. I would have spared her another year of embarrassment and ridicule."

"Damn it, Sam." White-faced and shaking, Angie pushed to her feet. "I agree with Molly," she snapped. "You're going to end up throwing away two little girls who need you. And why? Because of some noble-sounding notion about the spirit of the law? That's not the reason. This is about pride. You're setting pride above your daughters!"

He came to his feet in anger. "Stop right there. You're going too far, Angie."

"You're trying to prove something to yourself that no one cares about but you! Do you want to know something? What hurt the most was that you didn't come back for me. You left Chicago and you never looked back."

"I looked back a hundred times and you weren't there."

"In ten years you never came back for me. And I'll tell you why. Because nothing changed, Sam. You heard my father say that you'd never be successful, that you'd never amount to anything, and *you* believed him! You never asked if I believed him. You just walked away. And now you're going to walk away from our daughters for the same damned worthless reason! Because if you aren't successful enough to pay every penny of that doctor's fee, then you don't deserve your daughters. Like you didn't deserve a wife." Tears choked her. "And that's crazy wrong thinking!"

Molly turned to Can. "Let's go for a walk."

Can blinked. "It's after midnight. Besides, this is our house. If they need some privacy, they can go to their own house."

"We'd wake the girls," Angie snapped.

"Stay where you are." Sam spoke to Molly and Can, but he didn't move his hard gaze from Angie's flushed face. "We're finished here."

Trembling in anger and disbelief, Angie stared at his intractable expression. Then she dusted her hands together with a slapping sound. "Yes. We're finished."

Lifting her skirts, she marched across Molly's kitchen and out the door, slamming it behind her.

If his stupid pride cost him the girls, she would never forgive him. Never.

Anger, despair, and frustration kept her awake that night. Finally, near dawn she stopped fighting Sam's decision and focused her tired mind on trying to understand. The thing was, she did understand and a small part of her admired him. But she couldn't agree. However, one thing was utterly clear. Her opinion didn't matter.

Sam skipped breakfast rather than put himself and Angie through the charade of pretending before the girls that everything was all right. While he dismantled the bandstand, he reviewed what they had said to each other last night.

Once again Angie had chosen not to support him. She'd chosen to walk away rather than stand beside him and trust that he would do the right thing. That was what hurt most.

After a while he realized someone worked beside him. Straightening, he pushed back his hat as the sun shot over the peaks and lit the street.

"The guest of honor isn't supposed to do the cleanup," he said to Can. Irritation tightened his chest and made his shoulders flex. "Before you say anything, I still don't want your money." He narrowed his eyes. "And I don't want any advice."

Can swung his hammer and knocked two boards apart. Tossed them toward a pile. "You have to give a woman something to believe in, Sam."

"Damn it, Can. Stay out of this." He gave two boards a vicious smack with his hammer, prying them apart.

"Why haven't you told her how you're going to manage?"

Like it or not, he was going to get advice. "I have my reasons."

"They aren't good enough. She's worried and frightened." Can tossed two more boards onto the pile. "Most important, she's on your side. You're a blind fool if you can't see that."

Despite himself, Sam remembered Angie suggesting that they sell the house and live in a tent. Remembered her willingness to do whatever she could to earn money for the Daisy jar. And he remembered her blaming him for not sending for her. No matter what the subject, it connected somehow to the past.

He swung the hammer hard. "She knew where I was, I always made sure she had my address. She could have contacted me. She could have joined me at any point during those ten years."

"So you were too proud to beg for her to come, and she was too proud to beg you to send for her." Can straightened and wiped a hand across his brow.

"You don't understand all of it."

"I understand that neither of you are going to win a fight that's ten years old. And I understand that you think she doesn't believe in you because she isn't willing to blindly trust that you have a plan to keep your girls. Well, she's right. Angie's like Molly. They're both too smart to believe in a man just because he says Trust me. You and I didn't marry stupid women, Sam. If you want to keep Angie on your side, you're going to have to start trusting her."

"Damn it, Can. I trust her with my daughters, I trust her with my money, I trust her with my secrets."

"Then trust her with your pride. She wants to believe in you, son. Give her a chance."

"There's something about his plan that's bothering him, something he's not sure of. That's why he isn't telling you."

"He's testing me," Angie said wearily. "I finally figured it out. He wants blind faith, absolute unquestioning belief." It made her angry to think about. "I couldn't give him blind faith ten years ago, and I can't give it today."

Molly took a sip of coffee. "Every man ever born wants his woman to gaze at him with adoring eyes and gush, Whatever you say, honeyman." She smiled.

"Well, I can't do that. It was the same thing ten years ago. He wanted me to pick up and go west. He didn't tell me where in the west or what he'd be doing out here. Didn't tell me how we'd put a roof over our heads or food in our mouths. He probably had a plan then, too!"

"He probably did." Molly patted her hand. "Tell me something. Do you believe in Sam?"

"Of course I do." That had never been the problem, although Sam thought it was. "But how can I believe in a plan when I don't know what it is? That's the part that makes me crazy."

Molly shook her head and sighed. "Well then, all you can do is believe in the man." She studied Angie's expression. "Can you do that?"

Angie dropped her head in her hands. "What choice is there?"

The past used to be so clear-cut. Sam was to blame for their failed marriage. Period. Now she could see his side and could admit that she hadn't done right either. They were both at fault. Maybe it was the same now. Sam wasn't telling her his plan, and she couldn't muster blind faith. So they were stuck.

"There are always choices. You can believe in Sam and stand by him even if he's too damned stubborn to do right and tell you his plan. Or you can remain at odds with him, keeping both of you angry. Then for sure he won't tell you his plan."

"Maybe he doesn't think it's any of my business."

"Now you know that's not true."

"Then what is?"

"You may have been married for ten years, but you two are still working out living together." Molly smiled. "Each time you bump into a difference of opinion, you learn how to handle it better the next time. I imagine Sam is getting the picture that demanding blind faith isn't a good idea. And maybe you're getting the idea that you have to trust him to do right."

"At the moment," Angie said through gritted teeth, "I'd like to take that skillet off the stove and bang him on the head, drive him into the floor like a nail."

Molly laughed and looked toward the door when Lucy and Daisy skipped inside. "I've been waiting for you two. If we're going to finish that project we talked about, we need to do it today since Mr. Johnson and I are leaving tomorrow morning."

Angie's heart wrenched in her chest. "Oh Molly. How will I manage without you?"

"Abby, Tilly, and Dorothy have promised to keep you so busy, you won't notice I'm gone."

"I'll notice," Angie said softly. Before they both got teary, she stood and carried their coffee cups to the sink. "What project are you and the girls working on?"

"We can't tell," Lucy said quickly.

"It's a surprise." Every cell in Daisy's face and body betrayed that she wanted to tell Angie in the worst way. "I could give you a hint. . . ."

"No," Lucy and Molly said in unison.

After they went next door to Molly's house, Angie washed the dishes and cleaned up her kitchen, thinking about Molly's advice and about everything she'd considered last night.

There was no way around it. She had to believe in Sam's plan and believe that it would be successful. Truly she had no choice. But the bottom line was what she had said to Molly. How Sam handled his life and his daughters was none of her affair. He'd as good as said so. Heart aching, she went looking for him.

Sam saw her coming. She was heading toward Hugo Mueller's wagon wearing that tight-lipped fizzy look that hadn't yet boded well for him. He tossed the last of the bandstand lumber into the bed of the wagon, then took off his hat and wiped a sleeve across his brow before he walked forward.

"We have to talk, Sam."

"I know." She was beautiful when she was dressed to go out, but he found her the most desirable as she was now. Wearing a damp apron over an everyday dress, tendrils of reddish brown hair loose around her cheeks, her face flushed. Her lips were full and naturally rosy, an invitation to kisses, and her dark eyes flashed up at him in a way that made his stomach tighten.

"You're busy now, and I promised to help the women wash the dishes from the party. When will you have a few minutes?"

"Tonight. After the girls are in bed. By then, I should have something definite to tell you."

"Well, I can say what I have to say right now." She drew a deep breath and squared her shoulders, then looked him in the eyes. "I apologize for the things I said last night."

His eyebrows rose.

"I don't have a say. Lucy and Daisy are your daughters, not mine. I forget that sometimes, but last night you made it painfully obvious. Accepting help or not is your decision to make. It's your choice whether you lose them or not."

She pressed her lips together and lifted her chin. Then she turned on her heel and marched off to help carry the tubs of dirty dishes into Tilly Morgan's house.

Sam rubbed a hand across his mouth and watched her go, admiring the provocative sway of her hips and the way she carried her head, tall and proud. But he hated what she'd said.

If he lived to be a hundred, he'd never understand her.

Thirty minutes later, he headed down to the stable and saddled his horse.

Marcus Applebee was already waiting at the L&D when Sam arrived. Sam tied Old Brown to a tree and watched Marcus climb out of the main shaft, then he shoved his hands in his pockets and walked forward.

"What do you think?"

Marcus knocked his hat against his thigh, shaking the dust off, then nodded. "It's high-grade, all right. The assays came back on both drifts at well over five hundred dollars a ton."

That was as good as any mine in the district. "Then you're interested?"

Reaching into his jacket, Marcus pulled out a box of cigars, offered one to Sam. "My group would be willing to lend you some development money."

"I'm not looking for a loan." He didn't have time to develop the L&D. "I need an outright sale."

Marcus waved out a match and puffed. "At this point, you don't have much to sell. The drifts are just barely deep enough to show that at least one vein is likely ongoing." He slid a look at Sam. "But that vein could peter out in the next six feet. And you haven't dug far enough on either drift to know if there are other branches. Anyone who buys this mine is buying a wish and a hope. Not much else."

"Most of the mines around here are producing three hundred sixty dollars a ton," Sam said stubbornly. But he knew he wasn't negotiating from a position of strength. "I know in my gut that the L&D is going to be one of the richest producers in the area."

"Could be." Marcus turned to look out over the valley, his gaze following the train. "But I need more than your gut to justify buying blind. If my group buys the L&D, Sam, we're buying a pig in a poke. Right now nobody knows what's down there. Like I said, the vein could end in another few feet."

"Or you could hit a rich vug. Or the vein could have more branches than a willow."

"If you really believe that, then it's a mistake to sell." Marcus arched an eyebrow in Sam's direction. "You know that. You should beg, borrow, or steal the money to extend the drifts you've started and sink a half dozen more. Proving the promise is worth several hundred thousand dollars. You'll have something to sell."

"Like you said. I know that."

"Sam, we've been friends for several years. Keep your mine and develop it. I'll loan you whatever you need. Hell, I'll give you whatever you need. I'd rather do that than see you throw away a possible fortune."

He held the smoke on his tongue then slowly exhaled. Some would say there was a thin line between honor and stupidity, and maybe they were right. But he was in no position to take on debt, and his pride wouldn't accept the charity of a gift. He needed to do right by his daughter and by the spirit of the agreement he'd entered into. That was the only way he could justify Laura's trust, the only way he could believe he deserved his daughters.

"I truly believe the L&D will be a rich producer," he said at length. "But I suppose I could be wrong. I could spend thirty thousand dollars of borrowed money and come up dry. But it's a moot point, Marcus. I don't have the time to develop the L&D even if I had the money and an ironclad guarantee of hitting the jackpot." He pulled back his shoulders and focused on the ash growing on his cigar. "So. What's your best offer?"

"Damn it, Sam." They smoked in silence for a good five minutes, listening to the distant booms of dynamite and the train's whistle. "The best I can justify for a potential dry hole is five thousand dollars."

Disappointment bit the back of Sam's throat. Five thousand was a far cry from Cannady Johnson's windfall. But Can's mine had been developed enough for a buyer to know what he was buying.

"What kind of royalty?"

Marcus shrugged. "Two percent."

"Make it six."

"The syndicate will never agree to six percent."

"Why not? Six percent of nothing isn't going to hurt your group. And that's what you think you're buying. Nothing. I know you, Marcus. If you believed I had something here, you'd pay for it. Five thousand tells me you believe you're buying a hole in the ground and not much else."

In Marcus's mind, the five thousand was the same as a gift, and that irked him. Marcus Applebee wasn't seeing what Sam saw in the L&D. Then again, why the hell would he?

After a minute Marcus thrust out his hand to shake on the deal. "Five thousand up front and six percent royalty." He grinned. "If you're right and the mine comes in, your six percent is going to be the sweetest deal this district has seen. You'll be wealthy."

Sam gripped his hand. "I'll send Marsh Collins to your office to draw up the papers. How soon can I get the money?"

"It's a straightforward deal. Unless the lawyers tangle it up, I'd say you should have your money in a few days. Let's go to town and I'll buy you a drink." They walked toward the horses. "Either you just signed off a fortune for a pittance, or you palmed off a dry hole for a tidy piece of change."

Either way, now he had the money to keep his promises.

For the first time in a long while Sam was home to eat supper with his family, but it wasn't a particularly pleasant experience. Angie didn't say two words, and his daughters squirmed and pushed at their supper without eating much. Finally Lucy wiped a napkin across her mouth and asked if they could go.

When Angie didn't correct her as Sam expected, he said, "You know you're supposed to say, May I be excused from the table."

Lucy rolled her eyes, impatient to run out the door. "May we be excused from the table, please?"

"That's better. Where are you off to in such a hurry?"

"Mrs. Molly is waiting for us," Daisy said, sliding out of her chair.

"I want you home before dark."

Lucy and Daisy exchanged a conspiratorial glance. "We'll be back in a few minutes."

With the girls out the door and Angie not looking at him or speaking, the silence in the kitchen began to feel oppressive. Sam put down his napkin. "I guess you're mad at me."

"I was. I'm not anymore." Standing, she took the girls' plates to the pan in the sink. "Like I said, what you do is your own affair. I've already apologized for losing sight of that."

Sam listened to the weariness in her voice and studied the slump of her shoulders as she scraped the girls' plates. He would have preferred to see a flash of that Italian temper.

"The reason I didn't want to explain my plan is because I didn't know how it would work out."

"For a while I wondered if there really was a plan," she said without turning around. "Then I thought about it, and I know you wouldn't mention a plan if there wasn't one." She lifted her head and gazed out of the kitchen window. "You didn't tell me because your plan is none of my business."

Oh Lord. Standing, he started toward her, but the door flew open and Lucy and Daisy danced inside, sparkling with excitement. Their timing couldn't have been worse.

"Can't you come inside quietly?" Irritated, he changed direction and closed the door which they had left standing open to the flies and bugs. "Must you slam, bang, and run?"

They ignored him. At a nod from Lucy, Daisy skipped to Angie and tugged at her sleeve. To Sam's eye, it seemed that she dipped and lurched more tonight. "You have to sit down and close your eyes," she said excitedly.

"Whatever it is," Angie said in that tired, defeated voice, "can it wait until I wash up the dishes?"

Both girls turned stricken gazes toward Sam.

He cleared his throat. "Angie? Could you . . . ?"

"Three against one," she murmured. Then she flung down the utensils with a jarring clatter and wiped her hands on her apron. "All right. What is it you want me to do?"

Daisy took her hand and tugged her toward the table. "Sit here." When Angie was settled, not looking any too happy, Daisy gave Lucy a sparkling look. "Now close your eyes."

Frowning, Sam leaned against the sink, arms folded over his chest, wondering what this was about. Then Lucy came forward and he saw what she placed on the table in front of Angie. The irritation ran out of his chest like water out of the pump.

"Open your eyes," Lucy said, watching Angie's face.

"What . . . oh!"

Angie's hands flew to her mouth and tears sprang in her eyes. She looked at both girls, then carefully picked up the mended cup and saucer, holding them as if they might shatter in her hands. The glued cup would never be strong enough to use again, and a piece was missing near the handle, but her mother's cup and saucer had been returned to her.

"When . . . but how. . . ?" After cautiously placing the cup and saucer back on the table, Angie lifted the hem of her apron and wiped her eyes. "Oh my."

Daisy leaned against Angie's lap, smiling up at her. "I saved the pieces and Mrs. Molly helped Lucy put them back together again."

"I wanted to tell about it!" Suddenly Lucy went shy, looking at the floor. "I know it isn't good as new, but . . ." Now tears appeared in her eyes. "I'm so sorry. Angie, I'm so sorry. Mrs. Molly says the cup isn't strong enough to use, but you can still look at your mama's cup and saucer."

"Oh honey, thank you. Both of you." Opening her arms, Angie pulled the girls close in a tight, tearful embrace. "This is the nicest thing anyone ever did for me."

After a few minutes, Sam slipped out the door and sat on the stoop. He could hear them talking inside. Angie admiring the repairs, the girls relating every detail of gluing the cup and saucer and planning their surprise.

His daughters loved her. He'd seen that tonight, and he'd heard the love in their voices.

God help him, he loved her, too.

Chapter 19

"It was such a wonderful thing to do," Angie murmured, a hitch in her voice.

They stood outside in the darkness beside the clothesline pole, looking back at the house. Daisy's lamp stood in the sink, illuminating the mended cup and saucer on the sill.

"Are you warm enough?" Sam asked. At this altitude, the nights were always chilly, even at the end of August. But tonight an especially cold wind ruffled the edges of Angie's shawl. The wavering glow of the lamp in the window reached far enough that he could see her hand clutching the shawl close to her throat, but her face remained in shadow.

"I'll go inside in a minute. After you've said whatever you brought me out here to say." A gust of wind fluttered the curtains at the kitchen window. "I put a couple of small stones in the cup so the wind won't blow it off the sill."

"Angie, I need to tell you about my plan. What I've done."

She edged away from his hand on her arm. "That isn't necessary."

"Damn it, don't do this." The wind picked up, swirling cold dust around his boots. Sam didn't want to return to the house. He felt certain the girls were asleep, but just in case they weren't . . . "Come inside my tent, will you?"

Her fingers tightened on the folds of the shawl and he suspected she was remembering the last time they had been together in his tent, just as he did. Whatever that memory meant to her, it didn't extend to this moment. Her resistence was as tangible as his desire to hold her close to his body. "I only want to talk to you."

The faint light from the window slid across the gold band on her finger. She made a small sound, then slipped past him and walked toward his tent. "All right, Sam. But only for a minute."

Inside, he lit the lantern, then waved a hand toward his cot. "You sit there, I'll take the camp stool."

"You sit on the cot. I'll be more comfortable on the stool."

"Whatever you want," he said.

She sat down, arranged her skirts around her, and folded her hands in her lap before she looked at him. "Will this take long? It really is cold tonight." A gust of wind bowed the wall of his tent, died away, then came again. "Plus I'm tired, and I'd like to go to . . ." Pink stained her cheeks, and she waved a hand as if brushing something away. "Say what you want to say."

"I should have explained what I was planning, I guess I know that. I intended to, then we heard about Cannady's good fortune and I knew I wasn't going to come anywhere near his jackpot. By that time I'd already contacted Marcus Applebee and asked him to have one of his people assay the ore from the L&D. I didn't put off telling you because it was none of your business, Angie. Whatever happens here is your business." The lantern light shone directly on her face and for a moment he was distracted by her beauty. How had he ever walked away

from her? And how could he let her go again? "Damn it,
I feel like I'm towering over you."

He sat on the ground, leaned his back against the cot
and rested his hands on his upraised knees. The wind
blew a stream of cold air beneath the tent, and not for the
first time Sam wished things were different between them
and that he wasn't sleeping alone in a tent while she was
sleeping alone in the house.

Angie frowned. "What does Marcus Applebee have to
do with anything? Why would you ask him to have your
ore assayed?"

Speaking quietly, he told her what he had done.

"Oh Sam." She stared at him. "You sold your mine?
For only five thousand dollars?"

Only five thousand dollars. "And a six percent royalty." Now that the deal was done, doubt crept into his
mind. As sure as he was sitting here, he'd never see a
dime's worth of royalty. But he was enough of a dreamer
that it gave him something to hope on, however remote.

"You believed in your claim. Couldn't you have done
like Cannady and borrowed enough money to—"

Holding up a hand, he cut her off. "No, Angie. That
would be too much of a risk. If things went wrong, I'd
end up saddled with debt, and you'd never get your divorce." The word hung between them. When she didn't
say anything, he bit the inside of his cheek, thought
about that bastard Peter De Groot, and went on. "This
way, there's money for Daisy's operation, the divorce,
and enough left that I can move the girls out of Willow
Creek. Denver is booming; there should be plenty of
work. I plan to speak to Can about building his mansion."

"You've worked so hard on that claim." She looked
genuinely upset. "It was your dream."

He met her eyes. "I've thought about this. I'm never

going to be the kind of success that would have impressed your father, and that's what the dream was. You were right. I've wasted ten years trying to prove something to your father."

He pushed a hand through his hair, thinking what a fool he had been. Instead of focusing on what he loved, instead of using the years to build his construction business, he had drifted from mining camp to mining camp, tramping the mountainsides in search of an easy jackpot to impress her father. He doubted five thousand dollars would have changed her father's opinion.

"Do you know what galls me most?" He stared at her. "I didn't stick up for myself that night."

"I didn't stick up for myself either," she said in a low voice. "I just left the room when my father told me to."

"I should have told him that I might not be successful in his eyes, but you would never want for a home or food on the table and a few pretty lady things." Like the rose soap she loved so much. "But I let your father put it in my head that a man who worked with wood could never be as good as a man who worked with brick and could never deserve his daughter."

"I should have stayed in the parlor with you. I should have told my parents that I was a grown woman and married, and you and I would decide our own future."

"I've spent ten years treating my profession like a hobby that paid just enough to allow me to search for silver or gold." He watched the lantern light seeking out the red in her dark hair. "Consequently, your father's prediction came true. I haven't been successful. If I'd stood up to him and believed in myself, by now I might have been a prosperous contractor." They would have been together all these years.

"I'm sure you would have been. But—"

"What are you looking at?" She kept glancing at the wall behind him with a puzzled expression.

"There's a light on the other side of the tent, and it's growing brighter."

"A light?"

"I can't figure where it's coming from."

Sam turned his head to examine an orange glow that flickered against the canvas wall, receded, then flashed brighter and higher. For an instant he didn't register what he was seeing. Then he swore and jumped to his feet. "Fire!"

For a frozen moment neither of them moved, then they raced outside and halted in horror.

Whipped by the wind, flames leaped along the back wall of the house, licking at summer-dry wood. The curtains at the kitchen window blazed in tatters. Already the canvas ceiling above the sink was a sheet of racing flame. In seconds the kitchen would be an inferno.

Spinning on his heel, Sam dashed into the tent and emerged with a blanket covering his head and shoulders. Running toward the back door, he shouted over his shoulder. "Go to their window!"

Oh God, the girls. Angie's paralysis broke and she grabbed up her skirts and sprinted forward, then around the corner and into the darkness. Cold wind tore at her hair and skirts. Ringing filled her ears which later she would identify as the urgent tolling of the fire department bell.

On this side of the house, the ground dropped away. Screaming, "Lucy! Daisy!" she stretched up on tiptoe, but only her fingertips reached the sill. Swearing, gulping air, she frantically looked for something to stand on, but all she found was a boulder she couldn't possibly move. Damn, damn.

Smoke billowed out of the girls' bedroom window. Frantic, shouting over the heavy pounding of her heart, Angie screamed their names again and again, wringing her hands, unaware of frightened tears streaming down her cheeks.

Then Sam appeared in the smoke at the window, holding Daisy's limp body in his arms. "Angie!"

"Here! I'm right here!"

A soft whoosh preceded a sudden blaze of fire and light behind him. The blanket was gone. So was one of his sleeves. A finger of fire flickered on his collar. Fear and horror closed Angie's throat.

Before Sam turned back into the blaze behind him, he lowered Daisy as far as he could, then dropped her the remaining two feet into Angie's outstretched arms.

Daisy's weight sent Angie to her knees on the hard rocky ground, but she didn't notice. The child lay in her arms, limp and heavy, her eyes rolled up in her head.

"Daisy! Daisy!" Gasping and sobbing, she set Daisy on the ground and pounded her back. "Breathe! Damn it, breathe!" Daisy's head lolled on her shoulders. Grinding her teeth, half crazy with fear and terror, Angie pounded the child's back.

Daisy's small body convulsed, then her mouth opened on a sucking sound and her chest expanded.

"Angie!" It was Sam.

Stumbling over her skirts, she jumped up and reached for Lucy. Again she went down on her knees as Lucy's weight fell into her arms. But before she could try to revive the child, she had to smother the flames racing up Lucy's nightgown. Roughly, she rolled the unconscious little girl in the dirt.

Dimly she realized that Sam had jumped and landed beside her. "Move away from the house," he croaked, his voice choked and raw from the smoke. He slung Daisy over his shoulder and tugged at Angie's collar.

"Wait, wait!" His shirt was on fire. Oh God, oh God. Frightened, sobbing, Angie beat at his back with her bare hands. When the flames were extinguished, she scooped Lucy into her arms and staggered away from the house.

"No," Sam shouted. "This way. Toward Molly and Can's."

Now she saw that the wind snatched bits of ash and flame and flung them toward the unoccupied house on their right. Changing direction, Angie cradled Lucy next to her body and ran between the house and Sam's flaming tent.

When the darkness and cold wind told her that she was out of immediate danger, she sat Lucy on the ground and shouted the child's name and pounded her back.

Molly's nightgown billowed around her and Angie's nostrils pinched at the sudden stinging smell of ammonia. Molly waved the vial beneath Lucy's nose. "Come on, come on, come on."

Lucy's mouth opened in a gasp and she sucked air into her lungs. She coughed, struggled to breathe, then coughed again.

Sobbing, Angie pulled the child into her arms and didn't let go even when she felt Lucy's arms wrap around her neck and cling so tightly it hurt. Harsh ragged breathing rasped in her ear.

"Daisy," she gasped at Molly.

"Can took her to Abby Mueller's house. Come on, I'll help you get Lucy there."

For a moment Angie didn't understand. Molly's house was closer. But too close. If the wind shifted . . .

They hurried around the far side of Molly's house, well away from the flames, then crossed the street. Abby waited in her doorway, reaching for Lucy. "Daisy will be all right," she assured Angie. "Tilly's fixing warm water and honey for their throats." She ran a quick eye down the bare legs beneath Lucy's burned nightgown. "The burns don't look too severe. Doc Poppell will be here soon."

"Don't leave me," Lucy croaked as Abby took her out of Angie's arms.

"I'll be right back, darling." Lucy's face was streaked with soot and smoke. Red burned spots dotted her legs. "Stay with Abby for now and look after your sister. The doctor will be here soon to help. Try to be brave, darling girl." She kissed Lucy a dozen times before Abby carried her inside. "Where's Sam?" she asked Molly, fear in her eyes.

"Probably on the bucket brigade."

They stared across the street at a hellish nightmare. Sam and Angie's house was a solid block of fire, crimson flames leaped from the roof, lighting the night. And now the unoccupied house was also burning. Glowing ash floated on the wind, spiraling down on rooftops and into the street and yards.

As Angie and Molly watched, stunned with shock, horses drawing the fire wagon galloped down Carr, the bell atop the tanker clanging wildly. Faster than Angie would have believed possible, men had the hoses out and attached to the tanker. A volunteer brigade had also formed; a line of men stretched from the pump in Dorothy Church's yard and across the street, passing buckets of water toward the flames.

At first Angie didn't understand why the attention focused on the property beyond the unoccupied house. Then she realized their house and the unoccupied house had been given up as lost. The urgency now was to contain the fire and stop it from spreading and consuming the town.

Wind swirled her hem and when she looked down, she saw that falling ash had burned small circles in her skirt and shirtwaist. For the first time Angie noticed a large charred hole on her right sleeve. But right now she didn't feel any pain. She felt nothing but shock at what she was seeing and a numb pervasive horror when she thought about what had almost happened. Lucy and Daisy could so easily have died. A shudder wracked her frame.

"I need to get dressed," Molly muttered as if she'd just realized she was standing in the street in her nightgown and bare feet. She ran toward her house with Angie behind her.

"We should move your things outdoors," Angie called. "In case the wind turns."

Hugo Mueller stopped them at Molly's front door. "You can't go in there," he said sternly. "It's too dangerous. If the wind shifts, this place will go up like a pile of straw."

Can and another man were on the Johnsons' roof, stamping out bits of flaming ash.

Molly shoved Hugo aside. "If the house bursts into flame, I'll notice. Meanwhile, I'm going to get dressed."

"Molly Johnson, you stubborn old—"

Angie ran inside after Molly. "Stay there," she shouted to Hugo. "I'll pass things outside, you move them into the street."

"Just the boxes," Molly yelled, rushing toward her bedroom. "And my medical bag. The rest can burn for all I care."

Angie worked quickly, dragging the packing boxes to the door where Hugo hauled them to the street. Where was Sam? Was he all right? And the girls. How badly were they injured?

After Molly had hastily dressed, Angie left Molly and Hugo to finish saving whatever Molly wanted saved, and she ran to the bucket brigade, moving down the line peering into smoky sweating faces, but she didn't see Sam.

The house next to the unoccupied house burst into flame with a loud popping sound, and the brigade line veered. But Dorothy Church's husband saw her and shouted, "Sam's on the hose line."

Another tanker had arrived and Angie lifted her skirts and ran toward it, frantically seeking a tall man in a burned shirt. When she spotted him, tears of relief scalded her eyes. Thank God, thank God. For an instant their eyes met and she saw Sam's shoulders slump with the same relief that made her own heart pound. They stared at each other across the snaking hoses, the smoky orange light flickering on their faces, then Angie raced toward Abby Mueller's house.

Both girls were sleeping. Abby had washed their faces and she'd immediately applied molasses and flour to their burns.

"That's the best thing she could have done," Dr. Poppell said from Abby's sink. He dried his hands, but the tang of linseed oil still clung to his skin. "The molasses and flour protected the injuries and kept the air out until I could get here."

Angie lowered her head and raised a shaking hand to her brow. "How badly are they hurt?"

"Both children have burns on their legs. The oldest girl's burns are more serious than those of the girl with the clubfoot. The oldest may have some scarring, time will tell. But they were lucky. It could have been worse." He talked to her about changing the dressings. "They'll both have sore throats for a while, from the smoke. For the next few days have them gargle with the white of an egg beaten to a froth in a small glass of sugar water. I've given them doses of laudanum for the pain and so they'll sleep. I'll leave some with you." He laid aside the towel. "Now let's have a look at your hands, Mrs. Holland."

"My hands?"

Blinking, she extended her hands. Angry red burns dotted the backs, blisters had risen on her swollen palms.

"That's a nasty one on your arm; it's likely to scar," Dr. Poppell said, ripping open her sleeve. "We'll bathe the areas with vinegar first."

When he'd finished treating the burns and applying cotton and wrappings, he asked if she, too, would like some laudanum to help her rest.

Angie shook her head. With her hands bandaged, she couldn't help the women take water to the men, but she could stand in Abby's yard and watch her home burn.

The sun rose on blackened smoking ruins.

By the time the wind died and the men got the flames under control, four houses had burned to the ground. A brick chimney chase was all that remained of the Koblers' house. One wall still stood on the Greenes' place. The unoccupied house had burned to the foundation, and all that was left of Sam's house was a sludge of wet debris.

He stood near the charred grass where his tent had been pitched, staring at the devastation, at wisps of smoke curling out of the ashes.

"I'll kill the son of a bitch," he said between his teeth. As soon as he had his family settled, he'd take the train to Colorado Springs, find Herb Govenor, and beat him to death with his own hands. He didn't care that his hands were swollen and seeping. A bullet wasn't personal enough. A bullet was too swift an end for any bastard who would let his granddaughters burn rather than see them in Sam's care.

"Who are you going to kill?" The police chief, Darrel Connelly, handed Sam a cup of coffee, then rocked back on his heels and studied the smoking remains of Sam's house.

"I know who started this fire," Sam said thickly, his eyes narrowed into burning slits. "The same fricking son of a whore who started the fires at the Union Hall and up at Whittiers' place."

Connelly turned his head. "That would be Albert Wales, who's sitting in my jail right now." Sam stared at him. "Caught him red-handed, trying to burn down the new hotel three days ago."

"You caught the arsonist, but you won't get the man who hired him because I'm going to kill the bastard first." And he would enjoy it. Killing Herb Govenor was all he could think about.

"I know who you think hired Wales, but Sam, you're dead wrong. We've kept this quiet while we've been checking things out. Wales acted alone; he wasn't hired by anybody. He's ex-union, and he worked for Whittier until Whittier fired his butt. He went after the hotel because he heard Whittier was part owner." Connelly studied Sam's expression. "He knows you by sight, but he didn't know you were the builder on the union and Whittier projects. He says he doesn't have anything against you, and I believe him. When we first interrogated him about you, he didn't know who or what we were talking about."

A sinking feeling stole through him as the truth sank

in. Govenor had nothing to do with the fires. But Sam recalled the fire at the Dryfus place that no one knew about but him. It was something to ponder later. "If you're sure that Wales is the arsonist, and he couldn't have started this fire because he was in jail," he waved a hand at the smoke drifting off the rubble in front of him, "then who did start this?" Part of him refused to give up the belief that it was Herb Govenor.

"I think Dale can answer that," Connelly said as the fire chief walked up to them. "Tell Sam what you told me."

Dale Mercer waved Sam forward to the edge of the rubble. "From what you've said and from what we can see, the fire started here, on the kitchen side of the outer wall." Squatting down, he poked a stick in the debris. "You see this?" He found the sink, then stirred some glass shards and a melted lump of metal. "That was a lamp. Based on my experience, I'd say it's about a ninety-nine percent certainty that the fire started here." He gazed up at Sam. "I can't figure why you'd have a lit lamp sitting in the sink next to the window, but I'm guessing you did."

Sam stared down at the bits of glass and melted metal. And he remembered the curtains fluttering at the kitchen window. Angie saying that she'd placed a few small stones in her mother's cup so it wouldn't blow off the sill. He could hear the wind buffeting the walls of his tent.

The fire had been an accident. A result of wind, Daisy's lamp, and curtains blowing too close to the flame. Christ.

His shoulders dropped, and now he felt the pain in his hands and on his back. He had been so certain that Herb Govenor was to blame. Hatred had kept him going during all the hours on the fire line. He'd wanted to kill

Govenor so badly that the feeling was slow to dissipate even now that he recognized the truth.

"There's no doubt?" he asked finally. But he stared at the melted base of the lamp and knew the answer. The fire and police chiefs talked for another fifteen minutes, but he was convinced before he heard what they had to say.

Raising his head, he looked through the space where his house had stood and watched Angie crossing the street, picking her way through mud and puddles of standing water. She looked disheveled and exhausted, and he guessed that she hadn't gotten any rest since he'd last seen her shortly before dawn. Seeing her bandaged hands made his chest tighten. Thank God she and his daughters were alive. Nothing else mattered.

"The girls are still sleeping," she said after nodding to Connelly and Mercer. "There's a meeting going on at Tilly's house. They're figuring out where to put up the Koblers and Greenes. Molly and Can have offered us their house, and I accepted."

Her chin lifted a fraction as if challenging him to disagree. But hell, why would he? They had nowhere else to go, and Molly and Can had planned to leave for Denver this morning.

"I want you to come with me, and I don't want to hear any argument." She gave him a fizzy look that said she meant it. "The doctor's been waiting all night for you." She took the coffee cup out of his hands and tears filled her eyes. "Oh Sam." The skin on his hands was puffed and cracking. "Molly has breakfast waiting at her house. I expect she'll have to spoon-feed us, too."

As it turned out, her prediction wasn't far wrong. By the time Doc Poppell finished with him, bandages covered his back and parts of his chest. His hands were like

Angie's, thickly wrapped except for the tips of his fingers. After a few bites of Molly's flapjacks, he gave up trying to manage a fork.

"I'm not hungry anyway," he said, leaning back from his plate.

Molly gazed at him across the table. "Looks like you need a haircut, Sam Holland. That curl at the back of your neck is about gone. You were right lucky that the rest of your head didn't catch fire." She put down her napkin and stood. "I'll get my scissors. If I can find them."

Refusing any help, he picked up his coffee cup with his fingertips, had a sip, then told them about Albert Wales, the arsonist, and how the fire had actually started.

"Daisy's lamp," Angie repeated softly, falling back in her chair. She closed her eyes. "I should have thought of it. I put the pebbles in Mama's cup because the wind was blowing. Why didn't I think about the curtains fluttering over the lamp chimney? None of this would have happened if—"

"It's not your fault." Sam's voice was almost gone. His throat hurt like the devil despite the concoction the doctor had made him drink. The poultice beneath the cotton wound around his neck didn't seem to help much either.

"And the money in the jars." Angie rubbed her fingertips across her forehead. "I'll poke around in the ashes and see if I can find any unmelted coins."

"We'll be out of here as soon as I wash up the dishes and Can brings the wagon around to take our boxes to the depot," Molly said from behind him. He felt her fingers in his hair, then the slight tug of the scissors. "You can have the house as long as you need it. In fact, I'll bet

Can would sell it to you for a dollar and a promise to come visit us in Denver."

When Sam said nothing, Angie stepped in. "I'm not too proud to buy your house for a dollar. As soon as I find the coins that were in the jars."

"It's a deal."

"Thank you," Sam said after a minute.

Habit made him feel rushed, as if he needed to get going. But his claim now belonged to Marcus Applebee's group, someone else was building the school, and he couldn't solicit work until his hands healed.

As if she'd read his mind, Angie's gaze softened. "Get some rest, Sam. Things will look brighter after a few hours' sleep."

He doubted it. Next week he'd give her the money for her divorce, and she would leave him.

Chapter 20

By noon on Tuesday, the Willow Creek and Victor churches had organized donation drives to help the victims of the Carr Street fire. Housing was found for the Kobler and Greene families, and a steady stream of people appeared at the doors of the victims, bringing food, clothing, toiletries, and items such as body soap, laundry soap, tooth powder, and all the sundries folks required for civilized living.

Overwhelmed with gratitude but needing a brief escape from the constant stream of visitors, Angie left Abby and Tilly to answer the door and accept the welcome donations, and she took a cup of coffee outside to Sam.

She spotted him standing beside the debris and paused a moment to enjoy the look of him. Molly had left his hair long enough to brush the top of his collar, but he looked different without the curl at his neck. Sam Holland could never appear ordinary or less than heart-wrenchingly handsome, but her roguish pirate was gone. From a distance, he reminded her of the boy she had fallen in love with so long ago.

"Thank you," he said gratefully, accepting the coffee and holding the cup with his fingertips. "Are the girls still sleeping?"

"Yes."

Angie walked to the edge of the foundation and peered down at the charred and ashy remains. Everything she owned had been lost. Her clothing, the silver-backed hairbrush she'd received for her twentieth birthday, her hats and embroidered handkerchiefs. Her mother's cup and saucer. Peter's letters.

The fire chief had told them that tomorrow they could sift through the debris to see if any of their belongings had survived the fire. Looking at what little remained, she couldn't imagine that anything had.

"I'm keeping the girls dosed with laudanum. The doctor said sleep was the best thing. He stopped by this morning to help me change their dressings, and said he was pleased. He said we can lessen the laudanum dose tomorrow." She glanced at the wrappings on Sam's hands. "I need to change your dressings."

"Let's do it later. I'm meeting with Marsh Collins in about an hour to sign the papers on the L&D. Marcus is rushing the paperwork because he knows we need the money."

She didn't ask how Sam felt because she could guess. Despite Dr. Poppell's treatment, the burn on her arm was painful every minute; there was no respite. Her hands didn't hurt if she was careful, but she'd bumped them this morning and cried out in tearful pain. Most of Sam's burns were worse than hers.

She studied the bruised color under his eyes and the lines framing his mouth. "Sam, you need to get more than an hour's sleep."

Angie had borrowed a cot and set it up in Molly's small parlor area. They had put the girls in the single bedroom. Sam insisted he didn't need a place to sleep as the burns on his back and chest made it painful to lie down. When Angie had risen during the night to check on him and the girls, she'd found Sam dozing at the kitchen table, bent forward with his head cradled on his arms.

"If you'd take some laudanum, I think you could sleep on a cot."

"Maybe tonight," he said.

Definitely tonight, she thought, concerned about the exhaustion drawing his face. She would have said so, but a carriage rolling down Carr Street caught her attention. Her heart sank when she recognized Herb Govenor handing Winnie to the street.

"Sam," she said quickly, placing her bandaged hand on his arm, "please don't make a scene. They must have come because they're worried about Lucy and Daisy." Sam's face had darkened and his eyes turned as hard as blue marbles. "Whatever we think of these people, they are your daughters' grandparents. And Sam? This wasn't Herb Govenor's doing."

Winnie nodded toward them before she headed to Molly's door. Herb Govenor scowled, then skirted the crumbling foundation, looking out of place in his top hat and immaculate city clothing.

"What do you want?" Sam growled.

Govenor bowed to Angie, then glanced at Sam's bandaged hands. "I know you think I'm responsible for the fire, Holland, but you're wrong. I had nothing to do with this." He waved a hand at the ashy destruction. "I would never put my granddaughters in danger. I'll swear to that on a Bible."

"You let me think you were responsible for the fires at the Union Hall and the Whittier place."

One of Govenor's eyebrows rose as if he'd expected at least an argument, then he leaned on his walking stick. "I had nothing to do with that. When I heard what was happening to you because of those fires, I wished I had arranged them," he said flatly. "If you wanted to think I did . . ." He shrugged, then gave Sam a look of curiosity. "I was certain you'd blame me for this." A head jerk indicated the rubble.

"I did until I learned the arsonist was in jail. This fire started by accident."

"But you arranged the fire at Reverend Dryfus's site," Angie said, stepping closer to Sam. Herb Govenor had the same white-gold hair that Lucy and Daisy shared, but it was hard to warm to this man, even knowing it must have been difficult for him to come here today.

"Who lit the match isn't important, but his instructions were to harm no one and not to cause major damage." Govenor met Sam's unwavering stare. "I wanted you out of business."

"You got what you wanted. But you won't win custody of my daughters. Today I'm signing the papers for the sale of the L&D Mine," Sam said, speaking slowly. "After the signing, I'll go straight to the Sylvan Saloon and use their telephone to ring Daisy's doctor in Colorado Springs, and we'll settle on a date for Daisy's operation. Marsh Collins will inform the court of the date, which will be comfortably before the deadline. You've lost, Govenor."

"I already heard about Applebee's offer." Herb Govenor straightened his spine and pulled back his shoulders. "I also came to talk about the future." He hesitated. "I'm not a man to beg, Holland, and I won't. But Lucy and Daisy are our granddaughters, the only thing we have left of our daughter. I'm asking you to allow us to see them occasionally."

"Give me one reason why I should. One reason why I shouldn't tell you to go to hell and walk away."

"We're the last connection Lucy and Daisy have to their mother. We're blood kin. Our granddaughters have a right to know us, and we have a right to know them."

Angie's fingertips tightened on Sam's sleeve and she frowned up at him. "He's right," she said in a quiet voice. "I'm not betraying you," she said, seeing an accusation in his gaze. "I think it would please Laura if her family came together again. You'll raise your daughters, Sam. The major influence on their lives will be yours. But aren't they entitled to know their mother's side of their family, too?"

"Laura's parents turned their backs on her when she wanted to lead her own life!" His voice was low and harsh.

"We've all made mistakes." Her eyes locked to his. "What's more important? That you satisfy your dislike of the Govenors, or that your daughters grow up knowing their only grandparents?"

In the end it was his decision. She'd done what she could to influence him, anything more would be stepping over the line.

After nodding to Mr. Govenor, Angie gingerly lifted her skirts with her fingertips and returned to Molly's house. She came in the backdoor as Winnie was emerging from the bedroom, tears glistening in her eyes.

"When I think how close they came to dying . . ." She shook her head and pressed a trembling handkerchief to her lips. Then she slid a look toward Abby and Tilly. "Is there someplace we could speak privately?"

Ignoring Angie's protests, Abby and Tilly rose from the kitchen table and walked to the door. "We'll check in at our houses, then return in about an hour."

Despite championing the Govenors to Sam, Angie found it difficult to be civil to Winnie Govenor. She had to force herself to pour the last of the coffee into a cup and set it on the table in front of Winnie. If Winnie hadn't been a stiffly formal woman, she couldn't have watched Angie struggle to manage the pot and cup with her bandaged hands without offering to do it herself.

"I'll come to the point," Winnie said, twisting the hand-kerchief in her lap. "Mr. Govenor informs me that Mr. Holland will undoubtedly arrange Daisy's surgery to occur before the court's deadline. I won't say congratulations."

"I wouldn't expect you to," Angie said with a sigh.

"But . . . perhaps it's for the best."

That surprised Angie, being a greater concession than she had expected to hear from Winnie Govenor.

"I would have done my duty," Winnie hastened to add. "But perhaps it's best that children be raised by young people."

"Mrs. Govenor, I'm terribly busy. . . ."

She hadn't yet familiarized herself with Molly's kitchen. Donated clothing was piling up in the small parlor and it needed sorting and putting away. It was urgent that she contact Mr. Kravitz at once and arrange for new shoes for Daisy. They needed another icebox and more ice to hold the dishes of food arriving hourly. She had to borrow another cot for Sam. At some point he'd be able to lie down and they needed a place for him. Every few minutes she thought of something else that required her immediate attention.

"Mrs. Holland, please." Winnie's pride crumpled and tears swam in her eyes. "Please don't cut us off from our granddaughters. We want to be there when Daisy has her operation, and we want to be part of their lives. Please don't deny us access to our granddaughters."

"That's not my decision," Angie said softly. Despite the unpleasantness that had passed between them, and despite not understanding Winnie Govenor, she didn't want Lucy and Daisy to grow up without knowing Laura's parents. As much as she disliked the Govenors, denying Lucy and Daisy access to their grandparents seemed wrong.

"But you can influence Mr. Holland!"

She wasn't as convinced about that as Winnie Govenor seemed to be. But it didn't matter anymore. Angie still felt the chill that had chased down her body when Sam had told her that Marcus Applebee had been kind enough to rush through the money for the L&D.

"I'll be leaving soon," she said, testing the words on her tongue. Leaving Willow Creek, leaving the people she loved, leaving her heart.

"What are you talking about?" Winnie demanded.

"I told you the first time I met you. I came here to divorce Mr. Holland. He has the funds now, and the divorce can go forward."

Winnie drew back. "I don't like that at all."

Startled, Angie smiled. "You surprise me, Mrs. Govenor."

"A man like *him* needs a woman, that's plain. Mark my words, it won't be long before he marries again. And what sort of woman do you think she'll be?"

Angie blinked. This wasn't a subject she cared to consider.

"Heaven knows if she'll be fit to raise my grand-daughters!"

"As I recall, you don't consider me fit."

"At least I know you, and I know my granddaughters care for you. You're a plain-speaking woman, and so am I. We can speak our minds to each other. I know you have your faults, undoubtedly more faults than I'm aware of, but you remind me in many ways of Laura. Head-strong, stubborn, determined to have your own way." Pursing her lips, she thought for a moment. "I wonder if there's a way to get the court to prohibit your divorce."

Angie stood, signaling their conversation had ended. "Mrs. Govenor, stop trying to control other people's lives," she said gently. "It didn't work with Laura, and it won't work with me. As for your being present at Daisy's operation, I'll speak to Sam."

In fact, it was possible that she wouldn't be present herself, a likelihood she couldn't bear to consider. But remaining in Willow Creek until Daisy's operation meant continuing the present arrangement between herself and Sam. She didn't know how he would feel about that.

After Winnie left, Angie tiptoed into the darkened bedroom to sit beside the girls. Each wore half a dozen bandages, and each had several small red burns that weren't serious enough to require a bandage. Leaning over the bed, she kissed Lucy's forehead and smoothed her singed bangs, then kissed the side of Daisy's cheek.

Tears stung her eyes as she gazed at them. In the last five months she had learned that children were frus-trating, infuriating, and demanded enormous amounts of time, patience, and energy. They were also warm, funny, generous, giving, and loved in a simple straight-forward manner that squeezed one's soul.

She had learned that children didn't have to come from her body to be a part of her heart.

For ten years Angie had waited for her life to begin. She had believed life couldn't begin for her until after she divorced Sam, but she had been wrong. Blinking back tears, gazing at her sleeping daughters, she understood that her life had begun when she stepped off the train at the Willow Creek depot.

They had a picnic for supper, eating donated food in the girls' bedroom. Afterward, Sam delighted everyone by telling a bedtime story about a mother and father and two little girls who were accident prone. Someone in the family was always swathed in bandages.

"Like us," Daisy said, clapping her hands.

"Was the oldest little girl very very brave?" Lucy asked.

"Very brave," Sam said gruffly. "One day she fell down and skinned her knee to the bone. It hurt badly, but she just waved a hand and said, Pish, and carried on."

Angie hid a smile. "She said pish?"

"That's what she said. Pish."

Daisy and Lucy giggled and shouted "Pish!" over and over until they were all laughing. When it came time for goodnight kisses, the girls held out their arms to Angie, too, as if they always had. She kissed them both, her fingertips lingering on soft smooth cheeks, and she felt like crying.

At the doorway, she looked back into the room. "Daisy? Will you feel safe without a lamp in the sink? Your papa and I will be just outside your door."

Daisy yawned, immediately sleepy from the nighttime dose of laudanum. "I think so."

Angie blew them another kiss and quietly closed the door.

"I saw a couple of beer bottles in the icebox," Sam said. "Do you want one?"

"Thank you." She would have liked to go outside and

sit on the stoop as they always did, but Molly's house had only two steps and besides, the odor of ash was unpleasantly strong. They sat at Molly's table, and Angie smiled at the old faded oilcloth, remembering Molly's diamonds spread across it. "What's this?" she asked when Sam slid an envelope toward her.

"It's two thousand dollars." He rolled the beer bottle between his fingertips. "That should keep you comfortably during the year you're waiting for the divorce to be final."

Now it was real. But her life felt as if it were ending rather than beginning.

"I wish I could give you more."

"No, no," she whispered. "This is plenty."

Sam cleared his throat and raised his head. "I have a favor to ask. Will you stay until after Daisy's operation? I think it would comfort her and help her through the ordeal. And it's only another two weeks."

Now it was real. They were talking about her leaving.

"Some time ago I promised Daisy I'd be with her for the operation. If you hadn't said something, I would have asked your permission to stay until it's over."

"Asked my. . . ?" He shook his head and rested his bandaged hands on the tabletop. After a lengthy silence, he drew a breath. "We'll take the train to Colorado Springs. Stay in a hotel near the hospital."

"Did you decide to allow the Govenors to be there during Daisy's surgery?"

He didn't answer immediately. "I'd be happy never to see Herb and Winnie Govenor again."

"Do you think that's what Laura would have wanted?" Angie asked gently. "You said yourself that she hated being estranged from her parents."

"I can tell you this. If Herb and Winnie had won custody, they sure as hell wouldn't have allowed me to see my daughters!"

"That would have been wrong."

"Damned straight it would have."

She let his words hang on the night air. He wouldn't like it, he'd hate it in fact, but in the end, Sam Holland would do the right thing. Angie would have staked her life on that.

They sat in discomfort and quiet, the good mood of the bedroom picnic behind them.

"Are you still planning to move to Denver?" Angie asked finally.

He slammed the beer bottle on the table hard enough that the reverberation must have hurt his injured hands, then headed for the back door. When he didn't see his favorite hat on the hooks, he swore, then pushed one of the donated hats on his head.

"I'm going to the Gold Slipper. I'll see you in the morning."

Angie sat at the table until very late, remembering everything that had happened since she had arrived in Willow Creek. The tears and the laughter. The disappointments and the joys. Eventually she dropped her head into her bandaged hands.

She loved him. Loved him as deeply as she had known she could way back when she had first met him. She loved the look of him and the sound of his voice. Loved the gentleness in his gaze when he smiled at his daughters. She loved him for meeting life head on, for his thoughtfulness and dependability. She loved it that he could make her laugh. She even loved his stubborn, hard-to-understand sense of personal honor.

And she loved Lucy and Daisy. Laura had given her

daughters to Sam, but Laura must have known that someday another woman would step into Sam's life and into the lives of her daughters. There had been moments while Angie lived in Laura's house that she had fancied she felt Laura's gentle approval.

And now Sam and Lucy and Daisy were her family, too. Oh Lord. How could she live without them?

The two weeks until Daisy's operation passed in the blink of an eye. Although neither Sam nor Angie trusted banks, Angie had seen what could happen to money in jars. She put the two thousand dollars in the Willow Creek bank. Mr. Kravitz, bless his heart, set aside previous orders to make Daisy a new pair of shoes, and he threw in a new pair for Lucy because "the poor little burned-up girl needs a treat."

After ten days of healing, the dressings came off the girls and off her hands and Sam's. The new skin was raw pink and tender to the touch, but at least Angie could do most of her housework and cooking, and she could write thank-you notes to the many people who had given them the things they needed to make a fresh start.

The high point of the period was a visit from Molly and Can. Molly brought new fashionable hats from Denver for Angie and the girls, and an ivory-handled razor and new strop for Sam. Angie spent a wonderful afternoon hearing about Denver and big-city wonders, and she cried at the depot when Molly and Can left.

The hardest part of the two weeks was when Sam's back healed enough that he could sleep in a borrowed cot. Angie tossed and turned in the darkness listening to him breathing on the other side of the small parlor, and she longed for him. Hoped he would cross the chasm that separated them.

But Sam didn't touch her, didn't accidentally brush against her, spent as much time in town as he had when he was working. At mealtimes he teased the girls and maintained a running line of chatter, but he seldom addressed a comment or question to Angie, seldom looked at her directly. In the evenings he went to the Gold Slipper and didn't return until he thought Angie was asleep. If he knew that she was awake and watching him undress in the moonlight, he didn't say so.

It did nothing to halt Sam's withdrawal when a boy arrived from the Sylvan Saloon just as they were sitting down to noon dinner. When Sam answered the knock at the door, the boy asked for Angelina Bertoli, then informed her that she had a telephone call down at the saloon. Someone was calling her all the way from Chicago.

Silently Sam fetched her hat, cape, and gloves, then went back to his dinner. When Angie returned from town, Sam was gone and Abby was sitting with Daisy and Lucy.

Finally the big day arrived. Bags were packed, the house closed. The Muellers, Morgans, and Churches came to the depot to see them off and wish Daisy good luck. After the last-minute flurry of boarding, the girls hung out of the windows, waving as the train hissed and puffed and rolled away from the depot.

"Is it going to hurt?" Daisy asked after they were under way and everyone had settled into the wooden seats. She gripped Angie's hand and gazed up with large gray eyes.

"You'll be asleep during the operation. But yes, honey, I imagine it will hurt afterward. Nothing a brave girl like you can't handle though."

"You and Papa will be there every minute? You won't leave?"

"We'll be there during your surgery. I promise."

"They're going to cut Daisy's leg with a big knife, aren't they?" Lucy asked from Angie's other side.

Sam sat directly in front of them, and the way he held his head told Angie he was listening.

"I think the knife is very small and very precise."

Daisy swallowed hard, her small pale face framed by the straw brim of her new hat. "Am I going to die?"

"No, darling, of course not. The doctor has performed this operation many, many times." She hoped that was true. "You'll sail through this just fine. And after you heal, you'll have a new straight leg and foot."

Trembling, Daisy pressed her face against Angie's side. "I'm scared."

"I know you are. I would be, too. But when it's all over, you'll be so happy."

"But she *could* die, couldn't she?" Lucy leaned across Angie to stare at Daisy. "Missy Hamlin's brother died during an operation to remove his spendix." She looked up at Angie. "A spendix is right here." She poked her stomach.

"Daisy is not going to die," Angie said sharply, giving Lucy a be-quiet look. Which Lucy ignored.

She stretched an arm to shake Daisy. "If you die, can I have the red petticoat the church ladies gave you?"

"Lucy!"

"Daisy wouldn't need it anymore."

"Sam?" Frantically, she looked at the head in front of her and saw his shoulders shaking. At first she thought he was weeping, and that shocked her. Then she realized he was laughing. "Sam Holland, I could use some help here."

"You're doing fine," he said in a strangled voice.

Daisy leaned across Angie to speak to Lucy. "If I die,

you can have my red petticoat, but that's all. Anything else that's mine should go to the poor children."

"I'm your sister! You should give everything to me. Isn't that right, Angie?"

Narrowing her eyes, she watched Sam lean over his knees and raise a hand to his mouth.

She'd begun their reunion by hitting him. At this moment she itched to end it the same way.

But she couldn't bear to think about ending it.

Chapter 21

Sam hired a carriage to take them from the train depot to the Colorado Springs hospital. Willow Creek gold had built Colorado Springs. This was where most of the Willow Creek millionaires came to build their fine mansions and insist on paved streets, electric streetlamps, good schools, and theaters and dining establishments to rival any in the world. In Sam's mind, if the Colorado Springs hospital was good enough for a millionaire's child, it was good enough for his Daisy.

But he disliked the hospital immediately—the powerful odors, the crisp air of impersonal efficiency. He particularly disliked the children's ward. Rows of small forms lay beneath impossibly white sheets that looked too stiff and perfectly folded to be comfortable for a child.

Pacing in a small waiting room, he thought about the operating theater he'd been shown, and the ward filled with pale, silent children. He had focused on this day for nearly three years, but now that the day had arrived, he wanted to scoop Daisy into his arms and carry her away from what lay ahead.

Angie placed herself in front of him. "It's the right thing, Sam," she said gently, as if she'd read his mind.

"She'll be fine. And when it's over, she'll be able to walk and run and play like other children."

"I'd give twenty years of my life to spare her the pain," he said in a low voice. "Damn it!"

"I know." Her fingers tightened on his arm as a nurse approached them. "But your pacing is frightening Lucy. It might help if you'd pretend to be cheerful."

He couldn't think of one thing to be cheerful about. He was out of work, his home had burned to the ground, his daughter was about to undergo a difficult and painful operation, and his wife would leave him in a matter of days.

Every time he looked at Angie, a sharp pain invaded his heart. She was so much a part of him that he couldn't imagine his life without her.

But he couldn't imagine a life for her with him, and that was the problem. It might as well have been ten years ago. If her father had been alive, Bertoli would have pointed out that Sam was no more successful now than he had been then. He had nothing to offer a wife but a hardscrabble life, and what woman wanted that? Not a woman with Peter De Groot eager and waiting.

She'd asked if he wanted to know what she had said to De Groot when De Groot telephoned her. Sam had said no and walked away. Now a dark need to torture himself made him wish he'd listened.

"You may go inside," the nurse informed them.

Daisy looked tiny and frightened, swallowed by the long white bed. Whenever one of the other children moaned in the large, unnaturally silent room, she looked around with wide eyes and the color bled from her cheeks.

Even his irrepressible Lucy was reduced to whispering. "How do you feel?" she asked Daisy, staring at the hospital gown.

"Nothing's happened yet," Daisy whispered back.

For the next several hours they sat around Daisy's bed, talking in low voices, watching Daisy eat a sparse liquid supper, struggling to keep the conversation light and cheerful. When a nurse appeared to douse the lights in the children's ward, it was almost a relief to be chased outside.

"That's the most depressing place I've ever been." Even the smell of manure at the cabstand was more pleasant than the odors inside the hospital. Sam handed Angie and Lucy into a cab and sat across from them, glad to be relieved of the chore of acting cheerful.

Lucy sat on the edge of the seat, hands clasped tightly in her lap. "I'm afraid for Daisy," she said in a teary voice.

Sam watched Angie place an arm around Lucy's shoulders and hold her close. He wouldn't be the only one to miss this woman. Anticipating the girls' devastation was almost as painful as his own sense of impending loss.

"We'll take our mind off worrying by having a lovely dinner at the hotel," she said. "And then, we'll sleep on a bed as soft as a cloud. The hotel has beds stuffed with goose feathers."

"What is our bed at home stuffed with?" Lucy asked, interested.

"I don't know, something stiff and crackly. But you'll sleep like an angel tonight."

Raising her head, she met Sam's eyes, and he knew the night ahead would be as long and sleepless for her as it would be for him. With all his heart, he wished they could hold each other and find comfort in each other's arms.

But he had vowed not to touch her again.

Pride stopped him from acting on his longing. He

didn't want her in his bed because she understood his worry and pitied him. Worse, he suspected her heart had turned toward Chicago. It made him wild inside when he remembered that she was destined to be another man's wife.

Turning a brooding stare to the window, he chewed a fingernail and promised himself not to forget his vow no matter how deep his need for her.

He reminded himself again while he was having a drink in their sitting room, listening to Angie and Lucy laughing and splashing in the hotel room's bathroom. When they emerged, wearing wrappers, their hair swathed in white towels, he inhaled the scent of roses, a fragrance he would always associate with Angie.

"Papa?" Lucy halted on her way to the bedroom she and Angie would share. "Are you mad about something?"

He caught her under the arms and swung her in the air, then brought her close to his chest in a hug. "Just tired. Come on, I'll towel your hair and comb it, then tuck you into bed."

When he returned to the sitting room, Angie was seated beside an open window, letting the cool night air dry her long hair. If Sam had been a painter, he would have painted her as he saw her now: eyes closed, head turned to one side, drawing her fingers through long strands of damp hair. A hint of cleavage showed at the opening of her wrapper and made him swallow hard. The intimacy of seeing her with her hair down, wearing a wrapper, her feet bare, created an ache behind his ribs.

"Autumn is in the air," she said, opening her eyes. "The trees are starting to change color."

She had come to him in the spring like a bright leaf that would fly away in the fall.

"Would you like a drink? It might help you sleep." If

he stared at her another minute, he would embarrass them both by trying to kiss her.

"Thank you." She smiled and shook back her hair. "It's funny. I didn't used to like beer; now I prefer it and wish we had some." When he lifted an eyebrow, she shook her head. "No, don't ring for any. Whatever is on the cart will be fine."

"I thought I'd tell you my plans," he said after giving her a splash of whiskey. "When I arranged for Daisy's surgery, I also contacted an agent here in the Springs and asked him to find a house I can rent for the duration of Daisy's recovery. The doctor says he'll need to change her cast twice a week. When the doctor says Daisy is ready, I'll buy a small place in Denver. I spoke to Can and my first job will be the Johnson mansion. My prospecting days are over. Whatever my future holds, I'll find it in the building trade."

Angie looked down at her folded hands. "And now you want to know my plans."

"If you'd like to tell me." He tried to look as if he didn't really care. Tried to pretend that a clock wasn't ticking in his head, counting down the minutes left to them.

"I'd like to stay a day or two until we know for certain the operation was successful and that Daisy is doing well."

"Daisy would like that." This conversation tore his heart out.

"I might as well leave from here." Shifting on her chair, she gazed out the window at the night sky. "Everything I need to travel, I have with me." After a pause, she drew a breath. "I'd like to stay in touch with the girls, Sam. I'd like to write them occasionally, if you don't mind."

He hesitated, thinking what it would do to him when the letters started arriving from Mrs. Peter De Groot. On the blade of the knife plunged into his heart would be written her father's words: *You'll never be successful, you'll never amount to anything.*

"I have no objection," he lied.

"Well," she said after a lengthy silence. Standing, she placed her empty glass on the cart, then looked at him with an expression he couldn't read. When she finally said goodnight and turned away, he would have sworn tears glittered in her eyes.

He dug his fingers into the arms of the chair and made himself stay seated until he heard her close the bedroom door, then he bent forward and dropped his head in his hands.

He wanted her to say that she loved him. Wanted her to say there would be no divorce, that she would not leave him. He wanted her to tell him that she would rather live in a cottage with him than live in a palace with that bastard De Groot. That's all he wanted. Just the impossible.

"I'll release the tight tendons and ligaments in the posterior and medial aspects of Daisy's foot. We'll repair them in the lengthened position. Some lateral ligaments may have to be released as well. I'll make two incisions, a posteromedial incision and a lateral incision for the lateral structures."

Herb Govenor cleared his throat. "What happens after the surgery?"

"It's a long recovery program," the doctor said, speaking to the four people anxiously standing before him. "We'll recast Daisy's foot twice a week for six weeks. Then she'll wear a brace for another six weeks. If everything is as we hope it will be, for the next year she'll wear the brace at night. And then," he smiled, "she'll be as good as new."

"But if she isn't as good as new?" Sam asked.

"Then I'll go in again. It's possible I'll have to trim some bone. Right now I don't think that will happen. But it could." He addressed the next remarks to Sam and Angie. "Clubfoot is a treatable deformity and I've performed this operation dozens of times. Your daughter will come out of this with a plantigrade and flexible foot."

"What does 'plantigrade' mean?" Angie couldn't force her voice louder than a whisper.

"It means that Daisy will stand on the sole of her foot, not on her heel or the outside of her foot." The doctor glanced at his pocket watch. "Are there any other questions?"

"How long will the operation take?" Winnie asked.

"Two and a half to three hours."

"One more." Angie tried to speak louder, but couldn't. "How much pain will she be in? Afterward."

"I've ordered that she be given morphine. She'll sleep most of the next few days, and she'll be groggy when awake."

"How long will you keep her in the hospital?"

"I'd like to keep her for at least ten days. If there's a problem, we'll know by then." He gave his watch another pointed glance. "Now if you'll excuse me . . ."

On the way to the ward, Angie gripped Sam's hand. "It'll be all right. I just know it will." Stopping in the doorway, she looked down the row of beds to two bright golden heads bent close together, and her throat closed. The doctor had assumed Lucy and Daisy were her daughters, too. She remembered what Sam had said about being a parent, which made Lucy and Daisy her daughters as much as his.

Before they wheeled Daisy away to the operating theater, the Govenors wished her well and promised a treat when Daisy got out of the hospital. Sam held her close and ruffled her hair and gruffly told her that he loved her. Then it was Angie's turn.

"We'll all be here when you wake up, darling."

"They won't call me Miss Gimp-Along, Limp-Along anymore, will they?"

"No, sweetheart, never again." Blinking hard, she smoothed Daisy's hair back from her small face.

"Will I be able to dance someday? Like you and Papa when you went to the grand opening?"

Angie looked into those large gray eyes. "Oh yes. You'll dance and dance and dance."

"I love you, Angie."

"I love you, too!" She held Daisy close to her heart until Sam gently tapped her on the shoulder, then she stepped back and watched the nurses take Daisy away. When Daisy was out of sight, she turned blindly into Sam's arms and burst into tears. "She looks so tiny!"

"I'm afraid!" Lucy said, clinging to them.

It was the longest three hours in Angie's life, and she knew Sam felt the same. Perhaps the Govenors did, too. Sam and Herb Govenor smoked cigars and paced and occasionally exchanged a wary word. Winnie and Angie played card games with Lucy or read aloud from a newspaper someone had left in the waiting room.

At some point Winnie and Angie found themselves alone outside the waiting room door. "The custody question is decided," Winnie began. "And we're grateful that Mr. Holland invited us to be present today."

"But?" Angie inquired wearily.

"No buts. We're hoping today is an indication of improved relations between us and you and Mr. Holland." She drew herself up and spoke in a rush. "We'd like to keep Lucy with us for a week or two. Now hear me out. You and Mr. Holland will be spending a lot of time at the hospital, but this doesn't seem a positive place for a healthy little girl. We could keep her with us, entertain her, and bring her to the hospital to visit Daisy every few days. This would allow you and Mr. Holland to focus exclusively on Daisy."

Angie was too tired and too worried about what was happening in the operating theater to explain that she would be leaving soon. Instead, she merely nodded.

"I don't know if Sam will agree to an extended visit. On the other hand, he has a long list of things to do, and it might be helpful to know that he doesn't have to worry about Lucy. I'll speak to him."

Winnie pressed her hands in gratitude. "Thank you. I know that you and I got off to a bad beginning, but—"

A humble Winnie Govenor was more than Angie could cope with at the moment. She patted Winnie's hands and stepped back. "I believe the nurse said we could get some coffee downstairs. Shall we?"

She decided she had aged ten years during the last endless hours.

"She looks dead," Lucy whispered fearfully.

"No, honey, she's just sleeping." Sam couldn't take his eyes off the cast. The contraption seemed enormous. But it was also straight. Once again, he uttered a silent prayer of gratitude. His daughter would walk tall and gracefully. He dropped a hand on Lucy's shoulder. "Are you sure you want to spend a couple of weeks with your grandparents? You don't have to."

"Grandpa said he'd take me to the horse races, and Gramma is going to teach me how to play croquet." Lucy brightened somewhat. "I can have all the ice cream I want."

Slowly Sam nodded. He didn't like the Govenors; he never would. But he felt Laura close to him today in a way he never had before, and if it hadn't sounded foolish, he would have said that he sensed Laura was happy in a way he had never known her to be. He nodded again and sighed. The Govenors, damn them, were going to be part of his life. Maybe that's how it was supposed to be.

I kept my promise, he said silently, speaking to Laura. The doctor says he doesn't think another operation will be necessary. When the braces come off, no one will ever guess that she didn't always stand tall. I wish you were here, sweet Laura. This would have been the happiest day of your life.

If he were a fanciful man, he would have acknowledged a small sudden warmth on his cheek and an impression that a tiny breeze pushed him gently toward Angie.

Instead he looked at the woman sitting beside the bed, holding Daisy's hand while tears slipped silently down her face. He couldn't have said who was more beautiful. His angel daughter, sleeping with golden hair spread on the pillow like a halo, or his wife, her face wet with joy and love.

When a stern-faced nurse appeared to shoo them away, he placed his arm around Angie and led her outside, where the Govenors waited. For a long moment he and Herb Govenor stared at each other, then Sam kissed the top of Lucy's head and released her.

Govenor tapped his hat into place, scowled, then thrust out his hand. "I say let bygones be bygones."

"Let's take it one step at a time," Sam said, shaking Govenor's hand with reluctance. Frowning, he watched Winnie lead Lucy toward the Govenors' private brougham. With a crest painted on the door, no less. Making a face, he turned to Angie.

And it suddenly struck him. They would be alone in the hotel room tonight. And for the rest of the week.

"Sam?" She watched the brougham ease into the street traffic. "I can't stand this. If I'm going to leave, I want to leave tomorrow." Anguish tightened her expression. "I know it's cowardly, but I can't bear saying goodbye to Daisy and Lucy." Raising a glove, she dashed a tear from her cheek. "I can't stand to even think about it."

He wrenched his mind from the hotel room to a goodbye scene between Angie and his daughters, and winced. Lucy and Daisy had come a long way from disliking Angie and wanting her to leave. They loved her. They wouldn't understand how long she had already waited for her life to begin, or about that bastard De Groot, or that Angie wanted to be with another man. They wouldn't understand that Sam wasn't successful or that the only thing he could offer was himself. Himself hadn't been enough ten years ago. Why would it be enough now?

"I'll tell them good-bye for you," he said in a voice that sounded oddly hoarse. "I'll buy your train ticket and wire you the rest of your money."

Pressing her gloves to her eyes, she nodded. "Thank you."

Taking her arm, he walked to the cabstand and handed her into one of the hansoms. When he didn't enter behind her, she raised an eyebrow. "Sam?"

"I'm going to the nearest saloon, and I am going to get

very, very drunk. I'll fetch you in the morning and take you to the train depot."

"Is this what you want?" she whispered.

To spend the night in a noisy, smoke-filled saloon? No, that wasn't what he wanted. He wanted to be locked in her arms, kissing her until they were both dizzy and wild with desire, kissing her until it felt as if he would explode or die if he didn't love her with his body as hard as he loved her with his heart. He wanted to sleep with her in his arms, wanted to wake at dawn with the scent of her skin and hair beneath his nose. That's what he wanted.

"I think the first train leaves at noon. I'll pick you up at the hotel about ten-thirty."

After closing the door of the cab, he nodded to the driver and watched everything that mattered to him roll away.

Angie spent the night curled in a corner of the sitting room sofa, crying and watching the hotel room door. If she willed it hard enough, Sam would come. He would burst through the door and tell her that he loved her and tell her not to go, that he and Daisy and Lucy needed her.

At two in the morning, she conceded that he wasn't coming, and she moved to the chair beside the window. The rest of her life stretched before her like an endless road she didn't want to travel. There was no place she wanted to go. No one she wanted to see.

Chicago was no longer home, but it was the only place she could think of to go. She had friends there. And Peter was a gentleman; he wouldn't make things awkward for her. Perhaps they could still be friends. Bowing her head, she covered her face in her hands.

She loved Sam so much that it hurt her. Ten years ago her love had been romantic and idealistic. Now she loved with the intensity of maturity. She had seen Sam angry and disheartened and tired and cranky, and she had packed his lunch and washed his underwear and cleaned his house. And she still loved him.

She had stumbled around a ballroom in his arms, laughed helplessly on his shoulder, watched him run into a burning building, had seen the wetness in his eyes as he spoke to his daughter's doctor. And she loved him.

She had stroked his body and knew the firm, smooth texture of his skin. She had looked into his eyes as he led her into the mysteries between man and woman. She had felt his naked heart beating next to hers and had wept with joy. And she loved him.

Angie wrapped her arms around her waist and bent over. She felt as if she were dying.

"I went by the hospital," Sam said in the hansom cab. "They said Daisy had a bad night, but she was sleeping while I was there."

"I went to the hospital, too. I must have just missed you."

Faint purplish half-circles lay under her eyes, and her skin seemed tight on her cheekbones, as if she hadn't slept. A strand of dark hair had worked loose from the coil on her neck and curled on her shoulder. God knew what she thought about his appearance.

At 9:00 A.M. a saloonkeeper had awakened Sam from about an hour's sleep half-sprawled across a felt poker table. Breakfast had done little to quell the queasiness in his stomach and had done nothing for the headache pounding behind his forehead. He'd found a barbershop and paid for a shave and a haircut, but he looked only marginally better when he left the shop than when he'd arrived. His jacket and trousers were wrinkled and smelled of smoke and whiskey, his eyes were bloodshot, and his mood was foul.

"It's a nice day," Angie said, speaking into an uncomfortable silence. She kept her face turned to the window.

"Not too hot. Not too cool." Is that all they had to talk about? The weather? "Why do you keep pushing at your skirt?"

She gave him a quick glance, then looked down at her lap. "I'm concerned that it's a bit short and my stockings show."

Sure enough, he could see the tops of her little boots and a half inch of white stocking. The sight infuriated him. Angie had arrived with enough luggage and clothing to stock a small shop. After six months with Sam Holland she was leaving wearing ill-fitting, donated clothing and carrying one small valise. Disgust closed his throat. If he'd needed further evidence that she could do a lot better than him, all he had to do was look at that half inch of stocking.

The drive to the depot seemed endless. He pulled a hand down his jaw. "I'm sorry I was late."

Angie picked at her gloves, looking anywhere except at him. "I feel like I should say something about these months with you and your daughters. About . . ." She turned bright red then waved a hand. "No, never mind. Not that. But the rest . . ."

He thought he should say something, too, but nothing he wanted to say was appropriate.

"There's one thing. . . ." She drew a breath and met his eyes. "I'm not mad at you and I haven't been for a long time. What happened ten years ago was as much my fault as yours, more my fault."

"That's not true, Angie. I'm entirely to blame. I should

never have let you leave the room. And if I'd stuck up for what I wanted . . ." He shook his head. "Hell, it doesn't matter anymore."

"I understand about Laura, and I understand why you did what you did. And I'm glad, Sam, that you have the girls. They're wonderful."

He saw now why she couldn't bear to say good-bye to Lucy and Daisy. What she was saying and the finality in her voice tightened a vice around his heart. He couldn't stand this, and thanked God when the carriage finally stopped amid the bustle and turmoil swirling in front of the depot.

After handing her out, he paid the driver, then picked up her valise. But she didn't take his arm.

"You don't have to see me on board or wait until the train leaves."

"Don't be ridiculous," he snapped. His stomach hurt, his head throbbed, he felt hollow inside, and he was mad at the world. "Your train leaves in twenty minutes. I think I can spare twenty minutes to be a gentleman."

"Well, don't put yourself out on my account," she said sharply, sounding as annoyed as he was. Picking up her too-short skirt, she marched off in front of him, pushing through the crowd in that fizzy way she had, leaving him to follow.

When they reached the platform, the conductor took Angie's ticket, then smiled and tipped his cap. "There's still a few minutes before the last boarding call."

"I'd prefer to board now," Angie said stiffly.

If that was how she wanted it, all right. Saying good-bye now was better than standing around with nothing to say for five more miserable minutes.

She turned and narrowed her eyes. "Do you want your wedding ring back?"

"What?"

"I'm uncertain about the protocol, but I think the man is entitled to the return of his ring."

"For God's sake, Angie." He stared at her. "No. I don't want the ring back. Sell it. Throw it in Lake Michigan. I don't care. Just don't tell me what you did with it."

"Well, then." She swallowed and thrust out her hand. "Good-bye, Sam. I wish you a happy, healthy, prosperous future."

He shook her hand. "I hope you find the life you've been waiting for. I hope De Groot makes you happy."

A thin smile missed her eyes by a mile. "Peter telephoned that day to ask if I was certain that I wouldn't marry him. I told him I was certain."

His hand tightened around hers and he couldn't breathe. Then he realized nothing had changed. If it wasn't De Groot, it would be someone else. A woman as fine as Angie wouldn't lack for prosperous suitors.

Angie jumped and Sam twitched when the train whistle blasted and a hiss of steam drifted past them.

Angie took a hankie from her silly little bag and dabbed her eyes. "The steam," she explained, sniffing. "I . . . tell the girls I love them!" Turning, she bolted toward the conductor and let him assist her up the steps and into the train.

Sam handed Angie's valise to the conductor, then, feeling dead inside, he moved to the back of the platform and leaned against the wall of the depot.

That was it, then. His life had just become pointless. Expressionless, he watched the last-minute hustle and bustle, heard the clash of metal, peered through billowing clouds of hot steam.

Angie deliberately chose a seat on the track side of the train so she wouldn't be tempted to look out the window and see if Sam waited to watch her leave as he'd said he would. Besides which, she didn't want him to see the tears flooding her cheeks.

Damn him, and damn his pride. He had held her in his arms and made love to her. Surely he cared for her at least a little. How could he let her go? Again. How could he do that? How could he hurt her like this again?

Oh, but wait a minute. Her head jerked up and she lowered her handkerchief. *She* was doing the same thing. Going to her room. In Chicago. Instead of standing beside her husband as she'd vowed to do, she was walking away. Again.

Sam watched the cars roll by, desperately seeking a glimpse of her face at the windows. The calendar might as well have flipped backward ten years. That was the last time he had hurt this badly.

Abruptly he straightened. Son of a bitch. Damned if he hadn't done it again. He'd let her go without trying to stop her. He had decided she didn't want him, had decided for her that she didn't want what he could offer. Once again, it hadn't occurred to him to ask what she wanted.

He hadn't stood up for himself. Yet again.

He had to go after her, had to stop this. No, he couldn't do that, not until Daisy was coherent enough that he could explain he had to go to Chicago. No, that wouldn't do. He couldn't leave Daisy alone in the hospital. Damn it, damn it.

Frantic, he watched the caboose flash by and wondered crazily if he could run fast enough to catch it and swing on board.

Then a movement caught his eye and he saw her. Standing on the other side of the tracks, showing a half inch of white stocking and wearing that angry, fizzy look that he loved. He thought his knees would buckle when he jumped off the platform and ran toward her.

She met him in the middle of the tracks and jabbed him in the chest with a hard finger. "I am so mad at you that I could just spit! Daisy needs me. She's going to have a hard time managing that cast. And who is going to take care of Lucy when she comes home?" She jabbed him in the chest again. "And you need me! If you're going to start a new business in Denver, you'll want someone to set up your books and handle the money. You need help choosing a house because men don't know anything about picking out a house." Leaning forward from the waist, she narrowed snapping black eyes that fizzed and threw off sparks. "This is no time for a divorce, not when my daughters need me. We'll talk about the divorce after Daisy is well and when the girls are settled after the move to Denver."

"Oh God, I love you! And I do need you. I love you, I love you, I love you!" Wild with joy, he picked her up and swung her around, giving any lingerers an ample view of petticoats and white stockings. When he set her on her feet, he grabbed her and kissed her until applause broke out on the platform. "Listen to me. I can't give you a fraction of what you deserve, but I swear to you that I'll—"

"Oh Sam, you wonderful idiot. I don't care about anything but you and the girls." She held on to his ears and kissed him hard. "My life started with the three of you, don't you know that? You and the girls, that's all I want." Her hands flew over his face and chest, and back to his lips. "I love you. How can you not know? I've always loved you. Always, always!"

He threw back his head and shouted. "She loves me!"

Turning crimson, Angie cast a timid glance at the grinning people watching them on the platform. Leaning forward she cupped her hand around his ear. "I know where there's a hotel room that is going to be private for two whole weeks."

Instantly his body responded, and he smiled down into her shining eyes, loving her so hard that his chest ached. And suddenly the future looked bright and promising and everything was possible. How could it not be, with her beside him?

Scooping her into his arms, he carried her up the platform steps, past the depot, and put her into a cab. He offered the driver a bonus if he got them to the hotel in record time.

Inside, he kissed her until they were both breathing raggedly and shaking with their urgent need for each other.

"About the divorce," he said against her lips. "I think we should put it off until my business is well established." As if he would ever let her go again.

Angie nibbled his lip, driving him half insane, her face wet with happy tears. "Actually, I was thinking we should delay the divorce until the girls are out of school and can manage on their own."

Laughing, he pulled her onto his lap and kissed her again and again, unable to get enough of her, and wishing the cab had wings.

Somewhere deep inside a knot he had carried for ten years slowly unraveled and fell away. He was going to lay the world at her feet. With Angie at his side, he didn't doubt for an instant that he could be more successful than either of them had ever dreamed.

But he knew that he would never be richer than he was at this minute.

Chapter 22

"Mrs. Holland, dinner is ready."

Smiling, Angie swept a glance across her guests talking and laughing on the terrace, then looked out at the young people chasing croquet balls around a broad sweep of lawn.

"We'll wait another thirty minutes, Parker."

Winnie wouldn't approve of extending the cocktail hour, but Winnie also knew that Angie had never been a stickler for strict etiquette. Angie's dimples deepened when Winnie caught her eye and pointedly glanced at her watch.

They had brought Winnie to Denver two years ago and settled her a block away. But the starch had gone out of Winnie after Herb's death. Today she looked frail and round-shouldered, and Angie had noticed she sought the sunny spots on the terrace even though Denver was enjoying an exceptionally warm spring.

Molly ambled toward her, holding a plate heaped with hors d'oeuvres. "You know what I like best about being rich? Not having to cook. What are you thinking? You look pensive."

"I was trying to remember if Winnie will be seventy-five or seventy-six on her next birthday."

Molly placed a hand on the sleeve of Angie's new chiffon gown. "Winnie will outlive us all."

"It wouldn't surprise me," Angie said, smiling. "Have you seen our husbands?" She would have liked a glass of champagne since cocktails didn't appeal to her. But champagne wouldn't be served until after dinner, when the toasts began.

"I think they're in the library, talking business. You know how it is when Marcus Applebee comes to town."

Sam, Can, and Marcus would be talking about the mines and percentages that had made them all rich, and the myriad other business interests that had elevated riches to wealth.

Angie and Molly moved to the stone railing to watch the croquet game. The smell of spring flowers drifted from large marble urns that Angie and Sam had bought in Greece last year.

"Twenty years ago, did you ever imagine that one day we'd be living in huge houses with a staff of servants?" She smiled at Molly, who wore a short skirt and had taken to smoking pink cigarettes clasped in the end of a long cigarette holder. Molly's short silver bob was, amazingly, coming into fashion. Angie hadn't cut her own hair yet, but she was considering it. "Do you ever think about the Willow Creek days?"

"More often than I like to admit. Those were hard times and good times."

Speaking with quiet fondness, they reminded each other of the sounds and smells of those long-ago summer evenings on Carr Street. They remembered an oilcloth spread with diamonds, little girls running through sheets drying on the line, and the distant boom of dynamite in the hills. Remembered pennies counted into jars above a stove, and sharing chipped mugs of coffee sugared with hope. Remembered flames leaping in the night.

"Gramma, I'm hungry."

Angie smiled down at a toddler with gray eyes and wheat-colored hair. Lucy's youngest. Kneeling she straightened a tiny silk tie. "We'll eat soon. In the meantime, maybe Gramma Molly will give you a cheese puff."

"I hate to part with a cheese puff," Molly said, as if she resisted the idea. "But since it's you . . ."

Angie always knew when Sam entered a room. Her heart lifted as if a missing piece had found its way back to her. Turning, she gazed down the terrace, and saw him in the archway, smiling at her.

Gray streaked his temples now, but she thought the gray hair made him look distinguished and suited him. The tailored three-piece suit didn't. At least not in her opinion. She liked best those rare days when he donned his denims and flannel and a tool belt and joined one of the Holland Construction, Inc. crews that had helped to build Denver wider and higher. Keeping his hand in, he called it.

When he came up behind her and slipped his arms around her waist, she leaned back against his chest, loving the solid feel of his body. "Which anniversary are we celebrating tonight? The twentieth or the thirtieth?" he asked, nuzzling her ear.

"The twentieth. You know I don't count the first ten years."

They stood together, swaying slightly, looking down the terrace to where Daisy sat with a group of young mothers. As if she felt them watching, she turned her golden head, shifted the baby in her arms, and blew them a kiss. Later, when the dancing began, Angie would watch Daisy and Richard twirl across the ballroom and tears would gather at the back of her eyes. For an instant ghostly voices would singsong in her ear. "Gimp along, gimp along, here comes Miss Limp-Along."

"Mother, are we ever going to eat? Miles is getting whiny, and Gramma Molly is stuffing hors d'oeuvres into Charles. He won't eat a bite of dinner." Flushed from playing croquet, Lucy threw herself into a chair and pressed a handkerchief to her forehead. She'd been the first among her friends to crop her hair, and every year her hemline climbed with the fashion. If it hadn't been so, Angie would have been secretly disappointed.

Suddenly Lucy grinned up at them. "You two are a disgrace, hugging and touching every time you pass each other, gazing at each other with moony eyes."

Angie laughed. "Moony eyes?"

"Of course you've been doing that for as long as I can remember." She jumped to her feet and kissed them both. "If you're sure we're about to eat, Mother, I'll round up my boys and see to some hand-washing."

"They're beautiful, aren't they?" Angie murmured, watching Lucy stop to say something to Daisy. "Our daughters."

Sam turned her in his arms. "Not as beautiful as their mother." For twenty years she'd had an errant strand of hair that would not stay put. And for twenty years, Sam had been tucking it behind her ear. "You know," Sam said, giving her a certain well-loved look. "I was thinking."

Lifting on tiptoe, she kissed the corner of his lips. It was her anniversary, so she was entitled to make a bit of a spectacle. And he was so handsome. Blue-eyed, tanned, and as lean and muscular as he'd been when she married him. "I know what you're thinking, and the answer is no. At least, not yet."

Smiling, he edged her into an alcove and molded her hips close to his. "Tell Parker to delay dinner another thirty minutes. Or tell these people to go home and let's you and me go to bed and celebrate our anniversary properly."

Laughing she placed a finger over his lips. "We'll celebrate properly, we always do. But later, Mr. Holland." Giving in to temptation, she kissed him soundly, pressing hard against him. "Now . . . about our divorce."

Every year on their anniversary, he wanted to replace her plain gold band with diamonds and every year she said no. And every year on their anniversary, they talked about the divorce.

A twinkle danced in his eyes. "All right, here's my final offer. I'll agree to give you a million dollars, the house, the servants, the new automobile, and Winnie."

"Winnie?" She drew back in mock horror. "I have to take Winnie? I thought you were going to keep Winnie."

"No, she's all yours. I insist."

"Oh, well, I'm sorry, but this will require some lengthy negotiation. I'm afraid we'll have to delay the divorce until next year." The way he moved against her, his hands warm on her hips, made her wonder if another thirty minutes before dinner would really matter.

"Next year on our anniversary, we should talk about delaying the divorce until our grandchildren are grown. A divorce in the family would be too upsetting for young children."

"That's what you said when our girls were little. But . . . I believe you have a point. Perhaps we have a duty to set a good example for our grandchildren. But only until they're grown, of course. Then we'll definitely get around to our divorce."

Laughing, they held each other so close that Angie felt the steady exciting beat of his heart against her breast.

"I love you, Sam."

He framed her face between his hands and gazed into her eyes. "I love everything about you, my beautiful Angelina Bertoli Holland." A smile curved his lips. "Except that Italian temper and the way you eat your eggs."

Linking arms, laughing into each other's eyes, they led their guests inside. Together, as they always would be.